Book I

The Great
Balance

Beyond the Balance Saga

An Original Series

by Terrene A. Davenport

Sara,
I hope you enjoy this book.
Angie knows how much I love writing
so we are both sharing the love!!
Happy 2019!!
XO

PUBLISHING

ISBN: 1530567017

ISBN-13: 978-1530567010

For my first born son,

Gabriel

You were made from true love,

something that is so rare in this world.

We love you so much

To My Readers

Having a dream and never losing sight of it is so important. Never allow roadblocks to stop you from getting to your destination, you just need to find a clever detour.

With this being said, I have written this book and published it 100% percent by myself. Please, keep this in mind as you are reading through the chapters. Nothing is more difficult (in my humblest opinion, for me) than proofreading your own creative work. So, I know it's imperfect, being part of my first novel ever and all. It sounds fluid in my mind, yet I may miss some punctuation here or there. I apologize in advance for that.

One day I hope to be fortunate enough to have professional proofreaders and a wonderful editor. Until then, this is all me in my purest creative form, I hope you enjoy the adventure. Meanwhile, you have to be greater than the haters!

This is my detour, enjoy the ride.

Creatively Yours,

The Write Provocateur

Dedication

To My Amazing Best Friend & Husband, Roger

Without you, none of this would be possible. Your encouragement and feedback have made me and this beautiful idea come alive to its full potential. You have shown me so much love, passion, and adventure, that I was able to transform those experiences into words that became part of the story. I'm so fortunate to have such an amazing individual to call my partner in life. You brighten my day when I'm saddened by darkness. You make me laugh when I feel like I'm going to burst from anger, frustration, and tears. And you stick by me and give me room to breathe when I need it. You are my muse, bringing every creative bone I have in my body back to life. I'm so blessed to have you and thank God for it every morning and every night. Thank you for making me complete again. Cheers to us!

The Great Balance
Book I

T. A. Davenport

Contents

Beyond the Balance Saga: *BOOK ONE*

COPYRIGHT

Acknowledgments

* * * * * * *

My Dearest Sister

Thank you for constantly hearing every thought and future detail. You kept me level headed and calm. More importantly, thank you for taking on this enormous project. Nothing is more fun than working with someone amazing, and that amazing someone happens to be your baby sis.

My Amazing Proofreader, Edward

So very fortunate to have you on my side! I can't express just how invaluable your contribution was and will continue to be throughout this series. Having someone to depend on 100% is truly a wonderful feeling and I'm proud to now call you a friend. You helped me to polish this book and I couldn't have accomplished that without you!

My boo, Vanessa

Nothing can put into words what you mean to me or what your continued support has shown me. You once told me that I am such an inspiration to those around me that people are lucky to have me in their lives. Truth is, you help me to be that inspiration. What superhero can go on changing the world without their best friend and confidant?

My lovely twin, Ashley

You've supported everything I do from day one and with this book there were no exceptions. I can't describe how much love I truly have for you and what you do for me as a person. You are dear friend to me Ash, forever & always.

Prologue

Briellyn

Her face is barely recognizable. It's morphed into something much darker, more demonic. I don't know this face. The wind beneath her sweeps her long dark locks straight up into the air, yet I feel nothing. I'm panting, terrified of the situation. My heart beats so fast and hard that I can feel it in my ears. I have no idea what to make of this. Two men kneel before her. They mean something to me, yet I can't see their faces. Her long, dark claws dig into their shoulders on either side of her, keeping them subdued.

"Leave them alone," I yell out to her, staring into the eyes of this creature that strikes a sense of fear and loss within me. The darkness inside her has consumed her entirely and there's no humanity left in her.

"You get to choose who lives. Or if they both have to die. You can only choose one though, if you see it fit." Her voice sounds serpent like and has a faint echo. The room is so dark that it's difficult to see much of anything.

"Why should I have to choose? Please just let them go." I cry out, fear and worry dripping from each difficult word.

"One may live if we make a trade," her tone delighted by her offer.

"Will you take me in their place?" I huff audibly, willing to make the sacrifice for them both.

"*Only one!*" She hisses at me. "Would you give your second child in place of one of these men?" Her eyes grow darker, burning into me like a master branding his slave.

I nod my head yes.

"I need to hear it woman. *Speak up!*" Her words cause me to tremble, I can't keep my hands at my sides still.

"Yes," tears begin to fall and the words are challenging to voice, "I would give my second child in one of their place." It didn't matter. *I have no children.*

"Well then, kill the one that you don't want!" She screams out, pushing both men forward into the light.

"How can you make *me* choose? I love them both!" I cry out.

$$* * * * * * *$$

My eyes fly open as I stare into the dark abyss that is my bedroom. I lean up to glance at my phone. Three AM. My palm gently rubs my forehead. *Will these dreams ever stop?*

Admittedly, I haven't had one in a while. My anxiety is through the roof because of business. When I'm stressed, my mind displays it in a weird, violent vision. *Sigh.* Nothing I can't handle. Nothing out of the norm.

I leave my bed and walk to the kitchen to grab a bottle of water. After a few sips, I lie back down and attempt to fall asleep again. Sometimes I wish I could just get away from it all. If only just for a little while.

Briellyn

"Brielle? Brielle? Anyone in there? Earth to Brielle?" the distant words break my train of thought. I'm staring into space, getting lost in my book, when a familiar voice intrudes. I quickly swerve my chair around and take my glasses off. My business partner is standing at the front of my cherry wood corner desk with her arms crossed, tapping her foot. Rubbing my eyes, I stare at her, baffled as to why she couldn't read the sign on my door.

"What is wrong with you, I know my 'Do Not Disturb' sign is on my door…" I point to the door, merely twelve feet away. She stares at me, frustrated, not saying anything. "What *is it*?!" I raise my voice again.

She smirks and slams a magazine on my desk. *I'm on the cover.* "First off, you know that sign doesn't apply to me. Secondly, you made the cover! I told you it was a good idea to do that interview," she's overjoyed.

I turn beet red and clear my throat, looking at her with doubt. *Admittedly I'm jumping for joy on the inside that they thought me glamorous enough to put on the cover.*

She picks up the magazine and opens it, "And here I thought that beautiful brown skin couldn't get any prettier," she then covers her face and reads aloud. "After having the pleasure to sit down with this brilliant young woman, we have come to the conclusion that not only is Briellyn Donado the Donatella Versace of the business world, but she's as gorgeous on the inside as she is on the outside. Her radiance and confidence shine through her approachable exterior, but with the most amazing humility. Her fresh ideas and unique take on business attire is like a glass of cucumber water, chilled to perfection. This up and coming fashion genius is also extremely business savvy, having opened her line with only a few thousand and growing it to over a million in revenue yearly. She's currently in the market for an investor, and trust us, she's a pot of gold and platinum with only rainbows coming *and* going from her.... Blah blah blah, so on and so forth. You get the gist, I know you won't read it because heaven knows you can't take a compliment. Wouldn't kill you to accept a little flattery Brie. Which leads me to my next point as to why I'm here..."

Twiddling my thumbs and trying not to smile, I wait for a moment before replying, "Which is?"

"You were supposed to sign those papers this morning with that guy," she whines as she sits down in the cushioned red chair in the front of my desk.

"Oh right, because you so desperately want to bring someone else in our business when we are about to strike it big... 'scuse me for not being overly anxious to split the pot so much," I reply angrily, "Takes away from those that work for us. I don't even know this guy and I hate him already Ryn." I plop my face into my hands.

Eryn calmly grabs one of my hands from my face as I stare at her. "First off, it's *your* business that you've so graciously allowed me along for the ride. And don't worry, everything is going to be perfect. This is going to put you and me both in a very generous position. *Maybe* if you would've done the interview sooner, like I'd asked, you would have more options right now. We need to expand NOW and the buy in is more than we have. Isn't that the whole point?" she smiles at me, tilting her head sideways. Her bright red hair catching the light coming through my office window behind me; it makes it appear as if it were on fire.

I hated to agree with her, but I knew we needed to do something soon to aid in the business's growth; otherwise we were going to be in a world of trouble. I reluctantly smile, "I will call and schedule the meeting to get it done…"

"Today," she adds, standing up and walking towards the door of my office.

"Of course…" I grit my teeth together and roll my eyes as she begins to close the door; she turns around and blows me a kiss. "Read the article… you might turn a richer shade of red that we can market," she adds before shutting the door.

I grab the magazine from the desk and turn my chair around to stare out the window, "God please, if this is meant to be, please give me a sign." I look upwards and press my hands together in prayer. *I was never an every Sunday type of believer, but I live daily with a strong belief in faith.*

My cold office is being warmed by the sun coming through the beige window blinds. It's nice to have a floor to ceiling window in my office, the sunlight gives me a warm happiness I need right now. I lose myself in thought while watching the leaves blowing around outside and remember how fortunate I've been thus far.

Focus. I swivel my chair forward once again. My corner desk acts like a barricade between me and whomever comes through my door; protecting me, shielding me. I glance at my peace lily in the opposite corner on my left; the red marbled vase it's in just seems to burn into my soul. *I should get out of the office, I work too much.* Who would have thought being a clothing designer would be so demanding... said no one ever.

Suddenly my phone rings, I glance at it to my left from the corner of my eye; the black phone lighting up, beckoning me to answer it; the number unknown. I playfully swivel my chair left to right and stare at the phone. It continues to ring as I get lost in my thoughts once again, "Why must *every*thing be so extraordinarily difficult!?" I pick up the phone and press the button to answer the line, "Briellyn Donado." I'm intentionally stern and unfriendly to get whoever was on the other line to go away.

"Good afternoon Ms. Donado, my name is Eric," the very inviting deep voice on the other end cordially states. *Maybe too inviting, probably a sales call.*

"Look Eric, I'm sorry but unfortunately we are not in the market for whatever it is you are selling," I reply, lightening my tone while remaining stern.

"I'm sorry Ms. Donado, I think you have me mistaken," he insists, "I'm calling in reference to the sale of your business."

On one hand, I feel relieved; on the other, I'm now annoyed. "I'm sorry I haven't called you guys back, I've been deciding on whether or not to proceed with everything," reluctantly, I continue speaking, "Can we meet this afternoon to discuss the paperwork and the final cut?"

Nothing but deep, dark, silence on the other end; broken by a slight, very manly chuckle. Eric continues, "I still think you have me mistaken Ms. Donado, we haven't spoke before but from the sound of it, I would say that you aren't fond of whomever that you have me mistaken for."

I immediately begin blushing and pick up a pen to start fiddling with it, "Oh my goodness, I am so sorry. Yes, I indeed had you mistaken… anyway, my business isn't exactly for sale, per say. Um, what is it *exactly* that you are calling me about?"

Eric clears his throat, "I have heard about you… and your business, and I want to help."

Baffled and confused, I reply, "Help? I'm sorry, from whom did you hear this?"

"Well besides the wonderful article in W magazine, a mutual friend of ours by the name of Justin Vandegrift. He says that you are one of the most brilliant women he knows and that the economy crisis hit you a little hard. W magazine's description was more lighthearted of course.

From either perspective, with a little help you could easily recover and much more…"

"I'm so flattered…" I reply, elated with the thought that Justin would speak of me so highly. He is an old friend whom I care about very dearly. "Well… *now that you mention it*, I could use some help. *However*, I'm not interested in selling my business and becoming an employee."

Eric laughs, "Well…" He chuckles again. "You're in luck, because I wish to invest. Justin briefly went over your numbers from last year and I have to say, I'm quite impressed. I think you and I would work well together. Can you put together a small business plan discussing your recovery?"

A smile creeps onto my face, "Are you serious?" I sit here dumbfounded, I can't believe it. This is exactly what I need to prevent having to sell a huge chunk of my business to those criminals that Eryn deals with.

"Very, Ms. Donado. When do you think you might have it read..?"

Excitedly, I interrupt him, "Today!" I had to regain my composure. I then clear my throat, sit up straight, and calmly repeat, "Today… are you available for us… I mean me, to meet in person? I would really prefer to see exactly who you are and go over a few things with you."

"Absolutely. Can we meet for dinner at say, 7pm? I know this great place on 5th that has amazing food. I think it would be appropriate given the fact that I think we will be toasting to a new venture for us both by dinners end."

"I sure am!" I blurt out. *God, don't sound so desperate woman.* My thought is interrupted by Eric's laugh. It sounds so wholesome. It's the first refreshing thing I've heard all day.

"Great, here is my number. Please send me a text and I will send you the address. It is dinner dress though, just fyi. My number is (212) 323-1985."

I write the number down and begin imagining the way the night is going to go, "I will be sure to text you Mr.?"

"Windsor, it's Eric Windsor. But please, just Eric."

"Well, with that being said… please call me Brie," I smile wide, holding my breath.

"I look forward to seeing you in a few hours then… Ms. Brie. Until then," he says.

"Until then…" I hang up the phone. *Could my luck really be this good?* Excitedly, I call Eryn's desk phone to tell her the good news. I let it ring twice and then quickly hang up. Wait, what if this *is* too good to be true? I would feel incredibly stupid to tell Eryn I bailed on her guy and this Eric is full of it.

I see her calling me back. I pick it up immediately, "Hey Ryn, just wanted to let you know that I'm heading home for the day. I need to clear my head about this merger."

"Ok Brie, just remember this is important to *us* and everyone involved, I will schedule a meeting for tomorrow morning…" she replies quickly.

"Sure, we'll talk later," I hang up, irritated by her persistence. What does this guy have… is she sleeping with him or something? *Ok Brie, don't think like that… she's just trying to help.* I grab my phone and begin to text this wonderful stranger, Eric. "God, I hope you are the real deal," mumbling as I type. I stand, quickly leaving the office to head home.

* * * * * * *

I get home and pull into my garage, the base floor of my cute little corner townhouse unit in a gorgeous Stamford community. It's unnecessarily three bedrooms, but works for when my sister and her children come to visit. It has gorgeous dark Cherrywood floors throughout the whole home, golden sponge painted walls, a two-car garage, a cute little kitchen with white cabinets and granite countertops, and a tiny balcony, ideal for myself and a friend.

I walk up to the 3rd floor where my bedroom is and immediately start ransacking my closet. I need a dress that is powerful, sexy, and screams invest in me. *I'm worth it.* I absolutely *must* land this deal. He seems pretty interested, but what if he *is* full of shit? *I've had my fair share of fast talkers this past year.* Thankfully, in person it's pretty easy to discern.

What if it's some dirty old guy trying to get lucky? He didn't sound old though. I frown. I've been let down SO many, many times. I've built what I have all on my own and unfortunately the economy has just been a little unkind.

Think positive Brielle, this could be huge. I pause. *Or it could be nothing.* I despise getting my hopes up! I can't emotionally afford it, *again.* I breathe in deep and close my eyes. "Let go, let flow." I stare at myself in the mirror with a black knee length Herve Leger bandage dress held up in front of me. It's a sweetheart neckline with thick straps. I put it aside and then hold up a red lace Monique Lhuillier dress. It's a little shorter than the black dress and no cleavage, still very sexy though.

Decisions, decisions. I decide to go with the black dress because it's more low key and subtly sexy. Even if he's an older man, some nice cleavage never hurt anyone. *And black makes my dark auburn hair look beautiful.*

Being a business owner isn't easy. It may seem glamorous, but it isn't all that it's cracked up to be. The best part is being your own boss and taking responsibility for what happens, which is a whole lot more satisfying than any 9 to 5 I can think of.

You must be practical about everything. For example, I drive a 2015 metallic steel color Dodge Durango to help me haul whatever supplies I need. Like I said, *being a clothing designer isn't easy.*

And I may own a three-bedroom place, but it's more like a condo with tons of space. I keep myself on salary, and at the end of the year I award bonuses to everyone, including myself. But right now, money is tight.

I decide to drive into the city instead of requesting a driver because I knew it would cost me big bucks if I didn't. I grab two twenty-dollar bills from my cash stash for parking and hop into my truck. The drive into the city is always so pretty in the evening, and there's little traffic going in at this time.

I arrive at my destination at 6:55 and decide to valet so that I'm not walking in late. The valet walks over to my door and opens it, helping me out of my vehicle. I reach over to grab my purse before getting out. As I make my way to the front doors, I get extremely nervous. I start freaking out while rehearsing my approach in my head. How will I even know who he is? Should I text him and let him know that I'm here? *Yes, I should text him.* I grab my phone from my purse and proceed to send him a text.

'I just arrived, should I ask for you or meet you in a particular spot?' I type and hit send. Keeping the phone in hand, I slowly start to pace.

While looking at the sky I inhale deeply, then exhale and face forward, catching my reflection in the tall glass doors in front of me. I'm fixing my hair as a gentleman approaches me, "Ms. Donado?" I would know his voice anywhere, confident and calming. I coyly turn to say hello to the man who maybe my hero, only to find an extremely handsome, tall, dark haired, blue eyed, muscular figure. *Wasn't expecting him to actually look like a superhero.*

"You must be…" I stand there in awe of him. "Um," I lose my train of thought. *Train of thought, completely gone.*

He finishes, "Eric."

"Right, I was just going to say that. Sorry a lot on my mind," I hold my hand out to make his acquaintance, feeling sheepish that I'm in awe of his appearance. *Get it together, woman.* I've hung out with male models for goodness sake, *why am I starstruck?*

He smiles, "I'm sure you do," he proceeds to shake my hand and leans in to kiss my cheek. *Oh, my.* My eyes inadvertently brighten, and my eyebrows rise. The cologne he's wearing is absolutely divine. His suit's even more heavenly, perfectly tailored to fit his muscular physique. He looks to be about my age. Trust fund baby perhaps…?

"I hope you're hungry, this place is really quite good," he holds the door open and guides me inside, gently placing his hand on my lower back as we walk up to the hostess.

"Mr. Windsor, nice to see you again. Would you like to be seated in the usual area?" The hostess stares at him with a rather large, flirtatious smile. Eric acknowledges her and simply nods.

The restaurant is very posh and appears to be a lounge/hotel combination. The music is hip and the ambience is trendy and modern. The hostess leads us to where we will be seated. We walk past numerous cocktail tables to a narrow stairway, hidden behind a wall. As we walk up the stairs you can see everyone on the floor below; dimly lit table tops, and some people dancing on the open floor. At the top of the stairs there is a wide hallway equipped with huge, abstract lounge chairs lining its walls and small coffee tables. Eric is walking behind me as if to make sure I don't lose my way. The waitress stops in front of a glass door and opens it for us. Upon walking in, the ambient sounds dull out completely and I could hear my thoughts once again.

The table she finally brought us to has a gorgeous view of the garden that is centered in the middle of the building. It's lit up like Christmas, with white lighting and soft highlights on perfect landscaping. On the other side, we can view the high ceilings of the restaurant area, sofas and classy chairs lining the floor we were on, low lighting hides the intimate kissing shared between a well-dressed man and much less dressed young woman.

Eric pulls out my chair, "Please, have a seat my lady." I flirtatiously smile at him and sit down. He proceeds to sit across from me. "So, where is the paperwork? Unless of course, there's more to that dress than meets the eye," he asks as he puts his napkin over his lap and signals over to our own personal waiter. I blush. Before I can answer the first question, he asks me another. "Can I get you something to drink?"

I think to myself, no, but then I think again. It might take the edge off. *I need to take the edge off.* I smile at him, "Mai Tai please."

The waiter gets to the table, "Double McClellan, neat, and a Mai Tai for the lady," Eric hands the waiter something after he mentions the drink order. *McClellan? My drink seems childish in comparison. Maybe I should switch to a cran vodka?* The waiter promptly walks off. *Whelp, too late.* "So…" he turns his body to face me.

"The business plan is right here," I point to my head, "If you would like a hard copy after we speak this evening, I have it synced in my phone. All I'll need is your email and you can review it at your leisure."

He raises his eyebrows in response, "I see. I love a woman who's hands on about her business. I respect that."

I clear my throat again and fold my hand into my lap so as not to fidget too much.

A few minutes pass when the waiter comes back with our drinks. I've already begun discussing how much additional capital is needed in order to accomplish the years goals and what is in the works. "I'm willing to allow a 20% share in the company for the $250k investment, with payouts beginning in 15 months," I sip on my drink and smile at him.

"You're very persuasive…. I'll tell you what, after hearing the details of your plan, I'm very intrigued. You know how to get right to the point, and quickly," he raises his glass to me, "I'm excited to hear more, but first let us order." He takes a sip of his drink as I stare at him blankly. *I haven't even glanced at the menu.* I've been too busy running my mouth.

Quickly I grab for the menu and proceed to glance through it when Eric lightly grabs my wrist, "May I?" He smiles at me cordially as if he knew this would happen the whole time.

I smile back and nod, "Ok." A lady could get used to this type of gentlemanly treatment, it's so rare.

He turns to the waiter, "Will you please get my lovely dinner date the seafood delicatessen and for me, my usual," he looks over at me, "What kind of salad would you like?"

Immediately I respond, "Caesar, extra parmesan with sliced tomatoes, please."

"Thanks Jim," Eric says as the waiter scurries off. He turns back to me and sips his drink, "As you were saying…"

"Well you see, our biggest sellers right now are the reversible tunics that are adjustable at the waist. If we could get more colors and fabrics, our sales would almost double. When you add the NFL, NBA, and MLB licensing, it'll quadruple! And since the summer release is right around the corner…" I go on for what seems like an hour, it was really only about twenty minutes. I get so excited when I talk about my business.

Eric seems to know a lot about the fashion business and he is refreshing to speak to. He remains engaged in the conversation the entire time, genuinely interested in everything we're discussing. "So that's the main idea, nothing complex, just an increased marketing push to our newly targeted audience, the licensing, and a few new additions in production. The biggest push is getting a fashion show together, possibly overseas. But I'm curious, Mr. Windsor, you seem to know an awful lot about my area of expertise, what is YOUR background?"

He shuffles a little bit in his seat, "Well you see Ms. Donado, I haven't been entirely honest with you," he places his ankle on his knee, then his right forearm onto the table with his drink in his hand, and his left arm over the left back of the chair.

Oh no, here it comes. I knew it was too good to be true. I grab my drink and quickly suck the rest of it down.

He looks up and smiles at me, "I had no intentions of..." Just then the dinner arrives. *Saved by the dinner bell.* Our meals are placed in front of us with beautiful silver warming covers. The servers remove the covers to reveal this gorgeous platter of shrimp and lobster tail mixed with vegetables and some kind of potato. It smells delightful. *But I think I am going to be sick.*

I'm sure this handsome gentleman, Eric, is about to tell me he doesn't really want to invest *or* he wants different terms. The servers leave. Eric smells his food, as if taking in every distinct scent then looks over at me, "Please, try your food. I hope you like lobster."

A half-hearted grin graces my face as I grab my fork. I poke a piece of shrimp and the potatoes; it's dripping in this sauce. I place it in my mouth as Eric watches me intently. Immediately I'm in heaven, it is the most delicious thing I have ever tasted... *ever.* The shrimp is cooked perfectly and the potato just melts in my mouth. Whatever the sauce on top is, it adds just the right amount of flavor to make it delightful. It sends a sensation through my entire body, it's so good.

Eric can see the approval on my face, "That's what I thought," he points at me, "I figured you a seafood lover." He cuts into his steak and places a piece into his mouth. He then puts his fork and knife down and digs into the left pocket on the inside of his suit jacket. He pulls out a white envelope and puts it onto the table, keeping his hand on it; he slowly slides it closer to me. "This is for you," he says.

I take a deep breath and a long pull from the new Mai Tai that the waiter just brought me. What could be in the envelope? *Have a little faith Brie.* I slide the envelope to the end of my side of the table and grab it, then proceed to open it up.

Eric continues, "As I was saying, I had no intentions of leaving without giving you my investment up front. I knew I wanted to invest long before you and I had ever spoken. But I am changing the terms," he interjects just before I open the folded letter. A cashier's check falls out filled out to me in the amount of $300k. The letter had all the terms outlined in it. *With a final payout totaling $1.3M. Is he serious? Am I being Punk'd?*

I am taken back. Now this *IS* too good to be true. I don't know what to say and keep stumbling over my words, "Well… this is… um… more than I need but extremely generous of you."

Eric takes another bite and then pats his face with his napkin, "Well the additional $500k is for something I need you to do for me. And I only want a 10% stake in the company; you do enough without someone wanting to dig into your profits."

Almost choking, I sip my beverage. "Ok…" I begin, "What could I possibly do for you that is worth $500k?"

"$500k is only half; you will receive the other half upon completion of the task. Besides the fact that you can use the money to put your ideas into overdrive with no worry about funding, I'm in desperate need of your expertise and Justin told me that you would be exactly what I'm looking for."

"Justin has apparently told you a lot about me," smiling forcibly, I quickly grab my drink again, polishing it off.

"He told me that you have a very natural analytic ability and your mind is quick to solve puzzles and problems. Seeing things others can't, so to speak."

Funny he used those words. "So," I can feel the alcohol hitting my system, "there are many people who can solve puzzles and problems, catch things others may miss." I tried not to sound sarcastic there, but my confidence is showing. *Maybe my cockiness too.*

"Yes, but you are different, from what I understand," he reaches into his right pocket and places a small square picture onto the table, "tell me what you see in the photo."

I glance down at the picture then look again at Eric. He nods his head, encouraging me to proceed. I pull the picture closer, inhale deeply, and look at it. There are numbers that seem to pop up right off the table, like a 3D holographic. It's unlike anything I had ever seen before.

As my face lights up in amusement, I glimpse at Eric in delight and exclaim, "Now wherever did you find that? Interesting trick. The way the letters appear to fly off of it like that." *I really am amused by this.* I just don't understand his end game yet. He looks at me very intently and tilts his head. I softly shake my head as the smile disappears from my face, "What?" Worried that I may be coming across *too* confident. *Or possibly drunk.*

He leans closer to me, "Tell me exactly what you see."

Hesitantly I look down again, "Well, there's letters. An 'E'…looks like an 'M'… and a 'P'… I think, it's a little difficult making out these letters, I know I see the word royalty. And there's something about Canaries here…" Eric immediately grabs the picture away from me and places it back into his right inside pocket. "I don't understand, it was clear as day, anyone could have seen that Eric," I look up at him and furrow my brow.

He smirks at me, "Please, let's finish eating. I do hope you will consider my offer… *the additional* offer that is."

I grab my fork and poke another piece of shrimp, before I place it in my mouth I ask, "Are you going to tell me more about yourself and what's going on with that piece of paper in order for me to make an informed decision?" I resume eating after asking my question, staring at him with purpose and poise.

He gazes at me and smiles, "I will tell you, but we have a long time to get into those details, not tonight. Let us lighten the mood," he waves over to the waiter for another round of drinks. *Not another round.* Anymore alcohol and I'll be singing and dancing on the table for him.

I don't usually drink; in fact, most occasions, I have no want or need to drink. Tonight is different, Eric has given me very mixed feelings and I'm not sure how I should proceed with this. *Hence, the nervous sipping.*

Do I say yes to his mysterious offer? I mean, what exactly is it? Am I helping to solve a crime? *That actually might be fun!* Or maybe a treasure hunt… although, I don't think I would be good at that. Whatever it is, he is willing to pay me pretty damn good money to help. He seems pretty harmless… *Let's not forget incredibly handsome.* "Brielle?" I hear a familiar voice break my concentration for the second time today. Could it be? *No…*

I look over at the door and coming through is Eryn with some guy waving at me. "Oh no," I wipe my face and inhale deep. *Buzzkill.*

"What?" Eric asks as I stand up and proceed to stand in front of the table, *in front of him,* so that Eryn couldn't get a clear view of him.

"Brie, I thought you told me you would be home this evening? I couldn't help but notice you from downstairs…" Eryn accuses as she tries to look past me. Eric has his body turned towards me, trying to see around me at this other woman.

"Do you have a date and you didn't tell me?" She asks, moving me out of the way. "Hi, I'm Eryn. Brielle's best friend and business partner, how do you do?" she holds her hand out to make Eric's acquaintance, so he stands up to shake her hand.

"Eric Windsor," he says as he grasps her hand into his. Just as they shake, I feel a little winded. As if something takes my breath away, I stumble back. Eric let go of Eryn's hand so quickly that he is already standing beside me to prevent me from falling.

Eryn glances at the table to see the investment paper sitting there. "What is that?" she goes to grab the papers but Eric swiftly seizes them.

He sternly says to her, "It's something private… between Briellyn and I, actually." He forces a grin, her visual response uninviting.

"Well since you are here Brielle, I would like you to meet the new business partner… Fiorello," she flashes a devious smirk Eric's direction as the gentleman she came in with comes to light.

He's a very tall man with medium brown hair, slender build and stunning green eyes. I find it odd that him and Eryn actually look alike. *Maybe it's the booze.* "Pleasure to finally meet the brains behind the business Ms. Donado, I've heard so much about you. Please, call me Fiore," he holds his hand out to me. Eryn snorts and turns her nose up at his comment.

I take his hand, which he then kisses. "Pleasure's mine," I reply with a cordial smile graced upon my face.

He then proceeds to shake Eric's hand, "Eric." He gives a gentle nod with a firm hand shake.

"Have we met? There's something about you that is familiar," Eric states, raising one brow and tilting his head while staring at Fiorello's face.

"I don't believe so," is his polite reply. They simply nod at each other in acknowledgment of their meeting.

I cut the silence with my words, "I'm sorry I haven't called you or your people, but I don't believe the merger will be necessary after all," breaking up the odd glare the two gentlemen had between each other.

Eryn cut her eyes over to me, "Excuse me?!"

Fiorello raises his hand ever so gently as if to silence her. "Any particular reason for that my dear?" he asks smoothly.

"I found an angel investor who is giving a greater share and taking a smaller stake," I reply. I graciously look over at Eric who happens to be staring my direction.

Fiorello smiles, "Well that *is* wonderful news," he leads, he looks at me then looks at Eric, "But I do believe you'd be making a grave mistake by not partnering with me."

Eric places his hands in his pockets, prominently adjusting his stance, "And why is that *Fiore?*"

Fiore adjusts his posture in reaction, "Well you see, though you may be offering financial assistance Mr. Windsor, I have connections within the industry that can elevate her status in a much more significant way. You do have her best interest, don't you? Which is..." He motions at Eric as he briefly pauses, "*priceless*, as you say it?"

"But Fiore," I interrupt, batting my eyes and trying to seem polite.

Eric interrupts me, "I'm sure you have plenty of connections, but she shouldn't have to sell her soul and forget all of her sacrifices to get there."

Fiore looks at Eric accusingly, "Sell her *soul?*" he chuckles as he steps a little closer to me, carefully staring into my eyes, "I'd be willing to match his offer Ms. Donado." His eyes are very mesmerizing yet genuine.

"I... I... um," I stutter trying to think of a response; my eyes gazing back and forth between the two men inquisitively.

"Why change the offer now, why didn't you offer that to begin with?" Eric fiercely approaches Fiore, looking at him keenly. I glance at Eric, intrigued by his natural urge to be protective. *Kinda hot.* I focus back on the conversation at hand.

In agreement with his statement, I nod and add, "Yeah, why *didn't* you? Surely Eryn told you my numerous counteroffers, you wouldn't come down on the shared stake. Not for anything."

Fiorello grabs my hand, "I'll tell you what mademoiselle; I'm willing to not only match his offer but give you access to 50% of my existing clientele and hold off on all profit shares for the first three years. If I don't make you money, I will gracefully sign back my share." He stares deeply into my eyes. Something about it is telling me to say yes. *Just say yes.*

"Brielle, don't let him trick you into a last minute deal," Eric urges as it breaks my concentration on Fiorello.

"*ENOUGH,* both of you. At the end of the day, this is *my* company and I will do with it as I see fit," I raise my hands to both of them. Eric clenches his jaw and Fiorello puts his hands together, intrigued by my response. I continue, "With that being said, I graciously accept BOTH offers."

Eric and Fiorello both look towards the ceiling, assessing what I just said to them. Eric immediately states, "But you said it yourself, you only needed $250,000? Why…"

I motion to stop him, "Take it or leave it, we can all make money together. Eryn has put a lot of time and effort in with Fiore here and Eric your proposal is too good to say no. So…" I raise my eyebrows at the two of them and fold my arms together. Eryn is standing there in utter shock waiting to hear the outcome.

Fiorello perks up, "You are quite strong-willed Ms. Donado." He then turns to look at Eric, "Well, I look forward to seeing you at the quarterly investment meetings Mr. Windsor, after all, it's just business." He holds out his hand to shake Eric's.

Eric looks at me out of the corner of his eye and proceeds to shake Fiorello's hand. "Right, it's *just* business," Eric replies to him sternly.

"I look forward to meeting again. Ms. Donado... Mr. Windsor... I'll have my attorney bring over the paperwork," he shakes hands with me, kisses it once more, then proceeds to walk away.

"Oh Fiore," I add, stopping him in his tracks.

"Yes?"

"Make sure that contract states that you must make *more than* your shared stake in order to keep your share," I smile confidently at him.

He simply nods his head and smiles back, "Of course." Then takes his leave.

"You and I have a LOT to discuss Brie, I'll see you in the morning," Eryn mumbles my direction as she proceeds to follow Fiorello out.

I take a deep breath as Eric awkwardly twists his face, a smile somewhere in the mix, "Well, that was interesting." He helps me to my seat, which was just a few steps but I stumble. He asks, "One too many drinks?" *You have no idea, Mr. Windsor.*

I stare up at him and gingerly smile, somewhat embarrassed I reply, "I believe so, I'm not usually like this... *you...* this meeting... and now *that* meeting, it has all been incredibly stressful... and wonderful." Starry eyed I stare at him, *you're wonderful.* I shake my head. *Focus woman!*

He lightly angles his head and asks, "Why stressful Ms. Donado? Handling business and getting your way seems so... *natural* for you." He chuckles.

I adjust in my seat and take another bite of my food, I have eaten over half of the entre and clean my mouth with my napkin. "Well... *since you're asking*," I make sure no food is left in my mouth before continuing, "You're obviously this born to wealth, hot shot, who seems to be able to do whatever he wants, whenever he wants..." my tone is confident as I stare at him.

"I mean, I think any business owner with a good idea could only hope to have someone like you knocking at their door wanting to invest in their venture. Surely you know that though. You haven't told me much about yourself but I can tell you that you're probably third generation wealth, grew up in a great neighborhood, high-end education like Oxford, surely a master's degree at the minimum, given your extensive knowledge. Even though I didn't see you pull up in a vehicle, I'm sure you have a chauffeur at least some point in the day and at the very least three or four vehicles at your behest. I would say you are worth at least in the triple digit millions and if not yet, you will be one day through an inheritance of some sort. I'm not sure what you do for a 'living' but I'm sure you could lounge all day and never do anything, which I doubt you do because you are in such great shape…" with a cocky sneer and a twist of my mouth, I take another sip from my beverage and look at him sweetly, "Did I miss anything?" I say sarcastically. "Not all of us have such an easy life…"

Eric lets out a wholesome laugh as he wipes his face clean from finishing his food. He shakes his head in agreement, "Yes, I definitely could use your expertise. You're *saucy*, I like that. You were spot on about almost everything."

I flirtatiously motion at him as I take another sip, "Which one was I off on?" I never break my gaze from his eyes.

"Well for one, I have my doctorate. *Yes it's from Oxford.* And I'm worth billions Ms. Donado, thanks to my family wealth. But I bet you didn't catch that I'm not American…" he points at me as if to say, ah-ha, and shifts in his seat.

"Well excuse me… *Doctor* Windsor," I say sarcastically. Changing topics, I put my drink down, "I have to say, this was really delicious. Thank you for treating me to this delightful dinner and meeting."

"Treating *you*? I thought you were treating me?" He stares at me blankly but unable to keep a straight face, he begins to chuckle. "I'm just kidding. The pleasure is all mine," he finishes his drink.

The waiter comes by and gives Eric the check. Without skipping a beat he places something in the fold and hands it back. The waiter bows graciously and walks away. "Are you okay to drive?" he walks over to me, giving me his hand to help me up and out of my chair.

I smile at him while reaching for his hand, "Of course I am." *Hell no I'm not.* I take two steps while still holding onto his hand and almost fall sideways, "Ok, maybe not…" I add, trying to be more graceful and less like the terrible drunken date.

Eric is still holding my arm and laughing under his breath. "Ok. How about I drive your car home and I will have my driver follow us to take me home, would that be ok?" he asks as we board the elevator to get to the first floor.

I flash him a coy look out the corner of my eye, "I *knew* you had a chauffeur…"

He chuckles.

"That's fine," I smile like I'd just won a prize on Jeopardy for guessing the phrase. We get outside and walk up to the valet. Eric hands him my valet ticket and he dashes off to go get the vehicle.

Eric turns to look at me and cups my left hand into both of his hands, "Ms. Donado, I have had a fantastic time with you tonight and I truly hope that you give my proposal some serious thought after you get home. I…" he hesitates, "I need you on this. Your expertise would be graciously appreciated." He gathers himself to quaintly smile; patting his left hand over top of mine and then lets go. He then waves over his chauffeur with his left hand as he places his right into his pocket, and waits.

His chauffeur pulls around the corner. As he drives up, Eric approaches the passenger side door. The man rolls down the window and I can see the two of them exchanging a few words. Eric finishes speaking to him as my car is pulled up in front of me by the valet. I dig into my purse to pay the valet and he quickly shakes his head, "No ma'am, your valet was already taken care of by Mr. Windsor."

He opens the passenger side door for me and holds out his hand to help me inside. "Of course he did…" I mumble sarcastically under my breath as I sit in my vehicle and the valet closes the door. *Kind of sweet too.* I see Eric walking up on the opposite side just as the valet opens the other door. He waves at him in thanks and sinks into the seat. As he adjusts the seat and mirrors, I tease, "Been awhile since you've done this huh?"

"I was out driving this morning, I'll have you know," he quickly replies, amused. He glances at the navigation system in the center console and hits the 'home' button. "Ah," he says, "you're not too far from my home."

I laugh hysterically, "You mean you don't live in some fancy penthouse here in the city?"

He chuckles in response and nods, I hear him mutter, "Mmmhmm," under his breath. He drives off, making our way out of the city, his chauffeur is close behind.

"So..." I begin boldly, "I've been thinking about your proposal and you never mentioned exactly what it is I'll be doing."

He glances over at me and cocks an awkward, blushing type smile, "I'd like to think of it as important research, but for you, I think it will feel a lot like a vacation adventure. Lots of traveling... ya know, hotels and houses in private, remote locations. Kind of like a treasure hunt... but not really."

"Sounds fascinating," I tease, "I could use a little bit of adventure in my life. I'm such a bore and a homebody, I've never even had a real vacation before," I drift off into a brief thought while looking out the window.

"I'm also going to double the pay I offered you, are you *sure* you want to do this?" He keeps glancing at me and then back to the road.

I quickly turn and look at him, "Double my pay? Why? A million is already more than generous. Perhaps too generous. You just said it's only research..."

"I said you can *think* of it as research. But I believe that it's going to be a little more... *dangerous* than I let off..." he sounds hesitant.

"Dangerous?" I think quickly, and mockingly I reply, "I laugh in the face of danger ha-ha-ha-ha."

"Ha ha, yeah okay Simba, I'm being serious. Are you *sure* that this is something you want to do?"

"I'm 28 years old, I could certainly use some adventure. Let's do it," I smile at him, my words carrying excitement and certainty. *Please take me away from my normal life, you handsome stranger. If only for just awhile.*

He glances over at me with a very serious look on his face, "This isn't a game Brie, I want you to be sure…"

I couldn't believe he *finally* called me Brie, I smile sweetly, "Let me show you just how sure I am." I unbuckle my seatbelt and reach over to him.

He's looking at me nervously, "What are you doing?"

"Showing you," First I unbuckle his seat belt. I then pat his chest down. I can hear his breath quicken. I open up the right side of his jacket, pulling out the contract, then settle back into my seat. "What were *you* thinking I was going to do?" I lend him a flirty smile as I pull out a pen. I sign the contract and the back of the check. "I will be cashing this tomorrow. When do I start?"

"As soon as you are ready…" he replies confidently. I fold up the papers and lean over to place it back into his jacket pocket. I then re-buckle his seatbelt. *I can't believe I am doing this.* Eryn is going to freak out at me. "Something about sexy strangers that makes you do things you wouldn't normally do," I cynically mumble to myself.

"What was that Brie?" Eric chimes into my thought.

"I didn't say anything," I smile back. I'm looking over at him as his features gleam in between the street lights. Perfect nose, chiseled cheeks, masculine chin, deep dark hair, and eyes so deep blue you could drown in them, I snort to myself, 'there's not a chance he's interested in YOU.' But a girl can dream right? I lose myself in my thoughts for a moment.

* * * * * * *

"And it looks like we are here," his voice sounded like a boom in my head. The ride, *and the delightful thoughts*, are over. He pulls up into the community and I guide him to the front of my house. I open the garage and he pulls in. "May I walk you to your door, well to your first floor?" he shrugs. His sweet, handsome face is just so inviting.

"I'd like that," I reply.

I go to open my door, and he stops me "No, please, allow me." Again, I am taken back by his chivalry. He hops out of the car and quickly comes to the passenger side. I can see his chauffeur pull up in the rearview mirror just as Eric opens my door and lends me his hand.

"Ya know," I begin as I grab his hand, "Your mannerisms aren't like most men, a lady could get *very* used to this. I might mistake this for flirting." I smile as he helps me out of the truck.

"As a lady should be treated," he smiles back. *No hints about the flirting though.* I knew right then I wasn't his type. He walks me to the door that leads to my first floor and I pull my house keys out of my purse. I stick the key in the lock and turn it to open the door. "Well, thank you for the wonderful evening. I look forward to working with you," I hold my hand out to shake his.

He grabs my hand instead and brings it to his lips, kissing it softly and prolonged, "Until tomorrow." My heart instantly skips a beat. *Definitely can be mistaken for flirting*, I thought again.

"I will call you and let you know an exact date tomorrow," smiling as he lets my hand go. I turn around to go through my doorway and as I'm closing the door I wait to see him get into his car. His chauffeur is standing there with the door open and just as he is about to get into the vehicle, he pauses and looks straight at me, cracks a smile and waves. I politely wave back and close the garage door, then shut the inside door leading upstairs, pressing my back against it trying to catch my breath. *What an exciting evening!*

!

Briellyn

Making my way to my bedroom, I begin to get undressed. I think to myself, traveling, only God knows where, with a wealthy, handsome man. *How risqué of you.* Finally getting out my comfort zone though. This should be fun. *Eryn would be proud... or pissed.* I chuckle to myself.

What if he's some psychotic crazed killer? *Pfft. That'd be my luck.* This getaway...*this* is something women dream about but it never *really* happens. A handsome stranger whisking them away. I still have my doubts on its validity but I'll let this play out. See if it's more than just a tall tale.

As I sip my night time tea, I have a seat on my bed and pull out my laptop. I've never heard of the Windsor family and he claims to not be an American. Then what *is* he? He didn't have a defining accent. Perhaps I'll just Google him. There can't be that many people who are billionaires in the world.

I go straight to the Google search page. "Okay, let's see," I crack my knuckles and my neck and proceed to typing. E-R-I-C... space... W-I-N-D-S-O-R, enter. I scan the search page but nothing stands out. I decide to try W-I-N-D-S-O-R... space... B-I-L-L-I-O-N-A-I-R-E, enter. First entry is from ancestry.com. I click on the link and up pops a gentleman who looks like Eric's twin and it states within the brief explanation, born in 1895, the Windsor family was already worth millions.

"Well," I chuckle to myself, "at least he's not full of it." I begin to get butterflies in my stomach as I get excited all over again. I'm going to start packing tonight and post a job replacement right NOW. I don't even know how long I'll be gone.

As I sip my tea further and lose myself in thoughts of exotic beaches, I hear my phone beeping. I grab the small purse I had for the evening and see that I'd already missed three calls. *Eric perhaps?* I excitedly unlock the screen and press the phone button. Three missed calls from… Eryn. Wrong E-R name, last name I wanted to see. Why though I'm not sure.

Here is this dashing, handsome stranger who more or less swept me off my feet and single handedly saved my business and I *don't* want to talk to my best friend, this has never happened before. Maybe it's the idea that I know she'll be pissed that I'm leaving for a while. Just then, my phone rings again. It's Eryn. Should I answer it? *Ugh.* I'm dreading talking to her. I don't want to hear her lecture me but I know I might as well get it over and done with.

"Hello Eryn," my tone sarcastic as I roll my eyes and take another sip of tea.

"Um, why am I just now hearing from you?" she snaps.

"I just got home, calm down." I begin to pace in the room and set things up for the next day.

"Who was that guy you were with this evening? You told me you were going to be home…"

"Well *mother*, you don't have to worry. He's just a shareholder now, but of course you know that."

She went silent for a moment, "And when, pray tell, were you going to inform me about him?"

"Hmm, maybe this evening after dinner. Oh wait, you were at dinner so…" I'm sure she can hear both the sarcasm and smile in my voice.

"Excuse me Brie, but last I checked we were partners."

"Eryn, last *I* checked you were my VP and business confidant, partner is a term we use loosely. I still *own* the majority share along with my sister. You don't *own* any part."

"Oh I see..." she sounds almost hurt.

"Don't get all crazy, look, I will be doing interviews this week and I'll be going out of town for a while…" I bite my lip, clenching my jaw.

"Seriously, Brie? What are you *talking* about? I'm coming over."

"Um, no you're not, we will talk more tomorrow."

"Brie, you can't do this to me. I worked on getting Fiorello for *months* and this is how you repay me? You go parading around with some gorgeous stranger and just forget about me?!"

"If I didn't know any better, I would say that you were a little jealous. And it's nothing personal, it's just business. He took a significantly lesser share in the company than Fiorello was offering and gave us more money. Effectively, he convinced Fiorello to take a lesser share as well and now we have double the capital to work with. I'm actually thinking very clearly."

"Ok, prove it. Fiorello knows this type of business inside and out, let him hire your replacement." *Why you little…*

"Whoa now," I sit down on my bed, "Considering how important this is, I can't just leave it to anyone."

"Why don't you allow me to run it then and I will hire someone to do my job for a while."

"I love you Eryn, but I'll be hiring someone else. It's nothing personal, it's just…"

"Business. Right. Whatever Brie, I guess I'll see you tomorrow," she angrily hangs up the phone.

I look down at my phone and see it blinking that the call ended, "What a bitch!" I say loudly. I think to myself, I'm not going to let her ruin my night, no way. Just then I get a text message. I don't know if I should check it because it's probably just more of her negativity. I pull it up anyway. I have a soft spot for Eryn and even though she's a bit crazy right now, she's *MY* crazy bitch.

'Love you, I'm sorry and I can't wait to hear more,' it says.

I'm beginning to think she's bipolar, but I guess my news wasn't exactly like Christmas morning.. We've both been super stressed about what direction the business was going to go. I smile at the phone and put it down. It rings again, so I immediately pick it up. "Eryn, it's okay, I forgive you just..." I hear breathing over the phone. I pull the phone away from my ear to look at the number and it just says 'unknown'. "Hello?" I ask. "Eryn if this is your kind of a joke, I'm not amused."

A deep, husky, voice breaks the silence, "We are coming for you Aurecia." Then they hang up. *What the hell?* Inside I'm freaking out a little. I can feel my heart starting to flutter. It's that time of year though, October rolls around and the crazies roll out from the first to the thirty-first. I turn my phone off.

"Jokes on you, douchebag," I mumble to my phone, tossing it aside. I clamber into my bed and turn my bedside lamp off.

I laid there in the dark for about thirty minutes and couldn't fall asleep from all of the excitement. Eric's face was all I could see. I turn the lamp back on and open the drawer of my end table. The cashier's check sat there staring at me, it was a sight for sore eyes. I smirk and think to myself, I really hit the jackpot with this one... *lucky me.* So rarely can I make that statement.

I grab my phone and turn it back on. As it's loading up I'm staring off into space wondering what clothes I should bring on this 'expedition'. When my phone finishes loading up, it gently vibrates to let me know that I have another text message. I open it up to see that Eric sent me something… apparently shortly after I turned my phone off. *Of course.*

'I'm excited to be working with you Brie, please let me know if you need any help for this transition.'
-Eric W.

Even his text messages sound so prim and proper, I wonder if he has someone in mind to replace me… I mean, he did already have the check ready and he knew he was going to ask me to leave. *Now I feel like a hypocrite after just telling Eryn I didn't want a stranger choosing someone for me.* She won't know the difference, I feel like Eric just *gets* me. I open the keyboard on my touch screen and begin swiping away.

'I know you won't see this until morning, but before I decide to post on the job board, do you happen to know someone who may be able to fill my spot while I'm gone?'
-Brie

It's worth a shot if it saves me from weeks worth of interviews. He seems anxious to leave right away. *Shoot, I didn't even ask how long we'd be gone. That persuasive glare he had could erase my memory anytime.* I wonder if we will be back for the holidays. My mind is off pondering again as I reach to turn my light out. I place my phone on the end table and plug it up to charge, then drift off into the most wonderful dream.

* * * * * *

Birds chirping in the distance, the sound of the wind gently swaying the trees. Everything appears hazy because the sun is so bright. I'm in a gorgeous field filled with long ivory tulips. The smell is crisp and fresh. I can feel the flowers amongst my finger tips, like the finest woven silk, walking in the direction of the sun. As I get closer to the trees, there is a small stream. The trees shielding my eyes from the bright sun, I sit down next to the water. I run my fingers in this crystal clear stream, feeling the coolness it provides from the short walk. Animals are sipping from the refreshing creek; two fawns and their mother, a couple of bunnies, different types of birds grow alarmingly nosy. I smile at the one fawn looking over at me.

Suddenly the fawn falls over and the field dims. The other animals, except for the fallen fawn, quickly scurry away. I'm looking around frantically, trying to figure out what just happened. I go to stand up and make my way over to the fawn. As I step into the stream it seems as if the distance between me and the fawn gets wider. The closer I step, the further I seem to be. Once the water reaches my hips, it begins to turn red. The ivory draped dress I'm wearing is now blood stained. I look up to see the fawn is bleeding out. I continue to walk towards it and with my next step the ground disappears beneath me. I'm sinking infinitely into the water, the surrounding ground no longer there, drowning within its icy grip. I look up towards the surface to see a large dark figure hovering above the water as I take my last breath.

Briellyn

Tap, tap. Tap, tap, tap. My sleep is interrupted by the sound of something hitting my window. I'm gasping for air while grasping my blouse, trying to wake up, "Rrrgh, shut it woodpecker!" I glance at the time on my phone to see that it's 8:30am. "Jeez," I roll over to stare at the ceiling with my phone in my right hand, rubbing my eyes with my left, still trying to wake up as I'm going through each notification one at a time. Email after email, I mark it as either important or delete it. I then get to a text message response from Eric. My heart briefly stops.

'Actually, I have two people in mind. Care to do an interview or two at 9? I'll bring coffee and breakfast.'
-Eric W.

Wait. Like nine, like thirty minutes from now nine? I don't think I've ever gotten out of bed so quickly. I run into my bathroom and turn on the shower. While it's warming up I'm brushing my teeth and using the toilet. I must be checking the time every ninety seconds because I'm not sure if he meant at my house or the office.

As I continue to brush I walk into my closet to find a fashionable pant suit to wear. I mean after all, my signature suit collection is what got me linked into the fashion world. I find it to be extra powerful and sexy when a woman wears a three-piece suit that fits like a glove. I choose a wine colored pant suit with a pale blue satin blouse and hang it on the door. I spit the remaining toothpaste out and quickly shower up.

Once out the shower and drying off, I look at my phone again. 8:50. *This will be the fastest makeup session I have ever done.* I dab a little foundation all around to cover up any imperfections, blend it, dab some bronzer on my cheeks and atop my eyelids and then throw on some mascara. I top off my look with a pale pink lip gloss and a deep rose color on my cheeks. I unpin my hair; that I'm grateful I wrapped last night. Just as I'm putting on my heels, I hear a knock at the door. I grab my phone and glance at the time again. 8:57. "A little early," I mumble as I walk down the stairs to the door with my suit jacket over my left forearm, "But of course he is."

I open the front door and Eric is standing there in this spectacular pinstriped navy suit with a steel grey shirt and fantastic deep grey tie. He's holding two coffees from Dunkin' and a small bag. "Well good morning sunshine," he leans in to kiss me on the cheek.

"Come on in," I reply, kissing his cheek simultaneously back, "the kitchen is to the left."

He steps into my home and looks around, "So this is what a clothing designer's home looks like. I guess it's true what they say…"

He looks back at me, I smile. "Or I could just know a great decorator."

My response is teasingly swift. He hands me an iced coffee, "Touché."

"Well what do they say? Now I'm curious," when I glance at the side of the cup, it says my usual 'double extra cream, extra sugar, caramel swirl'.

"Um, ok," I furrow my brow inquisitively, "how did you know what I like?" I snark, "With precision." I squint my eyes at him in shock, forgetting completely about the previous conversation and hoping to God that he isn't *really* a crazy stalker.

"Oh," he smiles at me as he places the small bag on the counter, "I called your assistant. She told me what you drink since you never texted back this morning." *Disaster averted.* Clever man. Maybe *too* clever .

"I was hoping to catch you still in your bed dress…" he chuckles. *Bed dress? Really?*

"Seriously?" I reply teasingly, "who *are* you? Were you born in the 1800's." Laughing while repeating the word to myself, I notice Eric looking at me. "What?" I ask.

He tilts his head a little bit, "You have an absolutely radiant complexion. I couldn't quite tell yesterday evening, but here in the sunlight, you just have this… beautiful bronze glow." He smiles at me again.

I blush as I pull my hair back behind my right ear. *Bronzer does wonders my handsome friend.* Confidently I reply, "Why, thank you Eric." I grab some plates and open the small bag, quickly changing the subject, "So where am I doing these interviews?"

"Ah," he taps my hands away from the bag and proceeds to open it himself, "Well for one, I told the first person 9:30 because I hadn't heard from you. Two," he glances up at me with a devious smile, "I thought it more professional to interview at your office." He pulls out two small containers from the bag. The first one he opens, to my delight, is a mini ham, tomato, spinach, onion, and cheddar omelet while the second is a fresh fruit mixture of sliced grapes, strawberries, kiwis, and bananas. He puts the omelet on the plate and garnishes it with the fruit around it. He places the plate in front of me. "Bon appetit," he says cheeringly.

I work up a quirky smile and ask, "You're not eating?"

He sits down next to me, "I already ate, I had my chef whip this up for me to go… *for you.*" I let out a chuckle on the inside. A chef? *Spoiled brat.* "I hope you like it," he pulls his chair forward and adjusts.

Of course the omelet is delicious and made oh-so-perfectly. The fruit is so fresh you can taste the farm it came off of. Is this what it will be like traveling with him on this extravaganza? *The ultimate vacation.* I get to see how the other side lives for a change.

Thankfully the omelet is small, so I'm able to eat quickly while maintaining lady-like bites. I don't want to come across mannerless in front of a man who would put a nun to shame. *But I hate being late.* "I don't know what it is about you Eric, for some reason I trust you on a whole other level than most," I quickly walk into the living room to grab my purse. I come back and he's holding my front door open. "You're too good to be true," my eyes flutter at him and a subtle laugh escapes, "I'm still wondering why me though?" We both step out of the house and he stands there to watch my six as I lock the door. *Don't judge me on the lingo, I'm going on an adventure, gotta get into character.*

He gently touches my back and points to his car below. *A two-door, dark blue Bentley continental,* "Might I see you into work today?"

I look at him and smile coyly. "No chauffeur today?" I tease. My usual routine… *toast.* I shake my head and lightheartedly reply to his initial question, "Yes, of course." He walks me to the passenger side door and opens it for me, lending me a hand as I sit inside. He walks around the front of the car, *in my mind he's moving in slow motion.* He puts on these sunglasses that framed his face just right, the edge of them catching the sunlight. He's like a Hugo Boss supermodel. "It's just not fair," I mumble. He slips into the driver's seat and unbuttons his jacket. He buckles himself in. As do I the same, he presses the ignition. The car rumbles with a low, sexy murmur.

"One day, I will tell you why I chose you, until then, just enjoy the ride," he peels off. I'm not sure whether he meant it literally, metaphorically, or both but I was certainly going to sit back and do just that.

'Looking back over the past year, there's been another decline in births on a worldwide scale. The number has been declining rapidly every year for the last…' Eric turns the radio down as we pull up to the office.

"I'll wait outside, I'm confident you will hire at least one of them today," he smiles. "I'll wait outside, I'm confident you will hire at least one of them today," he smiles. I nod at him gratefully, opening the car door and stepping out. As I'm walking to the door, I can see Eryn staring at me from her office. I smile and wave at her, and though it was delayed, she waves back at me. I open the front door and make my way to my sanctuary, saying good morning to everyone while walking by.

My assistant isn't at her desk, so I just leave her a note stating to call when the first interviewee arrives.

I enter my dimly lit office and immediately put my stuff down so I can open the blinds. The suns warm embrace feels like the world's telling me everything is *finally* going my way. I don't remember a time when I've ever felt so good, and genuinely happy. I turn around and am immediately startled.

"I'm so sorry, I didn't mean to surprise you," a sharply dressed man says as he hops out of the guest chair in reaction to my scream, my heart beating out of my chest.

"Oooo weee," I exhale loudly, "it's… *okay*…" I raise my hand as if to stabilize myself.

He walks up, grabs my outstretched hand and chuckles, "I really am sorry."

"And who, exactly, let you into my office Mr.?," I lean toward him waiting for a name.

"Fiorello sent me," he states, "I'm his attorney, Laurence Steele, just dropping off the paperwork. As requested, ma'am." He holds his hand out to officially greet me. He continues, "And no one was at the desk, so Eryn said it was okay for me to wait in here."

"Oh did she? Well alright," I place my hands on my hips and look down at my desk, "I have a few interviews coming in and only a few minutes, so let's get this done quickly, shall we. Where do I sign?"

He pulls out the necessary papers and I quickly glance through them, double checking on the share percentage and the success clause. I initial where necessary and sign the bottom.

I stand up straight and look at him, "Is that all?"

He puts all the papers up, "Why yes ma'am, and this…" he pulls out a white envelope. I open it and glance inside. It's a cashier's check in the amount of $300k. The attorney asks me, "Is everything to your liking Ms. Donado?"

"Um, indeed, yes. Just one question, how does Fiore have such a prestigious lawyer to make house calls? You are *the* Laurence Steele from the firm Steele, Cyrus, & Rinke, are you not?" I reply to him, taking notice to exactly who he is. The name didn't ring a bell at first, but it suddenly dawned on me when I noticed the logo on his brief case.

He smirks then chuckles at me, "Indeed, one in the same. And Mr. Baron owns a rather large stake in the firm. If there won't be anything else, I'll be going now Ms. Donado." He waves at me as he walks out my door.

I shake my head in disbelief that I just signed a deal with a man who tried to take 40% of my company from me. Maybe this is what we need though. My phone rings and I answer it, "Good morning Stacey," I say matter-of-factly.

My assistant, Stacey, is letting me know that the first interviewee has arrived.

"Go ahead and send her in," I finish as I hang up the phone and sit down at my desk. Pulling up closer, I turn on my computer and grab a notepad and a pen from my left drawer. Not a moment too soon, this gorgeous woman walks in, brown skin, long dark curly hair, eyelashes for days, and a Hollywood smile. I stand up to greet her. "Hi, I'm Julia," she holds out her hand in front of me and I shake it.

"Please, have a seat," I point at the chair setting across from me as I proceed to sit down in my own chair. "Thank you for coming in for this interview on such short notice Julia," I pull out her resume from my folder that I had set on the desk.

"It's no problem at all Ms. Donado. I heard about this opportunity and knew it would be worth my time."

I look up and smile at her then look back down at her resume, "I see here that you have four years' worth of general manager experience, a Masters in organizational leadership, and several excellent recommendations including one from Mr. Windsor."

She nods her head in agreement, "Yes ma'am."

"So tell me, what brings you in for this opportunity? Filling in for the CEO of a small business is a big jump from a GM," I warmly smile at her.

"Honestly, I've heard so much about this business and your success in the tabloids. The way you are so real, how you help people to become better, it's such an inspiration. Even though I'm a little older than you and our paths have been different, I want to walk in your shoes. Be more like you. Most of the things you do, I have had training. Though I may need training in certain areas, I learn fast and I'm used to fast paced environments," she states confident. *I like her already.* She crosses her hands and fingers into each other as she sits a little straighter.

"Fabulous, I love the vibe that I'm getting from you. I'm also flattered you think of me so highly," I smile at her, "are you familiar with shopping cart platforms such as like BigCommerce or Shopify? Adding products, setting up photoshoots to display the products, et cetera? As a small business CEO you will be required to have your hands in many other positions, not micromanaging; but a sense of awareness of what goes on in other departments."

"After being a general manager, I realized how important it was to know everyone from the lowest paid to the highest paid, taking special care to show genuine interest and concern for those at the lowest. And in that position, I believe it to be quite similar to what you are talking about when you mention wearing many hats."

I beam at her as we continue to breeze through the interview for another ten minutes.

"I would very much love for you to hang out for about fifteen minutes while I interview the second candidate. Personally, I think you nailed it Julia, which is why I'm asking you to hang around for a bit. We have a very nice lounge that my assistant will show you to. Please help yourself to anything in there," I stand up to shake her hand and show her out the door, "Stacey, please show her the lounge area."

"Your next interview is here Ms. Donado," she points to a gentleman who immediately stands up upon hearing my name. I look over at him, and encourage him to come over. He's tall, slim, tan, and a total pretty boy.

As we walk into my office, I glance at the other resume on my desk to see his name, "Nice to meet you Javier." I hold my hand out to shake his. "Please have a seat," I motion at the chair and we both sit down.

"So tell me, what brings you in for this opportunity, filling in for the CEO of a small business is a big jump from a fashion director," I warmly smile at him.

"Well, I've been working my way up the corporate ladder and it's no longer for me. I met Eric and he told me about the many opportunities that he comes across and I asked

~ 53 ~

him to keep me in mind if anything were to come available. When he called me this morning, it was out of luck that I had requested the week off. I've never worked for a small business before but I hear it's a more humbling yet more rewarding experience."

"Indeed it is," I reply as I look at his resume, "Are you familiar with what we design here?"

"Yes ma'am I am, and I think I could be an asset because…"

He continues talking. But I can't help but notice how he seems to be more focused on the working for someone else concept as opposed to actually *being* the boss. We finish up the interview about ten minutes later. "Alright, well that about sums it up. I'm going to be honest Javier, I think you would make a great addition to my team but not for this position. *You're in luck*, I have wanted to create a new position for a while for a merchandising director and I think that you would be an *excellent* fit… if you're interested," I look at him curiously, hoping he will accept the offer.

"Perfect," I shake his hand before walking over to my printer to hand him a description of the position as well as the salary. "Everyone who comes in has to pay their dues the first six months and prove that they are worthy, become a part of the family. Afterwards, there is room for growth and very nice yearly bonuses."

He glances through the paperwork, "What *is* the starting salary, if I may ask?"

"With your experience and such I will happily start you at $74,000 a year. I know that may not seem like much but depending on the yearly end results, I offer everyone a generous bonus based off a percentage that is calculated based on contribution, years worked, position, and of course final product. Everyone is eligible for it the moment they are hired. Many members of our little family earn an extra amount equal to their yearly salary, so their pay pretty much doubles. And to help with taxes, it's distributed into their check throughout the following year. So, you could very well end up making over $100k if you play your cards right," I confidently hand him new hire paperwork and wink at him, "Get this back to us whenever you are ready."

"Could I borrow a pen please?" he asks as a huge grin graces his face. We walk out my office and over to Stacey's desk to grab a pen. He immediately goes to sit down and fill out the paperwork.

I walk into the lounge to see Julia patiently lounging on the chaise, legs crossed, coffee in hand. I knock so as not to startle her too much. She throws her legs over and sits upright, nervously staring at me.

"Congratulations," I walk over and hold my hand out, "You are the new Chief of Operations. I'm not formerly stepping down but you will fill in as the interim CEO and will hold the official title of COO."

She begins jumping up and down in excitement, I can see tears in her eyes, "Thank you so much for this opportunity. I promise I won't let you down." She leans in and hugs me. "When do I start?"

"Right now, if you like," I giggle, "there are many people here to help with your transition. I'm going to show you back to my office and get you set up."

I show her back to my office and begin doing a brief overview of what she will be responsible for. She shows me just how familiar with most of the operations she was by taking over the program. Oddly, it was like watching me outside of my own body. I know she is going to be a great fit here while I'm gone; she exhibits my same enthusiasm and positivity. "I will have Stacey introduce you to everyone, whenever you are ready. I will figure out a more formal office space for you before the week is out. I have a few things that I need to do, so please, take your time."

I walk out of the office once again to Stacey's desk. "Hey Stacey. I'm taking Julia on as the new COO and she will be my interim while I'm away. I'm going to have the decorator come by tomorrow and get her office squared away. Show her around and have her meet everyone when she is ready, make her feel at home," I wink at her, she winks back.

"I hope you have fun boss lady. You deserve it! It's about time you got out of here for a bit." I smile in thanks as she walks around the desk, running up to me to give me a hug, "Be safe."

I lovingly hug her back, "You be good while I'm gone and be sure to report to me *anything* that seems off."

She is the first person I hired. Her future means something to me so her college tuition is part of her compensation package. She's only 21 years old and has been here since I began my small expansion three years ago. Before that, it was mainly just Eryn and I, putting as much capital away as possible. That was when it was easy to handle everything ourselves.

I glance at my watch and remember that Eric is outside waiting for me. I couldn't wait to tell him the good news and how much I adore Julia. When I make my way outside, I loudly exclaim to him, "How did you know?"

"Know what?" he queries, his expression reeking of confidence from already knowing the answer.

"Know that those two would fit in so well," I finish approaching him quickly.

"Oh, it's what I do for a living. I see people who have potential, and place or recommend them where they can do the most good," he smiles sweetly, "and what do you mean two? You only had one position to fill."

"Julia is perfect to fill my position as an interim, I gave her the COO position. But Javier had such a quality about him. I knew I was going to be hiring for a merchandising director and had already created the job description, so I went ahead and gave it to him. So yeah, I hired them both," I start laughing as I cross my arms and lean my hips against his car.

He chuckles back, "Well I guess that means…" He was interrupted by Eryn walking out the front door and heading our direction. Her expression conflicted. She approaches us and quaintly smiles at Eric then looks at me,

"You weren't leaving without talking to me were you?" She looks sad.

"Of course *not*," I wrap my arms around her while rubbing her back.

She places her chin on my shoulder and glances up and over at Eric, "Please keep her safe, you have no idea how important she is to us. She's irreplaceable."

He nods at her in agreement as we release from our hug. "I hired a wonderful young woman in there that I know you will love. Please make sure…"

She places her finger on my lips, "Don't you dare finish. You know I will make sure she's good and the business is good… and everything will be good for your return." She smiles at me and hugs me again, "Don't forget to have fun. You should go ahead and go, I've got everything under control here."

I pull back and look at her, "Go ahead and go? Trying to get rid of me so soon? Plan on throwing a party right after I leave?"

"No, I'm not trying to get rid of you. *You* are the party. I just know that if you think about something too long, you'll back out so yes I'm sure, you deserve this! You're the hardest working person I know and all that money you've stashed in your house or whatever, you *never* spend. *Go… live* a little," she smirks at me. I gaze at her lovingly and jokingly pout.

I then look over at Eric, who puts his hands up, "Hey, I'm ready when you are."

This. I needed this. Everything is going so smoothly. It almost worries me. *Nothing could be this perfect.* I walk to the passenger side of the vehicle where Eric is holding the door open for me while Eryn walks back inside. As I sit in the car, Eric exclaims, "Well, let's go get you packed!" He shuts my door then walks to the driver side when I see Eryn come back outside with a small light blue box with a silver bow in her hand.

I roll my window down and she hands me the gift. She lovingly smiles, "So you don't forget about us here. It has two separate time settings on it so you will always know what time it is here." I knew immediately it had to be a watch.

When I open it up, it's one of the most unique trinkets I have ever seen; a double-sided watch bracelet locket. There's a heart with an oval inside of it on the front, and when opened, there are two clocks, one on each side. Inscribed on the back 'Not even time stands in my way'. I chuckle at the engraving. "Eryn, this is... absolutely beautiful," I immediately take it out of the box and she clasps it on my left wrist.

"It's made of platinum," she states as she adjusts it, "So no allergic reactions. It's also waterproof." She briefly glances past me at Eric, "Just in case you get wet." *Way to be obvious Eryn!* My cheeks become flushed as I stare at her in dismay. *She really just freakin' said that.* I blow her a kiss and she blows one back after which she says goodbye to me one more time and walks away. I didn't know what to think of her walking away so suddenly like that, but we've never had to say 'goodbye' before.

Just before we leave the parking lot, I ask Eric to wait, "Before we go." I look around taking it all in, unsure when I'll be back. I want to remember everything in this moment. The smell, where the sun is in the sky, how many clouds there are, the laughter of the kids playing nearby. I've worked *so* hard for this and now I'm *breaking* from it. *Feels like I'm cheating. But* at the same time, I'm happier than I've ever been. While closing my eyes, I whisper a quick prayer "I know God will keep it safe for me… Okay, we can go." I beam at Eric, wondering where my life quest is going to take me next

Briellyn

We are five minutes from my house when my cell phone rings, "Short cake! I was just about to call you, I have…" the voice on the other side stops me mid-sentence. "What?" I reply solemnly. The feeling of dread, guilt, and negativity suddenly engulfs me like a catfish sucking in its meal.

The voice repeats, "Dad died."

I'm trying my best to keep my composure. I take a deep breath and swallow hard, "When, Skyla?" I listen intently as she fills me in with the few details that she knows. Eric glances over at me as we pull into my community. He makes his way to the front of my house and I open the garage for him to pull his car into the empty space.

"Let me… ca-call you back," I hit the end button on my phone and lower my hand to my lap, staring at the wall in my garage, silent and still. Eric reaches over and touches my left arm, "Brie?" The touch sends a startling shiver down my spine as I recall a vivid memory of my father.

* * * * * *

"Briellyn! Get your ass down here!" I hear my father scream from the bottom of the stairs. A ten-year-old me walks down the narrow hallway of our home and stares at him from the top of the wooden stairs, his eyes piercing like daggers as my eyes cross their path. He gestures for me to come to him using his right forefinger. A terrified child walked down those stairs. As I came closer to the bottom, I could see the bottle of vodka in his left hand.

"Yes father?" I approach the third to the last step. He quickly grabs my left arm and pulls me down the remaining stairs, lightly hitting my heels as I'm lifted from my stance.

My eyes begin tearing up because his violence has no boundaries when he's drunk, and I'm horrified as to what he's going to do to me. I have no clue why he is upset. He brings me to the kitchen and viciously throws me to the ground, "Why the fuck are there dishes in this sink? And why are the clothes not done?"

I try to get up from the floor, my shaking arms pushing up from the cold tile floor, "I'm sorry father, when I got home I helped Sky with her homework and…" before I could finish my sentence, he slaps me across the face with the back of his hand, sending me back to the ground. I cry out, holding my face with one hand and extending the other in front of me to prevent another hard blow. "Please, father! I didn't mean to. I'm sorry! I'll do them right now."

He grabs my arm again to bring me closer to his face. Short, quick, audible breaths escape between my pleas. "Do you want something to cry about? Huh?!" he punches me in the chest. I could barely breath, tears streaming down my little face; all I could hear was Sky come running down the stairs screaming,

"Daddy no!" I remember reaching for her.

* * * * * *

"Brie?" Eric asks again while grabbing my left hand. I look at him, eyes filled with tears. He looks at me remorseful, "What happened?"

Blankly and slowly I reply, "He's dead. My father's dead."

"Oh my, Brie... hold on," Eric opens his door and runs to the other side of the car and opens my door wide. He quickly kneels down then embraces me. "I'm so sorry," he whispers to me. His words fade as I lose myself in another memory.

* * * * * *

I'm twelve years old, standing in front of the school under the overhead at the front of the building. It was warm but raining heavily that day. I had been waiting two hours for my father to pick me up. Seeing car after car pick up my peers but no one for me. The sun would be going down soon. The thunder was loud and I could see lightning strikes in the distance. Another day disappointed, *rejected...* he forgot about me, *again.*

I begin to walk home, my ten-mile journey, hoping the rain would wash away the tears and the pain. "When I grow up, I will never do this to my kids..." I mumbled to myself. I had seen a car out the corner of my eye and then a honk of the horn. I look up and manage to crack a smile, running

~ 63 ~

over to it and opening the front passenger door to hop inside, soaked to the bone. "I'm so sorry," my father rubbed the rain from my cheek and kissed my forehead. I smile at him gratefully.

* * * * * * *

"I can't go right now Eric," I speak softly. The words were difficult to voice, each one choking me harder than the last, "I have to go bury my Dad."

I stare off in the distance while Eric nods in agreement, "Well of course Briellyn. I'm here for you if you need to talk, or if you need help making arrangements, or just a shoulder to cry on. I know this is very hard for you." He helps me out the passenger seat to my garage door that leads upstairs. He closes the garage for me. I hear the notification on my phone going off. I glance down at it to see a text message from my sister,

I'm already at his home, but if you could get here ASAP I think it'd be best. XO'

I open the door to walk up the stairs, Eric following close behind. Walking straight to my bedroom, I put my purse down and gently sit down at the edge of my bed, staring at a picture that is sitting on my bureau. I was eighteen and Skyla, my sister, was sixteen when the picture was taken. The three of us standing together, dressed nicely, in our front yard. I had just received an award of appreciation from my school for the charitable work I did as a student council member. The school threw a formal dinner in honor of all students who received an award that evening.

It was the only night that I remember that didn't end poorly. My father had been sober for several months and his health was getting better. The last good evening we had before he spiraled out of control and became eternally angry.

I hear a gentle knock at the doorway to my bedroom, just in time to prevent me from soaring into another flawed memory. I subtly shake my head and fake a smile at Eric standing there. He leans on the left of the door frame with his hands in his pockets, "Are you okay? May I come in?" I nod as he strolls over to the bed. He gets down on one knee, to the ground directly in front of me, and looks up at me. "Do you need me to fly you somewhere?"

I don't need you to do anything for me. I don't want to feel like a charity case. Not now, not at *this* very moment. I shake my head no and softly reply, "No, I'll take care of it." I look down at the ground, past his face. The death of my father was like an odd wake up call to remind me never to trust anyone. Maybe this trip *wasn't* a good idea. Maybe I should try to get to know Eric first, figure out what this so-called expedition is about.

Eric can see that my mind is wondering. "Briellyn, I have a plane that can take you anywhere you want, whenever you're ready." His words were like a warm embrace amongst my thoughts, even though I didn't want them to be. My father would bring so much negativity into my life, which is why I had to distance myself from him. *Eric is nothing like your father Brie.* The way he's staring at me from below with those bright blue eyes is both aggravating and soothing at the same time. He seems like he means well. *Genuinely*, means well.

Do I *really* want him around during this hard time? Do I want my perfect image to unravel in front of him? Vulnerability is *absolutely* my worst nightmare. I don't even want to call Eryn and here I am with a virtual stranger. Maybe that'd be best; *a stranger won't pry too much.* He won't ask questions or bring up painful memories. Part of me wants to call Justin; he would know exactly what to say right now. *But Eric is right here.* Maybe keeping him around will make him more likely to tell me about the job he needs me for and that'll keep my mind off all of the bad. *And that's a good thing.*

"Okay," I mumble to him, "I will pack a bag and we can go. I would greatly appreciate the ride…" I'm leaning on my knees with my hands, rubbing my knee with my left hand. "And um," I stutter as I look down past him, "I would appreciate the company." I twist my mouth nervously, hoping he's okay with that and I await his response.

He smiles at me as he comes to his feet, placing his hand on my shoulder and the other in his pocket, "Whatever you need. I will call my pilot right now." He leans in a little bit, "You are strong, you *will* get through this." He flashes a concerned smile, kisses my cheek, then walks out of the room.

A half-grin tries to creep onto my face as I raise my fingers to touch the cheek he kissed. *He's dreamy.*

Focus Brie. I think my sister is withholding details. My father was only 65 years old after all. I was waiting for her to say, 'Oh, he drunk himself into a stupor and never woke up, or something.' I stand up and walk into my closet, first grabbing a black scoop neck maxi dress, then a black sheer blouse, another black dress with lace, and lastly, a pair of black dress pants. I throw my black ballet flats and a pair of heels into my travel bag. I fold the clothes and gently place them into the bag along with underwear, toiletries, and my favorite fragrances.

I then pick out a travel outfit, black lounge pants with the matching jacket and a pink tank top. I shut the closet door and proceed to changing into the lounge apparel. After I'm done changing, I grab my black sneakers and two pairs of jeans, two other tops and a sweater. I throw the sneakers onto the floor and slip them on, then fold the other items and place them into my travel bag too.

Just as I open the closet door, I'm startled to see Eric standing there about to knock. I jump backwards, grasping my chest after a scream manages to creep past my lips. *"Holy moly"* I wheeze, trying to catch my breath and recapture any dignity I still have.

Eric reaches out, "Oh, I'm so sorry. I didn't mean to." He grabs my hand as I hold it out to maintain my balance. *Second time today.* I chuckle and Eric cracks a smile in relief. "I just wanted to let you know that the pilot says everything is set and we'll be okay to take off whenever we arrive at the airport."

I smile and softly reply, "Okay." I pick up my bag and walk out of the closet.

"I'll just be on your balcony, handling a few phone calls okay?" he gestures for the stairs. I nod in acknowledgement and take a look in the mirror. My makeup had run just enough to blacken underneath my eye. I decide to just wash my face. Wash away all of the misery that comes permanently hitched whenever my father enters my mind, in hopes that it makes me feel just a little bit better. After I finish washing, I glance at myself in the mirror again. I already feel better and ready to tackle this... temporary *complication*.

I walk downstairs with my bags and wave at Eric on the balcony. He signals to me, walks in and grabs the bigger bag from me, and heads straight down the stairs to the garage. He's still on the phone. I will admit, it's nice knowing that I don't have to wait inside the airport to board a plane, or have to sit next to some stranger who wants to know where I'm going and what I do.

I lock the inside door and open the garage. Eric is finishing his conversation as he places my bag in the trunk, then opens the passenger side door. "Yes, but that shouldn't be a problem. Keep me posted, something doesn't sound right. Okay, bye," Eric ends the call as he grabs the other bag from me and places it in the trunk. I walk to the passenger side and sit down into the vehicle. Eric closes the door behind me and runs over to the driver side. He gets into the vehicle and starts the car. I buckle up and look over at him; his expression occupied with concern and worry. *All too familiar with that look.* He backs out of my garage, carefully looking behind him; hand on my seat to support his turned body. Each movement with precision as he clenches his jaw. *He's aggravated.* I didn't dare ask him what's wrong; I just assume that something isn't going 100% right concerning his business. Part of the trade is dealing with the bullshit and if it were me, I wouldn't want someone asking me a bunch of questions.

I close the garage with the button on my key chain and just sit in silence, trying to brace myself for anything and everything that is going to come my direction within the next eight hours. If there is one thing I know for certain, I need to be strong for my sister Skyla. I was always the one she looked up to, so I need to be ready to set a good example for her and a shoulder for *her* to cry on when I get there. I don't even know who to call right now or if I should bother calling anyone.

We pull up to a private airport, the rest of the ride remained in silence. The plane and crew is waiting for us, in all of its glory. I'd never seen a private jet up close in person but I've definitely never seen a plane this *color.* The entire under belly of the plane is a sky blue while the top side a rich midnight blue. The windows were all tinted the same color and the interior, which I could see from the car, boasts a rich golden tan hue. The stairs look like they were some type of golden maple wood and everything was trimmed in tan leather and suede.

The co-pilot is standing at the base of the steps waiting for us to stop. He's a rather tall gentleman, light caramel complexion, goatee, and rich dark hair. He looks to be Hispanic, maybe Puerto Rican, dressed in nice navy slacks and a navy jacket with two gold stripes upon his cuffs. He approaches my side of the vehicle as we come to a hault.

He opens my door and assists me out of the car. "Welcome to WindsorAire at Stamford.," he gently grabs my hand and helps me out of the seat, "I will grab your bags ma'am." After he assists me out of the car, he walks to the trunk to grab my bags. Eric steps out of the vehicle and the man greets him, "Good day Mr. Windsor, the cabin is ready for you. No cabin help, as requested." Eric simply nods as he makes his way over to me.

He places his hand on the small of my back as he guides me to the stairs. "I didn't request a stewardess, I hope that's okay. I figured you just want to relax, and anything you might need, I can simply get for you myself," Eric manages to crack a short-lived smile on his face to me.

I smile back gratefully, "Thank you."

I turn to look at the stairs to make my way up and notice the pilot standing there. To my surprise, she was a cute, chocolate skinned woman, with long black hair formed in this elaborate bun, a little shorter than me, dressed in a nice navy pant suit with the matching jacket. Not the typical pilots jacket either, the neckline was uniquely tailored to look like a cowl neck but it was a button up. She had four stripes on her jacket. "Hello there Ms. Donado, my name is Sheila Johnson and I will be your pilot this evening along with my co-pilot," she holds her hand out to motion to the man who greeted me, "Joseph Mendez."

"So wonderful to meet you Sheila," I beam at her. "I need to ask; where is the final destination so that I can land at the nearest private air strip?" She looks at me inquisitively. Female pilots are extremely rare and here is one, employed by a billionaire.

I reply to her, "Perkins Florida is where we are going, I believe the airport in Tallahassee will be easiest." She nods in agreement. Eric guides me along into the cabin. *The cabin is absolutely gorgeous.* Each circular tinted window has mini navy curtains. The entire cabin ceiling had lighting that curved to look like a snake of lights in a posh lounge. There was a bar immediately to the left with a granite countertop and several liquors secured by metal bars. To release the bottle, one had to push a button to loosen it. It had several wine glasses and whiskey glasses. It didn't take up too much space, maybe wide enough to seat two guests comfortably.

A rounded leather couch that could easily seat five or six people is next to it, part of which the back side of it is molded into two high seats for the other side of the bar. It has a small flat surface that could be used behind it, lit up with pretty blue light. To the right of the cabin are two huge reclining chairs that swivel around completely with the click of a button. A mounted round table with a granite top also stood between the two chairs. Past that section are two rows of four wide first-class looking seats, and on the other side of it a booth that would seat four to six people. Behind that is a wall, assumedly the bathroom. The whole ambience of the plane is like a five star hotel with wings. It's beautiful.

"Can I make you something to drink, it might help take the edge off…" Eric immediately walks behind the bar and begins whipping something up.

I nod, "That sounds great." I just keep looking at everything, taking it all in and decide to have a seat at the bar. Joseph places our luggage into the front closet behind the bar. "We'll be doing our pre-flight check and leaving in ten minutes sir," Joseph says as he closes the plane door and retreats to the cock pit. Eric finishes mixing my drink and looks up at me, "Would you believe their married?"

"Who?" I whip my head around to look back at him.

"The pilots," he hands me the drink. *Aw.* "To your father," he raises his glass up to toast me. I clink my glass next to his and manage to fake a smile. *I don't know if my father deserves a toast, let alone me flying there.* Eric consumes his drink in one gulp and pours himself one more.

Concerned, I ask, "Are you okay Eric?" He glances at me from the bottoms up glass. He finishes the drink and puts the glass up.

His lips curl as he braces for the after bite. "Yes, don't worry about me Brie. I'm here for you," he smiles, "Just a little bad business is all, no big deal." He grabs my glass and puts it up.

"If you want to get some sleep, there is a king size bed beyond the bathroom that is quite comfortable," he goes to walk over to one of the huge recliners. He flops down into the seat and reclines it. Relaxing, he looks over at me,

"These are pretty comfy too actually." I can see that he needs to get his mind off of whatever it is that upset him. Ever since that phone call he seems… off. I walk over to the other chair and sit down. "Wow," I lean back, "This *is* impressively comfy!" I beam at him. *I'm good at making others feel better.* It's so rare that I needed cheering up. It would make me happy to make someone else happy.

"So Eric, would you mind telling me a little bit more about this assignment you've hired me for?" I lean on my fist as its propped up on the arm rest of the chair. I grin at him like a freshman highschool girl excited to talk to her senior crush. He looks at me from the corner of his eye and opens the right side of his mouth. He continues facing the bar.

He clenches his jaw and presses the button to swivel my direction. "Are you sure you still want to do it?" He leans toward me while putting his elbows on his knees and laces his fingers through each other. I throw my right leg over the right arm rest and the left leg over my right leg, leaning over the left arm rest. "I understand if you don't want to proceed now. You know, given the circumstances," he continues. He maintains a solemn look on his face, almost as if he was awaiting my decline.

I flutter my eyes at him, "No." He puts his head down as I look down at the floor. "No, I think I need this now more than ever," I bring my head up to look out the window, sad but determined.

He looks up at me, "Well." A smirk creeps onto his face. "If that's true, I will admit that your assistance is essential. I know I said that to you before but I honestly can't do this without you." I could tell that it was difficult for Eric to vocalize that. The words seemed forced. "If it puts your mind at ease, you will first receive self-defense training with a close friend, because as I said before, it could be dangerous. We will then fly off to a place near Quebec City and after that the islands, then to London."

I pull my legs off the arm rest and sit up straight, somewhat leaning in towards Eric, "So it IS a treasure hunt?! But *why* would I need to learn self-defense?"

Eric looks around the cabin, "I mean, I guess, if you wish to call it that. We are actually trying to decipher coded messages to find a few things needed for something bigger."

"Bigger... *like?*" I curiously egg him on for more details.

"A project that I've been working on for a very, *very* long time. I can't tell you everything just yet. First, I must see how everything goes and... see if I can *trust* you completely," Eric gives me a serious stare. He finger combs his hair back with his right hand. *Trust me? Imagine that.* I'm still trying to trust *him.* I laugh to myself at the thought.

The pilot speaks over the cabin intercom, "Pre-flight check completed, please prepare for takeoff."

I could hear the engines revving up and the forward jolt of the plane moving. It made me sit back in my seat. My face displays a sudden disgust. *I hate flying.* Eric gives me a concerning look, "Are... you okay?"

I look back at him and get up. "I get motion sickness, I think I'll take up your offer on the bed in the back," I begin to walk towards the rear of the plane. He stands up to join me. As we pass the wall, the bathroom is indeed to the left and to the right is a refrigerator and a microwave. Past that it opens into a gorgeous small room accompanied with a king size bed, amber colored lights, no windows, a small space for changing clothes and hanging some up, and a beautiful navy and gold color bed set paired with the decorative pillows and all. The entire surrounding of the bed was made of cushion, so it's, in a way, a giant sofa. "Oh wow," I raise my eyebrows and stumble onto the bed, my tone with a hint mockery.

"It's really something right?" Eric smiles assuredly, "there's a switch on the wall there for the lights. It's about a four hour flight. I won't wake you until we are making our descent."

I couldn't help myself but blurt out my first thought, "So how many women have you brought back here? This is too nice for a man to want it just for himself." I joke, almost immediately regretting it as the last word left my lips.

Eric looks at me confused, then smiles, "I *still* think you have me all wrong Ms. Donado." He puts his left hand to his face and gently pinches his bottom lip with forefinger and thumb, "Let me know if you need anything." I coyly smile back at him as he walks out and closes the curtain. *Insert foot here.* I motion to my mouth as I take my shoes off.

Eric seems more and more mysterious. Oh my goodness, what if he's gay?! *What a huge gut punch for the female population that would be.* Well, if there's one thing for certain, he got my mind off everything and that drink gave me just the hint of relaxation I need. I get comfortable just as I feel the plane hit the runway. I turn the light out and feel us ascend into the sky. I only have four hours to clear my head, and I am going to take advantage of every minute.

.

Eric

I leave Brielle to sleep as I make my way back to the chair she was sitting in, pulling my cell phone out to call a friend. It continuously rings while I patiently wait for him to answer.

"Hey Kalil. I'm pretty sure I found her, the woman we've been looking for. Funny how someone can seem right, and then you think you're wrong, only to come back to the same one. I'm going to bring her to you for some training," Confidence and anger in my tone. *It shouldn't have taken so long, I hate doubting myself.* The thought of her last question echoes my mind again and makes me laugh.

Kalil replies, "Are you sure this time? And why does she need training, has something changed? Why can't you do it?"

"Questions, questions... how long have we been at this, Kal? I'm 90% positive she's the one. She can read the glyphs. And I need you to train her… *because I need you to train her.* I think someone may be on to us and I need to try to make contact to figure out what's going on. I can't risk her life. She needs to be able to protect *herself,* more than just her thoughts," I state assertively. *I hate it when he questions my authority.* We've been at this too long for him not to trust my judgement.

"Okay boss, whatever you need. You know I'm just giving you shit. When do you think you'll arrive?"

Sometimes, I think he reads my thoughts. "I'm not sure, her father just died. We are heading to north Florida to handle that. You're still in Texas, right?"

"Yes, I'm in Arlington still following that other lead."

"You can forget her, I'm telling you… *I can feel it*, she's the one. Much different than the others. I will give you a call twenty-four hours before we get there. Just be ready, I need her to learn hand to hand combat and how to shoot. Ya know, the works."

"I have a couple SEAL buddies who can assist with that. Who do you think is onto us?"

"I'm not sure, maybe rogue treasure hunters. I know something is *off*. I know if we don't accomplish this task soon, someone else will. We need to proceed with extreme caution."

"How much have you told her?"

"Nothing really, she knows where we have to go and why I need her. She knows about the training but that's all. I need to be sure I can trust her. Besides, I don't wanna scare her off."

"But if she's the one, then why do you need to be sure? The prophecy says…"

"I know what the prophecy says," I interrupt. My tone softens, "I just… imagined her different I guess." I picture her face from dinner last night. *Something about it, something about her.*

"Okay Eric, do you want to tell me what's on your mind? I get that you've been trapped here and we've been playing the shadow game, you've been trying to make contact forever, but you sound…"

"No Kalil, I'm okay. Can you get this done for me or what?"

"Yes sir, consider it done. I'll be waiting for your call."

I press the end button. *What is it about her?* She really does have me all wrong. I need to figure out who this person is who has suddenly taken an interest in my affairs. I can't put anyone in danger, I just can't. *Not after what's happened to the others.* My thoughts are interrupted by the copilot, Joseph, entering the cabin.

"Smooth flying here sir, mind if I sit?" I shake my head no and gesture to the other chair with my hand. "Sir, if I may, you seem edgy; much more edgy than I've ever seen you before. Is everything alright?"

I look at him sternly. His genuine concern for my well-being is… *heartwarming.* But why does everyone keep asking me that? I give him a reassuring smile, "Yes Joe, I'm good. And knock it off with the sir stuff. You've been with me ten years and you know how casual I prefer you to be."

"I know… Eric," Joseph sighs, "And in that ten years we've never seen this look on your face or feel the tension you are giving off."

"I thank you for your concern Joe, but I'm fine. I just hope that you and your wife are prepared to be away for awhile," I point to the cockpit, rather annoyed by all his prying. *Tension, pfft.*

"We knew this has been coming, long time now. We're ready."

"Great," I halfway smile and lean back in the chair to gesture that I'm no longer interested in conversing, "Is that all Joe?"

"Well," Joseph begins, halfheartedly smiling. *Here it comes.* "In all of our years of working for you Eric, we've never seen you fly with anyone else besides Kalil and Danny."

I perk my head up a little bit, swallowing hard, "What's your point Joe?"

"Well, she's very attractive, successful, sweet… I mean, could this be? *If I may be so bold…*"

I raise my hand and point to Joe with my forefinger, "That *is* too bold." I lower my hand, softening my tones, "Besides, it's not like that. I'm not attracted to her in that way." I recline once more and stare out the window; the only time I feel at ease is when I'm forty thousand feet in the air. *Close to my family.*

"I'm just making an observation Eric, you must be very lonely. You're never with anyone at any of the holiday parties you throw. You are always working. And here comes someone who is like-minded and you won't even consider her. Life is too short…"

"Please Joe," I interrupt, rolling my eyes, each word dripping with disdain, "It's so important that you not finish that sentence. I know how happy you and Sheila are, trust me, I can see it. But I don't expect you to understand. I just wish to sit in peace right now and get my thoughts together. We'll talk later."

Joseph gets up from his seat. He walks over to me and places his hand on my shoulder, "Do it for you, Boss. You need to relax." He turns around and walks back to the cockpit.

I continue to gaze out the window. Why was it me to get stuck here? I need to get home. I drift off into sleep as I feel comforted by the thought that I am one step closer to getting there.

* * * * * *

Briellyn

3 hours and 45 minutes later

I wake up in the dark room in the back of the plane unable to hear anything except the ambient noise of us still in the air. I hit the switch to turn on the light. A dark cloaked figure stands there at the doorway. As my eyes are trying to adjust I mumble, "Eric?" After gently rubbing my eyes, the figure is gone. I shimmy my way to side of the bed and bend over to grab my sneakers. I slip them on and stand up then *BOOM*, the figure is standing directly in front of me. I let out a loud scream and fall backwards.

"Brielle, Brielle," Eric is shaking me trying to wake me up. I open my eyes to see him standing over me, hands around my wrists. "You're okay, look at me... *you're okay*," he sits down and holds me. My heart is pounding so hard I think it's going to explode through my chest, like some gory scene in Alien. I'm panting and holding his arm that is wrapped around me with both of my hands. "You were just having a nightmare," he quietly comforts me. "Shhh, I'm here." I could feel a tear escape my right eye.

Again with the dreams. Like the universe is trying to tell me something. I can deal with the vivid night terrors but this dark figure keeps returning that I've never seen before, not before I met Eric. *It's freaking me out.* What if I can't trust him? What if there's something he has in store for me... and it's not good? But oh, the warmth of his body against me was soothing, calming. I instantly feel better with his arms wrapped around me; the negativity from the night terror just fades away into my distant memory. Something about it just feels familiar. Something this good can't possibly be bad, right? Maybe I should tell him about it.

"You woke up just in time, we've already started our descent and we are fifteen minutes out," he releases his grip a little bit and I sit up.

"Eric," I begin, as I scooch away from him a little and make my way to the edge of the bed to put on my shoes. I take a deep breath. "I have," I hesitate, "a confession to make." I tug my hair back behind my right ear as I slip on the other shoe. "I know this may sound crazy, but I've always felt like I have a special connection with God and I think, for whatever reason, he's telling me to stay away from you." I finish quickly, staring downward and then looking up at him, bracing myself for either a spurt of laughter and him calling me crazy or just a foolish stare.

To my surprise, a soft chuckle comes from Eric. He looks down and shake his head, "And why, dear Brie would you think that?" I look at him and instantly feel better. He is taking my accusation rather well.

"Well," I begin, I scooch a little closer and grab his hand and encase it between both of mine, "Lately, I've been having these dreams…" Eric's cheeks flush a little red and he has an awkward smile on his face. I correct myself, "Not those kind of dreams." Remembering what I said earlier, I blush, "I know what I said earlier was rather inappropriate." I glance away and around the room, anything but at him.

He lightly chuckles again and places his other hand over mine, "You can tell me. And I'm not worried about what you said earlier." I look up at him and his face was calming. I knew I could tell him and not feel judged. "Last night, I had a dream I was drowning while trying to save a fawn. This dark figure appeared at the surface but the water made it too blurry for me to see it. And just now," my eyes got wider as they tear up, "The same figure was standing where you were when you woke me." I regain my composure.

He rubs my hands with his, they felt rugged yet soft, like a man who works with his hands but still takes care of them, "What did the figure look like?" Eric's face shows much concern at this point.

I swallow hard, "It was dark, I couldn't see the face. The clothing was draped, black and oddly flowing, like someone under water. It made it appear very wide and intimidating. I think it had some type of hood, which is why I couldn't see the face," I'm gesturing with my right hand, "And I got a weird call last night and just, ugh," I brush it off and put one of my hands to my forehead, "I think it may be anxiety." I bring my hand back down.

Eric perks up, "What call?"

"Probably just some jokesters, they said they were coming for someone named Aurecia… I don't know anyone by that name so I'm sure it was a wrong number," I sniffle and smile at him.

He looks at me concerned and rubs my hands some more, "I'm sure it just anxiety." I can see him try to fake a half smile.

I lean in and hug him, "Thank you." He is taken back at first but then proceeds to hug me in return. His embrace made me feel safe. *And he smells so good.* I hate that I have such an attraction to him. I know he's handsome but damn, usually I can get a grip by now.

He mumbles to me, "Your welcome." I can feel him lean more into me, giving me more of an embrace and settling into a genuine hug. I think he needed one too. We release our hug and he mentions joining him in the main cabin.

"Sure," I respond. Just then I could smell my breath. *Have I seriously been breathing my bad breath in his face the whole time?* "I'll be there in just a moment," I come to my feet, "Just gotta use the ladies room." I smile and walk into the bathroom as he walks into the cabin.

"Okay," he cordially responds as he walks by. I shut the door quickly.

Even the bathroom is nice. And spacious. I immediately look in the first drawer under the sink. "Ah," I exclaim as I see toothpaste and on-the-go toothbrushes. Just as I thought, *perfect.* I begin brushing my teeth, making sure to brush them well. If he gets that close again, I won't have to worry about my breath scaring him off at least.

I finish up, washing my hands and take a paper towel to dry my hands and face. I look at myself in the mirror and try to pat my cheeks to make them appear a little flushed. If Sandra can do it in that movie 'The Proposal', maybe I can too. *I think that only works for more fair-skinned people, Brie.* I laugh at the thought. I open the bathroom door and make my way to the other chair that Eric was originally sitting in. It's difficult trying to get there because the plane is in a slight downward position.

"Brace for landing," I hear Sheila say over the intercom.

Eric smirks at me, "Just in time, Brie." I flop down into the chair and sit myself back completely. I grasp the arm rests hard and close my eyes. Eric looks at me inquisitively, "What are you doing?" He places his hand over his mouth as if to stop from laughing.

"Landings make me uneasy," I inhale deep through my nose and then exhale through my mouth. I was clearly overcompensating for the landing because it, by far, is one of the smoothest landings I had ever experienced. They eased right into it, no crazy braking or terrible bumpiness, just a gentle tug. Eric is looking out the window with a smile on his face. I glance out of the window nearest me to see that it's another private airstrip. I certainly didn't mind the exclusivity.

"I have a surprise for you," Eric comes to his feet. *Oh, you come gift wrapped?* The plane comes to a stop and Joseph comes out of the cockpit to open the doors.

I look at Eric as I prepare to stand, "A surprise... *for me?* What could you possibly surprise me with? You haven't had any time to plan anything." Eric reaches for my hand to help me to my feet. I grab his hand and stand up. He holds my hand and guides me to the front, leading the way. He walks to the exit and his muscular physique feels like it fills the entire frame of the entryway, blocking me from being able to see anything until he moves. As he begins to walk down the stairs and everything comes to light, I can see in the distance a man standing there. As my eyes finish adjusting I realize I'd recognize that face anywhere. Immediately grinning ear to ear, "Justin!" I quickly walk down the rest of the stairs as he runs over to me. I jump on him as he swings me around in his embrace.

"Brie," he holds me tight, "I've *missed* you woman!" He chuckles as he kisses my cheek numerous times.

He puts me down and I exclaim, "What are you doing here? I thought you were traveling or something." I pull the hair from my face and put it behind my ears. "Last we spoke you mentioned you were in California... *Mr. Big Shot,*" I continue as I playfully hit his arm with my right hand.

He grabs me again and hugs me tighter, "I heard about your father. I know how you are Brie, stop holding it all in. You don't have to keep it together one hundred percent, one hundred percent of the time."

Justin is my other best friend, the same one that told Eric about me. He, Eryn, and I have all known each other for over twenty years. I met Justin when I was four, and Eryn came into the picture two years later. Justin is, to this day, one of the best people I know, he keeps me humble. We talk three times a week and have never gone longer than four days without speaking to each other.

In college, him and Eryn dated briefly and had a fall out. Justin decided to go off and pursue his dreams and is now one of the most sought after sports rehabilitation therapists. He's become quite popular among big athletes and very wealthy individuals. He's about an inch taller than Eric, with a very muscular stature, thick, light brown hair, well-trimmed facial hair, and great cheekbones. He is one of the sweetest men I have ever known.

"I'm not ready yet," I wrap my arms around him in return, grateful for his words, "I'm not ready."

"Well, I've got all the time in the world for you. Why didn't you call me?" He releases the hug and pulls away to stare down at me. His expression shows me that he is a little hurt that I didn't call.

"I couldn't. I didn't want this news to affect anyone else I guess," I sourly look down.

He grabs my chin and gently pulls it up to look back at him. "I'm *always* here for you, whether it good or bad. But *especially* with the bad," he smiles at me, "Now that bitch Eryn, not so much."

I laugh aloud, wiping away a single tear, "Oh stop, you're not over that *yet*?!"

He puts his right arm around my shoulders as he walks me to the truck. I reach up with my right hand and hold his. He then opens the door and insists I climb in. I hop into the seat and he looks at me, "No, I'm not. I didn't even love her but what she did was just wrong." I chuckle as he shuts the door. I can see Eric off to the side. Justin walks over to greet him, a hand shake and then a hug. They exchange a few words and they both walk over to the truck.

Eric sits in the front seat and Justin sits in the back with me. We're in a black Cadillac Escalade, full black leather interior. The driver waiting for us as everyone settles in. "So," Eric says as he turns around to look at us. Justin's arm is around my shoulders again and I am leaning on his chest. "I knew you two know each other but I wasn't expecting that, are you two…?" Eric's looks at us so inquisitively.

Justin and I exchange glances and laugh, replying, "No," at the same time.

Eric raises one brow, "Have you two ever…?"

Justin looks at me and then back at Eric, "Really Eric? Are you eyeing my girl?," he chuckles, asking rhetorically, "Nah man, we are just great friends. I can understand your confusion though."

I look up at Justin and playfully hit him, "What did you tell him?"

"Well ya see, when Eric and I met, I was rehabbing a friend of his. I overheard their conversation about investment deals and such. Then they mentioned needing to continue trying to find someone who has a great talent with puzzles and memory stuff. And I remember you," he looks down at me, "talking about needing some financial help."

Eric quaintly smiles, "Yes, Justin here spoke of you quite casually, making no real mention of just how close you two were. When he said your name, I remembered it from that magazine spread you did with Forbes early last year. And of course the delightful spread from this year."

"Yup. This one," he shrugs me a little bit and looks back at Eric, "is as *single* as they come."

My cheeks immediately flushed from the embarrassment. I elbow Justin lightly in the ribs, "Shut up!" I aggressively say under my breath. Mortified but continuously smiling, I look up to see Eric's smile slowly disappear. He turns around and begins looking at his phone. *Definitely not interested in me.* That's okay; a girl can dream I guess. I clear my throat and begin talking to Justin again, "Have you spoke to Skyla yet?"

"I called her, let her know I'd be picking you up from the airport. She's very concerned about you."

"So you came down because she called you."

"No silly," he points to Eric, "*He* called me. *You* should've called me though. You need to stop that macho shit. You can be such a mule sometimes." He starts rubbing my shoulder with the hand that's wrapped around me as he looks off.

"Yeah, yeah. And you're kind of a nag," I mutter as I pat his stomach, "have you been working out? You're um, a little more buff than I remember."

"I guess I'll take that as a compliment," he adjusts in his seat, "I have actually."

I roll my eyes, "You look good Justin," I reply forcefully, "Where are you staying while here?"

"I'm over at this place called Duval, really nice. Not far from here actually," he continues to rub my shoulder.

"I think I want to stay with you," I say softly to him.

"I've got a big ol' king size bed that I'm willing to share," he smiles down at me.

I gently tap him on the chest, "Not in your room silly, I meant I'll book a room there too."

Eric erupts in laughter out of the blue. "I guess we will all be staying there then."

Justin shakes his head, "I don't know how the three of us will fit, besides, no offense Eric, you're a good looking guy and all; but threesomes are only appealing if I'm the only guy."

My face turns beat red as I sit up and look at Justin, "Would you stop?" I playfully hit him several times and grit my teeth, "You're embarrassing me."

Eric is up front chuckling away, "I find you equally attractive Justin, but that's one thing we can agree on."

His comment made me smile and stop thinking for a fleeting moment. It was the first time I had heard him make a joke. It made me think back to the bed on the plane. If there's one thing that very statement made clear; *he's certainly not gay*. The thought made me laugh. I thought about it a little longer though and hope he's not a boy toy like my buddy Justin here. Ever since he and Eryn slept together he hasn't had a steady girlfriend. I'm sure being a rehab therapist has its perks but he's a playboy now, and I know it. *And he knows I know it.*

"Where are we heading gorgeous, Sky's first right?" Justin looks at me.

I grin at him lovingly, "Actually could we check in first? I want to just freshen up and change." I sit back into the seat and begin fiddling with my nails.

Justin shuffles closer to me and leans in, "You know, I know you and your dad weren't close in the end but you can forgive yourself for that. He never made it easy for you."

Those words hit me like a ton of bricks. He always knew what I was thinking, and it irritated the mess out of me; in a good way. Immediately I begin to cry, holding my hands up to my face. Justin wraps his arms around me and begins to soothe me with a light shushing and holds me tighter. "I… just," I sniffle between breaths, "don't know why. he. hated. me."

"Come on Brie, don't be so hard on yourself," Justin assures me, "He never *hated* you, he was simply… confused. It was the alcohol. *Not* him."

I'm bawling my eyes out at this point, trying to tell myself to get it together but I can't. It was as if those few words just unraveled this little neatly knit barricade I had built to protect myself and I couldn't hold it up anymore. Justin is kissing my forehead and rubbing my back. Anything he could to soothe me. I calm down a few minutes later with my face pressed against his chest and my arms loosely wrapped around his waist. Just then, we pull up to the hotel. *That was fast.* I sit up and try to wipe my face clear of the tears. *I can't let anyone see me like this.* I pull out a mirror and see the horror that is my ruined mascara. *I can't let Eric see me like this.* I'm a complete and total mess. "Give me just a second," I tell the driver as he pulls up under the overhang and waits for us to depart the vehicle to check in.

"I got it," Eric states as he opens the car door and walks in through the front. I let out a sigh of relief.

"You *like* him," Justin exclaims as I'm trying to fix myself. He sounds so sure of himself

"No," I sniffle, "it's just business."

"You... liar," he smirks at me, "Girl, if you weren't milk chocolate you would've been a strawberry when I mentioned the threesome."

I pause and shake my head in disbelief, "He's handsome and like-*able* but I don't *like* him like that... he's nice to look at though. You said it yourself he's attractive," I continue trying to wipe away the makeup debris and deflect.

"You accepted the money, didn't you?" he grabs my hand and pulls it towards him.

I immediately put the mirror down and look at Justin, "Yes, why wouldn't I?"

"You accepted the terms of the entire contract then too?" He gives me a very serious stare.

"How do you know about that?" I snap.

He grabs both of my hands and looks me into my eyes, "Please be *very* careful and you call me if you need help or something seems off, you hear me?"

"If you were so worried, why tell him about me?"

"I'm not worried... necessarily. I just don't know what I'd do if anything happened to you because of me," he's so serious now, which is a rarity for Justin.

Eric comes back out of the lobby with a bellhop who opens the trunk. Eric opens my door and helps me out of the vehicle. He hands me a keycard and says, "You're in the room right across from Justin, room 603."

I gently take the card from his hands, "Thank you Eric, but I *will* be paying for this myself. I just want you to know."

He chuckles as I walk away, "It's really not a big deal Brie." He yells out. Justin walks from around the other side and they are both standing there as I wheel my suitcase in and make my way to the elevator. Justin has his hands on his hips, lifting his jacket up a little while Eric has one hand in his suit pants pocket and the other has his hotel key.

Justin looks at Eric and gently slaps him on the top of his back and grasps his shoulder, "Please take care of her, that woman means a lot to me. And if one hair on her head is harmed, I will hold you personally responsible."

Eric glances at Justin from the corner of his eye after I disappear from their view, "Justin, you have nothing to worry about my friend. I would never willingly put her in harm's way. I just need her help and I will return her home, safe and sound."

Justin pats Eric on the back in agreement. "Thank you," he says humbly.

"But," Eric turns to look at him, "If for any reason we need help, can I trust to call you?"

"Are you kidding me man?" Justin holds out his hand to show Eric respect, "I'm here, just say the word."

Eric smiles back at him and shakes his hand, "Thanks man." Eric grabs his bag from the bell hop and tips him. He looks at Justin and states, "I'm going to go get settled, just knock on my door when Brie is ready to go. I'm sure she'll come to you first. I'll be in room 710." He walks into the lobby and up the elevator. Justin walks in with him and stops to get a coffee at the snack stand near the front desk. He finishes making his coffee, adding a couple creams and sugars. He takes a sip and mumbles to himself, "It's going to be a long night."

Briellyn

I make my way into the elevator while Eric and Justin remained outside. With a need to shower and clear my head, I pray a little bit before this day goes any further. I glance at the watch that Eryn gave me and open the locket. *Not even time stands in my way.* The elevator door glides open. I step inside and press the button for the sixth floor, waiting patiently as a few other people join me in the elevator.

I couldn't help but notice this interracial couple amongst the small crowd of us. The woman is a beautiful rich shade of brownish red, with gorgeous jet black hair, and had the most striking green eyes I have ever seen; I'm almost positive she was of Indian descent. She, *all five foot nothing of her*, is snuggled up to this tall, slender, fair skinned Hispanic fellow with rich, semi-long, dark brown hair. They remind me of Sheila and Joseph the moment I lay eyes on them. They were cuddled up together, his hand wrapped around her and his chin touching her head. It's as if he's just standing there taking all of her in, her scent, her touch, her beauty. It's just beautiful. *Wish I had that.*

The elevator reaches level three and the loving couple, as well as two others, depart. All that's left is me and a handsome, sharply dressed, dark chocolate skinned gentleman and one of the hotel workers. I glance up and our eyes meet briefly, long enough for us to exchange cordial smiles before the elevator reaches the sixth floor and the doors slide open. As I walk out of the elevator I say to the gentleman, "Have a nice evening." He politely replies, "You too," and sort of bows his head.

I finally reach the front door to my room and swipe the key, opening the door to a gorgeous room. I hadn't taken the time to notice, but it suddenly hit me just how classy and modern this hotel is. The room is painted red with cherry wood accents, two cherry wood nightstands on either side of the bed, cherry wood bed platform base, and even a cherry wood headboard with black leather in the middle that engulfed the entire height of the wall and width of the bed.

Two ceiling lights hung low just above the end tables, giving off soft amber light. The bathroom, which is immediately to my right just as I enter through the door, has walls made of frosted glass with a sliding frosted glass door. The floors and inside walls are made of large, tan, square marble tiles. The sink has a clear glass top and open bottom, with a small shelf just under the piping to hold a tissue box and complimentary toiletries. The toilet is a typical run-of-the-mill, but the shower is glorious! It's a spa type with glass walls and a raindrop shower head. Everything in the room is put together well.

This glorious shower and I are about to have a hot, steamy date. I place my bags down onto the bed and dig my phone out of my purse. I unlock it and find my sisters' name:

'I just landed about 20 minutes ago, just hitting the showers and changing. Meet at the house in about an hour or so. Text ya when I leave. XOXO'

I immediately walk into the bathroom and turn the shower on, the droplets cascading like raindrops from a full gray cloud on a perfect spring day. I align all my toiletries onto the shelf noted below the sink and stick my body wash, loofah, and face wash into the shower. I peel off my clothes and throw them to the side, and put a shower cap on, tucking my hair in underneath it to keep it from getting wet.

When I open the shower door again, a gentle cloud of warm steam comes oozing out. I step into the shower and close the door. *Ahhhhhh.* I coo as the mildly hot water trickles over my delicate skin. This is exactly what I needed. The large water droplets beading across my body, falling further down with each additional drop. I lean on the side of the shower, facing the wall, and just let the water fall down my backside; like a water massage on the back of my neck. I stand there, unmoved, for about two minutes, letting the water put in the work. *The most action I've had in a very long time.*

This shower is starting to get to me. I begin sobbing, thinking of my mother and how happy my father was when she was alive. *It's all my fault, they're both dead cause of me.* At least that's what I've come to believe, my best was never good enough for my father. *And now he's dead.* Maybe I'll finally be free of the pain he caused, be done with all of his antics. *Or just feel guilty that I didn't do more.*

I can hear my phone buzz past the sound of the water. It must be Skyla. Every part of me wants to stay here and just sit in the shower; steam up or perhaps, maybe, doze off. I know I have more important things to take care of, and the phone buzzing is my reminder. Back to reality. I grab my loofah and lather it up with my body wash, the coconut aroma engulfing the steamy air. I quickly wash up and rinse, then turn the shower off.

I reach for my towel and dab the excess water off. The towel is fluffy and plush, not hardened like most hotel towels. *Justin sure knows how to pick'em.* Wrapping the towel around me and taking a couple steps over to the sink, I grab my oil and gently massage it into my skin. I feel better, like 98% percent better. I glance at the time and see that it's almost three o'clock. It feels later. The jet lag and sleeping in the middle of the day is always draining for me. I walk out of the bathroom to the bed where my clothing is, and gently unfold each item. I decide to put on the black maxi dress with the black and white poncho sweater I had. It's a little chilly outside so this should be the perfect balance of lightweight and warm. Once I finish dressing, I head back into the bathroom and rid myself of the shower cap. I fluff my hair out, add some lotion to my face and grab my phone to leave the room. I drop the phone into my purse, grab the room key, and head out.

Closing the door behind me, I walk diagonal across the hall to Justin's room and knock. *Knock, knock.* I patiently wait, but hear nothing. I knock once again. Still nothing. No ruffling behind the door, no shower running, just nothing. *Shit, no clue what Eric's room number is.* I make my way down the elevator to the main floor and pull my phone out to send them both a text. The elevator opens on the main level and to my surprise, Justin is standing in front of me waiting to go up.

"There you are, I was just going to knock on your door," he states cheerfully, a playful grin plastered on his face. I walk off the elevator, placing my phone back into my purse, discarding the text I was about to send.

"Well *I* was just knocking at yours," I reply with a smile. I hook my left arm into his right and walk him to the closest unoccupied coffee table. As we sit down, I ask where Eric is.

Justin leans back and puts his left arm up on the back of the chair, crossing his right ankle over his left knee, "He told me to go get him when you were ready. He knew you'd look for me first."

I lean back a little bit in my chair and pull out my phone, "I'll just text him and let him know we're ready."

I send out the text informing him we are downstairs in the lobby and resume talking to Justin, "So... how many appointments did you have to cancel to be here?"

Justin rolls his eyes and begins moving his suspended foot around. "Doesn't matter," he throws a small piece of debris my direction, "Nothing is more important than being here, you know that."

I shake my head at him, "You're a good friend Jus."

He smiles as he glances down at his phone, "Yeah, well."

I lean forward and place my hand on his right knee, "Why didn't you let me be there *for you* all those years ago?"

He glares at me with just his eyes, squinting, "What? Ya mean the situation with Eryn?" His smile is exchanged for a frown. He uncrosses his legs and leans in closer to my face, "You wouldn't believe me if I told you everything Brie." He sounds so sure of it. *Which almost hurts my feelings.*

I lean a little closer to his face until we are just a few inches apart and quietly challenge him, "With all that you know about me? *Try me.*" He doesn't break his stare, glancing from my lips to my eyes, and back to my lips.

"Am I interrupting something?" Eric approaches us, breaking the stare down between Justin and I. We both immediately lean away from each other and look up at Eric, who is now dressed in some nicely shaped straight leg dark denim jeans and a red cowl neck sweater. His hair looks a little wet, so he must have showered too.

I stand up and say to Eric, "No, nothing at all." I then glance over to Justin and say to him, "I'll be waiting to hear more later. You're not off the hook yet."

Justin rolls his eyes as he stands. "The driver was just for the airport, I have the rental parked out back," he motions for us to follow as he begins to walk in that general direction. Eric and I follow behind him.

On the way, Eric leans closer to me, "Are you *sure* I didn't interrupt anything?"

I glance over at him and smile as we continue walking next to each other, "Justin needs to tell me something, but I think he's afraid. You weren't interrupting anything. If *anything*, you bailed him out." Eric just nods his head in agreement. Out the back doors and a few cars later, we arrive at a black Chevy Equinox that Justin had rented. He unlocks the vehicle and climbs into the front seat. Eric opens the front passenger side door and allows me to clamber inside, then sits behind me. Justin starts the car after we both buckle up and pulls off without saying a word. He is genuinely upset I brought up Eryn again.

"I'm sorry Justin," I mumble to him, "I honestly just want you to know that you can talk to me about it when you're ready, I know you'd expect the same from me." I begin looking out the passenger side window, waiting for him to acknowledge my plea.

He glances over at me from the corner of his eye, "You mean that?"

I immediately snap my head back around to see his expression, "Of course." I smile at him, grateful to have him as a friend and in my life. Him and his brother are the only real family that Skyla and I have at this point.

"Okay," he smirks. I pull my phone out to text Skyla that we are on our way. After I text her, I watch our drive there and begin to remember my last time being here five years ago.

* * * * * * *

I flew in to visit my father just after I had graduated from college with my Masters in Business. I decided not to walk the stage because I knew none of my family could make it. Besides, I had already done it once for my Bachelors. I had just turned my business into an LLC and was excited to share the news with my father.

I flew in to visit my father, having just graduated from college with my Masters in Business. I decided not to walk the stage because I knew none of my family could make it. Besides, I had already done it once for my Bachelors. I had just turned my business into an LLC and was excited to share the news with my father.

I flew into town, rented a car, and showed up that clammy summer evening, knocking on the door. I didn't get an answer but the front door was open, so I just walked in. "Hello!" I yelled out. I could hear a slight ruffling noise in the living room to the left, so I walked in that direction. There was my father, laid out on the couch, *drunk*.

He had had his moments of sobriety throughout the years, but this was his worse relapse that I'd seen for myself. Skyla had just gotten married about six months ago and I knew he had a hard time with that. I twisted my mouth up at the sight of him, "Father..." I said quietly as I creeped closer towards him.

I could see him turn his head to look at me, "Aubrey?" he drunkenly asked.

"No father, it's Briellyn. Mom's not here," I replied as I knelt down at the couch and grabbed the bottle from him.

"You look so much like your mother," he said as he snatched the bottle from me to take another swig.

"Father, I came with some good news," I began to get excited, but as he took gulp after gulp, I knew he didn't care what I had to say. Concerned, I tried to take the bottle from him. *Only for the drunk fool to swing at me.*

Shocked, I sat back and stood up. "Enough of this dad! Mom is gone and drinking will *never* bring her back. All you have is me and Sky now. Please don't keep doing this to yourself. You need help. Let us help you!" He looks at me and tries to sit up. Clumsily he managed to do exactly that, never breaking his stare from me. He had this look on his face, that *'how dare you'* look. I remember it so many times as a girl.

He came to his feet and I backed up a little bit more. "HELP?!" he shouted at me, "I've never *needed* you. It's *your* fault your mother isn't here with me. I hate *you*!"

Shocked at his words, I took another step back and shook my head. "You've always blamed *me*. But we both know that she wouldn't have been driving back with me so late had you not been too intoxicated to come get me like you were supposed to!" I had to defend myself. Felt like I had to do it every time we saw each other.

"How dare you! After *everything* I've done for you. Get out!" He took a few steps towards me.

"Father," I pleaded, "You need help, *please*..." He threw the bottle at me, missing as I ducked.

He yelled again, "I fuckin' hate you, I've always hated you. It should've been you, not your mom. I disown you, leave and never come back!" Tears filled my eyes and my heart broken into a million pieces, never to be mended again. I left that night. Never coming back. *Until now.*

* * * * * * *

I wipe a tear from my face as the memory comes to an end and we pull up to my father's house. Justin parks right behind Skyla's truck. She gets out of the driver side and I see an officer get out of the passenger side. His police car is in the driveway. Justin, Eric, and I all open our doors at the same time and exit the vehicle. Justin being closest to Skyla, she hugs him first. Skyla then walks over to me and I hug her like I never have before, never wanting to let her go. She hugs me back the same way. I hadn't been to visit her in almost a year, but I always come spend time with her and her family for the holidays; so it was about that time.

My sister is a little shorter than me, fair skinned like our father's mother, long black hair, full cheeks, curvy, and soft spoken. She'd originally helped me with the first concepts of my business, rightfully claiming her small share of my company. She receives dividends every month, so on top of her husband's pay, she gets to be a stay at home mom and do what she loves; art.

Eric is patiently standing to my right as Justin has made his way over to stand on the right side of him. Skyla and I release our iron clad embrace as I glance over at the police officer standing there. "Deputy Givens?" I ask. I didn't recognize him at first, the uniforms were new. Givens is about six foot even, slender but muscular build, and dark brown hair. He is half Indian and half white, really tan skin but somewhat more European features. He has a rather unique look to him, so I am shocked that I didn't recognize him right away.

"Hey there Brie. Its Sheriff now," he tips his hat in my direction. I walk over to him to give a gentle hug; he's been a family friend since we had moved to Florida, just after I got out of high school.

"Congratulations," I exclaim as I release him, "well what are you doing over here? Don't you have more important stuff to do than offering condolences?" *Rude I know, defense mechanism.* He clears his throat and I suddenly remember my manners, "Oh, Skyla, meet Eric. He's our new investor." Eric politely shakes Skyla's hand as they exchange greetings. "And *Sheriff* Givens, please meet Justin, a very dear family friend and Eric another dear friend," I finish. Sheriff Givens shakes hands with both men. "Anything that needs to be said can be said in front of them," I continue. I can see Skyla glance over at me.

"'Scuse me just a moment," Sheriff Givens walks over to the passenger side of his vehicle to retrieve a sealed brown envelope along with some papers, and walks back over to us. The four of us stand in silence and wait. *What the hells in the envelope?*

"There's a few things I need to go over here ladies, the first being that this envelope had explicit instructions to only be opened with both of you present and in the event of Mr. Donado's passing."

I begin playing with the top collar of the sweater, nervous at the thought of what's in the envelope. He opens it and pulls out the piece of paper. Sheriff reads,

"Dear Sunshine and Moonstone,

I'm so sorry for the way I have acted ever since your mother died. I'm especially sorry for my lack of effort towards trying to seek help and get better. Neither of you may understand now, and may never understand actually, but when we lost your mother, most of me went with her.

I never meant to hurt either of you and I can't ever take back the cruelty or grief I've caused. I especially need to apologize to you Sunshine, my dear Briellyn. Did you know that you were named after your great great grandmother? She was strong and independent, even in the days where women weren't seen as much. You have always had her fighting will and spirit to one day help and change the world. Please don't ever change honey. I didn't mean it when I told you I hated you. I barely remember that night we last spoke all those years ago but that word stuck out to me. Countless times I would try to call you and say I was sorry, but I would only dial your number to hang up because I was too afraid you would reject me. I was also afraid that I would let you down once again.

I hid this letter from myself because when I drink I feel like a different person, sometimes in a better way, but in most times not so much. I'm passing this letter to the Sheriff so that it may get to the two of you in the event I never find the courage to do it myself. I love you both so much and you two have made me a very proud father. I'm undeserving of such wonderful daughters. You are so special, you have no idea. I hope you will find it in your heart to forgive me. Knowing that if this is being read to you, and not by me, brings me comfort in knowing that I can never do either of you anymore harm. I'm in a better place now, looking down over you both. Moonstone, kiss those beautiful babies for me. I'm sorry I didn't come to see them more. Please remember me for the good moments, though I know there are few. Feel free to talk to me when you're ready. I'm finally prepared to listen.

Love,

Your undeserving father

P.S. I don't have much to give either of you, but I have left a few things that were specifically boxed up in the attic.

I'm trying my best to keep my composure, but the tears escape me. I'm holding my sister and she's holding me. She's crying a little more than me, but I couldn't hold back anymore. All I keep thinking is, why couldn't he have told me this before? *Why couldn't he finish dialing my number?* "I take it all back," I weep softly to Skyla, "Every mean thing, *I take it back.*"

She replies between tears and sniffles, "It's not your fault, neither of us could have known." Justin walks over and hugs us both, kissing our foreheads and rubbing our backs. We both shift and let him into our crying circle. Eric stands there, but decides to walk over to us, unsure of what to do. I let go of Justin and Skyla, looking at Eric. Between tears and huffing, I'm able to manage a thank you. He immediately steps towards me and hugs me tightly. His hug felt so sincere and wholesome, again like he needed one too. I lay my head on his shoulder as he rubs my back; it was so soothing and calming. I immediately feel relaxed. *Damn it dad.*

"I'm so sorry for you both," Sheriff chimes in, "But there's more." Eric lets me go as I turn around to look at the Sheriff. Skyla glances at me.

I notice Skyla looking at me and look back at the Sheriff, "What do you mean?"

Skyla softly speaks, "They found his body. He'd fallen down the stairs." She begins crying again as Justin consoles her.

"Sheriff?" I ask, staring at him blindly.

He begins walking towards the door, every so often glancing back at me, "Well Brie, when I received this police report on my desk yesterday in the wee hours of the morning, I had to go and inspect everything myself. Neighbors called in and stated they heard a screaming and then sounds of glass being broken here at the house... watch your step there," he steps over some glass as he makes his way to the porch. I creep behind him, looking and listening intently. Eric is behind me, as are Skyla and Justin.

He continues, "He was found here at the base of the steps, cause of death is believed to be severe trauma to the head and neck from the fall, but you will have to give the coroner's office permission to have him autopsied to be sure. Nothing appears to be broken into, i.e. we don't believe there were any intruders or anything," he says as he walks up the stairs to the second floor, all of us still following closely. "But when I came back to do a thorough sweep, I had noticed that the bat was taken out of his room. It was out of place from the last time I had been here. I know he normally keeps it downstairs but it was in his bedroom. All of the windows and locks had been checked to be sure that it wasn't a break in and everything came back clean. No fingerprints of anyone else besides the old man."

We reach the top of the steps and he points out to the window at the end of the hall towards the front of the house, we all look over. "That's where the window was broken; he threw a bottle of Cuervo through it. That's why you saw all the glass just in front of the porch. The bottle landed in the middle of the grass," he glances at me, "the bottle was unopened." My stare shifts from him to the window.

"May I?" I ask, as I point towards the end of the hall.

I walk over as he continues talking, "All anyone is willing to bet is that he may have been drinking and simply slipped and fell down the stairs. And perhaps, in an angry fit he threw the bottle. The neighbors said they heard him screaming first and *then* the bottle. Time of death is believed to have been within a half hour of the time the call came in."

I look out of the window down below, seeing the broken bottle in the grass below, "Well what do you believe Givens? How do you know the bottle was unopened if it's broken?"

He walks over to me and stares into my eyes, "The top of the bottle where the cap is, was still sealed. And regardless of your fathers many relapses, he'd done quite well the past couple of weeks."

Eric walks over to us both, "Are you *certain* no one else was here with him?"

"It's as I stated before sir, our sweep of the house yielded no fingerprints, no tampering with locks or doors and all of the house was locked up when we arrived. Neighbors hadn't seen anything out of the ordinary either," the Sheriff replies as he walks back towards the stairs, "The other thing is, I know I mentioned it before, but I need one of you to come down to the coroners and identify the body and give permission, if you choose, to do the autopsy. I will leave you all to your thoughts." He ventures back downstairs to his vehicle.

"Mind if I look around?" Eric asks, holding my hand.

I shake my head no, "By all means." He sneaks off into my father's room while Skyla and Justin approach me.

"Who's going to identify the body?" Skyla sniffles, asking softly. Her expression tells me she doesn't want to.

"I can go for you, if you need me to," Justin insists. He puts his hands in his pockets and stares at me.

Skyla quickly responds, "I don't mind."

I continue to gaze outside and reply hesitantly, "I'll go with you."

He places his hand on my lower back and asks, "Are you sure? I can do this alone. It's really not a big deal."

I turn around and place my hand on Justin's chest, smiling at him, "I know, but this is something I need to do for him." I grab his hand and retreat down the hall towards the stairs, "We're going to take care of this right now," I say, rather matter-of-fact. "Sky, want to check out that box in the attic while we take care of this?" I yell out as we reach the bottom of the stairs.

"Already on it," she replies as she pulls down the attic door.

* * * * * * *

Eric

I can hear Briellyn and Justin walking downstairs, but continue looking around. Trying not to touch anything while in the process, I gently open one of the doors and catch a glimpse of the window. *Nothing.* I proceed to exit the room, but notice something behind the door. Upon closing the door, while still in the room, I begin to analyze it; then kneel to get a closer look, "Hmmm." I open the door and yell for Skyla in the attic, "Excuse me, Sky?"

She shuffles over in the attic and looks down the ladder, "Yes, Eric."

"Did you and Brie live here with your dad at one point?"

"Yes, Brie lived here for about a year after high school before going off to college and I stuck around for maybe three more years after that. Why?"

I smirk, "Oh okay, no, I was just curious." I creep off into one of the other rooms while Skyla goes back to looking for this box that her dad mentioned in the letter. There were, apparently, a lot of boxes he'd stored up in the attic.

I then find myself in Skyla's old room, a twin size bed, small desk in the corner, but not much else. Continuing into the bathroom, I take notice that it's connected to another room, a room filled with photos, nice bed setting, a desk, even some clothes and shoes. Briellyn clearly left everything behind. *Wonder what happened to make her just leave it all here?*

There was also a small chest on the floor that appears to be ransacked. *Oh, my, God.* Alarmed, I rush downstairs and go outside to call Kalil. I'm sure Skyla heard me, hopefully I didn't alarm her.

"Kalil, it was here..." I'm excited and worried.

"What?" Kalil replies.

"The termagant! In its raw form. It was here, at Brielle's father's house," I gesture while explaining.

"I thought that was just empyrean folklore?"

"My father used to tell me about them, I didn't think it was real either, just ways to scare me. But I can see it for myself right here in what I believe to be Briellyn's room."

Skyla gets to the bottom of the stairs and quietly stands at the front door. She overhears me talking to Kalil.

"But why would a termagant be in Brielle's father's house, I mean, what would it accomplish?" Kalil pleads.

"I am now 100% convinced that Brielle is indeed the woman we've been waiting for," I begin pacing. Skyla hides behind the wall so that I can't see her standing there, but I can feel her presence. "I gotta call you back," I immediately hang up the phone and proceed back to the stairs of the house. Skyla panics trying to think of a way not to seem like she was eavesdropping, but her heart is racing. *I can hear it.* As I walk through the door, she's just standing there; giving me a blank stare.

"Hey Sky," I cautiously smile, "How long have you been standing there?" Skyla continues to stare at me and begins to panic; her first instinct is to run. But I chase after her, catching up to her quickly. She's about to scream, so I cover her mouth. "Shhh, shh, shhh," I plead, "I'm not here to hurt you or your sister. Now, I'm going to explain myself, but I need you to be *very* open minded." I begin nodding my head and stare at her nervously, "I'm going to uncover your mouth and let you go now, if you promise not to run or scream again." She quickly nods her head in agreement.

* * * * * * * *

Briellyn

Meantime, on the way to the coroner's office, Justin and I are following Sheriff Givens car. I'm staring out the window, nibbling at my finger nails. "Hey," he glances over at me indulging in my nervous habit, "are you going to be okay? That letter was pretty powerful stuff."

I take my gaze away from the passing scenery, look over at him and grin. I grab his right hand, kiss it, and softly reply, "Thank you. Thank you for the countless nights of my incessant bitching. Thank you for dealing with my hardened personality. I can't begin to describe to you how much you being here is so necessary for me *and* Sky."

He smiles at me, quickly glancing back and forth from me to the road, "I want to tell you about Eryn now."

My eyes squint in curiosity, "Why now?"

Justin swallows hard as the words develop slowly, "Because I realize now that the year I left Connecticut was the same year you and your dad had that fallout. It clearly still haunts you and I left *knowing* that you were hurting. And in my selfish rut I left when you needed me most. So, I think it's time you know why."

I'm torn between wanting to know and not ever wanting to know. Here I am, hurting because the entire time I *thought* my dad hated me; when he was really trying to figure out how to make it right. *A real life Dr. Jekyll dealing with his alcoholic split personality, Mr. Hyde.* And now my best friend wants to tell me about why he left me alone when I needed him. We still spoke on the phone and all, but I was without his presence. And worse, he never wanted to talk about it. *I deal with my own issues by helping others through theirs.* Eryn, to this day, still will not speak Justin's name. She acts like he never existed. In fact, when I mention his name unintentionally, she will ignore me as if I didn't say anything at all.

My dear Justin clearly had a good reason for wanting to tell me this right now though. He would never want to tell me something at any given moment, especially like this, if he didn't find it either relevant or important. I cordially smile at him, "Go on, I'm ready when you are."

He reaches for my hand and I give it, putting it in his lap as my arm is snuggled under his. "I've gone over and over in my head how to tell you this, but I think I realize now that I should just say it before I lose my chance," he continues to look at the road, briefly glancing at me. "I want you to keep a very open mind when I tell you this." I nod my head in agreement, but he looks at me and insists, "No, I mean it Briellyn. Promise me you'll be open minded on this one."

I lift my right arm, signing, and persistently reply, "Scout's honor that I will be open minded. Do continue my love." I have only heard Justin call me by my full first name twice in the past, once when we met and once at his college graduation dinner. He stayed in Connecticut near me while I was still in college.

He continues, "Do you remember that night when the Huskies won the National Championship?"

I smile at him, "I mean, it was an amazing game that is hard to forget. But I'll admit, I was pretty drunk. Rare I know, but I think so."

"You and I were having drinks at that bar, right around the corner from our apartment building. The whole state seemed to be celebrating the win. You and I had been drinking and one thing led to another and we shared that kiss..."

I shuffle a little in my seat and swallow hard, "Yes." I pause very briefly then sourly reply, "You started seeing Eryn two weeks after that..."

"Anyway," he interrupts, "you may not have noticed Brie, but I stopped drinking after that. I wanted to be sure that if anything else happened that night, I could not only enjoy it... but remember it for the rest of my life. And to this day, *I will never forget it.*"

I'm starting to get nervous. *Did we sleep together and I blacked out?*

He continues, not once looking at me, "Before the kiss, maybe about eight months leading up to that, I had grown rather fond of you. We would go running together or hit the gym. You would tell me about all of your crazy, off the wall dreams. You were the only person I knew that had it all planned out and knew exactly what you wanted to do in life, how you were going to pursue it, and you were doing that start up in your senior year..." He bites his bottom lip, "You made a lot of college kids, including myself, some good money. And then you had briefly dated that quarterback..."

I sarcastically laugh, "Yeah, I remember." Not my best moment. *If only you knew, babe.*

"You were so heartbroken about finding out about that cheerleader that you told me you were no longer going to date, you were just going to let the right one come to you. After seeing your heart broken, yet again, something in me changed about you. I mean, I knew I had loved you. You've been my best friend since I was six. And right after your mom died, you just grew up. It was like you and I were the same age for the longest time, hell maybe you were older... but you were one of the guys. And then you just blossomed. Anyway, I was very fond of you and before I knew it, I had the biggest crush on you. That's why I started asking you to go out with me *all* the time. That night we shared that kiss, I thought to myself, she finally chose *me*. The look you had on your face was so sure too. You didn't look drunk, you looked at me like you *wanted* me."

I begin blushing while gazing at the road, avoiding eye contact.

He carries on, "I knew right then, I needed to stop drinking because this could be the first night of the rest of my life."

I whip my head around to see his face, astounded by his words.

"I was hoping it was real, and I knew it was when you leaned in and kissed me again. There was so much passion there, anticipation. I knew I had wanted that to happen for those last eight months and finally it did. And when I took you back to your apartment, two floors down from mine, I thought I should maybe ask to stay, but I didn't. You were still a little drunk and I wanted our moment to be perfect, ya know? So, I walked upstairs to my place and sat down on my couch and just thought about you, over and over again, there in the dark. And then I heard a knock at my door."

This is all news to me; he'd never spoken to me about this night.

"I open the door," he pauses and swallows hard, "and it was you. You walked in and kissed me so deep and so passionately, I... I just... went with it, letting you take the lead."

I slip my hand away and hold them up, shaking my head, "Hold on, I don't recall ever going up to your place. *I don't remember that at all.*"

"Open minded," he reminds me. I settle back down and he grabs my left hand again, this time leaving it in my lap. He inhales deeply, "That night I made love to a woman who I just knew was going to be my wife. But I woke the following morning to find Eryn lying next to me. I couldn't figure out what the hell happened. Was I imagining things? Was I drunk and didn't realize it? *Did someone slip me something?* Two weeks later, she told me she was pregnant. My future with you completely crumbled into dust."

"Oh, I remember the pregnancy thing alright. But she didn't tell me until about a month after you two began dating. I'm still on the part about you mistaking her for me though. I'm not sure how you expect me to believe that Justin." *I'm not sure how I'm supposed to believe any of this, actually.*

"Honestly Brie, *I'm* not sure how I expect you to believe it either, but it's true."

"I mean, even in complete darkness I would think the complexion thing would be obvious," I'm staring at him, waiting for him to smile or say that he's joking, but he doesn't. I can see in his face that he genuinely believed it was me. "Then why did you leave a couple months after that? Never to be seen again, until... well until a few hours ago. You never even would come down for the holidays when your brother would," I ask.

"When she lost the baby, she blamed me for it. The entire time we dated, I just felt drained by her. I hated every waking moment. The entire time, from the moment I woke up next to her, I thought to myself how much I fucked up. How maybe, had I just been honest with you to begin with, maybe it could've been you with my child. Not her."

I glance down, touched by his words. *The feeling was mutual.* I smile at the thought, but confused about the situation. How could I have not noticed? Could the man I'd been waiting for be the man I knew my entire life? I haven't truly dated anyone since the quarterback incident. I mean, I'd been on dates, but no one who I ever wanted to stay with. *And admittedly I had a crush on Justin, but that faded after hearing about Eryn.*

He continues, "To add insult to injury, the day I found out she wasn't pregnant anymore, I caught her banging some other guy. That just broke me. I went to stay with Marcus in Georgia and picked up in sports medicine, which happened to work out with my degree and I've been killing it ever since."

"She did *what?* She never told me about that... she told me that she was just so hurt about the baby she couldn't stand the thought of you," I sit back and try to digest this fairy tale gone awry. We pull up to the coroners' office. I unbuckle my seat belt, staring directly into Justin's eyes, "So why tell me now? Are you saying..." I look from one eye to the other and swallow hard, "that you still have feelings for me?"

He holds his head down, "I thought the feelings were gone but they are all still here, even after five years. I know you frown on me about my sexual exploits and I have *no* excuses for that other than I was trying to fill a void. Which *isn't* a good excuse but I would change my ways, right here, right now. If you'd be willing to at least consider me..."

I look down and think for a moment. I know I love Justin, he's my best friend and I've always kind of had a crush. But *in love?* Hell, I don't even know what love is. I've never said that word to any man but him, just never in *that* capacity. But after everything that has happened. I felt rejected when he and Eryn started dating after the kiss. *Our kiss.* But now I get it... *if what he says is true.* I still don't know how to explain the mistaken identity except that he was still drunk; which *I guess* is possible. Now he wants me to consider him and I don't know what to say. Hesitantly I reply, "Just give me some time, Jus," I caress his face, "you are the *only* man that has stuck by me through my emotional ups and downs. But this is a *lot* to digest. Will you just let me think everything through?"

"Of course," he joyfully replies as he opens his car door, "Just don't act all weird and shit now that I've said it out loud. I only told you I love you, which we say to each other anyway." *Good ol' Justin, always ruining a moment.* He exits the car and closes the door. I watch him as he walks around the front of the car to my side and opens my door.

Could I have just missed it all those years? I remember us joking back in high school before we moved here how if we both didn't find anyone by the time I was thirty, that we should just marry each other. *Is he feeling anxious?* I didn't get that vibe. *Not by that story.* He opens the door and holds out his hand and for a moment, just an evanescent moment; I imagine him in a tux and myself in a white gown, him holding his hand out for me as we arrive at the airport to board a flight to begin our honeymoon.

VII

Briellyn

Sheriff Givens shows us into the room where my fathers' body
is. The coroner is waiting for us when we enter. Justin and I
stand off to the side as the coroner slides the body out of the
cold, steel box. As he unzips the black body bag my father is
encased in, I find myself unintentionally holding my breath. *Was
his face going to be the one I remember from the day I walked out of the
house five years ago or just a shadow of his former self?* The coroner asks
us to step closer, so we did. I gasp at the sight of him. He looks
oddly thin, his mouth slightly open, eyes staring at the ceiling. I
immediately turn around and plant my face into Justin's chest.
He wraps his arms around me, holding me tight, leaning his
head atop mine. I begin to whimper, "How could I have left
him? I should have come back. I should have kept trying."

Justin comforts me, "It's not your fault, even your father knew
that." Tears begin streaming down my face again. First the letter
and now to see his horrified face. He looks like he died painfully,
unwillingly, not ready to leave. My sister and I know deep down
he wanted to be better for us. I let him fight this alone. It wasn't
fair.

"Should I go ahead and close it up?" the coroner asks.

Justin nods his head yes, but I let him go to interrupt, "No,
wait." *Suck it up buttercup.* I wipe my tears away. *I owed him this
much.* I turn around and stare at him, "I've read that when a
person dies with their eyes wide open, they've never found
closure. I need to give him closure." I step closer to the table so
that I can gaze down upon him. His face is forever frozen in

time like this, the time of his last breath. The look on his face gravely bothers me; but then I notice a mark that I'd never seen before, towards the top of his chest. "May I?" I look up at the coroner to see about pulling the zipper down a little more.

"Allow me," he replies nicely, zipping the bag down more until I tell him to stop.

"What is that?" I stare closer at my father's chest to see a rather dark mark, his skin raised like it was cut into the flesh, got infected, and scarred badly.

The coroner looks down, "What is it ma'am?" He stares closer.

I point to the symbol on his chest, "*That?* I don't remember him ever having that." I'm almost disgusted by it. Justin steps closer to see what I'm talking about.

The coroner stares at me, "Looks like a small mole or beauty mark, to me. Nothing out of the ordinary."

I look away from my father's body to the coroner, "You're kidding me right? That is not a beauty mark nor is it small *whatsoever*. This right here…" I circle my hand around the area to point it out once more. "You're trying to tell me you don't see this very obvious marking that looks like an intentional scar?" I protest. He shakes his head no and stares at me like I'm crazy. Justin glances at me curiously, he knows I can see something.

The coroner begins to explain, "Sometimes loved ones see things when they are grieving…"

Justin holds his hand up to stop the coroner, "Excuse us for a second." Justin grabs my arm and gently pulls me to the side.

Confused, I look up at him, "Please tell me you see the scar Justin, tell me I'm not losing it…"

He shakes his head and softly speaks to me, "I know you can, but I assure you that no one else can see it. You remember when we were kids and you would tell me how you could see things, but I never saw them? I always believed you right?" I smile at him gratefully and shake my head yes. "I believe you are seeing something, and I think maybe Eric may be the one to talk to about it. Just note it in your mind and whisper it to me and I will tell you if I can see it. I will touch your hand if I can't, or nod my head in agreement if I can," he smirks at me and kisses my forehead.

The two of us walk back over and thoroughly look over the body. I don't point at anything or make it obvious what I'm looking at. I simply lean over to Justin and put my hand up to whisper in his ear, "Do you see the purple mark in the middle of his bottom lip?" Justin softly touches my hand. I glance over again to see if there is anything else. I ask him again about the small purple mark on the side of his face and again he touches my hand. *Why is no one seeing this but me? Would* Eric know about the things I see? Would he believe me like Justin does or just think I'm bat shit crazy? I guess it'd be worth a try. *I've got nothing to lose, hell he's already signed the contract.*

"That'll be all sir," I told the coroner, giving him a forced, yet cordial, smile. He glances at me strangely and zips up the bag.

After he does, he mentions to me, "I have some paperwork for you to sign, to perform the autopsy. Sheriff if you wouldn't mind getting her to fill out the necessary paperwork, that'd be great."

Sheriff Givens walks us into the next room and has me sign a few forms. "So uh, what *did* you see in there Donado?" Sheriff's eyebrows raise in curiosity. Justin is standing at the door where the sheriff can't see him and I can see him shake his head. I smile at Sheriff Givens, "Nothing, I think I've just had a long day Givens." I sign the last form electing to have him cremated. "Anything else you need from me, Sheriff?" I pause before I walk out the door with Justin.

"No, but if you need to let off some steam, the paths around Piney Lake are great this time of year," the Sheriff states. I smile at him in thanks as Justin helps me out to the car.

Justin and I make our way back to the house. "I'm glad I got that over with," I exhale aloud to Justin, shifting a little in my seat, "I got to see him one last time." *Even though it gave me more questions than answers.*

Justin reaches over and holds my hand, "So you're going to talk to Eric about what you saw, right?"

Rethinking my decision earlier, I frown and reply, "What if he thinks I'm nuts?"

"It's what he recruited you for though, right? I think he'll be able to at least point you in the right direction Brie," he smiles at me reassuringly. I smile back and then gaze out the window. Why *do* I see these *things*? I've been seeing them since I was a little girl, as far back as I can remember, but got worse when I hit puberty. I am just ready to get back to the house to my sister, maybe go for a run to clear my head later. I turn the radio on with my free hand and just get lost in the music playing. *They play the best music during rush hour.* I know my brain will be entertained by music for the next twenty minutes until we get home, instead of pondering this issue. I sink further into my seat and just listen, holding Justin's hand in between mine and soaking it all in.

* * * * * * *

Briellyn

Twenty minutes later...

We pull up in front of my father's house to see Skyla and Eric sitting on the porch. Skyla's is propping her face up by her crossed hands, steadied by her knees and elbows. As we pull up, I can see her look Eric's direction briefly and him shake his head. She stands up, closes her sweater and crosses her arms as she shuffles over to me and Justin. "I opted to have him cremated," I blurt out. It was the first thing to come to mind for some reason.

"I couldn't find that box Brie, maybe you can help?" She looks down, virtually ignoring my comment, and shifts her right foot back and forth.

"What's the matter?" I ask her, worried that she didn't agree with my decision on our father's remains.

"Nothing," she glances up and scrunches her face, "I just..." She sighs audibly. "I just love you so much, that's all."

I immediately put my arms around her. "I'll always be here for you. Always have and always will," I kiss her forehead, "Let's get our minds off this and go find the box, yeah?" She smiles at me and nods her head yes. She turns around back towards the house and I wrap my right arm around her shoulders. She grabs my right hand with hers and wraps her left arm around my lower back.

"Reilly is on his way over by the way, he should be here in about ten minutes," she says matter of fact. I smile at Eric as we approach the stairs to the porch, then walk inside the house. He smiles back and stands up.

"So, how'd it go?" Eric asks Justin.

"As good as it'll go I guess," Justin nervously claps his hands together.

"Great," Eric states, about to turn around to follow us inside when Justin stops him.

"Hey man, Brie saw something there. I don't know if she is going to tell you or not but I know she sees things that others, including myself, aren't privy to; which *you* kind of know from our previous conversation. It seemed to freak her out a bit and I told her she should talk to you," Justin slips his hands into his pockets, and yields Eric a serious stare.

Eric steps a little closer to Justin, curiously, "Well what did she see, Justin?"

"She had a hard time explaining to me the mark on her father's chest, but she mentioned like a… purple mark on his lips and a small one on the side of his face. She said the mark on the chest looked like raised, infected scar tissue in this symbol…" Justin pulls out his phone and begins to doodle.

Before Justin finishes his sketch, Eric finishes Justin's sentence, "Kind of like horns coming out of a circle?"

"Yeah, something like that, what do you know about it?" Justin inquires.

"Not much really," Eric places his hand on Justin's shoulder, "Look, Justin, I know I haven't told you much about the mission or much about myself for that matter. But please trust me when I tell you, I think Brie may be a target because of me. I promise this was never my intent. But *I'm begging* you, don't let her out of your sight while we are here."

He steps back away from Eric, demanding answers, "Please tell me you have more to say than that? Dude, if she's in harm's way

I *need* to know how to protect her. And *why* she's in trouble. Who would be after you? *Are you into something that you haven't told me about?*"

Eric glances down and shuffles his feet, "I will tell you Justin, because I trust that your love for her is genuine. I will tell you on the way back to the hotel to be sure there are no prying eyes or threatening ears though. Fair enough?"

Justin nods his head still scowling, "Let's go check on them then." He strides onto the porch and walks up the stairs with Eric close behind.

When I approach the attic at the top of the ladder, I begin hearing a very high pitch noise; completely monotone, it never changes pitch. As I take my last step to completely stand in the attic and help my sister up, the noise gets louder. "What the *hell* is that noise?" I say aloud to Skyla, the sound somewhat deafening.

"I don't hear anything, what's it sound like?" she replies. I immediately roll my eyes and shake my head. *Here we go again.* I love being the weird one in the room. *Not.* I genuinely *feel* crazy. Lucky for me though, both my sister and Justin love me and believe me when I say I hear or see something. We affectionately have named it my *x-factor.*

As I step closer to one corner of the attic, the noise gets softer. So I turn back the other direction, towards the noise. In the opposite corner there were a stack of three boxes, none of them apparently labeled. As I stood directly in front of these boxes, the noise seems to turn into a beep. I move the box that's on top to the floor and the beeps get closer together. Then I move the second box, the beeps get even closer together. The top of the box had a shimmery blue glow. I turn the box around to see the year *1987* written on it in mom's handwriting.

"Well, I think this is the box…" I mumble to Skyla.

"Well open it up," she whispers impatiently. I open the box to see what's inside. The first thing I notice is the stuffed unicorn that my mother gave me on my third birthday. I can hear her telling me, "This may be an animal of imagination, but it's unique, just like you." It used to be a lilac purple, but for whatever reason it appears to be a shimmery shade of blue. I grab it and pull it out the box.

"What is going on with this thing? It's glowing blue." My sister shrugs her shoulders and just looks at the toy. I analyze it then put it down next to the box as I continue sifting through the items. There wasn't much in the box though; it when I was born, some newspaper clippings, my first baby shoes, and a few other things. As I continue sifting through the box, Justin had made his way into the attic with Eric right behind him.

As Eric reaches the top of the ladder, he looks my direction and his eyes widen, "Brie?"

"Yeah?" I reply still sifting, not paying him any mind.

"What is that?" he continues as he comes into the attic.

I whip my head around quickly thinking he saw some type of bug, "What?" I reply panicked.

He quickly walks over as he points to the unicorn next to the box, "*That*…?"

I look down at the stuffed animal and pick it up, "It's just a…"

"Unicorn," he interrupts, "But it's…"

"*You can see it too*?!" excitedly, I stand up and hand him the toy, smiling.

Justin walks over and stands next to Skyla, staring at the toy that Eric is holding. He mumbles to Skyla, "It's just a stuffed toy."

"It's glowing blue," Skyla replies quietly.

Justin whips his head around to look at her, "You can see it too?!" He looks back at the toy and at all three of us, confused. "Well, what the hell is wrong *with me*?" he mumbles to himself.

Skyla bursts out laughing. We all turn to look at her, inquisitively.

Between chuckles she blurts out, "Justin thinks I can see the glow," she catches her breath, "But I never said I could," she puts her hand to her chest from laughing so hard. She looks at Justin and gently grabs his arm, trying to control her laughter, "Brie told me what she saw before you walked up here, silly." She continues laughing, I find myself laughing too. Even Eric begins to chuckle a little bit. Within a few seconds, Justin begins laughing about it as well.

Eric begins to analyze the unicorn, carefully evaluating every stitch. When I finally catch myself, finishing my last laugh, I look back at Eric. I prop my hands up onto my hips and ask, "Well, what does this glow mean?" Before he could answer I could hear a car door slam outside. That must be Skyla's husband, Reilly. She begins to head downstairs. Justin starts after her to greet his old friend, we all were in college at the same time. Skyla met Reilly through Justin.

Just before Justin walks down the ladder he jokes, "I don't want to be the only one who can't see the damn glow. I'll be downstairs with the normal folks." He almost seems hurt that he couldn't see what both Eric and I could see. I know he and Skyla are firm believers, but I never knew that there was anyone like me. *Until now. It's quite exciting!*

Eric points to the bottom of the unicorn and says, "With your thumb and pointer, reach right in here." He's smirking at me with those pearly whites and his eyes are dancing with excitement as he stares into my eyes.

"Why?" I ask, clearly there is nothing there but stitching.

"Just trust me," he softly replies. I smirk back as he urges me on. I take my right thumb and pointer and place it in the area he told me to. I can see my thumb and forefinger bypass the stitching to reach inside the little unicorn's belly. My eyes light up in awe, staring at Eric in delight. He continues to smirk at me, subtly shaking his head. "Well how 'bout that," he mumbles.

"I feel something in there," my brow lowers as I focus on reaching a little further in, "It feels… *hard.*"

Eric chuckles, "Well…" he rolls his eyes, "pull it out." *Phrasing.* I laugh aloud and do as he says, securing the item between my fingers and gently pull it out of the unicorn. As I do, the unicorn dulls back to its original shade of lilac purple and the item appears to glow uncontrollably bright.

"What is it?" I ask, staring at its beautiful rich blue color. It appears to have some cracks to add texture and between those cracks it looks like lightning. It was about the length of a credit card and shaped like a pentagonal rod.

Eric grabs it from my palm, the brightness dulling down, "It's the aquari seraphic gem." His smile is intriguing, the genuine splendor further adding to my own excitement.

"The what?" I ask again.

Delightfully he repeats, "The aquari seraphic gem." The smile on his face is almost angelic. Like this is best thing he's ever seen.

"*Okay*," I begin, looking off to the side, "Care to elaborate for me?" Eric continues to gaze at the stone before grabbing a handkerchief from his pocket. He gently wraps the stone into the fabric and places it back into his pocket.

He then grabs my hands, "Brie," he begins, inhaling deeply, "A seraphic gem is an ancient stone. The story behind it is something we will discuss this evening, but to sum it up, it's one of four stones that when combined is the most powerful form of energy in the world. Some even, have thought to use it as a weapon."

I smile at him, bewildered and unconvinced, but intrigued by his description, "These vague details are killing me Eric, are you going to explain to me why that *gem* is glowing *now* when I've had that unicorn since I was three?" I release his hand and begin to pace, feeling a little frustrated, "Or maybe tell me why I can see these things that I thought no one else could, *until you came along?*"

Eric glances away from me and places his hands in his pockets. He makes his way over to me, "I know I owe you some answers at this point. Some I will answer now and others in due time. You are a very, *very* special woman. Apparently, a genetic anomaly that even I didn't know existed. *But one that I hoped existed.* I don't think you are ready for the whole story, it's a lot to take in. I promise you this; I will explain it to you when I know you can handle it." *Phrasing again.* I snicker.

He places his hand on my face, cradling it with his palm. I can smell the cologne he is wearing, embracing his touch and smell. *What is it about this man?* My best friend pours his heart out to me earlier, the only man who I've ever had strong feelings for. And I'm truly considering his offer. *But then there's Eric.* I barely know him, but he gives me this feeling of comfort that I just can't seem to shake. I manage to snap myself out of the minor trance, remembering that Eric has shown little to no interest in me *like that*.

I grab his hand and pull it from my face, holding it in my hands, "I trust you… *I think*. But it doesn't mean I don't still feel left in the dark. Can you at least tell me a little bit more about these gems? I know I already signed that contract…" *Probably wouldn't have hurt to have given is a thorough read through at this point, shame on me.* "But it would make me feel more comfortable proceeding."

Eric smiles at me and then steps a little closer, we weren't standing far from each other to begin with, so I get a little nervous. His face comes down to meet mine and my first reaction is to close my eyes and await a kiss. My breathing shortens and I swallow hard, leaving my lips parted. He kisses me softly; the texture of his lips just as soft as they appear to be. *My cheek is so grateful.*

He then whispers affectionately in my left ear, as I open my eyes, "The gems are what we are looking for. Will you join me this evening for dinner again, so that I may tell you the rest?" He steps back to where he was before, awaiting my response. Hypnotized I nod yes, trying to maintain my cool. *Friend zone. I repeat, friend zone.* He reaches his hand out to me and gestures for me to come with him, "Let's go rejoin the party." I grab his hand and walk towards the ladder. He goes down first and I follow, closing the attic and saving my thoughts, and numerous questions, for later this evening.

I can see Justin and Reilly conversing back and forth while Skyla just stood there. As Eric and I walk out of the front door of the house, I hold my arms out wide to Reilly, "Reilly, so good to see you!" He walks over to me and hugs me tight.

Reilly is a tall man with a lean muscular build, deep tan/ light brown skin, perfect waves in his dark hair, and a smile that would make any man jealous. I place my hand on his face, "Thank you for taking such great care of my dear sweet Sky during this tough time. It's amazing of you to come all the way down from Moultrie to be with us today *after* your shift." Reilly is an anesthesiologist.

"Of course," he smiles and then glances over at Eric. "And who might this be?" he asks suspiciously. Ever since that idiot quarterback in college, he's been more protective of me. Even more so after Justin left Connecticut.

I look to the left of me and reply, "This is Eric Windsor, an esteemed colleague of mine."

Reilly chuckles then smiles, "Oh, you are the one Justin was telling me about. Nice to meet you Eric." *Justin told him about Eric? Odd.* They make each other's acquaintance and I begin to yawn.

"It's been a very long and exhausting day for me," I extend my arms out, stretching my back. I am getting that urge to run it off; between anger and frustration I need some type of release. Everyone seems so oddly cheery and I just need to be alone for a while. *Just me and rock hard... pavement.*

"Sky, would you mind if I took your truck back to the hotel? I'm just going to rest a bit," I motion over to her truck. She quickly tosses me the keys and winks. I kiss Reilly on the cheek, "It was good seeing you love, we'll be doing a remembrance in the morning and I'll bring the ashes with me."

Justin approaches me, "Do you want me to go with you?" He asks.

I shake my head no, "I just need to be alone for a little while babe." I walk over to the driver side as he follows. He opens the door for me to get in.

"But I don't think you should be alone. Rrr mmm. You know, for numerous reasons," his expression speaks another agenda.

"I'm a big girl Justin, I can handle myself." I raise one brow as I step in the vehicle, wondering why he's being eerily clingy.

"Well then, while you're in your room, I'll go to mine. I think I want to shower anyway and relax." His persistence is unlike him. He shuts my door. *I don't want to hurt his feelings, but I don't want to be bothered at all by anyone, including him.*

"You can drive back with Eric after catching up with Reilly. Seriously, *I'll be fine!*" I try my best to be polite about it, but I know he can see in my face that no means no.

He cordially nods, "Alright then Brie. No problem. Just call me if you need anything. I'm here for you." Smiling, I blow him a kiss and drive off into the sunset.

* * * * * * *

On the way back to the hotel I make a quick stop to purchase some workout apparel from the sports shop. I didn't think to pack any this morning, because I was in such a rush. I buy three different sets of workout gear (three pairs of leggings in different styles, one workout hoodie, two half zip jackets and three tanks), three sports bras, and one pair of really nice running shoes. Everything is laced with a little bit of red.

I get to my hotel room and strap up quickly, removing all the tags from every garment. I begin with a light warm up and stretch before making my way back down to the lobby. I take off out the hotel back door; phone strapped to my arm and plugged in to my music.

As my feet hit the pavement, heel to toe, left and then right, I suddenly feel the weight of the world being lifted from my aching shoulders. Running is the only time I'm ever been able to completely clear my thoughts. My mind gets very cluttered, and running, or kickboxing, are the only times I can get a release from everything that I feel is bogging me down. I knew the trail that Sheriff Givens referenced earlier; there's a small park before it, so I head in that direction.

With each step, I could feel my body getting more in sync. This is exactly what I needed. *And then another date with that steamy, hot shower when I get back.* As I run through the neighborhood, I wave at the people sitting outside on their porches getting fresh air. It's nice seeing all the old stomping grounds. I get lost in my thoughts and memories with each mile I pass.

Forty five minutes later…

I glance at my watch. *It's already 6:30.* I should probably head back. It's still pretty well-lit outside, but the sun is going to set quickly; so I head back through the park knowing it would be faster. Just after I run past the ballpark and make the turn towards the hotel, I can see a dark figure in the distance standing in the running path. I stop cold in my tracks. Goosebumps creep up past every inch of my skin. The dark figure in the distance looks like the figure I've been seeing in my dreams the past two times I've slept. *But I'm not dreaming.* I blink my eyes several times just to be sure.

I turn around to look behind me and then turn back to see the figure is gone. *Okay, maybe I'm daydreaming.* I look behind me again to see the figure standing there, not three feet from me. Startled, I fall backwards, screaming for help; the scream much less audible than I wanted. Quickly I shuffle, trying to get my feet underneath me as I crawl away panicked. "What do you want from me?" I yell out. The dark figure hovers closer to me until it's above me and grabs at my arm as I try to shield my face. I close my eyes, praying it would all be over. I feel the wind gust up before suddenly disappearing.

I open my eyes to a darkened room, deep hues of gray all over the walls and cold, hard black marble lay beneath me. *This is no walk in the park.* But maybe the basement of someone's home, well rather large home. The room seems large and empty with no windows or possible escape routes. "*Hello?*" I whisper, the words manage to escape my trembling lips. I stand and try to gather myself.

Stay alive. I keep quietly repeating to myself. What is this place? Am I dreaming? These are the questions I keep asking myself. "Yes, this is very real," I could hear a very deep voice break the silence. Startled again, I stumble backwards, maintaining my balance. I try to look around the room but it's too dark for my eyes to see anything. That prickly feeling that people talk about in movies is taking over the back of my neck. I can feel my adrenaline starting to kick in.

"You are too far away for anyone relevant to hear you, and you're here because I brought you here," he finishes. My heart is beating faster than a jack rabbit on speed, my palms are uncomfortably sweaty, and I keep whipping my head around to try and see something, *anything*.

"Who are you?" I reply hesitantly, not caring to engage with whatever, *or whoever*, is talking to me. But I can't help it. The room feels icy cold. Tears flee my eyes out of fear, because I'm so afraid of what I *can't* see in this room.

The room suddenly lights up, ever so subtle, just around me, about three feet wide. I can now see my hands at least. I dare glance up to see where the light is coming from but I couldn't tell. I can feel the wind gust again right past my left shoulder.

"Who am I?" the voice replies, obviously coming from right in front of me, but I still can't see *who* it's coming from. "I think the question is, who are *you?*" his icy breath finding its way into the light.

This is in my head, I can close my eyes and tell myself to wake up right now and this will all go away. I close my eyes tightly. Tear after tear falls across my cheeks, freezing as they drop from my face. "You're dreaming," I say aloud, "Wake up!" I scream louder. I feel a cold hand rub my right shoulder. I don't want to open my eyes; I don't want to see. I can hear someone snap and suddenly I'm floating, just suspended above the ground only by a few inches. I soar towards the back of the room, leaving the light into total darkness.

I am pressed against something much softer now, but I can't move my arms or my legs. I continue trying to assess my location and look around, but it's still quite dark in the room. "Help," the soft word escapes my lips. I'm trembling as I can hear footsteps walking closer and closer, like Prada shoes in an empty building lobby.

I didn't know which way to look or what to expect. I close my eyes again, hoping to wake up and realize this was indeed all a dream. My hands are clinched up into fists and my feet are so cold, I can't feel them anymore. To my right, a curtain is opened, shedding light directly on me. I squint, attempting to adjust to the sudden burst of sunlight. Unfortunately, the light doesn't make me feel any better.

"Brielle, this would be much easier if you relax," the voice booms in my head. I can hear an accent in his voice.

Somehow, I find the courage to reply, "*What* would be easier?" Honestly, I didn't want to know. I'm not even sure why I asked.

A figure steps into the light, "I am Barbanon." He is a very tall, very large figure. I can't tell if he appears large because of muscle or if it's just his frame under the layered clothing that he's wearing. His skin is a deep shade of green and he has glorious deep, black, slicked back hair. He reaches for me, his long fingers and black pointy nails grasping my left arm. I realize that I am reclined on some type of red leather chair.

Barbanon stands above me to my left, moving his hand from my arm to my head. He uses his other hand to gently caress my cheek with his fingernail. "I need to figure out if you are the one I've been looking for all these years," he caresses my head, like he was a petting a prized puppy. When he smiles at me, I notice he has fangs.

"What if," I swallow hard, my voice trembling, "I'm *not* who you've been looking for?"

"Then you'll end up like them," he points to my right and I turn my head in that direction. I can see a fire conjure up, showcasing the bones of at least ten different individuals. I face forward and begin bawling, "Please," I plead, "I don't know anything." I begin to think about my mother and how she died. Then the thought of my father's gruesome face. Still crying, I gather my courage, "It was you, right…? The one who killed my parents…"

He wipes my tears from my face. His gesture seeming to be almost affectionate. "Oh my dear," he smirks, "I guess in a way, you could say that I'm to blame for that." *I'm going to die.* I'm going to die the day after my father, and Skyla will be all alone. I frown.

Barbanon moves towards my feet and the chair lowers, still reclined, but my feet are dangling, bending my knees. The back of the chair comes forward, so that I'm facing him. I sniffle and gather my courage again, I turn my lips up and I manage a few trembling words, "Do whatever you have to do, my mother wasn't afraid of you and neither am I." *I'm fucking terrified.* At this point the only thing I could think about was Sky; how I would never see her again, how I wouldn't see my little niece and nephew again. Justin. *Eric.*

Barbanon chuckles at my comment, "Well, I didn't exactly *kill* your mother, she was an accident. Technically, so was your father. The women in the corner there," he turns my face, "*that* was completely me. You see, the woman I'm looking for is the *perfect* reincarnate of a former deity. You wouldn't know anything about that would you?" he devilishly smiles at me.

I have no idea what he is talking about and I'm not going to entertain him; one thing is certain to me, I am going to end up in that pile of bones. He steps closer and places his hands on my knees, forcing them apart. He runs his thumbs up the inner seam of my spandex pants until he reaches about three inches from my crotch. I still can't move, every inch of me wanting to push him away. "This may hurt a little," he smirks as he kneels toward my right inner thigh. I can feel pressure and then a sting. I raise my head up to see his mouth sucking the blood from me. I let out a scream and close my eyes again.

I open my eyes, gathering I'm able to move my body again. Hysterically, I jump up only to realize that I'm propped up in my own bed back at the hotel room. I'm touching myself everywhere and look down to see my thighs are untouched. Two little beauty marks were where 'Barbanon bit me'. None of it was real. I could hear his voice saying to me, "Just in time." I glance at the clock and it says 6:55. I didn't remember getting back here, and I didn't remember showering. Did I shower and then doze off briefly maybe? I can hear a door open in the distance.

"Justin!" I clamber out of the bed and run to my door. As I open the door I exclaim, "Justin, I…" But it isn't Justin standing outside of his door. It's a tall woman, roughly my height, hair somewhat darker than mine, same caramel complexion, and same curvy build wearing a very sexy, *very little*, dress. It feels like I'm looking in a mirror. "Sorry, thought you were someone else," I mumble as I close the door. The woman smiles and walks off. I press my back up against the wall and tear up. *That bastard just can't let go of his playboy ways.* I can't believe after our conversation; he would bring someone back to his room. Could he just not wait for my answer?

Justin

Fifty-five minutes earlier...

"How do you expect me to believe all of that?" I wearily look at Eric after he explains to me Brielle's purpose in his mission as we are on our way back to the hotel thirty minutes after she left the house.

"Well, honestly, I don't *expect* you to believe anything. I *do* expect you to have faith though," Eric replies, disdain in his tone.

"Well given everything Brie has gone through, I guess it all makes a little more sense. Question is though, what makes you think someone is after you and not after *her?*" I like to think of myself as intelligent and quite analytical. *Damn good at it too.*

"What do you mean? She is simply a part of the equation, not the answer. These termagants couldn't possibly be after her... the only reason they would be is to get to me."

"Because of what you're trying to do? Using those stones?" *Don't play coy, pretty boy.*

Eric retorts, "Well, *you* wanted to know everything."

"Well, I wasn't exactly expecting a modern day version of Terminator 2."

Eric snickers at his comment, "Well, I trusted you enough to tell you Justin. You can run with it, or be in denial, either way it doesn't change anything."

"I believe you." *I think.* "It's just a hard pill to swallow. I think I'm going to come with you both on this trip."

"I told you, I would *call* if I needed your expertise. As of right now, I don't need you."

I sneer at him. I can sense the anger brewing deep down from that reply. "What if Brie *wants* me to go?" *Can't turn me away if she requests my presence.*

Eric shifts his head towards the window again, "Well… if it makes her feel better…" *Found your weak point.*

We pull into the hotel parking lot. *She'll want me to go, you'll see pretty boy.* We exit the car and head to our rooms, Eric continues on the elevator up to his floor as I venture to my room across from Brielle's. I stop in front of her door and want to knock on it to check on her, but she might be resting so I think better of it. I open my door and begin to get undressed. *I think I'll just order room service or something.* I sit down on the bed to take my shoes off. I glance over at the phone then the drawer underneath, opening the drawer to grab the menu from it and quickly glance over the options.

"I think I'll order dinner for two, have some food waiting for her when she wakes up," I find our favorites and proceed to pick up the phone. Just then, I hear a knock at my door. *That's odd.* I stand up and walk to the door. Looking through the peep hole, I see a woman standing there, she turns around and I realize its Brie. I swing open the door, shirtless, "Hey gorgeous, I was just about to order us some dinner. Want to come in?" She smiles at me as she nervously enters the room. I close the door behind her and place my hand on her back, "Are you okay? You seem a little shaken."

She glances up at me and nods, "Yeah, I just needed to see you." *Of course you did, I'm irresistible.* I gesture over for her to sit on my bed as I grab the chair that's at the desk. "I've been thinking a lot about what you said," she begins, "And I'm ready."

A chill runs up my spine to hear her say that. "Are you serious?" I try not to sound too desperate or anxious, but it's difficult to hold back my excitement. She stands up and walks closer to me.

As she stands next to me, she grabs my hands, "I think you and I deserve a chance." She wraps my arms around her so that my hands are on her lower back. Leaning in, she kisses me deeply, passionately. Her lips are soft and juicy, like a plush pillow pressed against mine. I've been craving that since that hazy night so long ago.

"Justin," her voice echoes in my head as she nibbles on my lower lip, "Take me." I pull her on top of my lap so that she's straddling me on the chair. My heart is beating wildly, my temperature rising in anticipation. I lift her up and bring her to the bed, continuously kissing her. I begin to unbutton her blouse, kissing her neck and then between her breasts until I reach her stomach. I notice a little mark just above her belly button, similar to the symbol that Brie had described to me at the coroners, except smaller.

I push the woman down on the bed, "You're *not* Brie…" *Wicked bitch.* I wipe my face of the kisses this she-devil just stole from me. *Not again.* "Who the hell are you?" I stand away from her, ready to throw her out. *I can't believe this is happening again.*

The woman morphs into something else right before my very eyes, she has a long winding tail with scales that look like gold armor, protruding fins about three to five inches long lining her spine, her skin a golden pale green, long flowing deep blue hair, and her breasts were covered by a single piece of cloth. The evilest laugh escapes from the she-devils lips, "Clever, clever. My aren't we quick to catch on." *Damn right I'm clever.* Her voice very high pitched and snake like, "I am what many have called a siren, but there are other less appealing names that I'm certain you're now aware of."

"Termagant," I mumble, thinking about what Eric told me. *Get the fuck outta here.* I shake my head and stare in awe.

"Precisely lover boy," the termagant wraps her tail completely around me, starting with the end of her tail at my neck, like the way an anaconda coils around its pray, *"you could've just went with it.* It's been such a long, *long* time since I've been with a human." She smirks, bringing me closer to her face and licking my cheek with her long, pointy tongue. I'm struggling to break free of her snake like grip, but the more I struggle the greater her grasp.

"You don't look like the termagant that Eric described to me," I struggle to say.

"Well that's because Eric has only heard *stories* of us, our true form is so rarely revealed."

"And this? This is your true form," it's getting harder to breathe. I stop struggling, my resistance futile.

"Oh no, I wouldn't want to scare you to death. Our true form is for when we come to collect a soul, but rarely has a mere mortal ever seen that. This is for show," she caresses my face gently with her curled up finger and then cradles my face with her hand. "Unfortunately my master says I can't kill you and take your soul, but you will need to do something for me… stay away from Brielle for awhile."

"If you hurt her I'll…" her grip tightens around my throat.

"As long as you stay away, your dearest sweetheart will be fine… for now." She smiles at me then proceeds to drop me onto the floor and changes back into her previous form. I gasp for air, trying to stand anyway. "Go to sleep lover boy," she blows something from her palm into my face that knocks me out cold. "Someone will find you… *soon enough*," she chuckles as she walks over my unconscious body to go into my bathroom.

* * * * * * *

Briellyn

Ugh. I'm so disappointed in Justin right now. First this nutty, far-fetched dream or whatever one would call that encounter, and now I run into a woman who looks just like me leaving Justin's room. Not to mention, my father's eerie appearance at the morgue, the letter he left, and that weird stone that Eric and I found inside my little prized stuffed animal. Eric is who I really want to see right now, *I need answers*. I need to know if this *Barbanon* character that has been popping up in my dreams happens to also be someone Eric knows about or is aware of.

I wipe the tears from my face and stand up. I know I've never been lucky in love; *hell I may just be one of the few women in the world who will never truly experience it.* Not once. And I have come to accept that. I walk over to the end table and grab my phone. To my relief, I already see a text from Eric.

'Dinner at 7:15? Meet in lobby, dress sent up. ~Eric'

Dress? What dress? I place my phone back onto the end table and suddenly hear a knock at the door. The timing couldn't have been better, *I'll give him that.* I walk over to the door and open it to see room service standing there with a black garment bag in her hand. "For you madame," the woman hands me the bag, "Have a good night." I close the door and walk to the bed, placing the garment bag over it. I zip it open to see this gorgeous burgundy strapless long peplum dress, zipper details at the waist, and a V cut down the front. I check the size, a perfect six. *How could he possibly know my size?* I see a small white piece of paper sticking out from inside the dress; I pull it out and open it.

'I called your assistant to find out your size, hope you don't mind. Didn't think you brought anything formal with you so I picked this up. Cheers, Eric'

Cheers. I snicker, raising the paper up. I glance at my watch to see its already 7:00. *This will be a makeup job like this morning.* Oh wait. Being fashionably late for a dinner date that isn't *all* business, isn't a bad thing. I know I could use an extra five minutes to make sure my look is pristine. I venture into the bathroom and pick out deeper shades for my eyes and a very nude, caramel shade of lipstick with a little liner. My hair was still in a ponytail, so I pull it down and grab my curling iron from my bag. I pin some of it back into an updo and I quickly add some bounce to the top, accentuating the layers, and pull some curls down each side.

I grab the dress out of the bag from the bed and slip it on as the bag slides to the floor. I need to fake some happiness right now and nothing makes me feel better than getting dolled up and being taken to dinner. *Though it's been forever, not including the business dinner the other night.* I glance at myself in the full size mirror that was adjacent to the bathroom. Sometimes I surprise myself, I grin. *I slay, I slay, I slay, all day.*

The dress fit my curves just right, my cleavage actually looks fantastic in this cut, the color makes my complexion pop, and the length was perfect, falling right at the knee to accent my hips nicely. The long peplum fabric is a nice touch. *Oh no.* I don't have any shoes. I glance at my watch to see it's already 7:16. I don't want to keep him waiting *too* long. *What to do?* As I walk over to the bed, I pick up the bag from the floor and realize that it still has a little weight to it. I glance at the bottom of the bag to see something golden still in it. I reach in to find caramel heels, gold on the stems, with the signature red bottoms. *He bought me Louboutin's.* I am so excited right now, like I just hit the lottery. I might make good money, but I never splurge on super expensive shoes for myself. *Never saw the point.* I sit on the edge of the bed and slip them on, perfect fit. I quickly grab my clutch and rush out of my door to get to the lobby.

As the elevator reaches level one and the doors open, I notice Eric standing in the middle of the lobby dressed in this three-piece tan suit; black shirt; a wide, patterned tie with hues of deep red, black, and speckles of gold pinned down by a diamond and gold pin. He had his hands behind his back, beaming at me with his perfect, angelic smile. My heart is beating rapidly and I can feel my palms become sweaty. I am nervous and I don't know why. *This isn't a date.*

As I walk towards him it feels like the entire lobby is in slow motion except for him. He takes a few steps towards me, before long we stand only a few inches apart. He glances at his watch and teases, "Ah, 7:20. I thought you'd keep me waiting all night." He grabs my hand and brings it to his lips, leaning a little closer to me, "You look absolutely lovely in that dress by the way." He kisses my hand.

I smile at him gratefully, "Why thank you. The man who purchased it for me seems to have exquisite taste."

He raises his eyebrows, "Indeed." He brings his other hand to the front, holding a flat, wide, black box. He opens it to display a gorgeous gold necklace that is an intricate knot in the middle and two dangling pieces, each bearing a rather large diamond and a pair of matching earrings. My eyes light up with excitement. "Now that is the second time today I've seen that look. I'm growing quite fond of it, actually," he says to me as I reach to gently touch the necklace. *Is this flirting, cause it feels like flirting.* My smile transitions into a smirk and I blush in reaction to his comment.

"May I?" He hands me the box, takes the necklace out and has me turn around. He brings the necklace above my head with both hands and lowers it to my neckline. I can hear the clasp release as he adjusts the necklace accordingly. He spins me back around, "The perfect touch… to the seamless look… on a flawless woman."

My eyes brighten; his comment is unexpected, but *absolutely* welcomed. "What's the occasion for such kind words?" I grin at him, admiring his lips.

"You'll see," he responds. He reaches for my watch, the gift that Eryn gave me, "Let's take this off, just for a little bit. You don't need to know the time tonight." He unclips the bracelet and places it in the box. I hand him back the box so that I can put the earrings on. Eric hands off the box to the front desk and urges me in the right direction with his left hand on my lower back, his right hand showing the way.

I notice a gentleman outside the lobby standing next to the car door of an American Aston Martin. We walk through the lobby doors and the gentleman opens the passenger door for me. "You are spoiled," I joke as I take a seat in the car and he walks around. *Admittedly I love reaping the benefits of it, for now.*

He sits down and looks at me, "*I'm* spoiled?" He motions at all of me, "Yet *you're the one* being wined, dined, and gifted." He smirks at me, forgivingly. I couldn't help but laugh aloud.

"I never…" I start.

"But, dh, dh, dh," he interrupts, "I know you'd never ask, and I know I don't have to. But I enjoy doing this for you, trust me." He smiles as I sit back, blushing.

The car is sleek but cozy. Once our car doors are closed Eric starts the engine with the push of a button. As the car purrs, I can my feel my heart starting to race again. *Nothing like a handsome gentleman driving a sexy car.*

We leave the hotel parking lot and speed off into the night. "Do I even want to know how you acquired this in such short notice?" I question as he shifts gears.

He looks over at me with a devilish smirk, "We'll be driving this to Texas when we leave here."

"Why not fly?" I inquire. *Not that I'm complaining.*

"We'll be doing a lot of flying here soon; I want to give my crew some time here," he shifts again. Light after light we pass, illuminating his face in soft amber colors, accentuating his dimples, "Besides, I wanna see how she rides."

Wait what? Me or the car? Smooth yet ferocious… the car that is. I chortle at his comment.

He glances at me curiously, "What? Do you know how to drive a stick? I could teach you if you don't."

His question and comment couldn't have been timed better. *Get your mind out the gutter.* I can feel my heart flutter for a moment. I need to change the position of my legs a bit just to take the edge off. I respond with a sultry look, then a flirtatious smile, "Oh I can handle a stick, it's been awhile though. Big engines too." I've already made the conscious decision to play it cool with Eric from now on. I have had the worst luck with men, given the circumstances with Justin. And I'm told I'm naturally flirtatious anyway, I'm just going to be myself and stop beating myself up over relationship failures. *Shit, I know I'm good looking.* But everyone has their own taste.

I lean over to him, crossing my legs in his direction and place my chin upon my propped up left hand, "What do you say I take the wheel on the way back, and uh," I shyly lick my lips and smile, "*You* can sit back and enjoy the ride."

Eric looks at me from the corner of his eye and chuckles, "If you think you can handle it…" *This conversation is spiraling dangerously out of control.*

I quietly laugh at his remark. Every moment him and I spend together, he loosens up a little bit more. It's nice to see him lighten up. He makes a right turn and then a left into a parking lot. A small restaurant hails before us as Eric turns off the engine. We both unbuckle our seatbelts and proceed to opening our car doors. Eric rushes over to my side to help me out of the seat. He places a very pretty golden knit shawl around my shoulders to keep me warm, "I wasn't sure if it was going to be too warm for this, but I think it's a little chilly."

"Thank you," I adjust the shawl and then stare at him in disbelief. He is almost *too* put together at times, like he has an oracle on speed dial. I grab his right arm with my left hand and he cradles it, gently grabbing my hand with his left as my arm sits snug into his. We walk to the front doors which are being held open by a very well-dressed man, "Welcome to La Provence, may I have your name for the reservation." The man queries in a French accent.

"Windsor," Eric responds, holding me closer. "Ah, Mr. and Mrs. Windsor, your table is ready, please follow me." Eric glances at me from the corner of his eye after the gentleman referred to me as the Mrs. I look down, a little embarrassed. I hear him quietly snicker and it immediately made me feel a little more at ease. He didn't correct the man. *I'll take it.*

The waiter leads us to a nice quiet area, away from most of the crowd. There is a little fireplace going and a decent size table for two draped in a white tablecloth with three candles lit, a small vase with a single rose, and two place settings.

Eric enters the room, holding my hand out as he walks, guiding me along. The waiter pulls out my chair and Eric helps me to my seat. He then walks to the opposite side of the table, unbuttons his jacket, slips it off with ease, folds it, and places it on the back of the chair. He finally sits down and rolls up his sleeves. There is something incredibly sexy about a man with rolled up sleeves. And then there is that vest. *I'm a sucker for a chiseled man in a vest.* My temperature is rising again. *Easy girl.*

He's moving his lips, those perfectly shaped lips that are close to a strong chin and even stronger jaw line. His dimples show briefly, with each pressing word. He's fixing his napkin, airing it out and placing it on his lap. With each movement, his shoulders seem to flex under the shirt, leaving me wandering. "And that is why I brought you here," I finally hear him say.

I gently shake my head and softly chuckle, "Come again?" *Damn it, phrasing.*

He smiles at me, "I wanted to get you out of your element for a while, I thought some food and conversation might help you through this..." He gestures his hands, "*trying* day," he repeats. I nod my head in agreement. He points to the menu, "Let's go ahead and order first, then I will fill you in some more."

Okay this phrasing is getting out of control! "Fill me in?" I smile, picking up my menu to cover my face.

"About the gems and such, you know, what we'd discussed earlier," he finishes, rubbing his chin effortlessly. The ring on his pinky finger showcases a symbol eerily similar to one of the hieroglyphs from the paper he'd shown me the first night we'd met.

"Oh yes, perfect," I smile. Gazing through the menu, all the food sounds amazing. I'm having a hard time choosing. "Eric?" I ask. He glances up at me from over his menu, I continue, "Any suggestions? Everything sounds so tasty, but I've never had French fare before."

He responds with a sexy grin and puts his menu down, "Why Ms. Donado," he playfully shifts his legs from left to right, "if I didn't know any better, I would say you're asking me to order for you…" he crosses his ankle over his knee, "*again.*" He clenches his teeth, flexing his jaw line.

I couldn't help but nervously smile. I immediately look away for a moment, afraid I might get suckered into his gaze once more. "Well," I finally look up, "you do have a rather well-versed palette."

He picks his menu back up and looks just above it, over to me, "You have no idea." *Please give me one.* I raise my eyebrows in response. I continue browsing through the menu anyway, just until the waiter arrives. A moment or so later, he comes in for our order.

Eric begins ordering for us both. *In French.* When I mentioned well-versed, I didn't think in different tongues. He speaks it like he's born to it. Maybe that's where he's from; he did mention he wasn't American. I decide to take a sip of water from my goblet as he finishes the order. "My goodness, did you order us a five-course feast?" I joke after the waiter leaves. I gesture at him, "You said so much there. I love food and all, but I don't want you to think I'm one to eat my worries away." I take another sip of my water.

"Maybe," he replies simply, "So let's talk." He kind of shrugs his shoulders, gently clearing his throat. I halfheartedly grin and bow my head to urge him on. "Well as you recall from earlier, the gem that you found today, I mentioned is one of four. I had no idea where the fourth gem was until today. I've only narrowed down a general location for the other three."

He shifts in his seat, leaning forward to better engage me, "Each one represents something different. There is the Aquari gem, which is blue, used to shape every water source known to man. There is the Eaviri, which is a pearlescent white, used to shape the skies. The Emaldi, a shimmering green with exotic features, used to shape every land mass. And then there is the Fieri gem, it's a radiating red and the most powerful of all four stones, it shaped the planets core. Each of these gems were placed in different parts of the world after it was created."

"Oh, you don't believe in the *big bang* theory?" I ask jokingly. *Corny almost, I know.*

He chuckles at my comment and shakes his head. *Glad he caught on.* I'm rather enjoying this phrasing game that I'm playing in my head. *Thanks Archer.*

He continues, "The story has it that God had created three angels in the beginning; each with their own unique abilities to aid him in structuring the world as we know it. Once the world was complete, he gave each of the angels a wife or two, to create mortal life. It is from two of them, and their wives, that all human life, different nationalities and all, came from."

"And the third angel?" I ask, setting my left elbow on the table and bringing my thumb and forefinger to my chin, listening closely.

"He carried a jealous trait that God didn't want to be present in man; he took away his ability to have children."

I frown, "That's horrible." I think for a moment, "But if that were true, how come envy is a sin? It's obviously a trait that man developed anyway." Even though I find the story fascinating, only parts of it I believe.

"Evolutionary characteristics. Supposedly, if the third angel were to have a child, the child would be…" Eric hesitates.

Would be… I stare at him curiously.

"Would be an outright demon. The antichrist." Eric stares at me, awaiting my response.

I think for a few moments, trying to grasp this concept. "So what are you trying to tell me, that the Bible has it wrong?" I'm not one to judge what others believe, but I don't easily sway from my own beliefs.

"No, of course not, it's simply a shortened version. There are always forces at work that we can't always see and they don't want or need any credit."

Okay, I'm intrigued. "Ah," I grab my goblet and take another sip. After today's encounter with Barbanon, I think I will further entertain this. But I still don't know for sure if my encounter was real. Before I could think of another question, the waiter comes in with our first course. As we both begin eating, I ask, "Well how do you know all of this if it remains unpublished and untold?"

"There were manuscripts that were found, long before the bible was written, that were locked away. I found them; *well my family found them,* and had them interpreted. Never to be shared with mankind. The information is too sensitive to become public."

"Is that how you became so wealthy? Family of treasure hunters?"

He laughs, "No, my family is wealthy through other means."

"Like?" I question him hesitantly, hoping it's not something outrageous.

"My great-great grandfather was a supreme court judge, his son a lawyer and a farmer, *his* son an inventor and railroad investor, and my father an investor. Collectively they invested right."

"That's an awful long line of successful men." Dare I say, "Any of them slave owners?" My eyebrows raise as I pucker my lips.

Eric almost chokes on his drink. He quickly grabs his napkin to cover his mouth as he coughs and gathers himself. I giggle. Between coughs he manages, "Why... *on earth...* would you ask something like that?"

I take another bite of my food, shrug my shoulders and smile, "I just figure the time periods match up. They were wealthy... assumedly white. Honestly, I'm just curious. I would never hold it against you if they were. Not all slave owners felt their slaves were inferior. Hell, some of them were even given land and wealth after the owners passed. And by all means, correct me if I'm wrong," I smile at him teasingly. I love getting a rise out of him, it's oddly entertaining.

Eric gathers himself, "Actually no, each of them rightfully *employed* every man or woman who worked with them or for them, of their own free will and with higher than average wages. My great grandfather actually fancied an Ebony."

"Oh really, his mistress perhaps?" I raise my eyebrows but look down and eat, snickering to myself. *I should stop teasing him, but he's so cute riled up.*

"No, they were together for a while and she disappeared very young, unfortunately. What is with this questioning?" Eric demands, unbelieving of my words.

"I'm just messing with you Eric, honestly I am, I may have gone too far, I'm sorry," I laugh aloud, reassuring him of my playfulness. I really didn't care what his answers were. I just wanted to get a rise out of him for my own amusement. *Terrible I know.* He angrily sneers at me, but lightens up after a moment. He takes a sip of his water. I adjust in my seat, "*So...* did these angels have names? In the bible they speak of the other angels, like Gabriel or Michael. Hell, even the devil has a name." I take a bite of my food as Eric answers the question.

"The eldest angel is Senon. The next is Palidon, and then the last, the exile, his name was Barbanon."

I stop chewing. *There's no way I could hear that name twice in one day.* What I experienced could not have been some type of a dream, it would be too much of a coincidence. "So, the devil, *Lucifer,* where did he come from if this *Barbanon* came first?" I inquire, anxious for an answer.

Eric shrugs his shoulders in a *well* kind of manner, "They are one in the same. He was banished from heaven and lost physical form. So he is like a lost spirit, at the most, convincing man to do his evil bidding. Just like in the stories, you never actually see him."

No. That's not right. The man, *or creature rather*, that I saw had a body, a *very* real touch. Maybe I was dreaming and he simply hijacked it, which is why I awoke in my own bed. The look of fright and contempt graces my face. Just then our main course arrives. The food looks amazing, but I feel so disengaged at this point. The smell makes me sick to my stomach. Eric notices my expression change and he waits for the waiter to leave to inquire.

"What's the matter?" he requests as he scoots closer to the table.

I look down, embarrassed. "Can I be straight with you?" I feel like I'm gasping for air.

"Of course," he gestures with his hand and sits back a little bit.

I take a deep breath. "I had another horrible dream," I begin, looking off to the side, "I'm a little embarrassed because I feel like it was more…" I bite my lip, "intimate."

I can see Eric swallow after I say the word. "I'm not judging," he replies kindly. I could tell that he's intrigued.

"Well, I went for a run earlier and I had been running for about forty-five minutes. I was on my way back to the hotel when I saw this dark figure, like the one I had mentioned to you before that was in the previous two dreams. It approached me, and then grabbed me, and then I was somewhere else all of a sudden. He called himself Barbanon," I quickly notice Eric shift in his seat and adjust his neck. His motions were concerning, but I continued, "And he had me pressed against this reclining leather chair of some sort, where I couldn't move anything except my head. He told me that he needed to be sure I was who he'd been looking for all these years…" I stop, embarrassed about the bite on my thigh.

"What?" Eric asks. His tone changes, his expression now filled with worry.

"He, uh, claims to take credit for my parent's deaths, well accidental and then he um," I stare at my lap before continuing; "he pulls my legs apart and... *and bites me.*"

Eric appears very uncomfortable. He shifts in his seat again, "Where?"

"My very upper inner thigh..." I begin, "But it was just a dream, I thought. I woke up in my room. I just didn't understand because I didn't *remember* getting back from my run *or showering.* I've never had lapse of memory like that before."

Eric sits back in his chair, thinking carefully. He then sits forward and whispers to me, "You have to show me the bite."

"What?!" I exclaim, not expecting him to say that. "Don't be ridiculous, *it was a dream.*"

"Brie, I know it's embarrassing where he bit you, but you have to get over that. I need to make sure you're okay. I need to know if this is a threat or not."

He's asking me to open my legs to him. Ha! Even though it's not for a sexual reason, there's no easy way to show him without me feeling vulnerable. Maybe it's because I find him attractive. I do find it rather riveting that he is jumping to my rescue though.

"The reason it's embarrassing is not what you think," I softly reply while shaking my head and looking down. Pushing my right shoulder up and holding onto the seat of the chair. My eyes glance over at him. His expression is more serious than I'd seen of him previously. I glance towards the ceiling and close my eyes hard. I suck my teeth and look at him, "I'm attracted to you Eric, so that makes it awkward."

Eric stares at me, shocked. "Come on, surely you knew," I egg him on. I place my face in my hand. *I thought my googly eyes were obvious.*

"I mean, I just thought you were naturally flirty. You have such a happy, upbeat, *confident* personality type, that may seem like flirting, but it isn't," Eric retorts, still a little stunned.

"I mean there's something about you, I thought maybe you were gay because I was showing some actual interest and you wouldn't display it back, but then the few comments in the car from the airport and then here. I have such... *mixed* feelings about you. You give me this very strange, *comfortable*, safe feeling. Like, I'm at home in your arms. But in my *mind*, I'm uncomfortable with it. There's no way I can show you the bite without feeling vulnerable to you. And I'm a very confident woman, don't misunderstand me. I just..."

"No, I understand," Eric interrupts. He reaches for my hand and takes it into his own. "Brie, I would never ask you to do something you weren't comfortable with. But I beg you, for the sake of your own safety; I do need to see the location where he bit you. I promise I will think of a way for it to be as comfortable and non-evasive as possible." He smiles at me. "Now eat," he commands.

How can I eat now? At some point tonight, I'll be showing this man something on my body that is in a location that is supposed to be discreet. But his touch made me feel safe again, comfortable. *This man is going to be the death of me.* My emotions can't keep up. My body tells me he's familiar but my mind tells me take it easy, you don't know this guy. I'd throw my rule book out for him if he asked.

Eric takes a bite of his food but keeps looking down and around, like he can't focus. I try to eat too, but with everything

I've learned, I'm having a hard time. "So, what are the gems for?" I blurt out the moment it comes to mind, trying not to think of my examination later.

Eric stares at me, pleased to have the silence broken and conversation resume, "They are actually for this machine that is being built. They are the key to making it work. Before you ask what the machine is for, I'm not going to tell you just yet. There are eyes and ears everywhere. But you will get to meet the scientists behind it, Dr. Lannister, Dr. Teegrit, Dr. Strassmore, and Dr. Reese. All of them fantastically brilliant in their own ways. And you're the perfect addition."

I gaze at him curiously. Me? *Brilliant amongst a team of doctors and scientists?* There aren't many times where I feel like the least qualified in a room, but I get the feeling I will know what it's like very soon. I want to know more about the machine, but I know he won't budge on his decision, so I ask instead, "When will I get to meet them?"

"When we reach Quebec City. They'll be awaiting our arrival." He grins, but then it turns more into a bothered stare.

"When will I see this machine then?" My eyes grow big with excitement, anything to get away from it all. It's something I need more than ever with all the weird shit going on.

"Not until London," he says promptly as he signals the waiter over. "Can we get our remaining entrees to go please? Something's come up and we have to leave as soon as possible." He wipes his mouth with his napkin then hands the waiter his card. I look at him and the waiter, confused.

"Um, what's the rush? Where are we going?" I inquire, nervous I missed something.

"Back to the hotel, I need to look at that bite Brie. I honestly can't even focus right now unless I know."

"Know what exactly? If I wasn't hallucinating, what does all of this mean? Again, I'm *pretty* sure I was dreaming. No marks or anything…"

"Barbanon is known to play many tricks. He's taught himself very intricate mind games over the centuries. Things that would be any man's nightmare. If he's bit you, I will tell you more about what's on my mind, but for now, I needn't worry you *if it was just a dream.*" He stands up and puts his jacket on, smoothing it out and making sure it's crisp. The waiter comes back with our food ready to go in a bag. Eric nods as the waiter returns his card.

"Merci, Monsieur Windsor. We hope you enjoy the rest of your meal," the waiter replies. Eric walks over to me and helps me to my feet. I'm nervous and anxious all at the same time. What could Eric be so worried about? *Should I tell him about the bones in the corner where Barbanon had me?* He places my shawl around my shoulders and grabs the bag with the food.

We make our way outside to the car and he stops on the passenger side. "Still want to drive?" He inquires, grinning at me. I am taken back because he insisted we leave in such a rush, I'd thought he'd forgotten. *Hell, I kind of did.*

"Hell yes," I reply.

"I figured it might take the edge off me seeing you naked here in about twenty minutes," he lightly chuckles and steps into car as I stop cold in my tracks. I'm blushing uncontrollably, yet feel oddly turned on by his bold statement. I finally continue to walk to the driver side and get in after he is already settled in the passenger seat.

He shrugs his shoulders and looks at me devilishly, "Pay back for the slavery and mistress comments."

I shake my head and laugh aloud. "If I didn't know any better, I think you're the one who needs to take the edge off. Don't worry, you just relax over there," I tease. We both know he's not going to see me naked. That wouldn't be necessary. But I might as well be in my underwear given where he will have to look. The last time I was in something so publicly revealing was my senior year of college. Hell, the last time a man has seen me scantily clad was over three years ago… and that was a drunken mistake that I didn't care to make twice.

"Are you going to start the car?" he teases back.

"Oh, right," I snap back into the moment. I press the start button and we pull off, "Like riding a bike," I murmur. Eric just chuckles as we speed off back to the hotel.

When we arrive, the doorman comes to open my door. As we make our way back around the vehicle, he grabs the bag of food from Eric. Eric then asks him to bring it up to his room, prepared on plates. He grabs my hand and says, "Let's get this over with so we can both stop being so awkward… *and worried.*" *Who are you tellin'?*

We board the elevator. If I didn't know any better, I would think he was nervous about seeing me partially clothed too. But maybe he's just worried about the bite. *I hope this is all just a figment of my imagination.* But the other part of me wants to know what the bite means and what Barbanon meant about making sure I'm the one, even if it isn't real.

I do want to get this over with though. I should've asked if we could stop by the bar. A shot might take the edge off a little bit. We reach the seventh floor and walk all the way down the hall.

There weren't but four rooms on the entire floor. He grabs his key card from inside of his jacket and waves it in front of the door lock. It clicks open to reveal this amazing suite, roughly four times the size of my room. He walks me inside and closes the door behind me.

"Wow," I nod my head in approval, "You certainly spare no expense. Do you Mr. Belvedere?" I glance back at him mockingly, I can see he's already removed his jacket and is now unbuttoning his vest.

"Would you, maybe, like to change into something more comfortable?" he inquires as he unbuttons his shirt sleeves and then his shirt.

"What'd you have in mind? Did you already call and have someone pick me up some pajamas. Journelle maybe?" I tease, wondering what amazing planned out outfit he had for me this time. *He plans for everything.*

He laughs aloud, "Oh my Ms. Donado. I *have* spoiled you." He reaches into his drawer and grabs a black tee of his and some of his satin boxers and tosses it at me, "I was thinking more like, something of mine."

I stare at it in my hands, "Oh." I laugh; embarrassed I made such a trivial request. "This will work great," I reply. He takes off his vest and his shirt, showing off his very muscular arms and chest. I find myself staring at him once more; this man is quite literally perfect. He looks like the gym is his home and he's always in the weight room.

He grabs something satin looking and walks into the bathroom, "I'll go ahead and finish changing in there so that you can change out here." He flashes me a flirtatious smile and I nod my head in promise as he returns to the bathroom.

He shuts the door and I immediately bite my thumbnail. This man would be the one that would make me break every rule that I've ever made for myself. *Seriously, every rule.* I turn around and put my purse and the shawl down on the bed. I sit down to remove my shoes as I stretch my arms around to my back to unzip myself. I slip off the dress, leaving me in just my bra and underwear.

I slip on the green satin shorts and the black shirt, which smells of that delightful cologne he wears. He yells out to me, "May I come out? Are you decent?"

"Yes," I simply reply. He comes out wearing a form fitting tank top and satin pajama pants. He has something in his hands. "Are you ready to do this Brie?" he asks.

My nerves are shot. "You wouldn't happen to have any wine or other alcoholic beverage, would you?" I'm rubbing my arm, staring at him bashfully, "I just need to take the edge off."

He opens his fridge and grabs a tiny bottle of rum. Giving me a peculiar look, he hands me the bottle as he sits next to me, "Drink up." I glower at him and take the bottle, shooting it quickly. I could immediately feel the sensation burning down my throat, then warming me up from my toes to my fingertips. Although I don't feel ready, I know there is no time like the present.

I pull myself further onto the bed, sitting legs folded in the center of it. I keep moving around my shoulders trying to relax. *Stop acting like you're about to lose your virginity, for goodness sake.*

He puts on a pair of pearlescent glasses and turns around to look at me. He carefully analyzes me, first looking at my left cheek and then my left arm. "Which thigh is it on?" he smoothly asks as I stare off into the distance trying not focus on what he's doing. I clear my throat and hike the shorts up on my right thigh just past the bite but before the curve of my hip is exposed.

I continue to look away as I can feel him very delicately touch me. *It immediately turns me on.* His touch wasn't sexual in anyway, but my body is longing for this man. *If I was a man, he would already know... thank God I'm not.* He takes off the glasses and stares into my eyes. "Well," he utters, inches from my face. But he doesn't finish. He simply pauses for a moment and continues to gaze into what feels like my soul. I know this face, this stare, those deep blue eyes, the raven black hair, the lips.

He leans in and presses his soft lips against mine. Tasting his warmth for the first time is like heaven. The feeling of excitement and anticipation rushing through me and around me is invigorating. I lean into him to bring him in, closer and deeper into me. I can feel him wrap his arms around me, drawing me into him, against his powerful body. I wrap my legs around him, portentous of me longing for him more intimately. He lays me down and climbs on top of me as he continues kissing me, his tongue massaging mine. My entire body is turned on. *If he rubbed my toe the right way, I could peak right now.* As the kiss grows deeper, there's a knock at the door.

He pulls away, quickly and suddenly. "Ignore it," I plea, trying to bring him close to me again, but he shies away.

"I shouldn't... *we...* shouldn't," he begins as he climbs off me, then off the bed. Flustered he adds, "I can't." He awkwardly walks towards the door and opens it. It's room service with the food from the restaurant. "Just leave the cart, I will pull it in, thanks," he states to the gentleman. He pulls the table in.

I'm staring at him, disappointed and worried, "What's the matter?" He brings the table in front of him in an attempt to cover himself and prevent me from seeing his interest. *But oh, I had already seen it.* "Did I do something wrong?" I probe again.

He looks down and sighs, "No, you did absolutely *nothing* wrong. We can't do this, you and I… *it's complicated.*" He sighs again. *What the hell just happened?* I just want to walk over and slap him senseless. I confess my attraction and this is what *I* get. *Thanks for the lady blue balls, pal.* He sighs heavily again, "I need to tell you something," he mutters out. Oh boy, here we go.

Briellyn

I swallow hard then mumble, "What is it?" Eric slowly walks over with the glasses in his hand and hands them to me. I look at the glasses, then back up at him and ask again, *"What is it?"*

He sits down a couple feet away from me and says, "You were definitely bitten, but it's much worse than that." He grabs the glasses and opens them up, "Please, put these on," he urges again.

I slip on the glasses and glare at him, "What am I supposed to be looking for here?" He grabs my left hand and pulls it in front of me, "Look at your arm." Clear as day, there are symbols all up and down my left arm. I pull the glasses up to look at my arm without their assistance, unable to see anything. I put them back on as I rush off the bed to examine myself in his full-size mirror. The symbols are up my entire left arm and onto the left side of my neck, even on my left cheek. The bite is also clearly visible on my thigh. *What. The. Hell?*

"Well what does it all mean or say?" I ask, staring at myself in the mirror. Eric stares at the ground so as not to make eye contact with me. I can see him in the mirror looking down, so I turn around. I place one hand to my forehead and the other on my hips and stare at him, "Am I going to *die?*" Eric immediately stands, rushing towards me. I motion for him to keep him away, angrily squinting at him, "The kiss, it was out of pity…"

He stood there, thinking for a moment, "No way, it's more complicated than that."

"Tell me what the markings mean, Eric," I plead, quickly changing the subject. He grabs my left hand and holds it in front of me. That immediate feeling of comfort overwhelms me again.

"The markings are in an ancient language that I don't fully know. I'm only familiar with three of the symbols. One means life, another means balance, and the last one…" he swallows hard and stares into my eyes. "Death," he states glumly. I could feel my heart drop into my stomach. His hand tightens around mine. That sense of security interrupts my feeling of anxiety and dread once more.

I stare into his eyes and then come to my senses. "What are you?" I ask accusingly, pulling my hand away from his, "Every time you touch me I… *it isn't normal.*" Eric stares at me blankly. "None of this began happening until you came into my life. Within twenty-four hours of meeting you my father dies and I'm cursed." *Ha.* Eric continues to stand there, silent. His expression is nothing short of regret. As I look at him, my hardened thoughts begin to soften again. My mind is trying to rationalize something that I don't understand while my heart tells me this isn't his fault.

"We cremate my father in the morning, after that…" I hesitate briefly, "Do you have any other resource that can interpret the markings completely?"

He looks at me, encouraged by my words. Softly he replies, "Dr. Strassmore should be able to decipher it… so you're *still* willing to do this?" Although he sounds hopeful, worry is more obvious in his expression.

I halfheartedly grin at him, motioning each of my words, "Maybe if we find what you want, I can break this curse. But I definitely need space tonight Eric. I haven't been with anyone in years and I can't *read* you so, *please*… give me that. You're reasoning is incomplete about the kiss, but I can't change your mind. You're going to think what you will. Being around you clouds my judgment though, so I'll see you in the morning." I head for the door, still in his shirt and boxers, grabbing the plush robe from the nearby closet. I walk back in his direction as I put the robe on and grab my purse.

"At least eat something Brie," Eric blurts out, pointing to the food.

I walk back to the door and open it, staring back at him, "Good night Eric." My tone drips with disdain and fury. I walk out of the room, the door immediately shutting behind me.

Eric watches me walk away. He slams his fist to the dresser and yells out a quick, shallow grunt. It's loud enough to echo down the hallway where I am standing next to the elevator. "I sure could use some help right about now, maybe some answers even," he speaks softly to himself as he leans against the dresser with his head down.

The elevator dings and I rush into it. I hit the button to go one floor down. The doors open and I walk to my room. I stand in front of my door and turn around, staring at Justin's door. As pissed as I still am about his exploits, there's nothing more that I want to do than talk to him right now. Finding out the bite is real tells me that I'm not safe in my own room and I don't want to be alone. I take two steps to reach his door and I give it three firm knocks. Listening closely, I hear nothing on the other side.

Justin picks his head up from the carpet, shaking off the remaining sleeping dust. I give the door two additional knocks and softly say, "Justin? It's me."

He climbs to his feet upon hearing the second set of knocks and sneaks to the door. He coyly peeks through the peep hole and can see me standing there. He goes to open the door but thinks twice. He places his back on the door and puts his hand on his forehead. "Go to your room Brie," he whispers to himself so that I can't hear.

Hurt and confused, I walk back to my door and let myself in. I haven't seen him since I left the house; I wonder if I hurt his feelings by telling him I wanted to be alone. As I open my door and close it behind me, I think to myself how I didn't want to be there. If I woke up here, that means that Barbanon has been in my room. Now, I'm afraid to fall asleep here. But I know I don't have a choice. Justin is still indisposed and Eric is… *complicated.* I decide to send Justin a text.

'Are you okay? Haven't seen you since the house, need to talk. – Brie'

I place the phone on the nightstand and turn on every light available in the room. I decide to keep the robe on and climb into the bed. *I feel so alone.* I quickly grab my phone and decide to text Eryn as well.

'I miss your face already. I hope you're having a better day than I did. –Brie'

I place the phone back on the night stand and wrap the blankets around me. While lost in my thoughts I manage to doze off. I find myself nestled to one side of the bed, comforted by someone's warmth behind me. "Justin," I mutter with my eyes still closed, "I was worried about you." I gently rock as I feel his hand slide over my stomach. Something doesn't feel right about it though. I carefully open my eyes and look down to see that my belly had grown. I appear eight months pregnant and the hand that cradles it is not Justin's hand, but green with long fingers and black nails. I roll over onto my back to see Barbanon's face in front of mine. He leans in and kisses me. *I kiss him back.* My stomach begins to ache terribly, so instinctively I sit upright.

Breathing heavily and looking around, the room is empty. I was dreaming again. I lean back and softly whisper to myself, "Lord protect me. I'm so scared right now and don't know what to believe or who to believe. Just give me a sign and guide me in the right direction." I rub my face with my right hand and then plop it down on my side. One small tear escapes my eye. I roll over and doze off once more.

* * * * * * *

The light from the morning sun grazes my face. Peeking over to the clock on the nightstand, I see that it's 7:30. I have the urge to go for a run, but decide on lifting weights in the hotel's gym to avoid another devilish encounter. Sitting up, I throw my legs over the side of the bed. Grabbing my phone, I check to see if there are any messages or missed calls. Nothing. *I have the worst best friends ever.* I decide to call the front desk and have them connect me to Justin's room. It's the only thing I haven't tried yet. "Can you please connect me to room 602?" I cordially ask the gentleman at the front desk. "Could you please verify the guest's name?" he asks.

"Justin Vandegrift," I reply.

"One moment please," he pauses for a moment. I can hear him typing into his computer at the desk. "I'm sorry ma'am, Mr. Vandegrift checked out early this morning."

"What? Are you sure?" I ask. *This is so unlike him.* He wouldn't do this to me again. *At least I hope he wouldn't.*

"Yes ma'am, I see here a checkout of around six AM," he waits for my response. "Anything else I can do for you this morning Ms. Donado?"

"Um, no. You have a good day sir," I reply softly and hang up the phone. Why the hell would Justin leave and not say anything to me? I quickly pull his name up on my phone and send him a text.

Justin, are you okay? I heard that you checked out this morning. How come you didn't come by? –Brie'

I should call him. I decide against it, instead head to the shower, and then to the gym. *He's fine.* He's a big boy and can take care of himself. *And I'm tired of giving a shit about everyone else when it seems I'm everyone's last priority.* I put on my workout gear and proceed downstairs. As I open the door to the gym, there are just a few people in there. I quickly scan for a free treadmill and lock onto one. I climb onto it and get situated. After a moment, I notice Eric out of the corner of my eye. I didn't even recognize him at first. I've only ever seen him in suits and sweaters.

He's wearing a navy UA shirt with some red shorts and navy anti-fatigue workout leggings. He's squatting. Perfectly, I might add. *Those delightful looking buns.* I try not to stare, but he's hard not to look at. He finishes his repetitions and walks my direction. I finish wiring my headphones around my shirt and set my station. Trying to still show him I'm upset, even though I'm not. "Morning Brie," he states nonchalantly.

"Eric," I address him simply.

"So, you're still upset with me then," he raises one brow and sneers.

I look down at him and play it cool. "No," I answer, "It's all good hun. No hard feelings." I flash him a quick forced smile. *Terrible liar.*

"Okay, what time should I meet you for the cremation? You never gave me a time last night."

"We can meet in the lobby at about 10:30," I reply. I can see the sweat slowly dripping from his brow, soaking his shirt and glistening his hair. He reminds me of superman with the way his muscles look so sculpted in the compression shirt and his dark hair slicked back. He has an S curl over his forehead.

He nods his head in agreement and walks back to the weights. He glances over at me, in between each repetition. I'm wearing a pair of charcoal leggings that make my rear end look fantastic and a red space dye long sleeve quarter zip. I begin running and finish in about twenty minutes.

Eric is still lifting, so I walk over and join him. "You even lift?" he inquires curiously. I nod my head in acknowledgement as I set up for some dead lifts. "Nice form," he murmurs as I bend forward to begin. *Pftt, whatever.* We both continue with our workouts, him finishing only twenty minutes later.

He approaches me, "You want me to order us some breakfast, about how much longer you think you'll be?" He's patting the sweat off his neck with a white towel.

I finish the last repetition I have and I stand up next to him, panting. "Well, I think I'll only be another five minutes or so," I lick my lips and place my hands on my hips, taking deep breaths through my mouth.

"Perfect, can I just bring it by your room then? In say thirty minutes?" he grins at me shyly.

I smile big, "Yeah, that'd be great." He begins to walk out of the room and I remember about Justin, "Oh hey, wait." I jog over to him.

He turns around and looks at me curiously, "What's up?"

"Did you know anything about Justin checking out of the hotel this morning? I went by his room last night, no answer. And then the front desk told me he checked out of his room around six."

Eric stares at me in the oddest way, "What? No. He mentioned meeting me in the lobby yesterday to go to the gym this morning. I just assumed he'd changed his mind. Have you called him?"

I look down and begin to worry about him. I shake my head, "Sent him a text last night and this morning and haven't heard back. I'm sure he's fine." I faintly smile at him and walk away. Eric watches me walk away for a moment and then proceeds to exit the room.

* * * * * *

Eric

I find myself hurrying to the lobby. Without hesitation, I pull out my phone and immediately dial Justin. *Straight to voicemail.* "Hey Justin, it's Eric. Brie just told me that you checked out this morning and you didn't meet up with me for the gym. What's going on? I hope this isn't about our disagreement about whether you could join us on this mission. Give me a call back. Brie's worried about you." I hang up. *Truth is, now I'm actually worried about the guy too.*

I continue glancing around the lobby for another moment or two. I then head for the stairs and continue onto the sixth floor.

Glancing around the hallway near Justin's room, I catch a glimpse of a green substance on the ground. As I bend down to get a closer look and rub it between my fingers, I realize exactly what it is. I rush off to get to my room and hastily dial Kalil.

"Brie and I will be there late tonight," I begin to pace.

"What's going on boss? You sound alarmed."

"You remember Justin right?"

"Of course, he's a good guy…"

"He's… well, missing. I found Empyrean sleeping sand on the floor outside of his room."

"*Oh* shit."

"Yeah, and that's not all. Brie encountered Barbanon yesterday. He bit her, explaining that he was looking for someone and thought she might be her. He also wrote an enchantment on half of her body, which I'm sure is a curse. I don't recognize most of the symbols so I'm hoping Dr. Strassmore can shed some light on it. It's ancient Empyrean, I'm sure of it. I feel uncomfortable leaving her alone at any point. I still don't feel comfortable telling her *everything* just yet. I think she'd have a hard time believing it."

"I've never heard you this unnerved."

"Barbanon has *never* made an appearance since our last encounter. Hell, we thought he was dead. *Well physically anyway.* I'll explain later, just ready her training for first thing in the morning. Focus on hand to hand combat, some use of heavy artillery might even be good. And of course, meditation. If she can better strengthen her mind, we might be able to prevent Barbanon from using her to do his bidding. Get Brie all the gear she is going to need for the expedition too. Sneakers, boots, clothing, jackets; ya know, the works. I sent over her sizes to you. Also, I need you to get those special bullets we discussed and the blades. Did you get the Amaranythian Amulet?"

"Yes, yes, I got it covered Eric. How long have we been doing this now? Don't ya trust me yet?"

"Too long, I just can't take any chances this time. If she's trained, she stands a better chance at surviving until the end."

* * * * * * * * * *

Briellyn

Meanwhile in the gym

I'm finishing my last set of curls. I can't get Justin off my mind. After finishing, I head back to my room. I decide to take the stairs as a cool off, slowly walking up each and every step while still listening to my music. I get to my door and open it, but stop before entering. There's a note on the floor with the hotel logo on it. I open the fold:

'Front desk at 4pm. No phone, no Eric. – M.V.'

What the hell? I had to think for a moment whose initials these are. After a moment or two, I realize they belong to Justin's brother, Marcus. But how did he know where to find me? *This looks like Justin's doing.* I remove my earbuds from my ears and glance at my phone. No missed calls or texts from Justin *or Marcus* so I decide to give Marcus a call. It only rings twice before he answers.

"Briellyn Donado," he sounds excited.

"Marcus…" I lead on.

"How are you sweetheart? I'm sorry to hear about your father. You and Sky have my deepest condolences. Wish I could be there for you both."

"Well aside from that, things seem to be going pretty well. Getting close to the holidays…" *Not to sound indifferent about his passing.*

"I know. Will I be seeing you and Sky again this year?"

"Um, well… probably Sky, but I'm not sure if I'll be able to make it this year."

"But we *always* get together, even without my feebleminded brother." *Even Marcus felt that Justin messed up with me when he left.*

"I know; I just have some business to take care of this time around. Speaking of which, did you leave a…"

"Yes," he interrupts.

"Yes what??" I had to be sure he knew what I was referring to.

"Yes, it's from me and I need you to follow the instructions with precision."

"Have you heard from…"

"Yes," he interrupts me again.

"Rrr. *Okay*…" I squint, annoyed by his interruptions. He is answering my questions entirely too quickly.

"It'll all be explained in due time," he says simply.

"Is everything okay?" I ask, wary of Justin's current location.

"Yes, just follow the instructions. I'm sure we'll talk again afterwards luv. But I have to go."

"Okay hun," I pull the phone away from my ear and hang it up. This whole situation just got weirder, but from what I can tell Justin is okay. *I hope.* I put the phone down on the nightstand, then quickly shower and get ready. I know that Eric will be back with breakfast soon and I want to be prepared to go when he arrives so we can eat quickly and head over to my father's house to meet Sky and her family. After I get out of the shower and change into my dress, I slip the security lock into the door and prop it open for Eric.

I finish up my hair just as I hear a knock at the door. "Come in," I yell out as I pin part of my hair up to keep it out of my face. *Of course he's right on-time.* I walk out of the bathroom to see Eric standing there with a bag of food. He is surprised at first, "Wow, you look... *amazing.*" He laughs as soon as he says it, maybe to lighten the mood. He smiles at me as he looks at my whole ensemble, from heels to hair. His eyes taking in the sight of me, pleased with their candy.

I'm wearing a black dress with a solid black hourglass plate up the middle of the front and back, tan on the sides that has a black lace overlay. It has a squared neckline and long black lace sleeves. A solid black crop jacket is layered over the top to compliment it. My hair is in gentle curls cascading down one side and I'm wearing the necklace he gave me last night. I'm trying to put my earrings in, pleased with myself at his continued gaze.

"Well thanks Eric," I finish putting the other earring in and grab the food from his hands. I begin setting it up on the little table, his eyes still fixated on me. "What is it?" I inquire as I turn around and look at him, eyebrows raised, shifting my hips to the side.

Somewhat baffled, he rubs his neck, "I wanted to give you more of an explanation about last night and…"

I hold my hand up and walk over to him, "Nonsense." *Work with me, I'm trying not to care.* I gaze into his deep blue eyes and groom him by flattening his collar and straightening his tie. "We are both adults Eric," I tighten his tie, "I don't expect anything. Just be glad it didn't…" I pause and quaintly roll my eyes for a moment, then stare back into his, *"Go further than it did.* It was the heat of the moment, we both got caught up. No regrets here. It's best to keep it professional." *Part of me really wanted you to blow my mind last night.* Eric closes his eyes and shakes his head no. He seems disappointed though. *That makes two of us babe.* I take notice, but move along without encouraging further discussion. Last night is in the past and I've slept off the frustration. *Well mostly.* I pull out the food and we both eat, barely saying much more.

When we get to the lobby after the quick breakfast, the valet had his car pulled up in the front waiting. Eric is walking next to me as the front doors open and I stop short at the passenger side. I'm about to open my door when Eric grabs my hand and pulls me against him. I stumble, falling into his arms. "Whoops," he beams down upon me, "Do you want to drive?"

Whoops, my ass. But yes I do. I will happily take bribes to ease the rejection from last night. I smile back and give him a gentle nod as I stand up straight, quickly fixing myself as I walk over to the driver side. I take notice in the parking lot that Skyla's truck is gone. Once in the vehicle I ask, "Where's my sisters truck?"

He looks at me and replies, "Oh they picked it up last night after we left for dinner."

We make our way over to the house, pulling up behind my sister's truck parked in the same spot it was yesterday. As we get out of the car, I look for her in the vehicle but she isn't there. I quickly turn my head when I hear the front door open and she is standing there with my niece Leah. She is only fourteen months old. My face beams with adoration as I rush to the porch to grab her from my sister's arms. As I get closer, Leah recognizes my face and begins cheerfully wrestling her mother to reach for me. I swiftly grab her and hug her tight, "My little Tinkerbell! Did you miss your Tee-tee!? Cause she missed you, beautiful." We video chat daily.

Eric smoothly makes his way over to us, and carefully watches me gush over my niece. He and Sky exchange morning greetings as her husband Reilly comes through the front door. He immediately walks over to me and kisses me on the cheek, then walks over to shake Eric's hand. I turn to look at Sky and ask, "Where's my little…?"

Then the front door bursts open once again as my happy yelling nephew Clayton comes barging through, "Auntie Brie!" He's almost four years old. My face lights up once again and I kneel down with Leah in my arms to give him a big hug and a kiss. Clayton begins going a mile a minute telling me a million things about bugs, birds, what he had for lunch yesterday. Then out of the blue, he just stops.

He stares at Eric intently, "Who are you?" His little voice sounds accusatory and innocent all at the same time. He walks towards Eric, gawking at him. All of us just stop and look at Clayton as he approaches him. "Why do you have those?" Clayton asks as he points accusingly at Eric.

Eric looks around, wondering what the child sees, "Have what little guy?"

Clayton puts his left hand on his forehead to shield his eyes from the sun, pointing just behind Eric with his other hand, "Those... *are they wings?*" His voice softens so no one else could hear him.

Eric kneels and the child adjusts to not having to look into the sunlight. Eric smiles and beckons him, "Come closer, I'm going to tell you a secret." Clayton curiously takes a few steps forward and leans in. Eric whispers into his ear, his sweet little face lights up with excitement. Eric urges him to tell him what he thinks quietly. Clayton whispers back to Eric. At the end of their whispering conversation, Clayton asks Eric to promise him and then makes him shake on it. The two shake and Clayton turns to acknowledge the rest of us.

"Well then," I stare at Clayton and then to Eric, "What was that all about?"

Clayton looks up at Eric admiringly, then turns to me, "Nothing Auntie, its top secret between us men." He pats his chest with his fist. Eric chuckles a bit as Clayton walks back over to his mother and I. *Oh Eric, you keep stealing sentimental pieces of my heart and it isn't fair.* Eric and I lock eyes for a moment before I can catch myself.

"I picked up Dad's ashes already, I figured wherever you wanted to go is fine with me," Skyla chimes in just as Clayton walks up to us. She helps me snap back to reality.

"I want to spread his ashes out by the pier, he seemed to always like it there," I respond while handing Leah back to her. "Give me a proper hug, kid!" I grab Clayton and hug him tightly, holding him off the ground. "Let's go see your grandpa off the right way, shall we?" I exclaim.

"Yeah!" he shouts as he runs away to the truck and hops into the back seat. The rest of the family clambers into the truck as Eric and I make our way to the car. Reilly comes over to us before we get in. "Is Justin not coming?" He looks at us both quizzically.

"Um, he's not feeling well." I blurt out before thinking it through.

"Oh," he walks away nodding his head. I can see him pull his phone immediately from his pocket.

Once Eric and I are in the car and the doors are closed he looks over at me and asks, "You spoke to him then?" I shook my head no. He can see that I didn't care to discuss it so he immediately places his hand on top of mine, as it's on the gearshift, and just softly says, "I'm sure he's fine." He didn't leave his hand there long though. *Even though I wanted him to.* We pull off, Skyla and family close behind, well on our way to the gorgeous Florida coast.

* * * * * * *

The six of us are standing at the edge of the pier. As the cool ocean breeze whips through my hair, I finish my dedication speech, "… Father, please know that Skyla and I forgive you. May you rest in peace knowing that we love you always, no matter what. And know, the Donado family traditions will continue through us and our children. Please watch over us through the rest of our life journeys and say hello to mom for us," I hand Skyla her flask, "Here's to you father!" Skyla and I toast each other first, taking a large quaff of the liquid and then hand our flasks over; Sky to her husband, and mine to Eric. Reilly knows the tradition, but Eric is completely unaware.

He grabs the flask and tips it to Reilly who proceeds to drink up. Afraid to ask the contents, Eric lifts the flask to his lips, bottoms up, and takes a big mouthful, following Reilly's lead. He puts down the flask and is amazed at how smooth the substance was. We stand in silence for a moment before releasing the ashes into the wind; it gracefully dances its way to the crashing waves below. "Rest in peace Dad," my words are soft, carried into the wind. I grab Sky's hand as a tear escapes my eye. It too, is whisked away.

I hand Skyla a small stemless glass as we make our way back to a more family friendly area on the pier. The glass she has, holds Italian wine. We toast each other once more and drink up.

With the loss of every Donado, it is tradition for everyone present sixteen or older to take a shot of a special mixture of juice and liquor. Children of the deceased who are five and older only have a sizeable sip of some Italian wine. This ritual represents the loss of half of their bloodline being absorbed into the next generation. It seems silly, especially when Skyla and I aren't drinkers, but we completely respect our ancestor's wishes and will continue to do so.

I remember sipping on the wine when our mother died, Skyla was still too young. At the funeral, I was told to take only three sips because I was so young, to signify past, present, and future. The remainder of my wine is then cooked up into a dish that I would have for dinner. It's really a beautiful tradition. Although I can't see it now, maybe I'll have kids one day that will carry on this tradition when I pass. *Doubt it, but a girl can dream.*

Skyla and I are standing about thirty feet away from the guys, the kids playing amongst their feet. I glance every once in a while over at Eric, Skyla catching me every time. "What happened between you two last night?" She asks, beaming her pearly whites toward me, taking another swig of her wine.

"What makes you think anything happened?" I ask her, defensively.

"You have glanced over at him like five times already; we've only been standing here a few minutes. You look... *conflicted*," she's obviously proud of her observation.

I turn around to stare off at the ocean instead of being tempted to glance over at him once again. "Well, we sort of," I pause and begin fidgeting, trying to find the right words to say.

"You little vamp. *You slept* with him!" Skyla exclaims, playfully slapping my butt with the back of her hand.

I spin back around, "*Of course not!*" I cross my arms in frustration, keeping the wine close to my lips, "We just kind of... made out." I sip from the glass, smiling nervously.

"*What!?* My sister who hasn't even so much as gone on a date in three years, makes out with a man she's known for maybe a week? Barely a few days. Lord help us, the world is coming to an end!" Skyla jokes, sarcasm dripping off every word.

"Oh, hush woman," I sip again.

"De-tails!" Her excitement is entertaining, like a kid in a candy store, waiting for the one thing she's never gotten from her big sis. *A love story.*

"I hate to disappoint, but it was nothing. There's nothing between us. Apparently on *both* ends," My expression sours. She comes closer to me and looks over at Eric.

"A mistake, sis? *You* are no man's mistake, and you don't make mistakes…" she says lovingly.

"I'm not sure what happened, one second we are having this passionate make out session. And it was amazing, I'll give him that. But then there was a knock at the door and WHAM. He went cold, turned himself off like a light switch, no explanation. Well he tried to give me one this morning but it's a new day, I didn't want to hear that shit. No sad love songs here. Besides, I have never done anything like that. EVER. I'm glad it didn't happen because I might have regrets today. I've only been with three guys and I made all their asses wait. Why should he be the exception?" I chuckle, mentally patting myself on the back for my restraint.

"That man there," Skyla says kind of drunkenly as she points, "Is in love with you and doesn't even know it yet."

I unfold my arms and glare at her amused, "Why would you say such a thing? You said it yourself, we haven't known each other very long."

"Have you seen the way that man *looks* at you? Or the way you glow when he touches you, or vice versa?! Come on Brielly!"

I laugh aloud, "He does have this thing. When he touches me it's like… I can't quite explain it. Like all is right in the world and nothing can hurt me," I glance over at him again and we briefly catch eyes. I look away as fast as I can, "I swear he's like a demon or something."

"Oh stop," Skyla says, gently nudging me, "When he looks at you, there's love in his eyes, maybe it's… love at first sight." Her eyebrows raise in sync, like they are trying to give each other a high five.

"Sky, stop wishing and hoping, it's definitely *not* like that," I urge.

"Fortunately, I know what love is and you don't. He's got the look, he's just not ready to accept it yet," she cheerfully drinks the remaining wine from her glass and smiles at me sweetly.

"*Or* he could be some insane devil trying to suck the life from me…" I glare at her slyly, swirling the wine left in my glass then drink it. One of Barbanon's minions maybe. *Not likely*.

"You are sarcasm at its best sis. Well, live a little and try it out. I'm sure he won't bite…" she adds. I chuckle at her remark, though it scared me a bit. "Besides, he's kinda hot. What do you have to lose?"

"Ha," I blurt out, "Man candy sent to *destroy* me. Indeed, he is hot, possibly perfect. But maybe too perfect in so many ways," I reply. *Gingivitis waiting to happen*.

Briellyn

I ask Eric to drive back. Skyla and her family went their separate way back home to Georgia. I sat in the passenger seat, lost in my thoughts. As much as I wanted to, I couldn't get yesterday out of my mind. My father's lifeless body, the gem in my toy, my abduction, the curse... *that kiss*. So much happened yesterday and I don't know where to begin or how to analyze it.

Twirling my hair with my right hand, I demurely glance over at Eric. I try not to make it obvious but I feel terrible for giving him the cold shoulder. He's actually been quite helpful and maybe has a great explanation for why we couldn't continue last night. Hell, maybe he's just very old fashioned and trying to be respectful. *Oh my goodness, maybe that's exactly it.* He's trying to be respectful! It makes perfect sense. He's so proper in every way. I definitely overreacted. Just terrible timing with everything that has happened, I wouldn't normally react the way I did. *Now open your mouth and say you're sorry.* I twiddle my fingers and look up and over at him.

"I'm sorry about last night... *and* this morning. I overreacted. You were trying to be a gentleman and I acted like a child," I'm calm yet hesitant. Admittedly, I feel *pretty stupid* now that I thought it through.

He looks over at me and softly smiles, "Don't be so hard on yourself, I take full responsibility. I'm a bit rusty at this."

Sure you are. To break the awkward silence, I smile and look out the window and ask, "What did you tell my nephew that's such a big secret?"

"Oh," he glances over at me looking out the window, "I told him that I was your guardian angel but he couldn't tell anyone because there were some bad people out there." He looks back at the road.

I quickly turn around and stare at him. A half-cocked smile creeps across my lips. "Why would you tell him such a lavish tale?"

"Well he thought he saw something that he couldn't possibly have seen, so I just went with it."

I laugh, "He's got quite the imagination."

"Indeed. I also let him know that I would train him to be a guardian one day."

"Aww, cute." *Why does he always know what to say.*

"Yeah, Clayton is a good kid," he looks at me once more out the corner of his eye and sees me still twiddling my fingers, "Is something wrong?"

"Well," I take a deep breath, then exhale, "Honestly, I'm worried about Justin. It's not like him to disappear like this. And I had another very weird dream last night. None of this began happening again until you showed up."

"I'm sure Justin is fine." He briefly pauses, "What was the dream about?"

"It wasn't anything long. I was pregnant. Practically full term, ya know, round belly and all. And Barbanon was there *again*," I peek over at Eric, embarrassed, "He had his hand over my belly and he leaned in to kiss me."

"Don't be so hard on yourself," Eric grabs my hand.

"Well I kissed him back," I reply bluntly. Embarrassed by my unconscious actions, I stare out the window again. I can feel his hand nudge me, beckoning me to look back at him. I turn my face to catch his eyes.

"It was *just* a nightmare." He sounds so sure, "It's no indication of how you truly feel."

I offer him a thankful smile. That feeling of security surrounds me again. Instead of pushing it away this time though, I embrace it.

"Why did you say 'again' earlier, about the dreams?" Eric says concerned.

I put my head back on the headrest and close my eyes. A tear falls from left eye as my voice cracks. *I'm too intoxicated to talk about this.* "It started when I was five, just after my mother died. I began having these dreams about a cloaked figure who would come and take me away. It keeps me locked away from everyone I know and love. At some point, this demon woman comes to take me. I refuse her so she tortures me. In each dream I die differently, painfully. Stabbing, drowning, poison, strangling... you name it. It would always feel so real. I wouldn't have the dream every night, but each time I did, it would feel like I never would wake up. The dreams stopped shortly after I stopped talking to my father. Anytime I dated someone, the dreams would come back and become more violent. Only when I was alone did they stop." I frown.

I can feel myself getting choked up but I continue anyway, "It's only now that I realize the cloaked figure looks an awful lot like the one from yesterday on the plane. The one I told you about. And at the park before my encounter," I swallow hard, "And it makes me believe that Barbanon has been watching me this whole time. My entire life. And *that* is a very uneasy feeling. And now he's cursed me and violated me. I mean I'm 28 years old and I have never been in a relationship for longer than six months. Right after I let my guard down and give into them, they'd always cheated or hurt me in some way. Even my own father cast me aside. I've only ever had Sky. And then of course, Justin and his brother Marcus who have always been there from a distance. Lastly there's Eryn, whom we've been attached to the hip since I was like five. I feel like the one man who has been in my life the entire time, as eerie as it is, is this devil, this fallen angel...*Barbanon*, or whatever you want to call him."

Eric grimaces, "Brie, you have to be the most brilliant and put together woman I've ever met. Building a business from the ground up despite all the adversity that I'm sure you encountered. You have ideas coming out your ears. Plus you're kind hearted, gorgeous, and very very special... given your unique ability. Don't let something that happens in your head affect who you *really* are." He takes a deep breath and sighs.

He glances back and forth from me to the road before continuing, "The thing that you described to me is what's called a termagant. I didn't want to tell you because I figured it was merely a coincidence. I told Justin what it was as a precaution. He wanted to then come on the expedition and I told him I didn't need him. I didn't want to take any chances with people you care about. You've already lost so much."

The cloaked figure has a name. I'm losing it. I'm unsure how to respond. "Why are you telling me this now?" I gaze down at his hand holding mine and swallow hard.

"Because I now know that the feeling that I've had the entire time must be true. I didn't want to alarm you if it wasn't necessary."

"What feeling? What the hells' a termagant? What aren't you telling me?" I want to be somewhat hysterical but I'm still trying to wrap my head around the concept of the devil.

"A termagant is a female demon or what has been come to be known in myths as a siren. They take many forms..."

"But aren't sirens supposedly these beautiful mermaid looking creatures that would lure sailors to their deaths?" I chuckle, thinking of the old tales that I was fascinated with as a child. But that's exactly it. They were just tales.

"They are one in the same except they don't take any one form. They are sent out to collect souls and do the bidding of their master. They can appear in many forms but they are *always* women."

"Are you sure, cause I think I've dated one..." I joke, thinking of that sleezebag, cheating quarterback.

"I couldn't be more serious Brie. I'm sure male demons do exist. However, I've yet to encounter one. It would make sense that Barbanon being who he is would only surround himself with females though. And worse, I believe that one is after you but I just can't figure out why."

"Why do you *think* one is after me?"

"Well, just like *you* can see things, I can see things that your eyes can't. There was slight termagant residue on one of your personal items in your old room. What I don't understand is if Barbanon has already abducted you once, why send out one of his demons after you again? It had to be prior to your abduction so maybe they are done but I don't know what he wants with you or why he would bother cursing you. Furthermore, Justin told me you saw markings on your father's body. It may be that one killed your father. But I just don't see the point of it all. Maybe it was to get you here to Florida, but either way, you're not safe until we can get rid of Barbanon for good."

"So what are you? *What am I?* Why is it that we can see these things and others can't?"

"Well in order to see the things you do, you'd have to have a special gene that you weren't supposed to from our original lineage. As I mentioned to you before, all humans came from the two, first generation angels."

"How do you know about all of this? I get the feeling that I was a bit off on my analysis of you." I sit and think for a moment then turn my head to look at him, "are you even really an investor?"

"Yes Briellyn, I'm really an investor. I'm really a billionaire and I'm really part of a family who knows the background of all religions. I simply took a fancy to it because of my ability and it lead me here, to you, and looking for these gems."

I let his hand go and cross my arms, "So tell me then, why is that every time you touch me I get this instant feeling of warmth and security, like euphoria. Why is *that?*"

He stares at me and back to the road like he wasn't sure how to respond. Hesitantly he says, "I'm not sure Brie. I can't answer that."

I'm sure he's telling the truth, I just don't know what to make of the cluster of things he just told me. My head is beginning to hurt, "I think I need to lay down for a bit when we get back to the hotel, it's almost 3:30 and I know we have a bit of a drive to Texas."

He nods his head in acknowledgment, "That's fine, whatever you need."

He seems uneasy now but I don't want to pry. We're only a few minutes from the hotel and I am curious to find out what's waiting for me at the front desk from Justin. I knew the only way to get Eric of my back long enough to follow the note, is if I said I was going to sleep.

* * * * * * *

Eric walks me to my room, "I know what I said is a lot to digest. But after your training, we are going to sit down with my team of scientists and I will explain everything. I promise." His hands are in his pockets and he's being a little distant. He stands off to the side of the door as I open it. "I'll be in my room, just send me a text or call me if you need me." He is careful not to touch me in any way.

I close the door behind me as he continues to stand there. I place my back to the door and sigh heavily. *Get a grip Brie. He's still just a man.* I turn around and look through the peephole to see him still standing there, hand against the door, leaning on it. He appears deep in thought, but then walks away. When I see him leave, I begin packing up my room. I change into something more comfortable, then pack up everything else in my room.

This way, I'm ready to go in case this meeting with Justin runs long. By the time I'm done, I glance at my wrist. *Damn it, Eric still has my watch.* I will have to grab it from him later. I pull out my phone instead, and its 3:54.

Before I can leave, I feel my nose running so I walk to the bathroom to blow it. When I do, the tissue is full of blood. *What the hell? I've never had a nose bleed in my life.* I blow my nose again and it seems fine so I throw the tissue away and continue on. I make my way to the front desk after putting my bags into Eric's car. Looking around cautiously, I approach the desk just as it turns 4pm. The woman at the desk is on the phone so I patiently wait, looking around the lobby.

She holds her hand over the receiver, "Are you Ms. Donado?" I look at her quickly, wondering if I should say yes. I shake my head in acknowledgment and she gestures for me to wait a moment. "I have her here now sir," she says on the phone. She then hands the phone to me.

"Hello?" I ask curiously. "Brie, I need you to come right now over to our old hideout. Be there within the next twenty minutes. Don't be late." The line hangs up before I can say anything in response to the request. It certainly sounded like Justin, and his non-direct commands tells me it would have to be him. I hand the phone back to the clerk and leave right away.

I decide to take Eric's car since I am pressed for time and without my own transportation. It also assures me that he can't follow me. Justin and I used to meet up at an old abandoned building out by the local high school whenever he would visit me. It was quite the hang out back when we were young. We put couches in there and made it the perfect covert spot. There's no telling what that place looks like now though. The building was small but had several rooms on the inside, functioning doors, and stone floors. Instead of building a treehouse, we had that. And only the cool kids would go there. I was never very popular but Justin always was, wherever he went.

When I pulled up, the grass surrounding the building had been mowed and perfectly maintained. The outside of the building was now painted, the roof top cleaned off, all of the weeds pulled up, and the windows look new. It looks like someone bought the place but it was hard to tell if maybe the new kids on the block just fixed it up on their own accord. I didn't want to just walk through the door if someone new owned it though. I decide to walk around the back to see if the rest of building looks renovated.

There is a tall garden maze in the back that had always been there but it definitely has been cleaned up. I creep closer to look into one of the windows and see old furniture. Justin had mentioned no phone so I couldn't try calling him to find out where he is. As I walk a little past the opening to the garden maze, I hear a noise. It sounds like someone stepping on sticks. *"Hello."* I yell in a whisper-like manner, *"Justin?" I'm going to kill him for bringing me out here in the boonies.* Even though it was still bright and sunny, there were so many tall trees around the area that it made it quite dim. This place gives me the creeps.

All of a sudden a hand covers my mouth, the other around my arms and chest, and I get dragged into the maze. Kicking my legs and fighting the figure with every step, I'm not doing much good. The figure uncovers my mouth as we stand there in the dark. "Shh, shh, it's me," Justin speaks up.

"You scared me to death!" I exclaim. My heart flutters, beating a mile a second. I try to regain my composure as I place my hands to my knees and gather myself. I go to stand up and without warning he leans in and kisses me, placing his hands around my face. His lips are smooth yet rough. I am so taken back by it, that I don't resist him. When he pulls away, he glares at me strangely. Once I come to my senses, I firmly punch him in the stomach.

"Owh," he groans. Between grunts he says, "I was just making sure it was you." He remains hunched over for a moment.

"That's for disappearing without saying anything," I point at him angrily.

"Ah, I… deserve… that," he continues to groan but proceeds to stand up straight. I then slap him on the left cheek, "And *that* is for kissing me without my permission!"

He rubs his cheek and stares at me. "I just needed to make sure it was you," he says again impatiently.

I blink my eyes and roll them at the same time, leaping in to hug him. "I'm just glad you're okay," I whisper into his ear, grasping his shirt as we embrace. I let him go, "And what do you mean make sure it's me, why wouldn't it be me?"

He grabs my arms and hunches down closer to my face, "Sometimes, I think you're bipolar."

I cross my arms and scrunch my face. He continues, "You're not going to believe the night I had."

I cross my arms and grunt at him. He wouldn't believe the night *I* had. A flash of the gorgeous ebony that came from his room last night crosses my mind again. "I was attacked by this… termagant… thing!" he blurts out, waving his hands around. "She told me to stay away from you and then knocked me out…" I've been trying to wrap my head around the idea of *female demons* since Eric spoke of them. This conversation immediately makes me feel uneasy.

"Wait, wait, hold on. Back up…" I interrupt, "You were attacked by one, meaning you actually saw it?" I stare at him inquisitively. I'm almost glad he's seen one. *Welcome to the club rookie.*

"Well, I think the better word may be threatened, let me start from the beginning…" he takes a deep breath and glances at the ground. He then looks up at me and grabs my hand, "Last night, Eric and I had a disagreement about me coming with you two on this expedition. After he explained the dangers involved, I felt I should go. He told me no, so I decided that I would order us some dinner and discuss it with you. Given our conversation earlier, I figured you might be game for dinner anyway and you would convince him to allow me to stick around. Before I could order, you happened to knock on my door. A happy coincidence. We spoke for a little bit and then we were kissing, one thing leading to another. Everything seemed to be going great… once more, but then I noticed this tattoo," he pulls out a sketch of the symbol that was on her stomach.

I stare at it curiously; it looks exactly like the symbol I saw on my father's chest. I can feel my heart begin to race as I grow nervous. All of this is a little too real for me.

He continues, "And immediately I knew it wasn't you. She turned into this enormous medusa looking creature and she said that if I didn't stay away from you, she would kill you. She then knocked me out with some sleeping powder."

"Oh my God, Justin. Are you okay?" I rub his cheek affectionately, my hand carrying a slight tremble.

"Yes, I'm fine. She said she wasn't there to hurt *me* according to orders, which is what worries me."

I swallow hard, "She's just a pawn." Immediately an image of Barbanon crosses my mind. Eric *did* mention they do all of his bidding.

"Exactly," he stares off, "But now everything makes me think about all those years ago, when I thought it was you that came to my door..."

My thoughts clear and I focus back on him, I raise one brow, "Wait, the story you told me earlier?" I roll my eyes, then angrily squint at him, "You can't be serious."

"Well, I mean... how else would you explain it Brie," he pleads. I walk away holding my hand to my forehead and the other on my hips, annoyed by the thought. He mumbles, "I always thought she was kind of extra anyway... seriously, she's a bitch and you and I both know it."

"Ugh," I stare at him even more annoyed, "Justin, *you were drunk.*" I couldn't stress that part about the story enough. I begin pacing.

"As I told you earlier, I wasn't. I stopped drinking that night. And if you really think about it, she's always been kind of jealous of us!"

"Eryn has *always supported us.*" I gesture at him and I, "She's been there... since we were... since *I* was a kid."

"Kind of a coincidence though, her coming into your life and then your mother dying the way she did..." Justin's smug tone creeps under my skin.

I turn towards him and give him a deathly stare. I huff loudly, pointing in his face, "You know my mother died in that crash, that is *not* fair Justin. Besides, Eryn was just a little girl. How could she have had anything to do with that!?"

"That's not how I remember it," he motions his head to the side.

"How would you know, you weren't there," a tear rolls down my cheek. His words continue to anger and annoy me as I continue pacing back and forth.

"No, I wasn't. But Eryn was that night. And I recall you elaborating a very different story to me… before she-devil got into your head and changed details. Think about it Brie… you told me there was a figure in the road. The next day, your sidekick wouldn't leave you alone and the story change to, it was just a deer. It may have not been her directly but maybe she was covering something up," He slightly raises his voice urging me to think by shaking my shoulders.

* * * * * * *

"Mommy, can we make cupcakes tomorrow?" a five year old me stares in the rearview mirror of the '93 Chevy Tahoe at my mother. Her brown eyes warm my heart as she stares back. In her angelic voice, she replies with a yes. "You hear that Eryn? We get to make cupcakes tomorrow!" I excitedly turn to Eryn. She is this petite little girl with fiery red hair and freckles with bright green eyes. She just moved in down the street from me and I've deemed her my new best friend. I can still see my mother looking at me as I look away from her at the road.

"Mommy look out!" I yell out, pointing to a figure in the road. My mother swerves the vehicle crashing into a nearby tree. I wake up to Eryn pushing my shoulder seconds later. My mother's air bag deployed but she is moving. She's okay. She looks out of her driver side window and panics. Turning towards the back, she calmly says, "Baby, I need you to listen to me very carefully. Go to the nearest house and find help. Don't turn around, don't come back without help. Get out and run, go now."

She is having trouble trying to unbuckle her seatbelt. I'm able to unbuckle mine as Eryn grabs my hand, urging me to come with her. I didn't want to leave my mother but the look on her face told me to obey without question. I nod my head helplessly as we exit. "I'll be right behind you baby," she reassured me. Eryn hops out the passenger side and I come out right behind her. I hear my mother's door open on the other side and then a loud smack. I fall to the ground to see her body lying on the ground on the other side. She was staring at me; those warm brown eyes, and in her silent way she was telling me to stay away.

The figure standing over her is a shadowy, dark clothed figure with long skinny fingers, black fingernails and a hood covering its face. It was what was standing in the road before we crashed. I wanted to help her but Eryn kept pulling me to come with her. As the figure hovered over my mother's body, she laid very still. I could hear it smelling her. She lipped to me, 'I love you' as the figure turned her face towards it. Her eyes became hypnotized as tears fell down her face into her hair. In that moment, I could see a small ball of light leaving my mother's mouth as her body shoke profusely.

Eryn managed to get me to follow her off. I wasn't sure what I had just seen but I remember reaching the nearest house and calling 9-1-1. Then I remember telling Justin what happened the moment I saw him but for some reason my thoughts were different. Almost like I can't remember what happened after we hit the tree.

* * * * * * *

"I remember now," I mumble, "The cloaked figure, of course." *The damn thing has haunted my nightmares ever since.* I stare down at the ground and think of my encounter with Barbanon earlier today. I digress, "But that would mean…"

"That Eryn isn't who we think she is," he says sadly, his hands still on my shoulders. I'm not sure if that's the conclusion that *I'm* ready to accept but I let him continue on. "Honestly Brie, I'm not sure if we should trust Eric either. He's sketchy. Him saying I can't go with you and then this demon woman shows up telling me to stay away, it's not a coincidence. You shouldn't go on this trip…" He stares into my eyes, he looks so sure of himself.

"But I'm *cursed*." I reply bluntly, staring into his eyes blankly.

"Excuse me, what?" He adjusts his stance and bites his bottom lip.

I raise my hand to my forehead and rub it down over my eyes. "I'm cursed. I've only wanted to tell you what happened to me all damn day and you've been MIA." I slightly step away from him and begin motioning every word. "I was abducted by Barbanon yesterday and apparently he *cursed* me. I'm sure he is who the termagant answers to and I think Eric may be the only one who can help me. I tried to tell you but…" I think about when I rushed to the door and saw the woman leaving the room. It's only now that I realize I saw exactly what *he wanted* me to see. "That son of a bitch," I whisper to myself.

"*Or* it could all be a ploy to get you to go somewhere he *wants you to go to*. How do you know you're cursed? Did *Eric* tell you that? *And* you were abducted! On his watch!" he's getting angrier with each word.

"Pause," I hold my hand up, "Yes, Eric is the one who told me I was cursed but I wasn't abducted on *his* watch, I was abducted on mine. I was out running when it all happened. The same creature that killed my mother, took me to Barbanon. And as far as Eric is concerned, I feel like I can trust him, no different than I trust you." My tone gets a little louder from my anger and excitement rushing in. "I'm a grown ass woman and I can handle myself."

Justin scowls at me, "Yeah? And look where it got you. Abducted and cursed." *You. Bastard.* He rubs my shoulders and tones it down, "Look Brie. I know the past twenty-four hours has been hard on you but I think, given everything that has happened to *both* of us, but especially you… you need to be somewhere safe… not with some *stranger*… regardless of how he seems, he *is* different from me. You think of us differently."

"If Eric truly wanted *you* to stay away, he wouldn't have called you here with the whole situation with my dad, don't you think?"

"Well, that was before he saw me as a threat to his operation." Justin rubs the back of his neck. He's pulling stuff out of thin air now.

"And if you got such a terrible feeling about him, you should have *never* told him about me to begin with," I pause for a moment. He looks at me regretfully. I sigh, "I just have a gut feeling he's one of the good guys here." I ball my fist up and push it on my stomach.

"I love you, but I'm going to need more than just your hunches. I'm not taking any chances with your life. I think he may be clouding your judgment. But to prove it, take this," he hands me a small chip. *How insulting.* I'm so angry with him I could spit. But I continue to remain calm, I know his hearts in the right place. He continues, "Put it in his phone, behind the battery. I will not gamble with your life, I'll be close by when you come to your senses."

"What the hell is this Justin? What's with all the secret squirrel shit? Last I checked, physical therapists didn't moonlight as 007." I glare at him.

"*Long story,*" he pauses, "But to make it short, during my times away I met some very interesting people. They owed me one and I'm cashing in on the favor now. I know this all seems bizarre Brie, but something more is going on and I don't know how to protect you and I *can't* let anything happen to you. Not when this is all my fault in the first place."

"You're right..." I reply simply. He smiles at my response. I look into his eyes and continue, "It *is* all your fault. I wouldn't be in this mess had you just kept me to yourself." *I mean that both literally and figuratively.* He stops smiling as I continue on, "I'll put the chip in his phone... but I'm doing it for me, not you. I need to prove to you that Eric *is* good. And you will keep your distance until more is revealed. I need answers damn it and I can't get them if I just run away. Eric may be a lot of things, especially mysterious but he *is not* bad, and this will prove it." *I hope.*

"Boy he's got your mind all out of whack, huh?" his judging voice chimes in.

"Maybe," I mumble, glancing down at the chip he handed to me. I look up scowling at him, "*And maybe your jealousy is getting the best of you.*" I immediately think of how I feel every time Eric touches me. When Justin questioned me about my feelings toward Eric when we first landed, I denied them all. And within the last twenty-four hours, Justin professed his willingness to change his ways just to be with me. Now I'm torn between the two of them. I shoot Justin a fake smile and head back to the car. He runs up behind me.

"If you're in danger, what signal will you give me." He looks at me carefully.

"Oh you'll know," I glance at him briefly, raising one eye brow as I step into the vehicle and start the engine. Justin stands there, arms crossed and frustrated. I pull away, deep in thought and worried that I am completely wrong about Eric. What if Justin is exactly right and Eric can't be trusted? *Why would anyone go through such a farce?* And Eryn. If she's a demon, she should get an Oscar for best supporting long-term actress. *Fuckin' Barbanon, that selfish imp.* He ruined my life. If I would have known the last thirty-six hours would be like this, I may have just taken my chances with Fiore from the beginning.

Someone just took a dump on my perfectly clean life and I let it happen. Everything is out of my control and I despise feeling this way. My mind is going a million miles a minute trying to make sense of Justin's conspiracy theory. If Eric was working with Barbanon, and Eryn is too, wouldn't Eryn have been more supportive about Eric? All the pieces to this puzzle don't want to fit in my head.

One thing is certain though, if my mother was killed by a termagant, admittedly by Barbanon. And then my father the same, the only way to truly find out what the point is in all of this, is to go through with it… *all of it.* Justin may want me to run away. But if I did, my parent's deaths will have been for nothing. I can't let that happen. I need to know Skyla is safe. If that means trading my life for hers, so be it. My phone rings, interrupting the diligent sorting of my thoughts. The number says UNKNOWN. I decide to answer it, "Hello?"

"Don't hang up, it's me," Justin spurts out quickly.

I immediately roll my eyes, I love him but this peer pressure is killing me, "*Yes Justin…*"

"I wanted to tell you I'm sorry. You *may* have been right about me being a bit jealous of the connection that you and Eric have and *may* have jumped to conclusions about him. I don't know what to think. Maybe he's not a demon. But... *something about him* isn't adding up. I just need to be sure, for your sake. However," he states, "I *do* believe that Eryn is no good."

His apology immediately cools my emotional fire and I feel better about my thoughts, "As much as I don't want to believe you," I exhale hard so that he can hear, "I think you may be onto something."

"Really? You believe me?" he sounds so relieved.

"Do you remember when you and I were starting to get close in high school and Eryn took it upon herself to hook you up with that really pretty Puerto Rican cheerleader?"

"Yeah I remember."

"Well, I had told Eryn that I was starting to have a crush on you and she made it a point to deviate from that."

"You had a crush on me in high school?"

"Stay focused Justin," I chuckle at his response, "And then when the failed kiss happened between us, I was just so removed from seeing myself with you that I felt every other guy was such a let down. I'd grown to love Eryn because I thought she always had my best interest at heart. But you may be onto something when you say she may have been double dealing. She's kept me focused on the business, which I thought was a good thing. But I feel like maybe she was just keeping me on a path that she wanted. The one that Barbanon ends up getting me in the end." I envision the pile of bones in the corner in his lair.

"Uh, second time you mentioned this name, who is Barbanon? I mean, other than the man who abducted you."

"Well, according to Eric, he's one of the first of mankind; well the devil according to the bible. He said he needed to be sure I was the one."

"The one for what?"

"That's the thing, I have no idea." I barely remember the exact words of the encounter because I was so terrified.

"So you think it's possible that Barbanon could have maneuvered your life, using Eryn to make you who he wanted?"

"Well, the thought crossed my mind. But if that were true, you would think he wouldn't need to know if I was the one or not."

"Right..."

"Well, either way I have to find out where this all leads Justin. I can't just walk away, scared or not. I will call you with all the intel that you need."

"There's a bag on the floor, underneath the front passenger seat in the car. Items you can use, like a pin for you to clip in your hair for me to track you and hear everything. I don't want to take the chance of you getting hurt because we *are* in constant contact. I will be able to hear everything as long as you have that pin. And I won't be far, so I'll have eyes on you at all times."

"You will be sitting down with me at some point and explain to me when you became 007, but until then… I'm glad you have my back." My smile can be heard in my voice.

"I always will, talk soon," he quickly hangs up the phone. I look at the screen and put it down. I pull up to the hotel and glance at the time on the dashboard. It's 5:30pm. I reach under the seat and do as the instructions say, placing the pin in my hair and hiding the rest in my weekend bag. Slipping the chip into my bra, I head straight to Eric's room. I had already checked out of my room so I can use that as my excuse for stopping by.

I knock twice and he cracks the door open. He has a toothbrush in his mouth and a towel wrapped around his waist. He looks at me cautiously, and in a muffled voice he says "Brie, come on in." I slip inside, immediately looking around to spot his phone. He closes the door behind me and walks up, "Everything okay?"

I flash him a reassuring smile, "I already checked out of my room. Figured I'd come up here and let you know that I'm ready to go when you are." He asks me to wait a moment as he quickly walks into the bathroom, spitting out the toothpaste. I notice his phone on the end table next to the sofa charging.

He wipes his face clean and walks back out to the bedroom, "I wasn't expecting you for another hour, give or take. You seemed really tired." As he stood there, I could hear the shower running. I'd seen him shirtless before but something about him being in a towel made me reminisce about the kiss last night.

I let out a nervous chuckle, "Sorry, I'm just a little anxious I guess." He smiles back at me shyly, placing his hand behind his head. "Anxious for the trip that is," I correct myself. *But I'd be just as happy standing here all night gazing at his impressive physique.*

"Well I shouldn't be long. I went for a run earlier and just want to freshen up before we leave. Have a seat wherever you'd like," he holds his arms open, gesturing for me to have a seat anywhere. I sit near his phone on the decorative sofa, eyeing it slightly. He walks into the bathroom and then quickly returns, grabbing his phone. *Damn.* I hear him hop into the shower and the door of it close. Fiddling with my thumbs again, I try to think of a reason I can go in there and take his phone.

After about three minutes I think, it's now or never. I stand up and head over to the bathroom door, knocking loudly. "Eric?" I yell.

"Yes," he responds, raising his voice so that I can hear him over the running water.

"May I come in, I just have to use the bathroom… its separate right?"

"Yes, it's to your left!" he yells back. As I push the door open, the room is completely clouded with steam. Eric is difficult to see within his frosted glass stall, which means he probably can't see me very well either. I take a quick glance around and see his phone on the pedestal near the shower. *Ugh.* I roll my eyes at the thought that I might be caught and lose his trust completely. I can tell that he is in the process of washing his hair. *Now is my chance.*

I quickly tip toe over and snatch his phone from the pedestal then cop a squat in the bathroom, closing the door behind me. I reach into my bra and crack open the back of his Galaxy Note, slipping the chip under the battery as instructed. I replace the backing and flip the phone back over, turning it on. "Come on, come on, come on," I mumble to myself. I can hear the shower turn off. *Shit. Shit. Shit.* The phone finishes booting up and I crack the door open. Eric is drying off within the shower stall but the bathroom is much steamier than it was now that he'd opened the door. *Thank goodness.* He's got the towel to his face as I slip over and place his phone back on the pedestal and creep out the door back to the bedroom.

Eric looks over at the pedestal and grabs his phone, drying his hair with the towel. He opens the door of the bathroom to see me still sitting on the sofa. "I didn't hear you leave the bathroom," he mentions, walking through the room in his towel once again, droplets of water still beaded on his skin.

Nervously I chuckle again, trying not to stare, "Sorry, I was really quick." *He's torturing me.*

"Be out in a moment," he replies, grabbing his clothes to take back with him to the bathroom. I exhale deeply as he closes the door once more, thankful that he didn't catch me. Thank God Eric doesn't have the ability to read minds. *For more reasons than one.* I patiently wait for him to get dressed so that we can go, anticipating our next stop.

Briellyn

Eric and I are well on our way to Texas. We've already been in the car for several hours. I must have drifted off while staring out of the window during the first thirty minutes after we left the hotel. I'm slowly waking up now. "Well hello there, sleepy head," Eric cheerfully peeks over at me, "We are about forty minutes out."

I sit up in my seat, "I was asleep for the entire ride?" I glance at the time and its only 2:00 AM. "Wait what? How fast were you going? It's only been 8 hours," I yawn, calculating the time in my head.

"Well you would know if you had been awake right?" he replies sarcastically, "Didn't sleep much earlier when I dropped you to your room, eh?" *There's no way he could know I snuck off.* I don't want to lie so I just shake my head no and look out the window.

"So are you going to be the one teaching me hand to hand combat?" I ask, changing the subject quickly.

"I wouldn't dream of fighting you…" Eric gazes at me, smiling. He has taken such care not to touch me since I'd mentioned the affect he had on me. I am beginning to long for it. "My buddy Kalil will be training you, he and his team will teach you everything you need to know," he assures me. *Kalil.* That name sounds entirely too familiar but I can't figure out where I'd heard it before at the moment.

"I don't have many clothes," I add.

"No worries," he looks over at me, "I've taken care of everything you'll need for the entire trip, down to your knickers."

"Oh," I reply simply. Immediately I feel guilty for bugging his phone. This man couldn't possibly be one of *them*.

"Oh and here ya go, meant to give it to you before we left," he hands me the watch bracelet Eryn had given to me. I take it out the box and stare at the engraving on the back. I don't believe Eryn is bad either, I think someone is trying to make her look like the culprit.

And Eric is good to me; he's always been a complete gentleman, gone out of his way for me, always listens, and comforts me when needed; I don't deserve his multitude of kindness. But his mysteriousness and my uncontrollable attraction to him frightens me. I don't feel like I'm in control of my own feelings when I'm around him and that makes me think that I need to watch him more closely.

We pull up to the hotel thirty minutes later. The Four Seasons, our home away from home for the next eight days. Kalil is waiting for us as we pull up. I knew I'd recognized his name, now I know why. "Hey I know that guy…" I say to Eric as I'm pointing at Kalil.

"Perfect, that's Kalil," he replies. The look on his face states he is happy to see him but I'm wondering why I knew his face. We pull up and he helps me out the passenger seat. The suit he is wearing says it all and it should. *I designed it for him.* Tailored to perfection to fit his muscular frame. I remember now.

* * * * * * *

A tall, tan, muscular gentleman, standing at about 6'5" is waiting in the lobby of my new building. Eryn and I were smack dab in the middle of our first expansion. Eryn excitedly came running into to my very bland office, "You absolutely must check out the hotness that just walked into our lobby." It was five years ago when we first decided to become an LLC in CT. Business was finally good enough to justify an office building.

I curiously approached the lobby, the only somewhat decorated room in the entire building, and saw the gentleman standing there waiting. He looked over at us, "Hi, I'm Kalil. I'm told that you are one of the best in town for a custom tailored suit. I'm hoping you can help me." He has one of the most perfect smiles I had ever seen. "Hi Kalil, it's nice to meet you. I'm Briellyn Donado and this is Eryn, not sure if you two have met yet…" I try to be as professional as possible.

He's so huge compared to me, I've never designed anything for a man this burly and tall, but I knew it'd make a great challenge. Eryn shook his hand after I did. "Come back to my office and we can sit and discuss your needs," I show him back to my plain Jane office and ask him to have a seat. Eryn was trying to chime in but he kept his distance from her. He politely asked to speak to me alone, stating that he was a shy guy. I, of course, obliged him and he took the time to tell me exactly what he needed. I then took his measurements.

But I remember how he couldn't stop staring at me. I smiled at him politely and asked, "What is it? You keep staring at me." He chuckles lightly and says, "Sorry, you remind me of someone I know. I'm caught a little off guard by it." I took his measurements and he begins asking me tons of personal questions about the business, childhood, and other random things. Oddly, I wasn't bothered by his inquiries; we became rather close over the next two weeks. And then he was gone. Never did see or hear from him again. *Until now.*

* * * * * * *

"I see the suit still fits rather well…" I playfully say as he grabs my hand to help me out of the car, "Hello again Kalil." *I didn't know whether to be pissed or flattered that Eric would go through such great lengths over such a long period of time to find me.* None the less, I am still fond of Kalil and give him a big hug.

"It's good to see you," he says as he wraps his arms around me, "You haven't changed a bit."

He releases me from the hug and I look at him intently, "So when you came to me for that suit, was it really for Eric? Was this all part of some elaborate plan?" I know it's blunt but I have to know.

He and Eric exchange glances and then he laughs, "Still have a hell of an imagination too. You and I have a lot to discuss."

Eric walks from around the other side of the car, "Well, since you two have met before we can skip all the pleasantries. Kalil, I'll be retiring to my room. It was a very long drive. So… you know where to find me. Please get Brie *caught up* and trained, I trust you will make sure she is well taken care of." Eric looks at me and cordially smiles, "I'll see you later." Eric stops by the front desk and makes his way to the elevators while Kalil and I remain outside.

"It's up to you, we can start a little early today or you can get some rest and I will come back," Kalil stands there speaking to me but I continue watching Eric as he disappears from sight, "Brie?"

I snap out of it and look at Kalil, "Now."

"I beg pardon?" he replies.

"We can get started right now; I'd like to know why you came to see me Kalil. Please don't lie to me. If you do, I'm on the first flight back to Connecticut," I cross my arms and glower at him. I'm desperate, longing for the whole story.

He looks saddened but replies, "Yes."

I tilt my head and inquire further, "Yes what?" I hold my breath, waiting for him to finish.

"Yes, I was working with Eric all those years ago," he replies flatly. He reaches into his jacket and pulls out a manila envelope, about 5x7, "In here, you will have almost all of the information you'll need to know about this mission. I realize you probably have a lot of questions but hopefully this will shed some light on a few things. This week will be quite a busy one for you as you'll be trained in methods of escape, hand to hand combat, defense techniques with both knives *and* a sword, intro to heavy artillery, honing your gifts using spiritual meditation, wilderness survival, and a crash course in stealth. Each evening I will answer *any* two questions you have truthfully. But you must adhere to the guidelines I set out for you. You must stick to this schedule and eat the way I tell you. You'll need your strength because this is going to be a very long week for you."

I nod my head in agreement. *Music to my ears.* Particularly the part about him answering any question I ask truthfully. *More than I can say for Eric.* Plus, I've known Kalil longer so I feel like I can ask him anything. Maybe this isn't so bad. I look at the envelope he handed me, "What do you mean by schedule? You mean like, you tell me when I can eat, sleep, and…"

"Something like that yes," he interrupts before I can continue to entertain myself. "Your training will start at 7AM and end at

6:30PM. You will be given your breakfast, lunch, and dinner. Nothing but the best foods to give you the energy you'll need without feeling fatigue from all the strain you're going to experience. Feel free to open the envelope and get to know who your trainers will be and more mission details. I'll walk you to your room and come back in about three hours. We'll start a little early today and end early."

I glance at the time, it's only 3AM. No wonder he looked at me funny when I said now. Once we reach my room, he hands me the key to the door. "Eric is just across the hall and my cell number is in the envelope, save it to your phone. I will be here each morning to pick you up for training 7AM sharp," he gives me a paternal glance. He's beginning to remind of my father. *On a good day.*

"I know, I know, you don't like to be kept waiting. I remember," I flash him a grateful smile as I open the door.

He chuckles at my remark and says, "Everything you need is already in here, all of your training apparel is in the closet. I'll see you in a few of hours." He walks off as I shut the door and turn on the light. *Major upgrade.* I've been given a decent sized suite equipped with a kitchenette, small dining room, living room, bedroom in the back with a huge gorgeous bathroom. Eric owed me one after that terribly long drive.

I take the pin that Justin provided out of my hair and speak directly into it, "If you can hear me Jus, I'm really hoping you're wrong about everything." I place the pin onto the coffee table and pull my hair down. Walking over to the dining area, I open the envelope and spread all of the contents out onto the table. Apparently Kalil had quite the team of experts to assist me in my training. I decide to read everything aloud to myself to help me remember it better:

'Daniel Rodgers (2nd in Command)'

'34 years old, 6'0", blue eyes, Caucasian, medium brown hair, lean muscular build, *easy on the eyes*, in charge of my escape and stealth training, former lieutenant commander in the US Navy, speaks three languages: English, German, and Russian, excellent marksman, has evaded capture five times, and carries a zero casualty rate.

'Jenna Fauxx'

'28 years old, 5'7", blue eyes, Caucasian, long blonde hair, great cheekbones and smile, in charge of my hand to hand combat training and a former martial arts and self-defense trainer'

'Camille LeVonn'

'30 years old, 5'9", brown eyes, looks Indian but is mixed with African American, long dark brown/black hair, in charge of my spiritual connection training to hone my abilities, former meditation therapist, can read the minds of humans and all land based mammals'

'Dominic Lopez'

'46 years old, *looks 36 years old*, 6'2", brown eyes, Hispanic, deep black hair, in charge of artillery training including small and large arms (Beretta, Glock, and a Ruger), Army brat, weapons connoisseur, former weapons trainer for Navy Seals and Army's Delta'

'Brendan Munich'

'47 years old, 6'3", green eyes, Caucasian, blonde hair, in charge of survival and SERE training, former Staff Sergeant in the Marine Corps'

'Eight days of training will include seven full days of training and one day of trial and review.

Schedule begins:

- PICKUP 7AM, breakfast on site;

- From 7:30AM – 10:00AM, escape and stealth training with Rodgers

- From 10:15AM – 11:45AM, spiritual training with Cam

- From 12:00PM – 1:00PM, LUNCH

- From 1:15PM – 2:45PM, hand to hand combat training with Fauxx

- From 3:00PM – 4:00PM, artillery training with Lopez

- From 4:15PM – 5:15PM, survival training with Kalil and Brendan

- From 5:30PM – 6:00PM, Drop off and DINNER

- 8:30PM, SLEEP

"Geeze, Kalil is a major control freak! Two and a half hours doing escape and stealth training? Am I learning to literally vanish? This can't be the schedule everyday…" I look further down on the dossier and continue to read it aloud to myself, "Schedule may vary by fifteen minutes either before or after the above scheduled times. NO EXCEPTIONS for all seven days of training… ah man!" I roll my eyes at the thought of how tired I am going to be but I'm actually looking forward to it. It'll keep my mind off of everything that's been happening and I'll be so occupied that this week will just fly by. At least here I know I'm

100% safe. There are certainly perks to living by an exact schedule.

I sift through the remaining papers: menu of what I'll be eating for each meal, a list of approved foods when not on the 'clock', after training do's and don'ts, what to watch out for health wise, and what items to wear each day. *Seriously?*

Today, for day one, I'm supposed to wear a black long sleeve dri fit tee and long black pant with the NIKE free bionic training shoes. I immediately get up and walk over to the closet and open it. A huge array of attire is in there, from a wet suit to the clothes required for today's daily activities. I glance down at my watch again, 3:30AM. *Ugh.* The time is going by insanely slow. But I'm tired so the times slow progression could prove useful for another nap. Just thinking about what this training is going to be like makes me edgy.

I walk into the bedroom where there is a huge King size bed waiting for me, modernly decorated in soft hues of cream and hints of gold. I walk over to the bed and undress, leaving only my panties and tee shirt on. I carefully slip under the cool sheets. I ask the front desk for a wakeup call at 5:30AM. That'll give me enough time to shower and dress accordingly, prior to Kalil knocking on my door.

* * * * * *

I wake up and shower, quickly getting dressed in the black long sleeve and black pant. The Nike shoes are like heaven on my feet; I playfully bounce up and down, loosening them up. I hear a knock at the door and quickly run over to it. I excitedly fling the door open, "I'm ready to go!" My excitement fizzles when I realize a woman, instead, is standing in the doorway. She has amazing, shimmery, white flowing hair, glowing blue-green eyes, full lips, and water-kissed skin. She is dressed in a blue, flowing long gown that literally looks like water. I am hypnotized by her appearance.

"Heed my words child, you are not safe. Everything you see isn't as it seems." Her voice is slightly eerie yet soothing.

Still hypnotized, I continue to stare at her. "Who are you?"

"Be wary of the face. Listen to your heart. Otherwise your fate will already be sealed, only to repeat itself once again." She sounds like she's speaking through water.

"*My fate*. Who are you?" I ask again, hearing footsteps behind me. I turn around to see the fiery red strands of a beautiful, exotic looking woman, with skin that appears to flicker between a light olive complexion and one that is teal. She had a Kris blade in her hand that she carefully stabs me in my lower right abdomen with. Applying pressure to my wound, I look back to see the other woman is gone and only the redhead remains.

"*Why.*" I manage as I fall to my knees, my muscles shutting down as I feel a burning sensation running through my veins. She snickers then kneels down and grabs my chin with her right hand, "Because you fooled me once." She pushes me down to the ground, flashing me a cynical smile.

* * * * * *

Panting heavily, I wake as I fall to the ground from rolling off my bed. My heart is racing and sweat trickled down my body. The room phone is ringing for my morning wakeup call. *Another nightmare.* The feeling of the stab still apparent. This one felt different from the others though. I stand up and walk to the bathroom, my abdomen in slight pain. I remove the two other items of clothing, hoping that a shower will help me focus and get my mind off of the women's faces.

I quickly shower and begin my morning ritual. Apparently, Kalil knew exactly what bathroom essentials I use regularly and stocked the place before I got here. *Very convenient.* As I go to put some of the oil on my still-tender stomach, I notice bluish veins were beginning to travel up my side and down onto my right leg. I can now see the teeth marks quite clearly on the inside of my thigh. I can't help but begin to freak out for a moment.

What the hell is this. I quickly finish putting oil on, attempting to ignore the newly emerged markings. I slip on the shirt I'm required to wear and the pants with the shoes. I hear a knock at the door then glance at my watch. 6:00AM on the dot. I quickly walk over to the door and glance through peephole, cautious after such a rough few hours of sleep. It's Kalil, standing there in a full black getup. I swiftly open the door and grab his wrist, pulling him into my room and shut the door.

"Whoa there killer, what is all that about?" he stares into my face. He can see the fear and worry, "What is it? What's the matter? Are you alright?" I want to panic and cry but I hold it back. I stare into his eyes and my face says it all. "What?" his tone deepens, traced with worry. I look down away from him and turn to the left, bringing up my shirt and showing him my right side with all the markings. "What the hell?!" he replies, trying to maintain his cool. The panic in his voice told me what I need to know about the marks. *That I wasn't hallucinating it.* "Where did these come from?" he kneels down to get a closer look at the markings.

I begin to cry. Not out fear but out of frustration, "I don't know, I woke up and they were there. Another weird nightmare and there it is."

He promptly stands up and holds me, "Shh, shh, there there. It's going to be okay. Neither Eric, nor I, would ever let anything happen to you. I promise." I lean into him, shaking, trying to stop thinking about the marks, trying to stop thinking about the faces. The woman that stabbed me, I could see such an enormous amount of hatred in her eyes. Beauty and anger bunched up into one tight knit package.

"It's the curse, Barbanon cursed me. It's seeping into my veins and I'm going to die," I manage, my voice cracking a little with each word. "Calm down. That's not going to happen. Eric was going to have Dr. Strassmore meets us in a few days but I think we require his expertise sooner. I will have him here this afternoon, okay? And you'll be fine. The man is brilliant, he'll figure this out." Kalil sounds so sure of himself, holding me close and laying his head on top of mine. I suddenly realize just how much I wish Eric was here. Odd that a complete stranger can leave me longing for his touch, someone that I've barely known for two days can make all of my worries go away completely. I'm sure Eric will be along shortly, given this change of events. *I'm looking forward to it.*

After sobbing for a couple more minutes, sifting through the thoughts and discarding them begins to calm me. Kalil looks down, "No matter what, we must continue on with today. You're not really going to let some silly curse get you down are you?" His smile is warm and friendly, I couldn't help but smile back. *Silly curse he says.* I shake my head no and lightly chuckle as I wipe the tears from my face. *But he's right.* I can't let Barbanon win. I can't show him, if he *is* watching, that I am torn down from this.

"Well what are we waiting for," I mumble, sniffling a bit more and pushing through to a smile.

"That's my girl," he wraps his arm around my shoulders, lovingly shaking me. *There's that reminder of my father again.*

Something about his personality, even from before, that just has this fatherly tone. He helps me to my feet and runs and grabs a wet washcloth to allow me to wipe my face. I clean off the tears and grab the hair pin that Justin gave me and we head out.

Once we get to his truck, a black on black 2016 Range Rover, I climb into the passenger seat and attempt to pin my hair up in a bun. As I clamp the decorative hair pin down in my mouth Kalil looks over at it and remarks, "Nice clip."

I smile at him and mumble, "Thanks," through my clenched teeth. *I was born ready for this, I can do anything, I am an unstoppable force.* As Kalil speeds off I can't help but ask if Eric is going to be there. Kalil shakes his head no, "He has other things to attend to today." Are the new markings on me not important enough to drop some of his *things* today? I catch myself, I can't be upset that he's a busy man. The more I learn about what's going on, the more I'm shocked that Eric could take the time out of his busy schedule to comfort me with my father's passing. *He has spoiled me.* And now, I crave his presence.

*   *   *   *   *   *

We pull up to a large warehouse type building. "What's here?" I point, looking around at the middle of nowhere he's driven me too. *One could hide a lot of chopped up dead bodies out here.* I swallow hard.

Kalil unbuckles his seatbelt and lets out a sigh of relief, "Training." If this giant warehouse is where training is, Eric has certainly been busy. The building must have been every bit of 6,000 square feet, maybe more. We hop out of the truck and I can see one other vehicle parked out front. "I asked Rodgers to be here early to give you a tour and start your training. Get to know him. Trust in him and his abilities. He has been training for this for two years. He's a good guy, I think you'll get along just fine," he urges as we walk towards the big steel door. He puts his finger up, "But not too close. Ladies fall for his charm quite a bit. So… *fair warning*." I snicker at his remark, noting in my mind that no man has ever been able to literally *charm the pants off of me*. Well, I suppose had the other night gone any further, *Eric would have been the first*. I raise my eyebrows at the thought as Kalil opens the giant door.

It reveals a boxing ring, tons of workout equipment, a cage with different types of guns and ammo, a room in the back that looks like a lounge, a climbing wall, and so much more that I can't see. "Whoa, this is…" I'm in awe when a dashing gentleman with striking blue eyes approaches us.

"Amazing, fantastic, extraordinary? Hard not to be in awe of this place, it is a state of the art training facility designed by yours truly." He places his hands on to his chest as Kalil snorts. "Oh, and Kal here helped." He puts his hand on Kalil's shoulder and flashes his perfect teeth. "Everyone on this mission had to come through here and endure our wrath. Looks like you're next doll face. I'm Danny. Kal here calls me Rodgers, but you can call me whatever comes to mind." My right brow raises and a smile creeps across my lips as he reaches for my hand.

I oblige his request and reach over to greet him. He bends over and kisses the back of my hand. I couldn't help but giggle, "Pleasure."

He rubs my hand and stands up straight after kissing it, "I would say I've been called that a time or two." We both laugh aloud as Kalil gives him a stern look. "Sorry boss," he shrugs, "You mentioned she was having a rough morning. Just trying to lighten the mood." He reassures him.

Kalil gestures towards the lounge, "Well, show her around, get her some breakfast and get started. The sooner the better. Dr.

~ 223 ~

Strassmore will be here later so I'm sure this extra hour will help." He walks off sifting through his phone.

Danny looks at me and grabs my hand, placing it under his right arm as he walks me towards to the right area of this giant warehouse. "Hungry?" he asks me.

"Famished actually," I reply.

"Great, I'll whip you up breakfast and then give you the tour, I was just chopping it up for myself so you can join me," he smiles. He walks me into the lounge area, which is impressively high end; sectional leather sofas for lounging, a ten seat steel dining table, a bar area, full stainless steel kitchen with an island, and a huge refrigerator. There's a cutting board on the island and a frying pan on the stove. He walks me to a chair at the table then makes his way back to the kitchen. He throws a hand towel over his left shoulder and continues cutting up ingredients, the smell of bacon wafting through the air.

"So what am I having? The smell of bacon is always a good sign." I peeking over to see what he's cutting up. He walks the cutting board over to the stove and puts half of the ingredients into the pan, "Oh you'll see Ms. Donado." I can hear the sound of the ingredients sizzling in the butter. He then cracks five eggs into the pan. *It smells delightful.* He finishes up and brings two plates over to the table, then walks back to the refrigerator.

On my plate there is a slice of whole wheat toast with butter on it, scrambled eggs with spinach, tomatoes, onions, and mushrooms, and two hearty slices of bacon. "Wow, this looks amazing," I exclaim. He grabs the orange juice from the fridge and two glasses. He places the glasses on the table and fills them up, one by one.

"Trust me, it is," he confidently replies, "Get used to it. For the week at least, Kalil has charged me with the luxury of your time and health every morning. I have to get your mind right for your long days." I shoot him a grateful look as he sits down. He reminds me so much of Justin. "Well, bon appetite, my dear," he urges me to take my first bite.

Everything about it is phenomenal. Everything tastes so fresh! There is no time to speak because the food is so good. Not whispering a word, just savoring each and every delectable bite. After I finish my last bit of food, I mutter to Danny, "You're quite the cook. Everything tasted so fresh!"

"Well, you're fortunate to have someone in your corner who cares so much for your well-being. All week he's having fresh ingredients delivered daily, just so you can have the best of the best," he flashes a smile at me before grabbing my plate. I'm not sure exactly who he is referring to but I could certainly guess.

I get up from the table and follow him over to grab the pot from the stove, "Surely you're joking, I'm certain this is every day for you." I hand him the pot to clean.

"No, no," he assures me, "We usually get a shipment once a week, maybe once every two weeks. But he said nothing but fresh ingredients every morning for Briellyn. I need her focused." *Oh yes, definitely talking about Eric.* I blush as I stare off into the distance briefly, feeling guilty again about bugging his phone. He turns around and looks at me, drying his hands off on the towel that he had thrown over his shoulder.

"Something on your mind?" he inquires, taking notice of the change in my demeanor. I shake my head no, blinking my eyes repeatedly hoping he doesn't see the truth about me.

"Well then, let's get started," he says cheerfully as we approach the door. He leans forward allowing me to walk through first, "After you my lady."

Briellyn

Training: Day One

Danny brings me to a small room. The room is entirely black;
walls, ceiling and floor. An eight foot long table with different
kinds of restraints on display is pushed against the wall to my
left. Directly in front of me are two different chairs, chains to
the walls, and a twin bed. *A dominatrix's dream.* I walk over to the
table to see the numerous types of restraints he has sitting there.
"Familiar with handcuffs at all?" he asks. I shake my head no.

"Ever been arrested?" I again shake my head no.

"BDSM?" his voice heightens. I laugh and shake my head no
while saying it aloud.

"Ah, you're no fun," he chuckles, "I'm just kidding about that
last one. Well last two actually. Even though cuffs are a dying
method for restraints, we are going to cover everything. Have to
make sure you can get out of a tight space, if necessary."

I smile coyly at him, thinking about Barbanon. "What about
magical restraints?" I inquire, pointing at the table.

Danny moves closer to me, "We'll cover that too. I heard you
were attacked two days ago."

I nod my head, "Something like that yes."

"*By the devil himself.* You must be quite special for him to go after
you personally and take a bite," he taps me gently on the middle

of my thigh, catching me off guard. I frown. "Does that aggravate you?" he probes as he approaches me.

"It makes me a little uncomfortable, yes," I try to be polite even though it angered me. I begin backing up towards the wall but he follows me closely, carefully invading my personal space.

"I'm going to be pushing you to your limits Briellyn. Pushing you to your breaking point. Past your breaking point. You have to know how to react when under pressure, when you feel most uncomfortable..." his voice softens and he places his hand on the wall and moves so close to my face that all I could see were his eyes. I'm unsure how to react or how to respond. I just want to turn away. So I do exactly that.

"I want you to know, that I'll be chaining you up in a few different ways," he continues his unreadable stare. I swallow hard. He then immediately walks away. His tone returns to normal, "I'll show you how to get out of those awkward and uncomfortable situations, including the one you were just in. You seem like a nice enough woman Brie, but on this expedition, nice isn't going to keep you alive. It's no secret that we *will* encounter terrorists, mercenaries, pirates, and possibly many other bad people. I need you to be able to hold your own," he gestures at me then turns his back towards me, facing the table. *I like his style.* I was uncomfortable, but I can see what the end game is. After what Barbanon did, I want to be able to maintain control if ever in that position again.

"I will die before I allow you to be captured on my watch. In the off chance that it happens and I'm not dead, you have to be prepared to defend yourself for as long as possible until we are able to find you. By the end of this week, I want you to be able to kick *my* ass," he states playfully then smiles.

Doubtful. I chuckle, and sarcastically reply, "Yeah, like I'll be able to do that." I've never been in a fight in my life.

"I have faith in you Ms. Donado," he declares, smiling while holding the hand cuffs, "Now have a seat."

I sit down in the seat with the steel legs and no arm rests, as he requested. He walks up to me and kneels down to look me in the face, "You see, when a woman is captured, her captor tends to try to expose her vulnerabilities. The more vulnerable she is, the more she's likely to break. The men we will be dealing with that oppose us may try to kidnap you to gain information and they will try their best to break you. This is why I'm teaching you how to escape from the most seemingly impossible situations; I don't want you to ever go through that. So, let's start with the basics shall we."

He stands up and walks behind me, grabbing both of my wrists and handcuffing me with my arms behind my back. He walks back in front of me. "Now, already you're exposed. Maybe not as open as you may think, but exposed nonetheless. Tell me, what's the easiest way to get out of handcuffs that are locked behind your back?" He stands there, pointer finger to his chin and arms crossed, just staring at me. *He's amused by this.*

I immediately think of every movie or show that I've watched in the past decade where a character had to escape from a similar situation. I have no clue how to pick handcuffs off, and even if I did, I don't have a pin or something readily available to use. "I have to figure out a way to bring my cuffs in front of me?" The moment I say it, I question my answer.

Danny begins to pace in front of me, "That's one way to go about it, but how would you do that?"

I look down and attempt to stand up, opening my legs so that I straddle the chair. He didn't cuff me to the chair, only cuffed my hands. After I stand up, I throw my left leg over the front of the chair so that my legs are together on the otherside. I then bring my hands up from behind the back of the chair . I look at Danny for approval. He nods, beckoning me to continue.

I feel so silly, standing in front of him like this. He is exactly right about the vulnerability, that's what I feel right now and he hasn't really said anything. I'm sure it could be much worse. I walk over to the wall and use it to sit down on my butt, sliding awkwardly down until I'm seated. I slide my cuffed hands under my butt and then pass my thighs. I roll my body so that my back is on the ground and slip my cuffed hands over my feet so that they are now in front of me.

Danny nods his head in approval, "Not bad Brie. Do you know how to pick a lock?" I shake my head no. He pulls the cuffs up near my face and shows me a small black pin. "You will have at least three of these on your person at all times. They are carefully constructed in the pants you are currently wearing; you have several pairs of these pants in your closet at the hotel for the mission. When picking a lock, you have two notches that you need to release. Behold." He places the pin into the hole of the cuffs and in three seconds flat, he unlocks one of the cuffs. He's certainly done this a time or two. He hands me the pin, "Now you try."

I take the pin from his hand and attempt to unlock the cuff from my left hand. "Locks can vary, sometimes you have to apply the rigid side clockwise, others are counterclockwise. So if one direction doesn't work, go the opposite way. I don't expect you to master this on your first try, but as long as you know the basics and can get it, I can live with that." He watches me intently.

I'm struggling. Fully concentrating on releasing these cuffs and by the grace of God, I get it open. Danny raises his eyebrows in disbelief, he raises his hand and rubs his face, "Well... seems you may be a natural." I give him a big smile, proud of my accomplishment. *Honestly more proud that I've shocked him.* I'm sure that doesn't happen often. "Well my dear, let's move onto something a little more difficult then," he replies, rubbing his hands together.

"One thing that you have to remember is that anything can happen and anything can be used to your advantage. You have a knife that will be in the heel of your boots," he shows me a military grade, black leather boot. Holding it closely so that I can see, he pushes on the front heel of the sole. The middle back of the heel releases gently, allowing enough space to pull whatever it is out. It's a short, wide one inch long blade. He points to it as he talks to me, "Be very careful with this Brie, the blade is extremely sharp. It will come in handy though if necessary. Use it to get yourself out of plastic or cloth restraints, or as a weapon in close combat. You only have one, and it's located in your *left* shoe. You can cut zip ties, Velcro, rope, and whatever else, *just don't cut yourself.*" He looks up at me smirking with his big blue eyes. I simply nod my head thinking and hoping I never have to use it.

"Let's move onto stealth since you'll need that skill more than escape as long as I'm around." He's so confident. I flash him a grateful smile.

"We will be heading to Canada, then the islands, and then London... but it looks like Malta has been added to our list of destinations as of yesterday. I'm told there may be ancient booby traps and such that we may encounter. None the less, grace and stealth will be your best friend. Although I can't see it help much underwater, I..." he begins.

I interrupt, "Underwater?" *Yeah… about that.*

"Yeah, Eric didn't tell you? Part of the mission will be at his giant underwater laboratory one thousand feet below sea level just off the islands. Routinely we will be going out in scuba gear looking for whatever necessary to find one of the gems."

"Um, excuse me a second would you?" I raise one finger up to him and quickly walk out of the room. I look around, trying to spot Kalil. I can hear his voice from a distance, so I hastily make my way towards it. I look around the bin and see a giant pool. Kalil is standing next to it on the phone, "Hold on one second." He places the phone receiver against his chest.

I look at him angrily, "It's off and I'm going home."

"Whoa, whoa, whoa, what happened?" he asks walking closer to me, trying to spot Danny.

"Eric never told me about going underwater in scuba gear, let alone a thousand feet!" the thought makes me want to vomit. I can feel my heart racing. All I can see is that water woman's face from my dream last night, and the drowning dream I had the first night I met Eric. *She mentioned a sign.* Maybe she's trying to tell me I'm going to drown. The thought is horrifying.

"We weren't sure if we needed *you* to do any diving, you still might not need to. You'll be perfectly secure in the underwater facility…" he bends down slightly to look me in the face, attempting to make me feel better.

"No. No way Kalil," I begin pacing, shaking my head.

He walks over and holds me still, "Look, I told you before Eric and I would never let anything happen to you. Danny and the rest of the team are trained to protect you from all things, land and sea. The facility is top of the line. Glass twelve inches thick and reinforced steel, you'll be transported down there by submarine. You'll be watching the divers from monitors. Most likely, you'll never even get wet at any point."

"Confined spaces *scare* me. And being underwater only makes it that much worse…" I stutter through my words. I can't begin to fathom what this is going to be like for me. I begin to hyperventilate as my hands shake uncontrollably.

"Listen to me Brie, *you can do this*. When we get there, you'll see. It's not even close to as bad as you think. You remember when you were unsure if you could design and produce a suit for a guy of my build, but you took the challenge anyway?" I nod my head yes, knowing that this situation is completely different. *Apples and oranges, Kal.*

He continues, "Well you are the kind of woman who is willing to take on a challenge; *nothing* stands in your way. Just breathe." He breathes in deeply through his nose and forms his lips to breathe out, coaching me along. "Come on, breathe with me," he encourages. I copy him, in through my nose and out through my mouth. The panic is beginning to subside and the shakes cease completely. I can hear Danny walk up behind me. Kalil looks over at him encouraging him to approach us.

"Now Danny here, also happens to be an excellent swimmer. Him, Eric, and I will always be by your side, at least one of us at all times. He's trained in all of the emergency procedures. The facility has been up and running for about three months now and we have had no mishaps. We'll be fine. *You'll be fine,*" he holds his hands on my shoulders and gives me a confident smile, "Now get your ass back to training. Fear is the essence of glory. I have word that Dr. Strassmore will be here close to noon."

I laugh, knowing just how horrified I truly am. *But I love a good challenge.* And the memory of my parents presses me along. I gather my thoughts and my courage, and glance at Danny, "Okay, I'm ready to get back to it." I flash him a fake smile. He guides me back to a different room. It's a massive room with many different levels and platforms. He pushes a button on the side of the wall and the entire room turns into a very real wintery forest on the side of a cliff. "Welcome to stealth and endurance training. Let's begin your first lesson," Danny's expression dripping with enthusiasm.

* * * * * * *

It's already 9AM. I couldn't believe how quickly the past two hours went by. Stealth and endurance training both kicked my ass and motivated me more. That 4D training that I just did made me feel like a B.A.M.F. but my muscles are screaming for mercy from the countless crouching, crawling, and balancing. Danny turns the simulation in the room off and tosses me a bottle of water, "Way to keep your head in the game, I'm proud to be your wingman." I flash him a tired smile, soaking in each second I have to rest. "The next hour and a half is going to physically be a breeze compared to the past two… mentally, *not so much*," he teases as he walks out of the room. I don't bother to follow because I recall my schedule having a fifteen minute interlude between each set of training. I guzzle the bottle of water and wipe my face, still slightly panting and still trying to regain my full composure.

A gorgeous Indian woman walks into the room, this must be Camille. She waves and then quickly approaches, holding her hand out, "Hello there Briellyn, I'm Camille. I'll be your spirit guide over the next week and over the course of this mission." I shake her hand and give her a big smile. I'm still unsure why a spirit guide is necessary *everyday* besides honing in on my ability to see these symbols, but an hour and a half seems wasteful. She appears sweet enough though and I'm truly looking forward to relaxation and meditation. She continues to pester me, "I know you're tired, but would you be willing to follow me so that we can get set up?"

No. "Sure." I reluctantly reply. I am completely unmotivated to move and she's making me do it a full ten minutes before my 'break' is up. *Ugh.*

We make our way through the entire warehouse, which is now buzzing with numerous personnel. *All of them training.* She takes me to the far side of the building into a room with a very thick entry door. Upon entering, the room resembles a sun room. Every wall is thick glass and the room feels remarkably warm. The floor is covered in rich hues of turquoise, green, and gold pillows. The one wall painted to resemble the sky. I immediately feel calm and relaxed. "Please, feel free to lie anywhere you please," she encourages me as she closes the door, encasing us in complete silence. The entire room looks plenty comfy so I carefully walk to the center of it, it just seems right. I lie down face up.

"So what do you need me to do?" I ask as she wanders behind me and slips an additional pillow under my head.

"Just relax as much as you can," she smiles. She places the forefinger and middle finger of both hands to my temples. *What exactly are you doing lady?* I just decide to speak up, "Just curious Camille, what is it that you are trying to do? Help me relax? We're meditating right?"

Her eyes are closed at first, but she looks down at me and chuckles, "Did you read my full bio in the package that Kalil gave you?" I try to remember exactly what I read about her, she can read minds. *Oh shit, she can read minds!* Immediately my thoughts shift to thinking about bugging Eric's phone. *And the sneaking away to see Justin.* I'm so screwed.

She begins laughing out loud, "Don't worry, you're secret is safe with me." I stare at her in confusion. She can hear my active thoughts like that? "Yes I can," she replies again to my unspoken question. I smile at her response, but I'm still concerned. "Okay Brie, I really need you to try to clear your thoughts so that I can begin your initiation. You and I are the same, a special genome allows me to read the thoughts of others, just as yours allows you to see Empyrean markings," she smirks. I adjust my shoulders as best I can while lying down and exhale audibly. I'm nervous but she seems pretty harmless.

I begin to clear my thoughts, trying to think of nothing is harder to do than I thought. I realize I'm getting lost at the thought of nothing. With my eyes closed with the warmth of the sun on my skin, and the scent of rose and chamomile fills the air, this is the most relaxing thing I think I've ever experienced.

Out of nowhere, a door stands in front of me. Someone is knocking on it; everything is so blurry, like the sun is so bright that my eyes are finding it hard to adjust. I open the door to see Camille standing there. "Very good, Briellyn." She wanders in smiling as she proceeds to hold my hand. "Where are we? How did we get here?" I ask, confused.

"We are in that fabulous mind of yours. You were a little trickier than the others I'll admit. Let's find out why shall we?" she looks at me, excitedly, but this is getting weird to me. *What others?* As we begin walking, the room doesn't change, everything remains white with no distinction of ground or ceiling. The door gets further away but we are literally walking to nothing.

"Um, where are we going?" I ask, getting impatient.

"You'll see," she smiles at me. I look back once more, no longer able to see the door. But when I return forward, we are standing in a clearing. There's a small river with weeping trees, plush green grass, and the sound of birds singing in the wind.

I marvel in amusement as I look around, "What is this place?"

"It's your minds own private oasis, everyone has one. The one place that your mind considers itself at peace," she explains as she walks over to the river, still holding my hand.

This suddenly feels familiar. Where do I know this place? "I've been here before," I mumble to Camille as she kneels down next to the rushing water.

"Indeed," she calls to me as she runs her right hand in the water. I kneel down next to her and she urges me to look into the water. When I look down into the water, I can see every memory I've ever had rushing through its clear flow. They look like movie snippets.

She tells me that I can catch them in my palm and relive them again if I want to. "Just use your mind to slow the river down so that you can catch the memory," she urges. I curl up the side of my mouth and concentrate. The river slows immediately. She chuckles, "Well I'll certainly give it to you, your mind is naturally very keen. Faster than the others."

Again with the others. I'll be asking Kalil about that later. For some reason, I choose the memory the night my mother died. Camille can see everything within the memory once I've grabbed it. It turns the entire room to where I was at the time yet, I'm still kneeling with the water in hand. I can see my mother lying on the ground as the termagant hovers over her.

I can't bear to watch so I turn my hand over, pouring the water back into the river. We are immediately surrounded by the oasis once more. "Okay," she begins, "You see over there, let's go."

She points across the river at a tree. *It's not just any tree.* It's the same tree from my dreams that the fawn was standing beneath when it fell over and began bleeding.

"Well how do we get over there?" I ask her. I'm not willing to wade through the water. *Not again.*

"It's your choice, imagine something that will help us get across, and manifest it," she explains. *Ah, the power of thought.* I immediately create a footbridge.

As we walk across it, I'm able to see every memory much more clearly. "Come on Brie, the memories are not why we are here," she commands. We reach the other side and under the tree are two small trinkets that resemble small Fabergé eggs, one is open.

"*And these are?*" I ask, worried about her response.

She kneels down next to them, "These are what make you so special. You see, Justin, and your mother, helped you to open the first one by believing in your ability to see things that others couldn't. This one is an additional genome that you have but haven't unleashed yet." She lifts up the unopened trinket and smiles at me.

I couldn't help but notice three additional trinkets nestled in the tree. "So are those unlockable traits or genomes too?" I point to them.

She stands up and turns to see them, staring in astonishment. "Yes," she tries to contain her excitement, "It's time for us to go back."

Within a flash, we are back in the room. My eyes fly open and I'm lying on my back again. I sit up, "Well that was abrupt." I frown.

She looks at me and asks, "Can you give me a moment? I will be right back." I nod as she gets up and quickly leaves the room.

I sit there patiently waiting for her to return. *I hope she doesn't sell me out about bugging Eric's phone.* Or maybe I'm some kind of freak show for having those additional genomes, if that's what they were. Either way, her abrupt departure had me uneasy all over again. I decide to sneak over to the door and have a peek to see if I can spot her.

She's ratting me out. She runs straight over to Kalil, barely able to contain her excitement, "Kalil, you will not believe what I just found out about our new girl."

He looks at her anxiously, "Well… don't keep me waiting." He smiles.

She returns her focus on him, "Oh sorry, she has *five* additional genomes! Plus I'm not sure why yet, but just like Eric, I can't hear her thoughts right away. When I touch her, I can access only active thoughts or ones that are going through her mind at that very moment. But memories and traits, she has to *give* me permission. And she's already very good at navigating and manifesting in her own mind, that doesn't come easy through someone's first meditation. She's amazing."

"Tell me more about this genome thing, you said she has five additional? How many does a normal person have?" Kalil inquires.

"Well, on average the normal human being has no additional genomes whatsoever. People like Danny or me, have one additional genome. And I expected her to have two additional genomes, like the others, one for sight, and we've never gotten to what the other one is for. Because, well you know… *but she has five!* It makes me wonder what looking into Eric's mind would be like, maybe we can..."

"Uh, I'm going to stop you right there. Eric is out of the question; however, he will want to know these findings immediately. I'm going to give him a shout and you finish up your session with her." He's trying to be nice about it, unable to share the same excitement because he's less familiar with genetic anomalies.

"I've been with you two for almost a hundred years and I'm still not able to do a trial run on him," she raises her hand, gesturing her words and anger in her voice. "It's fine, *I guess*. Just know, there's something more to this one. And if I have nothing to compare it to... well, it makes it that much more difficult to unlock. I'll let you know when I get her mind sorted and keep you updated on her progress."

Kalil nods his head in response and she begins to walk back to the room where I am. I couldn't hear anything but given Kalil's expressions, I doubt she told him anything about the stupid bug. I swallow hard. *At least I hope not.* I make my way back to the center of the room and have a seat where I had been lying previously. She opens the door and closes it behind her.

"Well my dear, with four of those traits still closed, we have some work ahead of us now don't we?!" she exclaims, rubbing her hands together and sitting legs crossed in front of me. She asks me to close my eyes and find one of the trinkets that are still closed. I close my eyes and try to clear my thoughts again. "Find the oasis without my guidance," she whispers.

My breathing slows as I turn my head left to right and side to side to loosen up once again, relaxing my shoulders and clearing my thoughts. It was easier the first time when I was lying down. Five minutes pass and I can't seem to find my way. "Focus Brie, you can do this. Your mind is a *powerful* thing. Think of something that brings you peace, focus on it, and then let it guide you." Her words are soothing, helping to guide my ever running mind.

I think of my mother's beautiful face. The smile she would always give me when we were baking or when I would say something funny that she liked. "Hi honey," the faint voice of my mother says to me. "*Mom?*" I feel like a child all over again. I can barely hear her voice but can see her; clear as day, standing under a tree, *my genome tree*, hair blowing in the wind. Her arms are open, beckoning me to come to her. She is on the other side of the river; where my trinkets are, where the dying fawn was. *Why can't I show up on that side from the beginning?* I begin to imagine the bridge again, not bothering with slowing the flow of the river or paying attention to the memories within it. At this point, I just want to be in my mother's arms. I begin crossing the bridge when a dark void appears in the middle of it. I can't get past it, no matter how wide I imagine the bridge to be. The void begins to take shape into the flowing black creature demon that took my mother's life. It makes me angry. I'm an adult now, not a scared little girl. And I know what it is.

I walk up to it, my skin boils from its black flamed, flowing robes. "You will never hurt anyone I love again," I command. The demon looks closer into my eyes, attempting to intimidate me. Reaching its long skinny finger towards my left shoulder and digging its nail into my skin. *It hurts.* Why does it hurt? My shoulder is burning! I begin to scream because I realize I'm no longer in control, the pain consumes me.

I wake to Camille shaking me. Panicked, I sit up quickly. "It's not real, it's not real," I keep mumbling to myself. Camille is holding a piece of cloth up to my nose.

"You're right it's not real. But your nose began bleeding, *a lot*, so I had to interrupt," she looks very concerned.

"Thanks," I hold my hand up to grab the towel myself, glancing at all the blood before bringing it back to my nose. The towel is soaked in it. Every time I see something related to Barbanon in my subconscious, my nose bleeds. It's got to be the curse doing this to me.

"I think that may be enough mind searching for one day, just tell me what you saw," she states, sitting upright in front of me with a wide bowl of white rose petals floating in water. I don't want the mind searching to end. I want to go back to my mother. Everything about it was so real and I was so close to just touching her.

I frown, "I was trying to get to my mother. She was on the other side of that river. But something was in my way. Somehow this thing caused me *pain* and I lost control of the situation." I look down, away from her in shame.

She grabs my free hand and cups it in hers, "I'm going to tell you something Brie that you may not be aware of just yet. You have additional genomes that I have *never* seen in *anyone* else before. If you are seeing demonic guards or things that you are afraid of as you are trying to reach your goal, it simply means you are on the right path of unlocking those additional qualities for you to be able to use them. Your mind fears the unknown and manifests things to guard them. It's not unusual."

"Well what could these other qualities be?" I inquire, still holding the towel to my face. *Great. I'm a freak of nature.*

"I'm not sure. You never know what they are unless they are unlocked and you're able to use them," she smiles.

"What if they aren't good?" I'm worried. *What if they're demonic?*

"Then we will, pardon the pun, cross that bridge when we get there." She looks so sure of herself. She pushes the rose filled water closer to me. "Dip the tips of your hands into this bowl. It'll balance your body's frequency to make the bleeding stop."

I do as she says, skepticism riddled all over my face. Somehow though, it works like a charm. The blood immediately stops trickling from my nose. I couldn't help but blurt out, "That's amazing. *What's in this water?*"

"I will show you in case you have another nose bleed and I'm not around," she replies. She takes the bloody towel and places it on a shelf outside of the room's door.

When she walks back to me, she pulls something out of her sweater pocket. It looks like a necklace. She holds it in front of me, allowing the charm to dangle at eye level then proceeds to sit down again. "This is an Amaranythian amulet. It protects you from evil spirits," she gestures for me to take it.

Evil spirits. "Right…" I couldn't help but feel sketchy about this, regardless of everything I've seen. And somehow I don't think this is strong enough to keep Barbanon or his demon bitches away from me. I'm beginning to grow tired of my sleepless nights. I look at the amulet, attached to this long golden chain. The charm is shaped like a seven pointed star with a purple center that's about two inches wide. The etchings within the charm look like purple veins.

I grab it and place the chain around my neck, the charms final resting place at the top of my cleavage. "I think you'll be pleasantly surprised," Camille interjects, "A great way to find your oasis is in the flame of a candle or by submersing yourself completely in water, which is unique to you I've noticed. I figured that by the rushing waters in your mind. The amulet should help you remain in control in the presence of those standing in your way. And protect you otherwise from demons." She stands up and walks towards the only wall in the room. There is a small cabinet door within the wall that has four small shelves filled with tiny vials. She grabs one vial from each shelf and walks back over to me.

She sits back down, "Everything is balanced in ones, twos, threes, and fours. There are four seasons, four 'corners' of the world, four hemispheres, four gems," she raises her eyebrows and looks deeply into my eyes, "well you get where I'm going with this. Even your amulet has four corners on its bottom piece. Everything is more balanced with four than it ever has been with two or three. When there is merely one of something, it may be more powerful than a balance of four. But that's rare. The other three points, these sitting on top of your amulet, are for the big three."

I raise my right eyebrow, "The big three?"

She smiles, "The three Empyreans who helped to mold our world. Senon, Palidon, and Barbanon. Here take these oils." She places the four two ounce vials into the palm of my hand. I hold my hand open staring at them. One is a slight hue of pink, another had a tinge of yellow, and the last two are mostly clear. She points to each one in my hand respectively, "This one is rose oil, this is helichrysum oil, this is peppermint oil, and this is juniperberry oil. Each one carries with it positive frequencies to help balance your body in a positive direction when evil or illness are lurking about. Add just *one* drop of each to a small eight ounce bowl of fresh water, preferably warm, and dip your finger tips and hands or your feet in it." I'm actually excited to receive all of this information; I didn't even know our bodies carried a frequency.

I mentally notate everything she's telling me. I saw first-hand what this did for me and I will be using these oils after every bad dream. I doubt the amulet will keep the nightmares away so these oils should suffice. Before this, I was never a believer in the power of herbs; I always thought it to be a bit farfetched. But, she has just given me an entirely *fresh* perspective on the matter. *Literally.*

"Since your mind seems overworked right now, we are going to call it a day. You have an additional thirty minutes before lunch to yourself," she stands up and puts her hands on her hips. For someone who is only thirty, she certainly seems to be spiritually in tuned as if she is sixty or possibly older.

"Do you mind if I just pick your brain a little bit?" I pry, staring at her curiously. She nervously chuckles in response,

"Well I guess so. What's up?"

I come to my feet and look her in the eyes, "You kept referring me to the others. Who are these *others?*"

"Oh dear. You have to ask Kalil about it tonight when you speak to him. I don't have the clearance to speculate on that," she replies, slightly shaking her head.

"*Speculate?* You said 'others' definitively, like you knew them first-hand. That doesn't sound at all like *speculation*," I glower at her, wondering why *everyone* is giving me a run around about this mission.

"Listen Briellyn, I'm sure you have a ton of questions. Each part of this training process is going to reveal more and more about this mission that isn't obvious in the packet. Each and every one of us, *including you*, has a definitive role to fill. In reference to importance, you are the key to everything surrounding this mission. By the end of the week, I'm sure you will be overwhelmed with the information you've received, so don't be too anxious. Sometimes ignorance is bliss."

Ugh, point taken. Her last statement hits me like a rock. My curiosity bought me to this very spot. As she walks out of the room, I get lost in my thoughts. *My need for adventure in my life is what made me sign those damn papers.* Hell, I wished for it. I'm getting all the adventure I could ever ask for alright; *curses, demons, the devil*... what's next? *Ultra-super powers, maybe I'll be able to fly!* Such a sarcastic thought, I chuckle to myself. *Come on Brie, this isn't Harry Potter.* Although right now, I feel like I'm living a Constantine/ Harry Potter clash and I'm the prophet detective with a twin being thrust onto platform nine and three quarters.

Take it in strides is the phrase that is repeating itself over and over again in my head. I close my eyes for a moment and take a deep breath. There's a sign on my wall in my bedroom that my mother used to tell me as a little girl, *'There is no challenge too great, nor task too small, that putting your mind to, and your best foot forward, can't accomplish.'* At this point, I sure hope that she's exactly right.

The door opens, startling me out of my thoughts. Kalil is standing there, "Hey Brie, come on out, I have someone I want you to meet." I quickly walk over to him and out the door.

There is a very tall, athletically slender gentleman with deep, dark hair and green eyes. He has a very friendly face and *striking* deep voice, "Hello there Briellyn. I'm Dr. Richard Strassmore, I'm told you could use my help."

Kalil chimes in, "This is the doctor I was telling you about, the master linguist who is going to interpret that curse and hopefully figure out what those marks from this morning are about. I'll leave you to it." Kalil immediately walks off, I could tell he has more pressing matters to attend to. I hold out my hand to make his acquaintance. Like the others, he kisses the back of my hand and slightly bows. He's such a large man though that it didn't seem like much of one.

"Nice to meet you," I giggle, gazing into his eyes. They seem mysterious and hypnotizing, yet soft and inviting.

"There is an exam room on the other side of the building just off the lounge, I can look you over in there," he smiles down at me as he leads the way.

The warehouse must have had over twenty people training in it at this point and that didn't include the assistants of the staff. It's no wonder Kalil had to have me on a schedule. I follow the good doctor all the way across the warehouse and then into the lounge. There's a door that I hadn't noticed the first time that read, *Medical Staff Only*, in large print. Dr. Strassmore pulls out a special key card and unlocks the door. It's a full lab. An X-ray machine, microscopes, exam table, and so much more that I am unfamiliar with.

"Have a seat on the table there," he points as he walks over to the counter to grab a set of rubber gloves. He then unlocks a cabinet and pulls out a set of glasses, similar to the ones Eric had in the hotel back in Florida. "Well, it'll be easier making these observations if you weren't in so many clothes," he slides over sitting on a wheeled stool.

"Well 'scuse me doc, I expect dinner or something before I take my clothes off for you," I smirk while making my saucy reply. The nervousness I'm feeling put me in a playful mood.

He reaches under the table and pulls out a robe and hands it to me, "Then by all means, I'll have to take you to lunch."

"Ha ha, very nice," I smile nodding my head in amusement and grab the robe from him. He promptly turns around on his stool. I hop off of the table and quickly get undressed, down to my bra and underwear, and throw the robe on over top. The robe is nice and plush, light blue, and short sleeved. I sit back onto the table.

"I'm ready," I state nervously. It's the first time I've been this naked in front of a man in quite a while. *Eric doesn't count.*

"Alrighty then, I'm going to examine individual parts so that you remain covered. I want you to feel as comfortable as possible, so just let me know if you need me to stop. This may take a few minutes," he puts on the glasses and pulls down the left sleeve. He ties the robe tight so the rest of my body remains covered. Quietly he looks through each symbol, writing it down on his little notepad that he has sitting next to me on the table. He studies the words around my neck and down my arm for a few minutes, then hikes up the robe a little to look at my right thigh. After he's done examining the words, he sits back down on his stool, puts the pen to his mouth and mumbles to himself for a few more minutes. My heart starts racing in anticipation. *When am I going to die?* I look towards the floor and start moving my feet back and forth timidly. I hope he just tells me straight, I'm not interested in a sugar coating.

"Well, this is certainly a shock," he sounds relieved.

"What? What is it?" I plead, overzealous to hear the interpretation.

"It's not a curse at all, actually," he slides over and shows me the pad. Pointing at each cluster of symbols, he reads, "May this allow protection from death, in order to live and allow life to begin. A safe haven surrounds this being, in the highest form of balance, to prevent physical harm. Let it be done."

What. My lip curls up and my nose creases. *Barbanon is trying to protect me.* From what? I'm not buying it. What could be more dangerous than him? "That's *really* what is says doc, are you 100% sure?" I probe further, unconvinced.

"That's what it says," he replies, putting his notebook down, "Now that we can put that to rest, let's take a look at these other markings." He pulls the entire right side of the robe open to expose my lower abdomen and upper thigh. "Poison, in your veins," he touches around, "I can fix that."

"Don't you have to know what kind of poison it is to provide me with an antidote or solution?" I ask, afraid he may give me the wrong medication.

"Every poison has their tell-tale signs. I happen to have seen this exact one before. I am curious, though, how you could be exposed to it," he stands up and strolls over to the cabinets. Opening them up one by one, he begins putting together a remedy.

"Can I be honest with you Dr. Strassmore?" I ask in confidence.

"Of course, between you and me. Doctor patient privilege… and please, call me Rick."

"Well… *Rick.* Last night I had this insane nightmare. I've been having these visionary terrors a lot lately. This woman approached my hotel room door and she was underwater, but not, and as she's trying to tell me something, this fiery redhead comes out of nowhere and stabs me with this wavy looking blade!" I'm gesturing with my hands.

He comes over, needle in hand, "That *does* sound rather outlandish. But please, do continue."

"She whispers something to me, um, something about, fooling her once… *OW!*" I screech as he jabs the needle into my stomach.

"Sorry love," he pushes half of the dose into my side, "Tried to catch you in the middle of a thought. One more." He injects the last bit into my upper thigh. "You'll notice the amount of darkness shrinking more and more each day until it's gone. Usually about three to five days at the most. You'll be good as new." He smiles and goes to put the needle into the biohazard bin.

"Ugh, whatever is in that, it… really… hurts!" I grumble as I step onto the floor.

"Get dressed, I know this fantastic place for lunch that Kalil would certainly approve of. Super healthy and insanely tasty. We'll sneak out the back," he insists, playfully gesturing at the back door, "He'll never even know we've gone!"

I nod my head excitedly, "If Kalil would approve, why not tell him?"

"Because you are supposed to be training all day, not out gallivanting with the likes of me," he grins.

He turns around so I can get dressed. *I could use some fresh air.* I reply, "Sure! Why the hell not?" My body may be in pain but finding out that I'm not cursed just lifted my spirits to a whole other level. I like this Doctor Rick, he makes me feel mostly normal and I need normal for a change.

Briellyn

We find ourselves in a quaint, healthy, stir fry place. The good doctor is sitting across from me as I gobble the last bite of my delicious food. "Oh my goodness, that was amazing Rick. This is exactly what I needed," I lean back in my seat patting my belly. The restaurant seems to be quite popular, filled with people from front to back near lunch time on a Tuesday. Only the freshest ingredients are used in all of the dishes, premium meats, and it's sautéed to perfection. It makes sense why it's so busy at lunch. Healthy alternatives to burgers and cheesesteaks are hard to find.

Rick chuckles, "I'm so happy I could help. I'm sure Kalil will have my ass if he finds out but at least I know he'd approve of the food."

I sip my water and adjust my right shoulder a bit, "Well, if he finds out, I'll just tell him it was my idea. That should take any heat off of you. Besides he owes me one after taking me out of my comfort zone to a mission I know so little about." I take another sip of water and watch as Rick methodically finishes the last of his food. "*So… Rick…*" I sit up and lean forward towards him, "Refresh my memory if you could. What are all of your expertise for this mission… besides Ancient Empyrean? And how did *you* get roped into this?"

"Funny you should ask," he begins, "I am a general MD, so I deal with all the medical work required to assure everyone training has a clean bill of health. I also have a generous background in mythology and ancient history, of course, and quite skilled at chemistry in many facets. Um, I speak over twenty languages, which can get tricky." He chuckles as he continues, "And I've traveled to over fifty countries in my short 37 years of life."

I point to him nodding my head and smiling, "That was going to be my next question. Your age. You read my mind."

"I got roped into this, *as you say it*, because I was following a lead about Empyrean history. It's very hard to come by you know," he leans forward, lowering his tone.

I whisper to him, "Before this I never even knew about Empyria, I guess in the sense that it's supposed to be anyway. This all sounds so crazy, like some bed time story we tell to children to get them to go to sleep. My favorite was always Atlantis," I snicker, motioning the words with my hands, keeping my voice down.

"Why my dear, Atlantis... *was a very real city*, no fairy tale there." He leans back in his seat, drinking from his glass.

"Oh no, you don't really believe that do you? I mean, I love mythology and fantasies but it's just that, a child's bedtime story." I cross my arms and lean back, cocking my foot up on the chair next to me.

"Where do you think I got my lead about Empyrean?" He smiles wide.

"You're kidding?" the smirk on my face screams both disbelief and hope.

"No, no. I don't joke very much. I'm actually quite bad at it really. Children's bedtime stories, *as you call it*, are merely elaborated stories that have been passed down so much that they seem to become more imagination than history." He sighs as he looks at his watch, "But I must be getting you back, Kalil will think I've chopped you up into little pieces with as long he *thinks* we've been in the lab." We both get up as he pulls out his wallet to leave the money for the check. I didn't have any cash or credit cards on me so I guess I'll have to just take this treat in stride today. The warehouse is just a quick eight minute drive back and we'll be walking through the doors just in time for my next lesson.

* * * * * * *

"Hey Jenna, has Brie checked in with you yet?" Kalil walks up to the ring where Jenna and a colleague are training.

She shakes her head no, "Nope, not yet boss." She continues her training scuffle as Kalil walks away.

He immediately walks into the lounge, "Hey Danny, you see Brie come out of here yet?" He points to the door, aggravation, curiosity, and nervousness all in his voice.

Danny is sitting on the couch with a bowl of something he whipped up, looking through a National Geographic magazine. "Nah, no activity out here. Least, not that I noticed," he replies nonchalantly.

Kalil begins ravaging his own pockets to find his master key. After about a minute he finds it and approaches the door. He swipes his key, anxious to get the door open. Two red lights flash, denying him access. He swipes it again and the light flashes green, unlocking the door. He throws the door open and sees me standing next to the table as Rick hands me a small Ziploc bag. "These will keep you balanced on the inside, just in case you have another nose bleed," he looks over at Kalil as I grab the bag from his hands.

I walk towards the door, "What's the matter, you look…
worried?" I try not to sound too sarcastic while walking past him.
"Danny, can you tell me where to find Jenna?" I ask as I walk
away before Kalil has a chance to say anything.

"Well geeze Doc, what took so long? I was…" Kalil says and
then stops himself, "*Nevermind.* Is she going to be alright? Were
you able to determine the markings?"

"Well Kalil, it would seem our little secret weapon had managed
to encounter Ahkmedah poison, a type of mixture of poisons
between snake venom and a poisonous herb. We're lucky we
caught it. I didn't alarm her, I thankfully had the remedy here.
She'll be good as new in just a few days."

"And the curse?" he raises his brow and puts his hands into his
pockets.

"Well," he begins as they walk further into the lab, "It's not
really a curse *at all*. He actually cast a protection spell on her,
believe it or not."

Kalil frowns in confusion, "Why on earth would he do that and
bite her?"

"Well, I can't speculate on that but it would seem the devil is
playing a very interesting hand. And we are blind to his poker
face."

"Interesting choice of words doc. Hang around, a few guys need
their exit physicals. You'll be flying back with us. By this time
next week, the mission will be in full swing, finally," Kalil smiles
and nods as he leaves the room. Dr. Strassmore assures him he
will get whatever he needs done with a simple nod in return.

* * * * * * *

Danny walks me over to meet Jenna. She dismisses her trainee then strolls over to the far side of the ring where we are, sitting down at the edge. "Jenna, meet Brie. Brie, this is Jenna," Danny points at her then at me. "You too get acquainted. Let me know if you need anything," he nods his head and flashes a flirty smile at her then walks off.

She smirks briefly until he's out of sight then glares down at me. "Come on up." She sounds so smug. Jenna is a gorgeous blonde, about my height, and has an elite female fighter's body. She's not someone that anyone would want to cross. *Certainly not me.* I climb into the ring, as she requested, and walk closely behind her as she walks to the other side.

"Let's get one thing clear, okay princess?" she turns around, clearly irate with me.

"*Um,*" I begin. *Really?*

She interrupts, "You're here for one thing, and one thing only. Hand to hand combat. I don't show mercy… *on anyone.* So that includes some innocent, little school girl type like you. You can either keep up or get the hell outta my ring, ya got it?"

Well who pissed in your corn flakes sunshine? I nod, blinking my eyes repeatedly to keep my cool.

"I don't understand what's so special about you anyway. All of this money and training for *you*? *Ha!* I have to admit, you're not at *all* what I was expecting. What a waste," she flashes me a sinister sneer while leaning against the ropes.

I can feel my blood beginning to boil from anger. *This is my show, she can't steal my thunder.* This *is* all for me. And I will be sure she remembers that. She takes another sip of her water and hands it to her assistant, a pretty Latina. "Let's get this over with," she grumbles. "Come on, just follow my lead and do exactly as I tell you to," she signals me to the center of the ring. I follow her, ready for her instruction and still annoyed by her attitude. This is going to be the longest hour and a half *of my life*.

"Close combat is life or death most of the time, so pay attention. We're going from zero to sixty on a lesson plan that should be done over the course of three weeks. So let's hope you can keep up, *'kay pumpkin*," she puts her hands up near her face, gesturing for me to do the same. "Keep your hands balled into a fist when you're not using them, it'll get you into the habit of eventually punching with your fist. For now, open hand slaps will do fine," she commands, "Always be aware of your surroundings, look at your opponents face and their body language. It'll never fail you." She rocks side to side on her tiptoes, keeping a fluid hop in her step. I attempt to mirror her, show her that I have what it takes. I've done kickboxing so hopefully that experience helps here. She yells over to her assistant, "This one thinks she's cute." Her assistant begins taunting me by blowing kisses and cat call whistles. "Go ahead, take a swing," she teases, "Let's see what you're made of."

I want to hit her in that smartass mouth. Who does she think she is talking to me any kind of way? She gestures at me again but I continue to keep my form. She lowers her hands to her sides and looks at me undaunted, "That's what I thought. *You're too chicken shit to swing.*" Immediately I growl as I swing my right arm at her. She dodges the blow quickly and pushes me in the back forcing me to the ropes. I bounce off and hastily try to regain my form.

"Uhh ohh, maybe I was wrong. *You're a step above chicken shit.*" She taunts again. I want to swing again but she hasn't taught me anything yet. Continuously putting myself out there will only make me look like an idiot. But this *chick* is testing my patience. I attempt to swing again with my left hand this time, but she grabs it, lightly punches me in my stomach then twists me around until she has me in a chokehold. I can barely breathe, struggling to get her arm loose. It all happened incredibly fast. "One thing you'll learn princess? The best offense," she throws me to the ground, "Is a good defense." I'm coughing and trying to catch my breath as I turn red from frustration. "You've got some spirit though. I'll give you that," she motions at me as I'm hunched over. She glances over at her assistant, "Layla, give her some water and place her towel in the corner here. I think our little princess is ready."

Layla hops into the ring and hands me a bottle of water, "Don't worry sunshine, she's like this with everyone." She smiles at me then walks away, sliding back outside of the ring. *If looks could kill, Jenna would be passing her last breath right now.* I don't know who she thinks she is, *or who she thinks I am*; but I know for certain, anger will only get me knocked to the ground... *again.* I struggle to come to my feet, my stomach a little tender.

"You have me wrong Jenna. I don't think I'm better than anyone here. I honestly just want to help," I struggle to say as I continue to pant. She chuckles at my attempt to break the ice. I continue my plea anyway, "No, seriously. I'm brought here; long after all of you have been training. My level of importance merely equates to the level of dedication shown by you and the others. I feel so... *humbled* by what's going on; my *life* is completely in *your* hands. I'm at your mercy." Jenna's expression changes. *And so she has a conscience.* My words are working. My inner self beams, grateful for that strategic communications class in grad school.

"Alright, alright," she gestures for me to come closer. "Hands back up, get in your stance," she motions, "Offense or defense, always remain ready. I'm going to show you the best defensive moves that will help get your attacker on the ground and you in control. You want to always remain in control." I nod my head, listening carefully to her instruction. This is going to be fun, especially if I get to pay her back for this wonderful introduction by the end of the week.

The hour came and went as she finishes kicking repetitions with me. "Okay princess, that's enough for today," she lowers her gloves. I'm trickled with sweat and my heart is racing after some excellent cardio training. Good thing I enjoyed working out before this. I take a seat at the edge of the ring as Jenna walks off.

Layla is standing there and approaches me, "Good job today, way to hang in there."

I gulp some water, "Thanks."

"Hey, um, where'd you learn to negotiate like that?" she asks, staring at me the way a child would when their anxious to know something.

"Grad school." I take another swig. "And daily business requires it. Can't let people push you around. You have to learn to talk them down," I reply, chuckling at the question, "Thinking quick on your feet is necessary when dealing with people in my line of work. Why?"

"I've just never seen Jenna look so stumped... *or guilty.*"

Ha, ha. Good. She shrugs her shoulders, smiling, "I'll see you later." She immediately marches off. I take another gulp of water and recap the bottle.

I gently dab my face and the back of my neck with my towel as Danny walks up, "*So,* how ya feelin'?" He looks like he's trying not to laugh.

"Today has been quite the challenge, but I'm game for more…
What?" I inquire, noticing the silly look on his face.

He laughs a bit, "Jenna is so pissed."

"Why?" I thought her and I squashed our differences. *Well
mostly.*

"She didn't like the way you made her feel. On the inside. She's
a raging bitch though so don't even worry about it," he replies,
laughing it off.

"Why would you want someone like that on the team then?" I
ask.

"Well, she is *the best* at hand to hand combat that I have ever
seen. She's trained up every single one of the people on this
mission and deep down, she's really kind. She just has this tough
outer shell. She only knows you from the mission statement and
of course the gossip," he smiles at me, like I'm supposed to
know what gossip he's referring to.

I raise my eyebrows, insisting, "Well, are you going to fill me in
on this *gossip* about me? I thought we were buds. I've been here
for less than a day and I already have rumors about me…"

"Yes, *little miss popular*," he teases.

"Yeah, lucky me," I uncap the water and take another swig,
rolling my eyes.

"Well, between you and me, she has the biggest crush on…"

"Kalil!" I interrupt, looking over at her as she is talking to Kalil.
Her body language is completely different with him.

"Ha ha, no. Actually it's Eric," he glimpses over at her and Kalil. "You see; Kalil has run interference on her attempts to get close to Eric from day one. But that is Kalil's job. Eric has many women who are quite fond of him apparently but no one ever sees him with anyone… *well romantically anyway.* I just have Kalil point them my direction," Danny laughs and then points to Layla, standing off to the side staring at Jenna. "*And Layla* is in love with Jenna but Jenna is *mostly* straight. They hooked up once when Jenna had a few drinks and poor Layla has been bowed ever since."

"Oh geeze, poor thing," I glance over at Layla.

"But that's not all," Danny turns and looks at me, "Jenna overheard from a little birdie that you and Eric were off on a few dates and it just… infuriated her."

"Well who told her that?" I ask, irritated that anyone knew of our personal encounters. I'm sure if he knew about the kiss, he would have mentioned it.

"She overheard a conversation that him and Kalil were having. So *are* you and Eric…?"

"No," I interject, lowering my brow. I clear my throat, "No. It's strictly professional with us."

"That's a *liiieee* if I ever heard one," he smiles at me rocking his shoulders, "He's a tough man to get close to but I would say he fancies you big time. Him and I have shared many a conversation but he's a very private man. If he's interested in you, you should be extremely flattered."

Pfft. I should be flattered? Try the other way around. "Why, because he's rich?" I reply mockingly, rolling my eyes again.

"No," Danny shifts his body again, "Because he's genuinely a good guy. I would take a bullet for him. Can't say that about many people, except for Kalil and *maybe you*. He's done a lot for me and my family."

"Family? You're married?" my eyebrows raise in surprise.

He laughs aloud, "*Me?* No! Never! But I have a sister and then there's my mom. I'm a mama's boy big time. And an overprotective brother. Eric bought my mother a house, pays all of her bills, pays for my sister's education, pays for all of my travel to see them *and* still gives me a generous salary. He talks to me about them, speaks to them to find out how they're doing. *He's all about family*."

Now there's a surprise. I lean in closer to him, "Do you know any of Eric's family?" I'm hoping he can maybe tell me about Eric's parents at least.

He folds his arms and leans his back towards me, "He doesn't have any here. Kalil is as close to family as it gets for him."

"Aw, poor guy," I pause, "How is it *you* know so much?" I probe, wondering his source.

He leans up off the edge of the ring and helps me down, "Because I hear and see everything." He smiles confidently, "Nah just kidding. Kalil, Eric, and I have all hung out quite a bit hashing out the details and locations of this mission over the last two years. So we're all friends. I've seen the other side of Eric that no one sees. It would catch you off guard. But the man is a genius. I can't wait to see all this planning finally come to fruition."

So Eric is a lone wolf. *Only adds to his mystery.* No family to speak of but enjoys helping the families of others only adds to his charm. Jenna's hostility towards me is now amusing because I know where it stems from. I'm sure Eric would not approve of her tactics today if he found out, so I'll keep it to myself as long as she doesn't push me too much. I'm hoping I'll be able to put her on her ass by this time at the end of the week.

"We need to get you to your next lesson my dear," Danny holds out his hand for me to grab, "You'll like Dominic, Nick 'the quick' for short. He's Layla's brother. Very, very laid back and an *excellent* instructor. You ever fire a weapon?"

"No, I've never felt the need…" I reply hesitantly.

"Oh, well he'll tell you quick, everyone should not only know how to handle and fire a weapon, but a woman should have a small one for self-defense at all times when possible. He's going to teach you how to use a gun and later this week, he and I will teach you hand to hand combat with knives and swords."

"Why on earth would I need to learn to use a sword?" I laugh, thinking of the old musketeer movies.

"If everything goes well, you may expect to be in a very different time." We walk past the pool through a door that leads to an outdoor range, "Hey there Nick, come on over to meet Brielle!" Nick is slightly off in the distance collecting his kill. He shot a rattlesnake and is dragging its carcass back our direction.

"Damn snakes," he drops its limp body into the trash can and wipes his hands on his pants. He's got a rugged, Latino Richard Gere thing going but with jet black hair and a rich tan complexion. "Nice to finally meet you Brie," he reaches his hand out to shake mine. He gives me a nice firm hand shake.

"She's had zero weapons training or handling so you'll be starting from scratch with her. I have another group to train so when you two are done for the day, Kalil will be taking over," Danny walks back into the building.

Nick grabs a gun from his side and places it in my hand, "Get used to the weight of it. That's what power feels like, *respect it*. You can take another man's life very easily with that, but only use it if you need to when we are not training. *Ya got it?*"

I nod my head. It's heavy and the metal is warm, something about it makes me extremely uncomfortable. I inhale deeply then exhale. Nick just looks at me like he's waiting for me to say something. I flash him a fake grin. He turns the gun over and continues his lesson, "Here's your safety. When holstered, be sure that it's on. In most cases, you absolutely will *not* need to use your weapon. So make sure your safety is always on. Even if it is, you never point your weapon at anything you don't intend to shoot and try not to drop it. Okay?"

"Okay," I reply, getting more and more nervous with each second I hold it. Nick walks over to a metal case filled with equipment, he signals me to come over. "I'm going to put you in a gun holster that wraps around your leg and waist," he pulls out a black holster. I nod my head giving him the okay to put the holster on. He quickly assembles it and shows me how to properly holster the hand gun. He then hands me hearing protection. "Okay, prior to putting on the muffs, I'm going to show you proper stance, how to holster, how to aim, and how to hold the weapon when you're ready to fire. Then we'll pop off a few rounds. Then I want you reload and fire some more. Here's the button you press when you are ready to reload, it'll eject the magazine so you'll be able to put a new one in; which can be found in this part of your holster," he points to two small pouches on my left side.

After showing me how to stand and handle the weapon properly, he has me put on the muffs and hands me some protective glasses. He stands very close so that I can still hear his directions. "Just remember, this round is just to get you comfortable with firing a weapon. Don't worry about your aim. Ya ready?" he yells, holding up his hand for the signal. I nod my head yes, turn the safety off, and look through my sights to take aim. He throws his fist down and I immediately begin firing. With each shot I feel like I'm having trouble preventing my forefinger from slipping on the trigger. I continue to fire anyway. Even though I'm not hitting anything, I feel a rush of emotions come over me. The only thing I could possibly be learning this for is to potentially hurt or fatally wound another person. The thought is overwhelmingly disturbing.

I'm empty already. I push the button to release the magazine, open the pouch, grab the new magazine, pop it in the gun and continue firing. I can feel tears streaming down my face as the thought of shooting someone begins to consume me, but I keep firing until the chamber is empty.

"Nice work," Nick says as I lower the weapon, put the safety on, then holster it. "What's the matter?" he inquires after he looks at my face.

I wipe the tears and sniffle, "Nothing, I'm good." He puts one hand on my shoulder and asks, "It's a lot of power in your hands isn't it?" I stop and stare at him. *Too much power.* I nod my head repeatedly as a few more tears make their way out. I wipe them away, "Yeah, it's a bit overwhelming actually. More than I thought it'd be." I sniffle and pull myself together, "Sorry." I frown at him. *I'm not a wuss, I promise.*

"It's totally fine Brie. You're not the first first-timer I've had cry on me and you sure as shit won't be the last," he flashes me a forgiving smile so I give him a hearty chuckle. "Let's go see how you did shall we?" he pats me on the back as we make our way over to my paper dummy. He puts his hands on his hips and counts the holes. "Not terrible for your first time but uh, we've definitely got some work to do," he chuckles.

The following firing rounds went much better. I got the anxiety out with the first round and have felt fine ever since. I actually find shooting kind of fun and soothing. I even turned out to be a pretty decent shot. "Way to recover today. I thought after that first round you might be a lousy shot," Nick jokes. I curl the side of my lip and give him a crooked smirk. He continues, "You have a holster in your room, figure out what the comfortable fit is for you and make sure you bring it each day."

I nod my head, puckering my lips, "I can certainly do that. This was the most fun I've had all day."

He laughs and puts his hand on my back, guiding me back inside the warehouse, "Well good, I'm glad. The more fun it is for you, the easier it will be to get your aim down." Danny was right, *Nick is a great instructor.* Very laid back and easygoing.

We find Kalil right by the pool with another older gentleman. "Hey, hey, hey, if it isn't the lady of the hour! How'd shooting go?" he walks up to us and shakes Nick's hand.

"It was… surprisingly fun," I reply excitedly.

"She is actually shaping up to be an excellent shot. Takes instruction well. I'm looking forward to seeing how she does with the tank later in the week," Nick chimes in.

I quickly turn my head to look at Nick, grinning, "Tank? Is that really necessary?"

He laughs, "I'm just kidding. She's all yours Kalil. I'll see you tomorrow missy." He waves goodbye and heads to the lounge.

The older gentleman that Kalil was sitting with stands up and walks over immediately after Nick leaves. "Brielle, meet Brendan. He and I are going to go over some survival training with you and then you will be done for the day," Kalil seems anxious for the day to be over. Brendan and I shake hands and exchange greetings.

He's an older gentleman as well, salt and pepper hair with a goatee. We begin walking into the main part of the warehouse as Kalil explains to me what I need to learn, "If, God forbid, you ever get separated from the rest of the group and need to survive on your own, we need to make sure you know how to use external resources to feed and keep yourself hydrated. In most cases, you'll never be alone anyway. But in the off chance you are, you'll be prepared. The islands are going to be mostly an underwater excursion and in Malta we will be in the temples. Eric managed to convince the people who run the tourism on the island to shut it down for ten days for us to be able to do our research. Malta is small enough that you couldn't possibly get separated from any of us so this training is mainly for Canada's crusade. Once the gems are all found, we'll be heading to London to put everything we've found together."

"Can I forfeit one of my questions later to ask a question now?" I look at Kalil curiously.

"Are you sure you don't want to see if the question happens to get answered in this lesson?" he replies.

"I know it won't be," I state confidently. He nods, silently telling me to continue. "Were there others before me?" I look at him nervously, biting my bottom lip. He stares at me blankly then looks at Brendan, "Brendan, uh, would you excuse us for a moment?"

Brendan replies, "Sure," then quickly walks off.

"If you're wondering why I ask, Camille happened to mention it when she found out about my additional genomes; I know she told you."

"Look Brielle, I told you I would be honest with you and I plan on keeping my word. But I'm not sure you really want to hear the answer to that question," Kalil looks reluctant to continue.

Reluctance speaks to my curiosity buddy, spill the beans. "No I do, I can handle it. Whatever it is," I smile, reassuring him. I'm honestly unsure if I *really* want to know.

"There are many women, similar to you; that came before you. Some even looked eerily similar in appearance," he frowns.

"What's so bad about that?" I inquire, wondering about his previous statement.

"They're all dead or missing," he sadly replies, putting his head down.

"*What?* How?" I look at him with dread.

"We'll discuss that over dinner. I need you focused for now, okay? I promise I'll explain. And that question won't even count against your quota for the evening..." he gives me a forced smile. I won't be able to stop thinking about what he said. But Kalil is good at redirection. I nod, upset with the lack of fulfillment from the answer. I follow him into the lounge where Brendan is waiting for us. There's fresh fish in the sink.

"Have you ever skinned a fish?" Kalil asks as if we didn't just have an awkward conversation.

"No," I stubbornly reply, crossing my arms and leaning against the counter. Kalil tilts his head and raises an eyebrow when he realizes this is me pouting.

"Brendan here, is going to show you how to skin one," Kalil points to him and stands in the background. I walk closer to the sink as he picks up a fish and begins skinning and cutting it up, guiding me with his words as he goes along.

"Remember, a fish is one of the few animals in the wild that you can eat raw. Just try to avoid the bones," Brendan smiles at me. I grin back, showing that I'm actively listening. After he finishes his lesson, he has me try. I follow along with his instruction. "Very good," he praises.

Kalil puts a huge backpack on the counter, "You and everyone else will have a climbing pack in Canada." He begins pulling items out and describing what they are to me. "Just FYI, this pack weighs about twenty-five pounds; you have one in your closet. Danny will have you training with one on your back for a few drills for the rest of week, get you used to the weight of it," He glares at me, concerned.

They go over a few other details with gadgets that are in the bag and we finish a couple minutes early. Kalil cooks up the fish for dinner and sits me down to eat. "Eat up and I promise we will talk once we get out of here. This conversation that we are about to have is for your ears only," Kalil insists. I perk up and speedily eat my food, anxious to hear about these other women. He laughs at me but follows my lead, not wasting anytime on chewing.

We are leaving the facility and getting in the car when I notice Jenna and Brendan briefly kissing as they say goodbye. "Are they… um, together?" I nosily ask Kalil as he closes his door.

"Yup," he replies, backing out of his parking spot and heading down the road, "I kind of frown on the age difference but that's out of my hands. If it keeps her out of Eric's face, I'm okay with it."

"*Ha!* I heard about that today. I find it comical. So what are *you* to Eric, his bodyguard?" I tease.

"Very funny. Once you get to truly know Eric, you'll realize if there is anyone on the planet who can handle himself, it's him."

Interesting statement. Eric seems so laid back, not really the feisty type. "So about these other women," I ask, quickly changing the subject.

"Right," he pauses, "So… There was a prophecy foretold a very long time ago, that a woman of your description would be the only one to have the capability to find all four seraphic gems. She would have the special gift of Empyrean sight, *unknown to even most Empyreans,* allowing her to conquer the challenges involved with unearthing the stones. Her sight allows her to see ancient signs left only by God himself of the locations of the seraphic gems. Her success is foretold to be necessary in order for the human race to continue. There's more but that's really the meat of it."

I put my left thumb in my mouth and begin biting at my nail, "That's some heavy shit." I scrunch my brow and adjust in my seat. I think it over, "Well if that's the case, how come the others died or were unsuccessful? How many others have there been?"

"Well," he clears his throat, "There have been twenty-one other women, you are the twenty-second." He continues looking forward at the road, unwilling to look at the expression on my face as I stare at him. Eyes wide, mouth gaping open, complete astonishment and disbelief.

"How is that possible?! You've had twenty-two different women come through that facility in the past two years? It doesn't make any sense!"

"No, Brielle," he begins, "There have been twenty-two women, including you, over the past two hundred and forty years. You're the only one to get training."

I stare out the window, shaking my head in disbelief, "But, how does it date back so far? How do you keep track of something like that?"

"Files, historical documents, research. Eric has many resources. The prophecy never gave an exact year to when the woman would be born or come of age, only a birth date. A month and a day, a description of her appearance and of course her unique ability. There was another woman here in Texas who could have potentially been in your shoes. She wasn't the one though; your abilities have proven more worthy than others. We've been tracking and narrowing down candidates for the past five years when we found you. The first time we met, I was vetting you and came to the conclusion you weren't one. You seemed too normal. Then when your name came up from Justin when Eric inquired about women seeing things, the chances were too high to ignore. So we came back to you as a potential candidate. Little did we know one of the gems had been in your possession the whole time; thanks to the gift your mother gave you. *You* are the one the prophecy is speaking of."

I want to puke. Little miss boring and unpopular all through high school goes onto to save the entire human race. *Lucky me.* "Is there a possibility that my mother knew what I am or uh, what I'm supposed to be? Did my mother know the gem was in the doll?" I ask, my mind running in a million different directions.

"I couldn't tell you Brie. Your mother passed away before any of our people could have spoken to her," he gives me a concerned look.

I sink into my seat, "What if I don't, ya know, what if I'm *not* the one? What if…"

"Stop trying to psyche yourself out. Just keep moving forward and do your best. The Big Man doesn't make mistakes my dear. Unfortunately, *we have.* But you are finally with us," he smiles at me and grabs my hand, trying to comfort me. I give him a concerned smile. In a way I feel relieved. I finally know what my role is for the mission. I grab the amulet and begin twiddling it in my fingers as I look out the window trying my best to clear my mind.

Briellyn

Kalil walks me to my room. I'm exhausted from the long day of training but I have two definitive questions that I know I want to cash in on before he leaves, so I invite him into my room. "How's Eric? I haven't seen him all day…" I nervously ask as I stare at my door knowing he's right across the hall. I've gotten so used to seeing him that it's weird with him not being around.

"He's good," Kalil nods his head, "I'm going to go over and debrief with him here shortly." He slips his hands in his pockets. I take a seat on the couch and lean forward, elbows to knees and fingers laced together staring at him still standing. "Well um, you've told me so much and I'm trying to narrow down my questions to the ones I've found to be the most important… and necessary," I continue, twiddling my thumbs and pressing my lips together. I release my finger interlock and start rubbing at my knees, "I, uhm, would like to know how you were able to narrow down locations of the other three gems if I'm the only one capable of finding them?" Kalil stares at me as if he's astonished by my question.

He nervously chuckles as he begins his answer, "Uh, well. That's a great question Brie. You will see the generator when we reach the base in Canada. Each of the gems that are still within the earths crust emit an energy source that's about five miles wide. The energy uses the earth to camouflage itself within its surroundings. We were able to track the energy using a combination of different seekers, which wasn't easy. The only gem we were unable to find or narrow a location for was the Aquari gem, and that was because it was no longer within the earths crust. We are actually unsure of which gem is where out of our locations but we know they are there. We also piggybacked off of the research of some great minds dating back centuries, using the technology to pinpoint more exact locations… In reality, it's really just speculation that we're all hoping is right."

I raise my eyebrows, "We are doing all of this on a hunch."

"Isn't everything just a theory until it's proven? Most of it is indeed speculation from the research. We won't know for sure until it's *your* eyes on scene. You're the only one who can see the signs. Unlocking those other genomes in your mind might be exactly what we need in order for this to be successful. But we won't know until their unlocked and you're pointed in the right direction," he smiles at me, carefully sitting down across from me on the chair.

"Okay," I reply hesitantly. I've never cared for uncertainty. Believing I was cursed was one thing. But, it was Eric who gave me the idea. I laugh at the thought. *Hunches can be favorably wrong.* This, unfortunately, is a scenario where the hunch *needs* to be right.

"Is there a timeline for when these gems *have* to be found? Am I working against a deadline?"

"Well, we estimated that it could take up to a month to find each gem, aside from the one in Malta. With Malta being a much smaller site, we hope it won't take longer than two weeks. If it does, we don't know how much longer past the two weeks we can hold the island. But it's certain we'll be working through Christmas, New Year's, and most of January."

"That doesn't answer my question," I sit back and fold my arms.

"February 20th will be the last day that we can get the gems into the machine for it to work, and we will need at least a week before that to make sure everything is working properly so if it's not, we have time to work out the bugs. So February 13th is when we need to be done with our research."

"That's barely three months, what if we run into complications or the locations are incorrect?" I'm beginning to get nervous all over again. *I haven't felt this much pressure since I was asked to design that spring collection four years ago entirely from scratch in only ten days because another designer got caught doing insider trading.*

"Guess you have to have a little faith," he raises his eyebrows and has a smug little smile on his face. *What have I gotten myself into?*

"Well, if you have any other questions, write them down for tomorrow night. You should get some sleep. You have had a long day and tomorrow is going to feel that much longer because you're going to be sore from today. Nice work today by the way," Kalil gets up and goes to walk out the door. Before he closes it, he looks over to see me with my face cupped in my hands still sitting on the couch, "Hey Brie." I quickly lift my face from my hands. He smiles and throws a small bag at me, "I have complete faith in you my dear." I shoot him a forced smile as he shuts the door.

I look in the bag and see it's the oils that Camille had given me. I must have forgotten them back at the warehouse. I quickly stand up and begin pacing, biting my fingernails. *You know what; I'm going to take a warm bath.* I head straight for the bathroom and shower up quickly. After I get out, I wrap myself in a robe then walk over to run the bath, pouring a drop from each of the oils and some soaking milk into the running water. The aroma instantly made me feel better, more relaxed. As the tub is filling,

I begin to walk back to the bedroom. Just as I open the door, I'm scared to death and almost slip, startled by the figure standing before me. The figure catches me and tries to calm me. "Justin?" my eyes focus as he helps stand me back up. Adjusting my robe, I scold him, "What the hell are you doing here? You almost scared me to death. How'd you get in here?"

"Sorry, sorry. After I had heard everything today I figured you might want to talk or get your mind off things or something," he replies, "And I kinda stole one of the maid's master keys…"

I quickly hit his shoulder playfully, laughing off the idea that I could have very well slipped and fell. He frowns at me, concerned, "How are you?"

"I'm… okay I guess. All of this information makes my head hurt. But I'm glad to see you," I lean in and kiss him on the cheek.

"Told you I wouldn't be far," he grins.

I walk into the bedroom and glance in the closet. Some of my things from home are in there. Eric uses Stacey as his resource to get me things I need. *Clever man.* I grab a set of pjs off of the shelf and walk back to the bathroom. "You can grab that chair over there and come talk to me while I soak," I point to the chair that is sitting at the vanity in this amazing bathroom. He grabs it while I grab a hand towel off of the rack. He puts the chair up near the head of the tub and sits in it. I clear my throat and promptly signal him to turn around. He chuckles and then does as he's told, turning around and shutting his eyes. I quickly disrobe and swiftly sink into the enormous tub and its milky white water, placing the hand towel over my body and covering myself. "Okay, you can open your eyes now," I state playfully. He opens his eyes and turns around. He straddles the back of the chair, crosses his arms and leans his head down on top of them.

"If I would have known a long day of training would end in me seeing you naked in a tub with just a hand towel covering you, I definitely would have recommended it sooner," he gives me that boyish grin I've grown to love.

I shake my head and roll my eyes, "You're such a perv."

He chuckles, "I'm just kidding. So how was all that training today? Very top of the line," Justin begins, paying careful attention to maintain eye contact with me.

"It was fun honestly... well mostly. That chick Jenna was testing my patience though," I point to him and smile.

He laughs aloud and teases, "Come on now Brie, you've never even pushed someone seriously let along hit anyone."

"Oh but I wanted to hit her, knock her lights out," I reply boldly, "I've never wanted to hit someone so bad in my life." I sit back in the tub and I get lost in thought for a moment.

He stares at me in silence. "What's the matter?" he asks after a couple minutes.

I snap back to our conversation and look at him, "Nothing really. I'm actually glad you're here. There's no one else I'd rather kickback and relax with after a long day." He chuckles at my comment. I lightheartedly say, "What I wouldn't give for a pizza!"

He mimics the act of scolding me, "Now that's not part of your eating regime for the week!"

I giggle at his reply, "Thank you."

"For what?" he asks. I reach up to him for him to take my hand.

"For always being there, always believing in me even when I didn't believe in myself," I smile as he takes my hand, "I couldn't ask for a better friend. You've been my rock for as long as I can remember."

"Me either," he smiles back. "And I do believe in you, more than you know. I think Kalil is right. If there was anyone who could save the world, it would be the most ambitious and kind-hearted woman I know." He kisses my palm and stares at the ground.

I look up toward the ceiling. "Ugh. I don't want to hear that from you. At this point, I wonder what life would have been like had I just been normal. Would my mom be alive? Would my father and I have been closer? Would you and I be…," I turn to look at him. Concerned I ask, "What is it?" staring at him nervously.

"It was selfish of me to ask you not to continue with this. I was so worried I might lose you that nothing else mattered. Most of what you learned today, I already knew," he frowns. I continue holding his hand.

"How?" I inquire.

"Eric explained most of this to me already, well at least your importance. It was the same night he explained demons to me," he continues. "I worried more about losing you, than all of mankind. But I see now that," he takes a deep breath and swallows hard, "it was the same me saying that I don't believe in you enough to take care of yourself and accomplish this on your own. I've never been so inspired by anyone before and you have always accomplished everything you set out to do. I realize now, I've never really had to worry about you. You have always found success; you've always found a way, even if you have to box up your feelings in order to accomplish a goal. You may not be a *physical* fighter but you have one hell of a fighting spirit. And if I truly love you, I need to help you set it free, not try to keep it boxed up."

My eyes swell with warmth as tears begin flooding down my cheeks.

"I'm so sorry," he finishes.

"No. Thank you for that Justin, it means so much to hear that from you," I stare at him for a moment. As I continue to stare, I notice that he becomes more and more blurry and my eyes begin to burn. "Justin? I can barely see you." Panic begins to set in as I try reaching out to him with my other arm. He's talking but I can't understand what he's saying, like his words are being muffled through the water. My vision continues to blur until everything is black. I can't feel the rest of my body; I don't even feel like I have a body even though my first urge is to thrash around. *Get a grip Brie.* I calm myself and begin trying to focus.

Once I'm focused, I realize I'm underwater. My naked body is covered by shells and kelp. I can breathe normally and my body freely floats within the clear blue depths. I can see a figure drifting towards me. "Hello again Briellyn." I attempt to swim closer to her so that I can see her. *It's the woman from my dream earlier this morning, the one standing in the hallway.* "Are you a siren?" I ask her angrily, realizing that her presence before was a distraction from the redhead. Since Eric told me termagants and sirens are the same, she must be one of Barbanon's demons.

She shakes her head no, "We've met before child."

I chuckle, "Yeah, this morning before the crazy redhead stabbed me with a knife, poisoning me."

She continues to smile, "You really don't remember. Its ok, I'm not here to hurt you. I'm here to guide you."

"Guide me where? How did I get here? I was just in the bathtub talking to my friend and now I'm here," I probe, wondering if I fell asleep on the couch and never made it to the bathroom. I mumble to myself, "None of it was real." *Damn these hallucinations.*

"Oh it was all real. You, indeed, are very special. Your mind is forever working in different directions all at the same time. This just happens to be one of them," she blinks at me and smiles. I just stare at her in confusion. "The direction that is. You're at the right age. Exactly the right age as a matter of fact; *ten thousand... three hundred... and forty-four days old.* I was hoping you would make the right choices to get to here. To get to me," she begins swimming around me.

"And who exactly are you? You know so much about me, but I have yet to know even know your name," I watch her carefully as she swims around; elegant and beautiful. It looks like she's gracefully dancing in the air, but the way her clothing drapes around her is more distinct of being underwater.

"I'm Rhea," she gleams, "I'm the Seer, an oracle of the water. The only born from the blood of Palidon. One of three."

"Three?" I ask her curiously. I begin to swim around with her, hypnotized by her deep blue eyes. They remind me of Eric.

"Why yes," she chuckles, "Balance comes in different forms, as you discovered today. One and twos. Three's and fours. Even I have two equals."

I think for a moment, "So if you are the only born from the blood of Palidon, then you have an equal born from Senon?"

She nods her head, smiling blissfully, "Very good."

"But if you have *two* equals that would mean… but that's not possible. I heard the story. He has no children," I hesitate, remembering Barbanon's inability to create life beyond his own.

"My equal from Senon is an oracle of land, she is like a sister to me. The Orator, the voice of God. She acts as a medium or vessel for Him to interact with humans. She takes many forms, one to which I'm sure you're familiar with. Mary, ring a bell?" she stares into my eyes. My eyebrows raise when I hear the name, she continues, "And Barbanon, though unable to reproduce directly, created a very dark magic with which he was then able to clone himself in female form. She is also sterile, because she is of him directly. She is the Slayer, killing men by the thousands. She corrupts the thoughts of man, killing their hopes and dreams. Once they succumb to her dark ways, she collects their souls for souvenirs. You have, unfortunately, encountered her wrath."

"The fiery red head that stabbed me in the dream," I frown, shaking my head, "But if she works for Barbanon…"

"Don't think too much of it child, it'll burden your mind with negative thoughts. You need to focus on your own mind and unlock those beautiful mysteries within you," she rubs my face exactly the way my mother would when she comforted me as a child. I close my eyes and embrace the touch, only to then open them to see my mother there. She is in Rhea's clothes and we are still underwater. It is as if Rhea transformed into her. My eyes begin to water; I stare into her eyes as vivid memories of her pass through my mind.

I remember her holding me as a baby, singing to me to soothe me. When she would lay me down, she would whisper, "My darling daughter, the world is so great and chaotic. I pray that you bring balance to it one day."

I remember her entering us in a talent show. Her and I did this interpretive dance that ended with a standing ovation. That night when she hugged me, she told me, "Did you see? You light up an entire room. You just shine so bright, it's hard not to see you."

I then see her face once more, lying on the ground the last night she was alive. I was so scared that I guess I repressed the memory. She said something else to me, "I'm protecting you."

I open my eyes and look directly at her, "You were protecting *me*. The termagant was after *me*. That's what dad meant. You knew? You gave your life for mine." I lean into her arms crying. She begins stroking my hair as I cry into her embrace.

"The greatest balance of power comes in ones and fours. You carry the future of mankind within you, and with that future you carry me. You will never know the power of love until you're ready to give your life for someone else. It's the greatest power of all. I'm so sorry you haven't felt true love yet, but you will."

My body feels like its on fire. The same sensation that I had in my eyes before I lost sight of Justin is now radiating over my whole body. I am in a dark place once again and Rhea, along with my mother, is gone. I can hear a distant voice that's slowly getting louder. My vision is coming back, less and less blurry from this dark place. I'm back in the tub and I can hear Justin scream in agony, "Ah!" he yelps.

I sit up in the tub, panicked, "What? What just happened?"

"What happened? Woman you just shocked the shit out of me is what happened," he's standing up trying to shake it off.

"So you heard everything?" I gasp, asking him excitedly, trying to comprehend how long I was gone.

"Heard what, you said thank you to me and then you shocked me; more like electrocuted. I'm not sure what happened but it was like grabbing an eel or something, I think. I wouldn't know what that's like but I imagine that's what it would feel like. Maybe not *as* bad, but… *shit*," he is pacing back and forth trying to regain feeling in his legs. His hair is standing on end. For him it was like I never blacked out.

I think for a moment, "I'm so sorry hun. I think…" I give him a weird smirk. "I think you and my mother together, somehow, helped me to unlock another genome," I feel like I'm glowing. Wait. *I am literally glowing.* I stare at my ambient, glowing body still submerged in the water.

"I've seen some weird shit over the last couple days, but this glow you have is freaking me out a bit," he pinches his bottom lip between his forefinger and thumb and puts his other hand on his hip. He grabs my robe and hands it to me, "Get out of the tub now. Please." He is careful not to touch me as I grab the robe from his hands. He's clearly aggravated by my unintentional shock.

"Thank you," I say after I take the robe. He walks out the bathroom. I look at my hand and stare at my golden glow. I quickly hop out of the bath, slip on the robe, walk over to the vanity, and look at myself in the mirror. I'm definitely glowing and the room appears different to me. Everything I touch gives off a type of energy, like shooting stars from my fingertips. I can feel it coursing through me. *Amazing.* I continue to admire the glow of my hands front and back. I walk out of the bathroom to Justin. He's standing there, tapping his foot as he stares outside. He's freaked. "Justin?" I ask, carefully walking up to him. He looks at me, cautioning me to stay away. "Please don't shy away from me now," I plead, slowly walking closer towards him, "I didn't mean to do anything to you, my mind was elsewhere."

He shakes his head no, holding his hand out, gesturing me to keep my distance. I immediately grab his hand and completely focus on him. He begins to glow a little bit too. He turns his head to look at me, "How are you…" he stares at me, his eyes glowing a shimmering green. He immediately calms and his entire demeanor changes.

Excited and cautious, I reply, "I don't know exactly, but I know I don't want to hurt you again. I'm hoping to calm you. Is it working?"

He shakes his head and smirks, "Oddly yes." He leans in and hugs me. I'm surprised by his gesture, but quickly wrap my arms around him too. He smells of sweet amber and spice. I can hear his heart beating rapidly, each breath through his nose, the warmth of his thoughts. It makes me hug him tighter. He slowly releases my hug and stares down at me. He wants to kiss me but he leans in and kisses my forehead. "Get some sleep," he whispers, holding me in a very loving embrace. Then he quickly releases and walks out of the room. I stare at the door as it slowly closes shut. I can't help but feel that I have somehow genuinely hurt him. He doesn't seem to know how to act around me anymore. Saddened and frustrated, I slip on my pajamas, crawl into bed, and stare at the ceiling. "Thanks mom," I whisper as I roll over and drift into the best slumber I've had since I met Eric.

Justin is walking towards the staircase when Kalil opens the door across the hall at Eric's room. He sees him upset and closes the door again. He turns around and looks at Eric, "I wonder what that's about…"

* * * * * * *

Eric

Thirty minutes earlier...

I open the door before Kalil even knocks and invite him in. I linger a moment and stare at Brie's door before shutting it behind him. Kalil walks over to the couch and has a seat. "Well, how's she holding up?" I ask as I walk over and sit down across from Kalil.

He crosses his fingers and leans in, "She's trying. I think she's having a hard time grasping with the idea that her whole sense of normality is no longer her reality. But I'm sure she'll be fine. She's got the amulet on and she's aware of how to balance her energy now. There were a few things that I wanted to talk to you about that I couldn't call or text you in regards to."

Hmm. "Shoot," I lace my fingers together and listen judiciously.

"First off, Justin took the bait. He asked Brie to bug your phone... and she did," he smiles, "We can track his location through the same chip that he's using to listen to your calls and view your texts, as planned."

"So her loyalty is as strong as we thought. *Excellent,*" I try not to seem too anxious to move on to how Briellyn's day was.

"Secondly, Camille told me something that I'm hoping you can shed some light on," he hesitates, "Brielle has... an *unusual* amount of additional genomes, apparently."

I lower my brow, "By *unusual amount,* you mean... how many exactly?"

"Three more, to be precise. Camille has never seen anything like it and it has her very curious. Maybe too curious. She wanted to get into your mind to compare but I told her no. But she says she can't read Brielle's thoughts without physical contact and even with that it is difficult… the same thing she happened to encounter with you."

I lean in, my interest peaked, *"Like me* huh? That *is* very interesting. I'll look into it further. I'm not sure what that means because I can't say I've ever heard of it before. Friday the 13th is the last day of the full moon, I will find out then. Anything else?" *Get to the good stuff.*

"Jenna gave Brielle a hard time today. Roughed her up a bit," Kalil begins.

I immediately perk up. My protective instincts overwhelm my failed attempt to play it cool, especially with her, "Is she okay?" *I should fire that girl.* I try not to look too concerned.

Kalil chuckles, "She's fine. She's a tough one." He analyzes my body language. "I've never seen you so… *caught up* with any of the other women. We've done this before but you're… you're *different* with her."

"I can't explain it Kal," I lean back in my chair and cross my ankle onto my knee, leaning my chin into my palm. I think about our car ride. "You know she told me today that when I touch her she has this overwhelming feeling of comfort and security. She accused me of being a demon." I chuckle. *Truth is her comment is unsettling for me.*

He looks at me, smirking, "Well what'd you tell her?"

"Nothing, I just stared at her," I shrug, staring off, "I don't know what to tell her. The stranger thing is though… *she does the exact same thing to me.* I can't explain it because I've never felt this way before. She's unlike anyone I've ever known." Not to mention she's absolutely gorgeous. *I'm smitten with her.*

Kalil stares at me, one brow raised, "Well, with that aside, I certainly think she is going to help you get where you belong… *finally.*"

I force a smile, still deep in my thoughts of her. *Don't let him see your feelings for her.* I turn my head away again. Kalil continues, "She *is* the one the prophecy speaks of. She's got to be. And we're running out of time."

I wish the prophecy mentioned my unlikely attraction to this chosen one so as not to be blind-sided by this. I gently nod, "Yes, I agree with you there."

"You want to hear the strangest part of today?" Kalil asks.

I cut my eyes to him and grumble, "There's more?"

"Those symbols on her that Barbanon cast? *It's a protection spell,*" He stares, anxious to view my reaction.

"What?!" I lower my brow, surprised and confused.

"Doc is sure of it, he showed me the translation," he shrugs it off.

I come to my feet and begin to pace, "Why would Barbanon have any interest in protecting Brie?" *I can't wait to be rid of that nuisance.*

"I think, if anything, it's a good indication that she is definitely the woman of the prophecy if someone as ancient as he is, is trying to *protect* her. Could work in our favor."

"Yes but *why*? First we thought he'd been banished from physical contact, now he's casting protection spells and engorging himself in blood. *Her* blood. The bite was too intimate to ignore. And what would she need protection from if not from him or one of his demons. What's the connection? What would he need her for? There is an end game here and we aren't seeing it damn it!" I slam my fist on a nearby table. *I can't believe I let that happen while she has been under my protection.*

"Calm down. Maybe…" Kalil comes to his feet, "he needs her for the same thing we do."

I roll my eyes and bring my hand to my forehead, "Of course, that would only make sense. No one else could want those stones more than me to go back in time, *other than him*. He's the only person who knows what they can be used for. Missionaries and pirates have been after them for years, decades even. Probably all with the promise of riches or fear from his wrath. He got others to do the dirty work for him, staying in the shadows. Making us believe that we had succeeded in banishment the first time. *Sly devil*. Get the last bit of trained men you have and get them out to Canada *before* we get there. With Justin trailing from a distance, hopefully he'll see anything that we can't. We can't take any chances this time. If we lose her, humanity is done and we can welcome the apocalypse. I don't know about you but I can't watch the world waste away, *I just can't*." *And I can't lose her.*

Kalil pulls out some documents, "I will give the order after we're done here. I also need your signature on each of these before I go."

I go through word after word of the three, five page documents; signing and initialing where needed. We hear something in the hall so we stop what we're doing. Kalil sneaks over to look through the peep hole only to see Justin leaving Brie's room. Justin is clearly upset. After he walks down the hall, Kalil carefully opens the door to ensure its just Justin walking away. He then closes the door, "I wonder what that's about…"

"Did she leave her room?" I inquire. *I hope not.*

"No, *Justin* just left her room and he looked pretty upset. He was obviously trying to be quiet judging by his exit. One of my guys said they thought they'd seen him in the hotel earlier today. Maybe I should go check on Brie," Kalil worries about her like he's protecting a baby chick. He walks back to grab the last signed document from me.

"Justin would never hurt Brielle. And if anything was wrong, *he* would suck it up and knock on my door or call me. *Trust me on this one,* she's fine. Stick to the routine the rest of the week and just keep me posted." Part of me hopes it isn't a *lover's quarrel.*

"So you're avoiding her?" Kalil's brows raise.

Of course I am. "In a way, sure I guess," I shrug, "I don't want to make her uncomfortable when I'm around her. And I can't help but want to touch her when I am. I can't subject myself to that everyday knowing it's not what *she wants.* " I've never felt this way before. *About anyone.*

Kalil looks at me carefully and walks over, placing his hand onto my shoulder, "Your heart will never steer you wrong."

"Easy for you to say, Kalil. You know it's not that simple for me," I sternly reply. *I only wish it were.*

"If there is one thing I have learned about life Eric, the way someone makes you feel inside is as *simple* as life gets, "Kalil shrugs, "Get some sleep boss."

I smile as Kalil leaves the room. I head into my bedroom and lay down once he's gone. With my arms folded and placed behind my head, I gaze at the ceiling. I imagine Briellyn's face from the other night. Staring into her perfect almond-shaped eyes, with her curvy lashes reminds me of why Cleopatra was so enticing to most men.

But her gaze has innocence about it, her kind and caring soul speaking through them. *Her fearsome body language protects her true identity.* I can see the hurt and distrust of men in it, yet the willingness to still put herself out there. A gorgeous, powerful, intelligent woman who is secretly unsure of herself on a more personal level. I could feel her uncertainty when kissing her velvet soft lips, her mind conflicting with what her body was telling her she wanted. The taste of her tongue still lingers on mine.

Her delightful curvaceous body pressed against mine as she indulged my hands with the touch of her. Those magnificent full breasts and ample ass are only accentuated by her petite waistline, creating the perfect hourglass shape. And those long legs that she is so obviously discreet about when she wears clothing that compliments her so well, I want to feel them wrapped around my hips once again. But it's the way her complexion radiates when I touch her, that subtle golden glow on her bronze skin that leaves me wanting more. *Much more.*

Many women have shown me interest and I've cared little to nothing for their advances. But Briellyn, the purity of her intentions that are so obvious to me. Yet she holds back and remains poised. Such restraint she displayed, so different from any other woman I've met. Any other would have continued to try to seduce me, yet she just walked away. Something about her feels familiar, which makes me want her that much more. But I know once I have her, nothing will be the same. "Give me strength, Lord. Allow me to focus so as not to fail you," I take a deep breath and drift off into a slumber.

Briellyn

Day two and three of training were the most difficult. I'd been getting great sleep but my body has been extremely sore. I found it more difficult to control my 'electric' abilities when my body was exhausted. Camille had explained to me that it's a genetic anomaly that must have descended directly from Senon. Even though all humans are the product of him and his brother, the genes were never supposed to pass down. Genetic anomalies cause things like her telepathy or my electricity to be employed through lots of psychological training. Without mental focus, the genes would never surface. My Empyrean sight is a naturally occurring gene that surfaces without assistance.

Her and Kalil further explained to me the importance of the big three and the gems, according to history. Senon wielded the Emaldi gem, which allowed him to create landmasses. It is the second most powerful gem of the four, it was used to surround the blistering core of the earth with crust, rock, and stone. Helping it to harden and keep cool was the Aquari gem, which was wielded by Palidon. And the Eaviri gem encased the earth in its atmospheric safety net, protecting it against the sun's harmful rays and any debris from the universe. The Eaviri gem was wielded by Barbanon.

The electricity running through my veins is merely energy collected from the earth's surface into my body. I'm then able to exert the energy against anything I focus my mind on. Unfortunately, it's finite; it drains my energy when I use it in excess. As Camille stated to me, it was never meant for a mortal to have.

By day four, my body is used to the vigorous training and I've gotten my new gifts under control. I managed to shock Jenna a few times because she upset me, and it took everything in me not to laugh about it. Let's just say, I got her pretty riled up and the training got quite intense. But she calmed down. It's now day five and we have just finished up training. Danny comes to join Kalil and me for dinner in the lounge.

"Hey, hey there superstar! How's my main squeeze?" he says playfully and gives me a fist bump.

Kalil is finishing up dinner, "Will you be joining us this evening Rodgers?"

"Most definitely Kal. This woman killed it today, she's a freakin' rockstar. I'm not impressed often, but lady you have genuinely blown me away with your dedication." He looks back and forth between Kalil and I, pointing at me the entire time. He turns towards me, "I'm so very proud, your review will be a breeze on Saturday." He leans in closer to me and whispers, "We should celebrate." My eyes light up. *My sentiments exactly!* I could use a break.

Kalil walks over with two plates and places them in front of us, he walks back to get his plate and some bottles of water. Danny leans in again and whispers some more, "I know this great dance club that you'll just love." Excitedly I nod yes, making sure that Kalil doesn't see my expression so as not to suspect anything. Kalil walks back over and sits down, placing a bottle of water in front of each of us. "You're damn right she's a rockstar," he raises his water bottle to the middle of the table, "To Brielle's success and the continuity of mankind." Danny and I raise our bottle in toast with him, "Here here," we both say. I still find it hard to believe that finding the stones will somehow save humanity but I'm enjoying the idea of being the world's savior.

We eat our food in silence, enjoying the onion, celery, and pepper chicken stir fry that Kalil whipped up. Once we're done, I grab everyone's plates from the table and walk over to the sink to put them down. "I'll go warm up the car. See you in a moment Brielle," Kalil points behind him then waves at Danny, "Goodnight Rodgers, see you in the morning." Danny rushes over to me.

"He seems like he's in a really chipper mood tonight," I suggest as I finish cleaning off our plates.

"Well I would hope so, Camille's going to keep him distracted while we all head out to the club," Danny has a huge, devious grin on his face.

"Kalil and Camille? How poetic!" I giggle, unaware that they are in a relationship together.

"They aren't like official or anything but they've been 'hooking' up for a while now. Ya know, monogamous and everything but no titles. I couldn't get tied down like that," Danny shakes his head to exaggerate his point. "I'll come pick you up about fifteen minutes after Kalil drops you off. You have any questions for him tonight?"

"Nope, I'm full to the brim with information. I'm just ready to get on with this mission and if questions pop up from there, I'll ask. But heading out tonight sounds like a lot of fun. I need it after this crazy long week. Are you sure he won't find out?" I slightly twist my face as I finish washing the last dish.

"Nah, Camille has him wrapped around her finger. And it's been awhile so I'm sure he's dying to just relax with her. It'll be a piece of cake!" Danny's laid back demeanor is refreshing.

"I don't have anything to wear though. Kalil didn't request my assistant to send anything... *appropriate* for a dance club," I frown. Just because I'm out of my element with this training doesn't mean I don't want to get dolled up tonight.

"No worries. I'll have Layla give me one of her dresses; she's got some sexy ones." He raises his eyebrows as he awaits my reaction.

"Wait, huh? I thought she...?" *Wasn't the girly type.*

"No, no, no. She is in love with Jenna. But only Jenna. She's mostly straight and still girly as it gets. Oddly enough... and she *loves* dancing. It's her and her brother that turned me onto this club. There are a lot of very attractive women that frequent this place. And it's my favorite spot to..." he stops and stares, "Ah, nevermind. Anyway, I'll have the dress in the car and you can change in the downstairs lobby or whatever. Just focus on sneaking out of the room. And don't worry; I won't leave your side tonight." He winks at me and goes to walk away.

I reach out to stop him, "Oh hey..."

He steps back and turns to me, tilting his head upward, "What's up?"

I glance at him, feeling silly for asking, "Have you... *happened to speak with Eric recently?*"

He nods his yes, "Yeah, we've gone over your progress and the training you've had with me. Why?" He sticks his hands in his pockets and grins at me.

"Oh, just curious I guess," I shrug my shoulders and playfully roll my eyes, trying to hide my interest in Eric's affairs.

"Let's have some fun tonight, 'kay? You deserve it for working your ass off this week," he walks up to me, "You'll see him a couple days." I nod my head as he walks off again.

I'm actually really excited! *Finally, something spontaneous and against the rules.* I feel like such a rebel! The thought of breaking Kalil's rules is actually more exciting than I thought it would be. I rush outside and hop into the truck with him. "You seem awfully chipper all of a sudden?" he accuses, staring at me oddly.

"Nothing," I reply hastily, "Excited to get some sleep. Lately it's been my favorite thing 'cause you guys work me to death.

He presses his lips together and smirks, "Okay then. No questions tonight?"

"Nope, you can head home and relax," I grin at him. I feel like I'm lying to my father.

We pull up to the hotel and he walks me to my room, the same as usual. After I shut my door, he slips something under Eric's door and makes his way back to the elevator. I Once I know that he's gone, I shower quickly. Pulling my hair down and running a comb through it with some curling mousse, allows it to curl up in its natural state. And lastly, I smooth out my face with some lotion and put on some mascara, light eyeshadow, and chapstick. I grab my phone and send Justin a quick text, suggesting he come out for a dance or two. I sit next to the window and wait for Danny's R8 to pull into the hotel parking lot.

After a couple minutes, I see him turning into the lot. I creep over to my door and make sure all of the lights are out. I open the door, put the do not disturb sign onto the handle and slip out quietly. Once I'm down the hallway, I rush into the elevator and hit the button for the lobby. I let out a huge sigh of relief, and excitedly blurt out, "Oh I need this so bad!" I begin laughing to myself. In the midst of my excitement, I notice the elevator lights and nearby hallway lights flickering. *Whoa there, tone it down.* Controlling my fluctuations of energy when my emotions change is tough, but I need to prevent any unnecessary power shortages in the hotel in order not to be found out.

Once I reach the lobby, I run out to the car and put my purse in the front seat. "The dress?" I ask. Danny reaches behind his seat and pulls out a gorgeous lace and chiffon mid length skater dress. It's a gold skirt with a gold lace overlay on the black bodice, a straight neckline, and thick straps that crisscross in the back.

"Oh my God, this is absolutely beautiful," my eyes just light up at the sight of the shimmering gold color, "I'll be right back!" I run back inside to the ladies room off of the lobby. I find the first available stall and slip into the dress and my shoes. I open the stall door and gaze at myself in the mirror. *Tone down the glow Brie.* I try to tune down my excitement so that the glow would subside but I find it difficult to contain. Finally, I manage to get it down to a realistic glow and proceed back to the car.

Danny's standing outside of it on the passenger side. His eyes light up when he sees me. He whistles, "Hot damn Brie, you clean up quite nicely." He opens the door and helps me sit down into his coupe. Then quickly gets to the other side and slips down into the driver's seat. "I'm going to show you off tonight, and you're going to love every second of it," he brags, then flashes me an encouraging smile.

I'm not the flashy type but that was Danny's form of a compliment. He has a cockiness about him that I find amusing. I can't believe women fall for it though. *His pretty boy looks must make up for his humorous charm.* All in all, I know he's a good guy and I've grown fond of him. We are at the club in about fifteen minutes when he pulls up to the front. There's a very long line. "Oh no, we'll be waiting forever. How is there a line and it's not even eight o'clock!?" I pout.

He parks directly in front of the club, "Oh, there's no wait for Danny Rodgers." He hops out of the car, tips the guy some money and hands him his keys. He then opens my door and helps me out. It's like everyone in the line tuned their voices down a notch or two. I lean into Danny, "I'm not glowing too much am I?"

He shakes his head, "No, not at all. You have this amazing, look-at-me-I'm-hot radiance going on right now. Very natural though. You just know how to light up a room is all." I blush. *Interesting choice of words.* The bodyguards at the door greet Danny by name and let us through. We walk down a dark hallway and come to a giant room with high ceilings, multi–level dancefloors, kickass music, and an amazing bar. Nick, Layla, Jenna, and Brendan are waiting for us at the bar nearest the hallway entrance. Layla walks up to me and hugs me, shouting in my ear so that I can hear her, "You look great in that dress, I knew you would. So glad you could make it!"

She smiles at me and I grin back, "Me too!" I shout.

Nick rushes us over to the bar and there are five shots waiting. Danny hands me the glass and brings his lips closer to my ear, "Don't worry, I'm rationing your shots and they know it!" Presently, I'm not worried about getting drunk. I know my limits and I just want to have a good time. I look around at the amazing dancers scattered about, like a scene from 'Dirty Dancing'.

Danny grabs my hand, breaking my focus. He pulls me out to the dance floor and whips my body close to his, "Just follow my lead." He puts his arm around my waist and our hands cupped together. Step, step, step, twist, then he thrusts my hips left, then right, twist out and pulls me back against him. *Now I'm the one who's impressed.* I can't stop smiling and laughing from the fun we're having. Between the twirls and dips, I glance over and see Rick standing at the bar with Layla.

As we continue to dance, I ask Danny, "What's Dr. Strassmore doing here?"

He glances over at the bar briefly, then dips me and whips me back up. "We invited him. Don't let the good doctor fool you Brie. He's quite the stud. Women just throw themselves at him, possibly even more than at me if you can believe it. I'm not sure what it is," Danny smiles and spins me around twice, pulling me back with his arm around me and his hand on my belly, my back against his stomach. "I'm sure he'll want to get at least one dance in with you before the night is out," he says as we continue.

Jenna and Brendan are twirling, grinding, and making out hardcore, not even ten feet from us. *They couldn't keep their hands off of each other!* Normally I would find it distasteful but at the moment it's oddly entertaining. First time I've seen Jenna relaxed and not being rude. *Brendan, please break her off so she can ease up on the rest of us.*

Regardless of their public display, it made me long for Eric once again. Danny's touch as we dance is graciously welcomed by my inner woman, even though I'm not enticed by his handsome face or muscular physique. And judging by the way he moves his hips, I can see how any woman would swoon over him. But his presence is helping me to work off some of the frustration from the other night with Eric. *I may have even imagined for a fleeting moment that he was Eric.*

Layla and Rick get on the dancefloor and take it over. They both are amazing dancers, making what Danny and I are doing look like child's play. I smirk and Danny notices. "See, I told you," he shouts into my ear. Women are just staring at him in awe and Layla is the belle of the ball. We move in close to them and Danny throws me at Rick as Rick throws Layla at Danny.

"Why hello again Ms. Donado," Rick smiles big as he dips me only two feet from the ground.

I beam, "Hello indeed Doc." I sway my hips left to right, following his lead. The entire crowd is clapping to the beat and watching us dance. It's certainly not me running this show, he's got a hold on everyone. For an older, *and taller*, man he's impressively nimble. As he swiftly tosses me around, I try to see if I can spot Justin. *No sign of him.* I thought for sure he would come but I haven't seen him or heard from him since my first night after training.

"Is everything okay?" Dr. Strassmore shouts at me, taking notice to my slight change in demeanor. He twirls me out and then pulls me back in, placing his hand on the lower part of my hips. My temperature begins to rise the more we dance. There's something about him that is very seductive. I feel hypnotized by his movements.

He spins me around, placing his hand to my chest. He then dips me and when he does his hand caresses downward, grazing my breasts. He's so focused on dancing, embracing his body against mine. I don't believe he's intentionally being erotic; he's just into the music. I decide to just enjoy it. *A little dancing never hurt anyone.* Danny interjects and it snaps me out of my dance trance. He steals me away from Dr. Strassmore as Layla is swung into his arms. Danny and I then continue to dance for another thirty minutes before we stop for a water break.

We rush over to a table near the bar, both of us glistening with sweat. "Are you having a good time?!" Danny asks as he sucks down an entire glass of water.

I wildly nod my head, raising my eyebrows, "Hell yeah I am!" I sip on some ice water then take a piece of ice and rub it on my shoulders, my décolletage, and the back of my neck.

Danny raises his eyebrows, "You know, I could do that for ya if you want," he jokes. I can tell there is a hint of truth to it though. I'm sure he's not used to being turned down. *But my sights are currently set on a particular billionaire.* If they weren't, *and I was a coquette,* I might just take him up on the offer.

I playfully push his shoulder. He glances over at the bar, not a few feet away, "I'm going to grab us our last shots for the night." I acknowledge by nodding my head as I take another sip of water. I listen to the music, bob my head, and toss my hips to the beat as I watch Layla and Rick continue to stun the crowd. Rick keeps looking over at me, signaling me to come over. I motion to let him know that I would be there in a moment, after I take another shot with Danny.

"Excuse me miss, might I enjoy the next dance with you?" a man's voice breaks my focus on the music. A chill travels up my spine as goosebumps take over my body. He's standing behind me but I'd know that voice anywhere. The entire room slows, coming to a standstill, as my heart begins to race and my breath quickens. *I've been caught.* I turn around to see Eric's handsome face. Every inch of me wants to embrace him because I haven't seen him in five days. But I can't read his expression. I can see Danny from the corner of my eye and I signal for him not to bring the drink over.

"What are you doing here?" I nervously shout, trying to play coy.

"I guess I should be asking you the same question," His sarcastic, flirtatious smile doesn't ease my nerves. He's standing there in a black tank, unbuttoned long sleeve and black slacks.

Definitely disappointed in me. I frown. Defensively I try to explain, "This wasn't their idea, it was mine. Please don't punish them. I just... needed to get out. I was feeling... *claustrophobic.*"

Eric smirks at me and shuffles his shoulders. He holds his hand out, "So are you going to dance with me or continue to explain yourself?"

I'm not sure if he's joking with me but I grab his hand. He guides me to the dancefloor and pulls me in closer, "I'm not upset with you. I've been watching you for almost fifteen minutes, having a great time. And I think it's rightfully deserved. I heard you leave the hotel earlier, so I followed you to make sure you weren't getting into any trouble." We are shuffling our feet, faces only a few inches from each other. *Oh, how I've missed his touch.*

"I'm sorry Eric, you must be so disappointed in me," I glower. *I feel so irresponsible.*

"Au contraire my love, you've surprised me. I didn't think you had this, sneak out and dance routine in you. I'm sure Rodgers is partially responsible here. I won't tell Kalil if you don't." His smile is dreamy as he dips me low, waiting for my response. *Please kiss me.* I beam back a flirtatious grin to signal to him that I agree.

If I thought the feeling of him holding my hand or hugging me was irresistible, he and I dancing is the ultimate euphoria. We are dangerously close, allowing the music to take us over and let our bodies do the rest. His hips guide mine to the rhythm of the music, his hands control my twirls as I spin away from him only to be pulled back to him, his body inviting mine with every move. Our forms move like they're flirting with each other.

Danny found some cute blonde and began dancing with her since I became occupied. Four songs later, Eric asks me if I would like something to drink. It's a little shocking, seeing him like this. It's no wonder Justin didn't make an appearance, he'd probably seen Eric come after me and didn't want to get caught. We head over to the bar and he orders us both a shot. I stare at him as we wait for our drinks. "What?" he gives me a strange grin.

I tilt my head, "This isn't like you…"

"Technically, this isn't like *you* either; which is why I'm okay with it," he smiles and I can't help but stare at his lips. *My evening's enjoyment is now complete.*

"How come I haven't seen you all week? Have you been too busy to come say hello?" I tease with a hint of sincerity and concern.

"Honestly," he clenches his jaw and looks down at me, "I wanted to give you space after you told me about how my touch affects you. I didn't want to continue to make you uncomfortable."

Uncomfortable? Try pleasantly aroused. I beam at him. There's nothing sexier about a man than one who respects a woman's boundaries. I didn't realize that my words sunk in so deeply. The bartender places two shot glasses on the bar and takes the twenty dollar bill that Eric left for him. Eric grabs both glasses and hands me one. "To the most amazing woman I've ever met," he shouts. I carefully scan his eyes down to his mouth, soaking the moment in. I raise my glass to his and we take the shot, sharing the same sour expression as the alcohol trickles down.

Just then, the DJ makes an announcement, "It's that time of night everyone, let's see who can show us something new!" The DJ changes the music up to a swinging, upbeat jazz, and everyone begins fighting for the limelight. Rick and Layla had been the center of attention all evening so it wouldn't surprise me if they continued their reign. Eric grabs my hand and rushes to the dance floor. "Have you ever done any swing dance?" he asks.

"In high school, some in college maybe, but that was years ago…" I reply, yelling over the music.

He grabs my waist and pulls me into him, pulling my leg up onto his hip, "Do you trust me?" My pulse quickens. That feeling of something deep within me gets a little out of control as I begin to radiate a little more.

Excited, I shake my head, "Yes". Eric places his hand onto my chest over my heart and closes his eyes for a moment. My glow begins to calm and simmers down, my thoughts clear and the room clears. I only see Eric now. How is he doing this to me? Like a perfect dream, he serenades my physique with his own. The twirling and spinning, picking me up and jumping over me; it's like we are completely in sync. The entire crowd is cheering us on, including Rick and Layla. Before we realize it, it's 10:45.

Danny walks up to us with his new blonde beau. "We should probably go," he suggests.

Eric raises his eyebrows, "I'll take Brielle home. You go have fun." He winks as Danny gives him a grateful devilish grin in return. Eric urges me to walk with him, taking me out to his car.

He hands the valet his ticket and walks back over to me. "Did you have fun tonight?" I can tell that he's hoping I'll say yes. I frown and look down. He quickly grabs my hand, "*You didn't have fun...*"

"It's not that. *I had a great time,*" I look into those deep blue eyes. *I suck at communicating my feelings.* "I was never uncomfortable around you, Eric. I just wasn't sure what to make of my very mixed feelings about you. I'm so sorry if I made you think I didn't want to be around you."

He pulls me closer. Something's animalistic and possessive about it. *I'm yours for the taking.* I continue, "Honestly, I've missed you this week, not seeing you has drove me crazy. And tonight was perfect, thank you."

"You're very welcome Briellyn, I'd prefer nothing more." He looks from one of my eyes to the other. My lips begin to curl and smile but slowly shut from him leaning in closer. *HONK!*

Rudely interrupted by Jenna and Brendan. We immediately separate from each other. "You guys shouldn't stand out here, get going!" Jenna scoffs as they drive off. The valet pulls up right after. Eric opens the passenger door for me and helps me climb in, then quickly gets to the driver side. We drive back to the hotel and walk up to our floor.

When I open my door, I glance back at him, "Thank you again for tonight. You're full of surprises. I'm beginning to love that about you." *What don't I love?* I give him a sweet smile and kiss his cheek. "Goodnight, Eric," I whisper into his ear.

Eric stands there with the sweetest look on his face as I disappear behind my door and close it carefully. "Goodnight dear Brie," he mumbles under his breath, holding one hand over his heart. He snaps out of it after a moment or two and turns around to let himself into his room.

I run into my bedroom and jump onto the bed, landing face first. I joyfully scream into the pillow and begin laughing to myself. A deep breath escapes as I place my hand over my heart, which continues to race. *I finally have my mind and body mostly under control but then Eric comes in and tames it completely.* I roll onto my back and get off the bed, quickly undress, then wash up and climb back in. He's the only man that makes me feel shy like a little girl and a confident woman at the same time. When he stares into my eyes and bares those pearly whites, my knees grow weak and my heart begins to flutter. Maybe now that he knows I've missed him, he'll make a debut tomorrow. I close my eyes and think of his face as I rollover to get some sleep.

Briellyn

The next day is the same as usual. Kalil on the other hand, has some extra pep in his step. He sang along to the radio on the ride to the warehouse this morning. It was entertaining, him singing Taylor Swift. Now Camille was a different story. She seemed a bit strange after our session. Jenna is pissed at me, *for assumedly my affections with Eric,* and tried her damnedest to take it out on me in the ring. When she caught me in a chokehold and tried to put me to sleep, I zapped her pretty good. That landed us both in trouble with Kalil. We're now sitting in the lounge waiting for him as Danny plays the mediator.

"What the hell were you thinking Jenna? Why would you do that?" Danny asks, scolding her. He's pacing left to right staring at us like we're a couple of catholic school girls.

"She's upset over the relationship Eric and I share," I interrupt, pissed that we are being scolded because of her uncontrollable jealousy.

Jenna gets up and tries to hit me again but Danny grabs her, "Enough Jenna."

I cross my arms as he sits her down. Kalil walks in and slams the door shut. "All things considered, I've been having a fantastic day. Everything has been going according to plan, my breakfast was great, *and then I hear about this high school bullshit.* Whatever is going on between you two needs to stop," his voice is deep and stern.

Jenna deviously smiles and looks at Danny, "Should I tell him or will you?"

Danny's eyes narrow at her. Kalil chimes in, "Tell me what Rodgers?"

"Romeo here took Juliet out last night until eleven pm..." Jenna blurts. Kalil's expression goes from annoyed to angry.

"Is this true Rodgers?" Kalil stares at Danny.

"Look, she'd been working hard..." Danny begins.

I interrupt, "Don't blame Danny. It was my idea. I wanted a night to blow off some steam before this mission was fully underway. I wasn't sure if I would ever have the chance again." I think twice about mentioning Eric's presence, "I was home by eleven, but I'm here. I didn't get drunk or out of control, just a little dancing. I was up on time this morning, ready to go. Nothing out of the usual." *Hopefully that will suffice.*

"You two," he points at Jenna and I, "Squash whatever differences you have right now." He glares at Jenna, "if this is about the relationship that Brielle and Eric have together, I assure you, I will fire you right now. You're my best fighter and your services are needed, but not required. We *can* and will manage without you if necessary. Hers, however, are essential to this mission. If you can't be professional about this, you're gone."

Jenna crosses her arms in frustration. I'd never seen her pout before. She then nods her head, "Fine. I'm good. No more of this, *I got it.*"

"Now go," he commands Jenna. She immediately stands up and walks out. He then scowls at Danny, "Did you even once think about the consequences if anything were to have happened to her last night?"

Danny's eyes shift toward the ground, "Of course I did Kal, I never even let her out of my sight. When she went to the bathroom, Layla went with her and I stood right outside the door! But you have to realize, she's a person… a woman, not an animal or a child. You've kept her locked away in a tower like she's Rapunzel. When I took every precaution necessary to ensure her safety *and* allow her to blow off some steam."

Kalil twists his mouth. As much as he wants to be angry about it, he lets go. I can see it in his face. He exhales audibly, "Fair enough. Fair enough. I've always trusted your judgment and that's not going to change now. But next time, come to me first." He puts his fist in front of Danny.

Danny replies, bumping his fist against Kalil's, "Sure, you got it Kal. No harm, no foul."

"I have to talk to Brie for a moment. Let Nick know she'll be heading over momentarily," Kalil finishes. Danny glances at me and then walks out of the lounge, closing the door behind him.

Kalil sits down next to me. I sadly twist my face from feeling guilty, "I'm sorry, I shouldn't have asked him to take me. I just…"

Kalil holds up his hand and smiles, "There's no need to apologize. Danny may be a lot of things, personally, but he cares about people like no one I've ever seen. I can tell he's let you into his very small inner circle. He's gotten to know you through intel and now that he's met you, *finally*, he sees the goodness in you. And he's exactly right, I should have given you a night off."

Oh, thank goodness! I smile and scoot closer to hug him. Feels like I just got cut some slack from dear old dad. "Look, there's something that I need to tell you. It's for Eric's sake because I know he wouldn't tell you. *Not in a million years,*" Kalil begins. I release the hug and stare at him, holding my breath hoping it isn't bad news. He swallows hard and then continues, "Eric is... *unique.* Like you, he's not like other people you've ever met before."

"Right, I know we both can see things that others can't," I lean my head in, wondering where he's going with this. *I mean, I think I'm a little cooler, with the electric abilities now.*

He shakes his head, "No, more than that. *Much more.* You remember when I told you that there were other women over the last couple of centuries like you?"

"Yes..."

"Well," he exhales deeply and closes his eyes, "Eric and I... have both been around for over two hundred years."

I burst out laughing, "That's a joke right. Oh my goodness, I thought you were going to say you two were like, into each other or something. But over two hundred years old... come on. Immortality is for suckers. *Do I look like a sucker?*" My laugh fades, waiting for him to tell me it's a joke. His face remains unchanged.

"It's not a joke," Kalil stares sternly, "I've been trying to figure out how to tell you. Eric isn't human... *he's an Empyrean.*"

"You're serious?" I glower at him, scrunching my eyebrows together and staring into his eyes, "How?"

"I told you that we've been looking for a woman, born on July seventh, who resembles you physically... and there have been twenty two, including you, over the past two hundred and forty years. Eric has been searching all of these years based on a prophecy that was told to us back in 1776. Eric is trying to get home to Empyria. He was sent to the British Isles to find a demon that was causing havoc amongst the people. Eric is *the* Empyrean of war; his job is to help settle wars created by demons. So if there is ever demonic presence, Eric is sent to take care of it. He's like Ares mixed with the angel Gabriel."

He's not kidding. I'm utterly blown away, "So are you an Empyrean too? One of his commanders or something?"

"As a gift, his grandfather, Palidon, made me an immortal. I'm not an Empyrean by any means. I am however close to two hundred and eighty years old. Camille is also an immortal, she is about a hundred and thirty. Her immortality was a gift from Senon."

"Well that explains the relationship between you two. Are you married?" I disregard that Danny had told me they don't use titles.

"Something like that," he swallows hard.

"What about before her? You're almost twice Camille's age. Who were you *before* immortality?"

"I had a wife when I was still mortal. She died protecting our children when our village was raided by mercenaries. I was leading a hunting party in the mountains, like we did every year, preparing for winter. My daughters and my younger sister were all taken. I found out later, that my sister happens to be your great great times eight grandmother." His eyebrows immediately raise.

I smirk and roll my eyes, shaking my head, "Wait, I'm sorry. *What?* You're tell me that my sister and I are kin to you?" He nods. "Through my mother or my father?" I probe, still somewhat unconvinced.

"Father," he replies.

As weird as it is, it makes sense to me why him and I connect the way we do. That odd feeling he gives me like I'm talking to my father. I don't want to believe it. *But if I can believe that I can shoot lightning bolts from my hands, I guess anything it possible.* I give him a halfhearted smile then hug him. "Now I understand why you're so protective," I chuckle as we continue hug tighter. He gently pulls away after a moment or two.

"Eric is afraid to connect with you, thinking you would turn him away if you knew what he really is. I don't believe that. I've watched him over the centuries we've been together, never has he experienced love or infatuation in anyway. He's tried though, if anything to blend in. But his feelings for you are relentless and he's having a hard time coping. If you truly care for him after what I've told you, like I think you do, let him know. Only when you're ready though. I don't think you two can go too far but maybe you can become better friends through all of this." Kalil kisses my forehead and stands up. "Get back to training," he commands, smiling at me.

I stand up as he walks out of the lounge. *An Empyrean.* I think about what he told my nephew about him being my guardian angel. *He wasn't lying.* Maybe that explains why his touch is so intoxicating to me. But now I know the feeling is mutual, and that is invigorating in itself. I try to clear my head and walk out to my next training session, thinking of how much more complicated my life becomes.

* * * * * * *

Later that evening after Kalil drops me off to my room, I begin to wonder what life would be like with someone like Eric. If he's trying to go home to Empyria, what does that leave for me? *Heartbreak and disappointment of course.* I frown. Maybe it's in my best interest not to pursue it any further. I don't want to make Eric feel like he has to choose between me and getting home. I lay my head down and go to sleep, my day of review is tomorrow and then the final test is the next day.

I wake to a frantic knock on the door. I glance at the time to see it's not quite six o'clock yet. I hop out of bed and slip on my robe, quickly walking to my door. I look through the peep hole and see Eric standing there. Panicked, I throw open the door, "Eric? What's the matter?"

He shakes his head as he walks into my room, "We are going to have to shorten your review and squeeze in your real life run through today."

I close the door and blink my eyes several times, "Why what happened?"

"I just got a call from our base of operations in Canada. It was attacked early this morning."

"Attacked by who?" I inquire; I've never seen Eric so panicked. *It's making me anxious.*

"I'm not sure yet exactly. I'll be taking you over to the warehouse today so I can review the security footage. Someone will be coming by this room to collect all of your things while you're gone. We go to Florida tonight to head to Canada in the morning."

"Ok, I'll get ready right away," I say to him. He stops pacing and stares at me for a moment. *Those dreamy blue eyes just see right through me.*

"What is it?" I ask, approaching him slowly then place my hand on his arm, "I've never seen you so panicked, are you going to be alright?"

"I just don't want anyone getting hurt because of me, most certainly not you," he frowns, such sincerity in his words.

"It's going to be okay," I reassure him, "We can fix this. We'll get you home." My tone is pleasant, comforting almost.

Eric squints at me, staring curiously.

"I'm going to shower and get ready, you should do whatever you need to do so that we can go ahead and leave when I'm done," I redirect his thoughts.

"Right," he walks to my door and opens it, "Meet you in a few minutes." I nod and proceed to get ready; showering, getting dressed, and reviewing the list of things I need for my run through today. Once I have everything I need, I grab my gear and meet Eric in the hallway. We quickly get to the warehouse where everyone is already waiting outside.

Danny opens my door as Eric hops out and runs off with Kalil. Danny begins briefing me as he grabs my things from the car, "Okay, remember what drills we've run all week." He shuts the door and we hastily make our way to the lounge. "Today, they are going to drown you as part of your final and a very real fight; but I know you're going to do fine," he encourages. I begin taking deep breaths and pacing to calm myself as I feel my heart begin to beat faster and my palms start sweating.

Danny walks over to the microwave, grabs a plate out of it and hands me some food. "Eat something," he demands. I grab the plate from him and begin taking tiny bites. I am entirely too nervous to finish the food so I take a few more bites and put the plate down. *I could see the dread in Eric's face; does the God of War usually panic?* The situation must be *really* bad.

Danny walks up to me, "You alright? You look a little blue?" *I want to puke actually.* I nod, reassuring him I'm good and not nervous about the final. I'm ready for a controlled scenario. *I'm not ready for an uncontrollable scenario afterwards.* Danny guides me out of the lobby and gathers everyone to proceed with the review.

The review goes smoothly and without any issues, not even from Jenna. It seems everyone is a little edgy and ready to go, given today's event. It's about noon and they are preparing the last little bits for the final run through. The scenario is that I get lost from the group and I'm trying to catch up. I run into a mercenary, at some point, who attacks me and tries to kill me. It'll be the first time I use my new shocking talent as defense during a real fight.

They place me in the scenario room where I've been training with Danny all week. My test begins. I'm climbing the side of a mountain and make it to the top, tracking footprints and keeping a good pace. There's a river up ahead so I decide to make camp before the sun goes down. I'm setting up the tent when I hear something close by. I take out my gun, switching the safety off and aiming in the direction from which I hear the noises. My heart is pounding; I can barely breathe. I'm hate the idea of shooting someone, fake or not. A deer pops out of the bushes, startling me. I relax my stance and roll my eyes, whispering, "Thank God." I endeavor to put my gun back into my leg holster when someone pops up behind me and chloroforms me. *I never saw it coming.*

"Rise and shine," a bearded man mumbles to me as I come to. A fire is raging in front of me and my hands are tied behind my back. "Hey there, it's about time," he continues.

"How long was I out?" I ask, wondering based on how dark it is.

"About thirty minutes or so, not too long," he grins. "You have some information I need and I'll be on my way. I don't have to hurt you if you just cooperate," he continues. "I'm told that you know where to find Eric?"

I didn't think they'd use Eric's name in the scenario. "What do you want with Eric?" I stubbornly ask.

"That's my business, missy. I just need you to tell me where I can find him," the man is picking his teeth with a very sharp hunting knife.

"I don't know off the top of my head. I'm using a tracker, it's in my tent there, in my bag," I motion my head in the direction of the tent. Hopefully my overly helpful demeanor doesn't raise any red flags.

"You are very cooperative... *I appreciate that,*" he gives me a smug look and walks towards the tent, "Where in the tent?" He flings the door of it open and crawls inside.

"In the bottom of the pack that's on the floor," I begin moving around, trying to get out of the restraints. Once I realize I can't slide the restraints over my legs to bring them in front of me because my winter gear is too bulky, I decide to try something that I hadn't attempted in training. I focus my energy to singe the zip ties. *It works.*

I get up and jump on the mercenaries back, attempting to get my arm around his neck. He pulls me over his back and throws me to the ground. He attempts to stab me with the knife but I roll over, then run out of the tent. He follows me and sees me standing by the fire. I'm in my fighting stance, ready for his attack. He attempts to punch me, but I dip and push him off using his momentum. While throwing another punch my direction, I manage to give him a shot to the ribs. He then tackles me to the ground, straddles me across my stomach, places his hands around my neck, squeezing tightly. I use my shocking ability to send a threatening pulse through his body. He releases me as if he were just tased.

I try to catch my breath for a moment and spot my gun. The pulse didn't last long, he sits back up within a few seconds. I roll over, attempting to come to my feet while I continue to catch my breath. He grabs my foot and pulls me to him, back down to the ground. I manage to kick him with the opposite foot and he lets go. I run over to grab my gun and he rushes me from behind, holding my arm out to prevent me from pointing it at him while placing his other arm around my neck. I try to jump and pull him forward up over me but my efforts fails. He has more mass than me.

I zap him again but my mind is panicked, the shock isn't very strong. Fortunately, it's strong enough to make his body release the hold but not to stun him. I try to run away but he grabs my jacket, throwing me into the river. He rushes me quickly and I shock him again, this time mid-punch. The blow hits me in my jaw, knocking me on my ass. It takes me a moment to recover. He then grabs my jacket and holds me down under the water. I struggle as I'm losing air. Just as I begin to black out, he pulls me out of the water, limp and slightly unconscious. Danny runs up to me, sliding over. He leans down to listen to my heart. He begins to perform CPR and get the water out. Three thrusts to my chest and then he breathes into my mouth.

I gasp as the water shoots up and out of my mouth, my lips darkened from the cold. I cough profusely. He rolls me over onto my side. His sights then turn to my attacker. "Did you have to hit her in the face that hard!? That wasn't part of your job!" he gets up and shoves my bearded attacker. Jenna and Nick run in to hold him off.

"It certainly wasn't intentional," the bearded man replies, "She sent a different type of pulse through me, I couldn't control myself."

The simulation is turned off as Eric comes running in. He leans down next to me and sits me up, wrapping a towel around me as he caresses my face. "Brie, look at me. Are you ok?" He places his hand under my chin, encouraging me to look up at him. I nod my head, shaking from the cold. "You passed. Nice work," he holds me close to his chest. *I would do it again to be rewarded like this.*

He calmly walks over to the bearded man, while everyone is distracted by Danny still screaming at him, and coldcocks him. The man is unconscious and laid out on the ground. Everyone stops and stares as Eric walks out of the room. Danny and Layla help me to my feet. Layla accompanies me to the showers and helps me get cleaned up. I'm given a pair of comfy sweatpants and a sweater from her. Afterwards, I'm brought to Rick to examine any injuries.

"Well, you can certainly take a hit my dear," he says, carefully holding the sides of my face and analyzing my jaw. "You have bruising and swelling on your jaw and light bruising around your neck," he adds, "You'll have to take it easy the next couple of days. Foods that are easy to chew might be a good idea, an ice pack to reduce the swelling, and here are some Ibuprofen to aid in reducing the swelling and cope with any pain you might have." I take the pills from him. He then takes the rubber gloves off. "You don't have any remaining water in your lungs and no internal damage, you'll be good as new in a few days," he continues. He hands me a mirror. I frown when I see the swelling of my jaw.

"You weren't supposed to get hurt like that," Eric's voice tears me away from my brief moment of vanity. He walks into the examination room.

I glance at him, slightly embarrassed by my rugged appearance. I put the mirror down and attempt a smile. "It's no big deal," I stutter, keeping my mouth mostly shut, "But seeing you knock that guy out cold was totally worth it."

Eric playfully rolls his eyes and continues to walk up to me. He carefully holds up my chin so that he can get a better look at the swelling, "Well, he deserved it." He clenches his jaw, "The car is already loaded up and everyone is ready to go." He helps me off of the exam table.

"Wait," I look at him, "I know things are crazy in Canada right now and it might be really selfish of me to ask but… Can we possibly see my sister before we go? It'll be very brief, I promise. We're driving to Florida right?"

He shakes his head, "No, I had the plane fly here and we'll be departing from the private air strip thirty minutes from here. But…"

"*Please*. I need to see her one last time," I put my head down for a moment to hold back the tears. I glance back up, into Eric's eyes, my voice trembling, "If anything were to happen to me on this mission and I didn't properly say goodbye to her and the kids, I would never be able to forgive myself."

Eric grabs my hands and stares back, giving me a caring smile, "We'll fly there first, no problem. I'll have the pilots plot a flight nearest her home. I'll give the rest of the crew the option of taking the cargo plane out or taking the detour with us."

I close my eyes, "Thank you." Eric leans in and kisses my lips. It takes me by surprise. *Finally.* I slightly lean a little more into him, keeping my eyes closed and savoring the moment. He then holds me a little tighter, kissing me deeper.

He slowly leans away and caresses my cheek, my eyes slowly creep open, "You're very welcome." He grabs my hand and walks me out. *I'm officially in heaven, almost literally.* Everyone is standing by their cars waiting for us. Eric raises his hand, "Hey everyone, change of plans. We'll be making a pit stop into Georgia to see Brielle's sister..." I glance over at Kalil, as Eric continues, "Anyone who doesn't wish to go can ride the cargo plane straight to Canada. That plane will have to make one fueling stop in New York and pick up some additional cargo. Everyone else who doesn't mind making the stop can feel free to proceed with me as planned."

* * * * * * *

We make our way to the airstrip and Eric makes sure I'm the first to board the plane. He takes me to the back room and lays me down. Tucking my hair behind my ear, he says, "Try to just take it easy. I'll let the pilots know about the stop. There's an ice pack in the fridge right here and a few bottles of water to take the Ibuprofen." He points to a button next to the bed, "Just push that if you need anything at all. I'll just be in the next room." He covers me with a blanket and kisses my forehead. I try to get comfortable as he leaves the room.

No one is going to decline a private flight. Everyone came, including Jenna, so this is the first time his private plane has been full of people. Joseph beams from all of the excitement, anxious to get to Canada. Eric approaches him and lets him know about the stop in Moultrie, Georgia. He immediately goes into the cabin and begins replotting the flight. Joseph yells out to Eric, "It's about a two hour flight to get there. Arrival time would be about 6:30PM." Eric gives him the thumbs up as he walks back out to shut the plane's door.

Eric raises his voice once the door is closed, "Ok ladies and gentleman. Within the next twenty four hours or so, we'll be in Canada. As you all well know, our base of operations was attacked early this morning around 2AM. What we are dealing with is indeed, supernatural. Marauders with the help of demons. You all have been trained in extraordinary combat and you will be armed with unique ammunition that can kill demons so remember all of your training. Unfortunately, we are down twenty men. I had to make calls to eight families this evening and offer them my condolences. The other twelve will live, but they are in pretty bad shape. You are my closest comrades, so watch your asses. I don't want any of you getting hurt out there because of foolishness. Kalil will give you any additional information you need to know." Eric points over to Kalil to direct the attention to him and then walks to the bathroom. He pulls out his phone and dials Skyla's number.

"Hello?" Skyla asks when she answers the phone.

"Hey there Skyla, it's Eric Windsor. You know, Brielle's friend?"

"Uh huh, I remember you. Is everything ok?" She's nervous.

"Everything is fine. I was wondering if you could meet us at Moultrie Municipal airport around 6:30… Brie wanted to see you before we left the country so we are heading that way here in a few minutes."

"Oh, of course I can!" she exclaims, "I'll see you all soon!"

Eric hits the end button and mumbles to himself, "Perfect. So now Justin knows where we are going and I can recruit him too." He leaves the bathroom and walks into the back room.

I lift my head up, "Is everything ok?" He approaches me and leans down, "Shhh, everything is fine. I just called your sister and she knows we'll be there in a couple hours. I figured I would come lay with you. If you don't mind."

Um, does a bear shit in the woods? My mind begins to wonder for a moment. "Of course, sure," I mumble as a smile creeps across my face. I immediately scoot over. He sits down on the bed and removes his shoes then throws his legs over onto the bed and leans his back against the headboard. "Come here," he motions for me to lay my head down on his lap. He begins caressing my hair, "I forgot to mention how gorgeous you looked the other night. I hadn't seen you in so long I got lost in your beauty."

I blush, enjoying each of his gentle touches. I change the subject, rubbing his leg, "You didn't tell me what happened in Canada."

"Don't worry yourself, I have it under control. I just want you to rest," he answers pleasantly. *Ah rest.* After being drowned and roughed up, I am quite tired. And Eric is amazingly comfortable. Within moments, I'm fast asleep as he continues to indulge me in his soft touch and enchanting smell.

XVII

Briellyn

I wake up to see Eric sleeping while still sitting up. I can feel the plane descending so I glance down at my watch to see that its 6:25PM. He looks so peaceful sleeping that I don't want to wake him. I gently caress his cheek. "Eric?" I whisper. He slowly opens his eyes and stares into mine. His eyes try to adjust to the sight of my face. "We're descending sweetheart," I whisper.

He grumbles for a moment, like he's not quite awake, "Reese."

"No, it's Brie," I squint and gently push his shoulder a little to wake him up more. He jolts and starts smiling at me then sits up. He raises his arms above his head and yawns.

"I'm shocked I feel asleep," he states, "I haven't been able to sleep very well in weeks. You're so comfortable."

"Uh huh," I reply coyly wondering why he called me by the other name. "*Just curious*, who is Reese?"

He sits forward and swings his legs over the side of the bed, "The doctor?"

"No, you called me Reese when you woke up," I add.

"I don't know why I would call you that. The only Reese I know is the doctor you'll meet in Canada and she looks nothing like you."

"Oh," I reply. *Who cares Brie, leave it alone.* It doesn't make any sense for me to pry.

"Prepare for landing," Sheila's voice booms over the intercom.

I lay down and brace myself, waiting for the planes wheels to hit the runway. Eric just sits there, staring in amusement. The plane touches down and begins to slow. He immediately stands up and turns around to help me out of the bed. When I stand up next to him, he grabs my chin and takes another look at my jaw.

"Nothing a little makeup can't cover," I assure him as I gently pull his hand down off of my face. He silently acknowledges my statement with a forced smile. I walk over to grab my shoes as he bends down and puts his own on.

"Your sister should be waiting for us," he slips one shoe on and is working on the other. He stands up and glances down at me.

"Perfect," I reply as I put a little concealer on my face so that my nephew doesn't notice the bruising. There's nothing I can really do about the swelling but hopefully he doesn't notice it. Layla gave me a scarf to use back at the warehouse, so I'll wrap that around my neck to cover the bruises there. Eric walks up behind me and places his hands on my shoulders, gently rubbing them, "I'm going to go check on everyone." I give him a simple nod as he leaves the room.

Kalil is sitting up, waiting for Joseph to open the plane's door while Danny, Jenna, and Layla are all sleeping. Nick is sifting through his phone and Dr. Strassmore is staring out of the window. Eric approaches Kalil and whispers, "I'm not sure how long we'll be here but I don't think longer than an hour or two. I'll let you know. I'll bring back food for everyone though." I walk into the main cabin and quietly shut the door behind me. Eric signals for me to walk over so that we can disembark the plane. I can see my sister in the distance. I run off the plane and rush to her, hugging her tight. "Hey Sky," I mumble in her ear.

She hugs me back and chuckles, "Hey you. I can't help but notice you're glowing in the dark right now Brie, what's going on?"

I release her from my grip and look down at myself. "Oh, it's my new um, specialty. Besides the vision, ya know?" I focus on getting my emotions under control to tune down the radiance.

Eric kisses her on the cheek, "Hey Sky."

She looks at him and smiles, "Hi Eric." She points back to her truck, "Well lets go, I know you two can't stay long." We follow her back to her truck.

"Mind if I drive?" I ask, hoping she'll say yes so that she is seated on my right side where my swelling isn't noticeable.

She nods, "Sure," and throws me the keys. Eric hops in the backseat and we begin driving to her house. Thank goodness it's only a few miles away. "I have the nanny watching the kids, Reilly is on his way home. We should just about meet him there," she holds my hand.

"Perfect," I reply. *Good, this way I can say good bye to them properly, altogether.*

About eight minutes later we pull up in front of the house. I park at the curb instead of in the driveway knowing that we have to go back to the airport soon. Eric looks around while Skyla and I just stare at each other. I lay my forehead on the top of the steering wheel and look at her. "I hate that I'm going to miss Christmas with the kids," I pout.

She rubs the top of my back, "Oh, I know. Don't worry though. We'll celebrate when you get back." We are blinded by approaching lights but see that it's Reilly. He turns and pulls into the driveway. Reilly hops out of his car and waves at us as he begins to walk our direction.

I wave back and about to open my door when I hear glass break and a sharp sudden piercing noise. Reilly stops cold in his tracks and his shirt becomes laden with blood. I see him drop to his knees as my sister screams in horror. *What. The. Fuck.* Eric reaches in the front and tells us to keep our heads down. My heart skips a beat or two from the replay in my head.

Eric hops out of the back seat on the passenger side and creeps towards the front of the vehicle. "Stay in the car!" he yells outs.

"My babies are in the house," my sister keeps repeating between her tears and terror. Eric pulls out a gun and makes his way to the front door of the house. The shot came from *inside* the house. Eric can see a bullet hole through the side of the first story window and a dead woman on the floor but no sign of the kids. I put my finger over my mouth to quiet my sister and attempt to look up over the bottom of the car door's window. I can see Reilly lying in the driveway and Eric at the front door. He kicks open the front door and runs for the staircase. I hear three more shots fired as I tuck back behind the metal casing of the car door.

Eric reaches the top of the steps and calls for Clayton. "Eric?" his frightened whisper escapes from the hallway closet. Eric quickly walks over to the closet and sees him hiding there with Leah in his arms. He picks Leah up from him and then grabs Clayton. Whoever it is that is firing, is making its way up the stairs. I peek up again to see if I can spot anything else and I notice Reilly twitch. "Reilly is alive," I whisper to Skyla who is having a hard time maintaining self-control. My adrenaline kicks in. I glance over to the kicked in door and see what appears to be a mechanical human on the second step.

Eric, with the kids in his arms, runs into the back bedroom and barricades the door. He puts Clayton down so that he can grab a blanket, "Ok, now I need you to hold your sister and I will hold you both." Clayton nods, grabbing his sister from Eric. Eric then begins wrapping them into the blanket. I hear another shot.

"Fuck this," I take a deep breath, start the truck, and quickly reverse it into the driveway. "Hop in the back," I command Skyla as I push the trunk button to open it. I throw open my door, and hop out; staying low to the ground as I creep to Reilly. I place my forefinger and middle finger to his throat, looking for a pulse. *Slow but steady.* I hear another window crash as Eric glides down to the ground at the backside of the house. Two additional shots are fired as he runs for the vehicle. He has a golden aura around him and the kids that I've never seen before. I grab Reilly under his arms and try to get him into the trunk. Skyla opens the back door holding her arms out for Eric to hand over her children. Eric then runs back to me, "I told you to stay in the vehicle!"

"Help me get him in the back!" I plead as I continue trying to drag him. Eric picks him up and throws him over his shoulder. "Get us out of here!" he quietly screams at me, signaling me back to the driver's seat. He gets Reilly in the back area and shuts the trunk as I climb back into the front seat. Two more shots are fired and then two additional shots, from what sound like a different weapon. I speed off to the end of the block and notice a car speed off from the house, following our direction. I quickly make the turn to head back towards the airport. Eric pulls out his phone, "Kalil, we are on our way back. Tell Doc to prep, I have a gunshot victim and he's in and out of consciousness. Something attacked us at Skyla's house. We'll be there in five minutes!" He lifts Reilly's shirt to get a better view of the wound, "It's a flesh wound. None of your organs were hit." He rolls him over, "Bullet went straight through, you're just losing a little more blood than I would like. Stay awake for me Reilly; I've got some help for you on standby."

Eric takes off his shirt and balls it up to apply pressure to Reilly's wound. I keep glancing in my rear view mirror and see the head lights. "I think we may have company," I yell out to Eric. He looks behind him and calls Kalil again, "We've got someone following us, be ready." Leah is screaming and Clayton is trying to be as calm as possible. He looks toward the back of the vehicle and sees all the blood from his father. "Is my daddy going to die?" he sadly asks Eric, terrified by all the blood.

Eric gazes at the fearless child and flashes him a comforting smile, "Not if I can help it. You remember what we talked about right?" Clayton nods his head yes and continues to stare at his father, who's growing weaker by the second. Eric continues, "You were very brave today, keeping your baby sister safe. You will earn your wings in no time."

We arrive at the airport. Danny and Kalil are posted up with their weapons; Danny crouched down near the ground and Kalil standing up ready to fire. I stop the car as close to the plane as possible to provide them protection if they need to tuck behind the vehicle. I quickly get Skyla and Leah on the plane with Clayton following her close behind as Dr. Strassmore helps Eric get Reilly on the plane. They take him to the back room where doc had already setup a care station with lots of towels and such. Nick is standing at the planes entrance with his weapon ready and hands me a gun. We wait for the car that was following us from a distance to pull up.

Within thirty seconds of me standing there and ready to shoot, the car pulls up and comes to a screeching halt. "Get out of the car or we will shoot!" Kalil demands. It's difficult to see who, or what, is behind the wheel with the lights so bright. I hear the car door open. Danny is low to the ground with his rifle, he has a better line of sight than the rest of us because of the lighting.

"Slowly step out of the vehicle, hands above your head," Danny yells.

The figure steps one foot out, hands above his head, then the other foot. He stands up and yells, "Don't shoot. Brie it's me!"

I lower my weapon, "Justin?" I walk to the bottom of the steps and say to the guys, "It's okay." I trot over to make sure I can see him and that it's actually Justin. It is but I'm wary. "You followed us from the house?" I glare at him cautiously.

"Yes, I gave you cover fire. The last two shots were from me," His sad, shocked face tells me it's really him. I quickly embrace him as he holds me tight. "Is Reilly going to be ok?"

I shake my head, "I don't know yet but I think so. We happened to have our doctor on board and he's looking at him right now. Eric said it looked like a flesh wound."

I quickly walk him back to the plane, "Justin, this is…"

"Justin, good to see you again man," Danny interrupts, giving him a fist bump.

"How do you two know each other?" I ask, blurting out something so unimportant at the moment.

"Long story but we go back a ways," Justin says.

Everyone waves at him as he walks with me on board. Kalil and Danny load up and get the plane's door shut. Kalil shakes Justin's hand, "Good to see you brother."

Justin looks at him and replies, "Good to see you all but we should probably go. No telling how far behind that thing is." Kalil notifies the pilots to take off. I begin to walk to my sister, she's on the couch holding Leah and crying her eyes out. But Clayton runs to me and hugs my legs. I pick him up and sit next to Skyla. "Hey, hey, shhh. It's okay, you're safe now. You're *all* safe now. I know Reilly will be fine, he's in great hands," I wrap my left arm around her while still holding Clayton in my right.

Justin greets Layla and Jenna before approaching us. "Hey Sky," he leans down on his knees and grabs her free hand, "It's going to be okay."

Eric finally comes out of the back room. "Reilly will be just fine," he rolls his sleeve down. I could see he had a bandage on his forearm. "He's sedated but he's going to be just fine."

I have Justin sit where I am while I stand to walk over to Eric. "Are you okay?" I stare in his eyes and then at his arm.

"I'm fine, Doc just needed to give Reilly some blood is all," he gives me an encouraging smile and looks at Skyla, "You can go back there now Sky." Skyla hands Leah to Justin and tells Clayton to stay put. She disappears into the back room.

"Can I speak to you," I query Eric, "In private… for just a moment." I glance at him desperately and he follows me into the bathroom. I cross my arms as he shuts the door and locks it.

"Do you want to tell me what all happened back there? My father dies last week, by a termagant no less, and now my sister and her family are attacked… at *her* home," I quietly caution him. This can't be coincidental.

Before he can say anything I continue, "And how is it that you are able to give my brother-in-law blood?" *You know, because you're an angel and all.*

He looks at me strangely, "I'm O negative, I can give blood to anybody."

More lies... I'm not supposed to know his secret. But I do and I want answers now. My sister and the kids, and now Kalil, are the only family I have. I would die inside if anything were to happen to them. "Do you know why Barbanon would go after my family? That... *machine.* What was it? I've never seen anything like it," I ask, toning my accusations down.

"I've never seen one either but it is certainly the work of dark magic. A camouflaging spell making it transparent to the human eye, poisonous rounds. I'm honestly not sure why they would come after your family Brielle," he comes closer to me and lightly caresses my jaw, "But I promise you, I will keep your family safe. I'll put them up in a nice place where Reilly can rest and get better. He'll need a few weeks to recover. But you have to trust me, I never meant for any of this to happen."

I sigh. Arms crossed over my chest and staring at the wall. I decide to blurt out, "I bugged your phone."

"*What?*" he asks, his lips curling slightly.

"I bugged your phone. That's how Justin knew how to find us," I say again, staring with tears in my eyes, "I should have trusted you. But I was worried that you weren't telling me everything. I felt horrible the moment I did it but I think you should know now. For the record, I trust you *now.* Although I'm sure with my confession, you don't trust me."

He pulls me in close and kisses me. It's unexpected but my body welcomes it with a tingling burst of goosebumps across my skin. His hands gently cradle my neck and face as his lips carefully massage mine. I uncross my arms and wrap them around him. He releases the kiss, "Thank you." *Well that's one way to seal a loyalty deal.* "You have just made me the happiest man alive," he smiles then kisses me again. He leans in closer. I can't help but to back up towards the wall as the plane ascends from the ground. I have never experienced the feeling that I get when he kisses me. All of my worries disappear, my heart flutters, my mind goes blank, my knees grow weak, and it feels like every inch of my skin comes alive. *If I believed in love at first sight, I know Eric would be the one.* But my inexperience in the romance department leaves me reluctant to pursue my feelings with him. I have always ended up disappointed and something tells me he will be no different. It would surely lead to nothing but frustration and disappointment once he returns home.

The others I've dated are just men and even Justin is but a man. But Eric is not, he's so much more than that. I want more from him but the only outcome is his return to Empyria. "Come on," he suggests, unlocking the bathroom door then grabs my hand to leave. When we walk out, I glance over at Kalil who gives me an approving nod.

"I'm going to go check on Reilly and Sky; I'll be out in a moment," I whisper to Eric as I point to the back room door. He nods his head and makes his way to the main cabin as I open the door and walk in the room. Skyla is laying behind Reilly with his head in her lap. He's awake. "Hey there Brie," he mumbles as I stroll over and hold his hand. I sit on my knees next to him. He manages, "That was a brave thing you did for me. Thank you."

I motion with my head trying to hold back tears and mumble, "Of course. I would never leave you, *any of you*, behind. You're family." Skyla smiles down at him and leans in to kiss him, carefully cradling his head. "You both have had an exhausting evening. This bed is very comfortable, try to get some sleep. If you need me, just hit this button and I'll come running," I point to the same button that Eric had shown me earlier. It dawns on me that had we not decided to see her, she could very well be dead and I'd be getting a call from the local police station. *Thank God for Eric's generosity.*

I stand, briefly watching her and Reilly interact with one another before leaving the room. The way he is hurt and the concern on her face. This was me and Eric with the roles reversed not even two hours ago. I walk out into the main cabin, and look over at Justin holding Leah. Clayton clambered into Eric's arms, holding him like his life depended on it. Eric looks relaxed and happy, pressing his face against the top of Claytons' head. Baby Leah is fast asleep in Justin's arms. *Both men I care about holding two precious parts of my life.* 'Uncle Kal' and Danny are creating new plans for where my family is going to stay. Layla and Jenna are making something to eat in the little kitchen and Dr. Strassmore is staring at me. I lip, "Thank you," to him. He winks at me as I sit across from him, leaning back in the seat and turning my head to look at Eric once more. Maybe Eric and I *do* have something more between us. I'm not sure exactly what it is yet but for once in my life, *even amidst the recent danger*, I feel balanced and complete.

*   *   *   *   *   *

Three hours later…

Everyone on the plane is sound asleep with the exception of the pilots. Joseph strolls into the main cabin and quietly taps Eric on the shoulder. He radiates a light shade of blue as Eric looks at him and gently lays Clayton down onto the couch. Joseph proceeds to walk into the kitchen but stops when he sees me, sleeping. He stares at me for a moment then proceeds into the kitchen area, with Eric close behind, and shuts the door. Joseph may be standing in front of Eric physically, but the glow molded his appearance to a different man, "I expected to hear from you late last night," Eric sternly states, keeping his voice low.

"I'm sorry. The moon wasn't at the right alignment until now. How are you, Royce?"

"Grandfather, have you seen what's been happening? I'm far from fine. Someone is after Brie's family and I'm sure it's to get to Brie. Can you tell me why anyone would want to kill her entire family? This isn't anything like the others, I feel like I'm being left in the dark here..."

"Barbanon has many tricks and isolating her from many who have gotten close has been one of his schemes. She is growing more and more powerful each day she's around you, killing her family would send her, *and her new talents*, spiraling out of control."

"I've thought about that."

"Something about you is different. That's not what you really want to ask me," Palidon probes.

"I know the rules, but... is it ever possible for Empyreans to fall for a human?" Eric stares at his grandfather's spirit concerned yet hopeful.

"You know you can only fall in love once, Royce. Empyreans are created to watch over humans. They may have been born from us in the beginning, but we are incapable of experiencing true love with them. Have fun if you need to. Soon you'll be home, where you are meant to be."

"Fun? You think that's what this is about or what any of this has been for me?! Interacting with countless women to find twenty one near matches and then the last one after two hundred and forty years on this planet happens to be so remarkably different, that I'm…"

"No you're not. Her genetic anomalies are simply clouding your judgement. We won't have this discussion again."

"But why *her*, grandfather? Why does the fate of humanity rest in *her* hands?"

"The child in the other room, you know, the one who was laying on you? He and his sister are part of the last generation of mankind. God has taken away their ability to procreate over the years and Skyla's children will never be able to have life beyond their own. Neither will anyone else born within the last fifteen years."

"But what has that got to do with Brielle? I know that you mentioned her saving humanity but I thought that was from apocalyptic circumstances. Not infertility."

"Oh, the human race is in for a heap of trouble with both if you are unsuccessful in your quest. Once those gems are found, you will be able to go back in time and kill Barbanon. For good this time. It's believed he's found a way to produce his own children thanks to stem cell research using human women as hosts. It would mean war for Empyria if he succeeds. So He's gotten rid of the ability to give birth for women altogether. The gems will help you and Brielle to travel back in time and kill Barbanon for good. The moon is almost out of alignment, we'll talk again on the next full moon. Don't get caught up in the idea that you're in love with her, *because you're not*. It's impossible."

Joseph faints momentarily. Eric grabs him to prevent him from falling to the ground. He regains consciousness almost immediately, "What happened?"

"You were getting a glass of water and as I came in, you fainted," Eric quickly responds.

"I don't even remember getting up out of the cockpit," Joseph holds his hand to his head and stands up.

"It's okay, it's been a long day for all of us," Eric replies.

Joseph walks out of the kitchen back into the cockpit. Eric stands there, shaking his head, clearly aggravated by Palidon's words.

* * * * * * *

Palidon's spirit returns to Empyria. He is sitting in this golden chair next to Senon. Senon looks at his brother, "Well?"

"It's her. It's exactly her. I thought you said this wasn't supposed to happen, that it couldn't happen."

"Surely it can't be that bad, brother. It may not be what you think."

"Oh no. It's worse, much worse I fear. I think it's time we pay a visit to that daughter of mine, Rhea."

XVIII

Briellyn

It's midnight in Quebec City. The plane ride was annoyingly quiet but we made it there safely. My sister and her family are carted off the moment we land to a safe haven for Reilly to recuperate and heal, while the rest of us are on our way to the local château to rest before driving to the base at 1:00PM.

"So, I wanted to ask you," Eric begins, holding my waist as I wave goodbye to my sister and our transport pulls up, "Briellyn, I would prefer it if you would stay in my room while we await the transport this afternoon, if you don't mind. I don't want you out of my sight with everything that's going on and…" He hesitates, "if that's uncomfortable for you I can…"

"Shhh," I hold my hand up to his face and smile, "No, I can't think of anywhere else I would rather be. I know I'm safe with you." I stare at him coyly as the entire crew climbs into the large passenger van. Eric and I are the last to board so he and I are closest to the door. The cargo plane with all of the gear, new vehicles, and remaining crew won't arrive for another couple hours and it will take a little while to inventory everything and clear it through customs. Meanwhile, we will be getting some rest before leaving Quebec City to get to the base, which is about a three hour drive inland.

We arrive at the Fairemont Le Château and check into our rooms. Eric's lingering concerns stem to all of the crew, pairing everyone together in either a studio suite room with two beds or a suite with two bedrooms. He doesn't want to take any chances given what we are dealing with. Jenna, Camille, and Layla are paired together, as well as Danny, Nick, and Dr. Strassmore; Kalil and Justin; Sheila and Joseph; and lastly Eric and I. Our rooms are all on the same floor.

Eric opens the door to our room and we enter a gorgeous French modern décor in hues of gold and blues. The bedroom is a separate room in the back and the front room is a quaint parlor space that has a bathroom of its own. The space easily sits ten people, perfect for our rendezvous with the rest of the team prior to the transport pick up. Eric shuts the door behind me and utilizes every lock. He puts our bags down and looks around, then locks his eyes onto me. "Is this ok?" he asks as I continue to admire the décor.

Still not used to the pampering but I'm not arguing. I nod my head, giggling, "Yes, this is beautiful. You've been more than generous."

He lets out a wholesome chuckle and walks to the bedroom, opening the doors for me to enter. "You can have the bed, I'll take the sofa," he suggests as I walk past him into the bedroom. I turn around to look at him and grin. He's such a complete gentleman; I'm not sure how I ever doubted him. But I guess someone who's lived through the end of the 18th century through the 21st century *would* be a complete gentleman. It certainly explains his classy tendencies and use of certain words.

"I'm going to hop in the shower. I still have a little bit of Reilly's blood on me. *But...* Did you want to shower? Because I don't mind if you wish to go first," he mentions to me as he grabs the bags to bring them into the bedroom. I look down and see some blood on my pants from when I tried to move Reilly.

"Good idea," I mumble to him. *My inner vixen wouldn't mind showering together though.*

He smiles and gestures towards the bathroom, "Ladies first." I smile back and grab my bag from him, making my way into the bathroom and closing the door. I quickly undress and shower while he waits for me to be done.

Eric begins to undress; throwing his bloodied clothes into the trash then wrapping a towel around his waist. He grabs his toothbrush from his bag and brushes his teeth in the bathroom that's attached to the parlor. After he's done, he removes the cushions from the sofa bed and pulls out the mattress to prepare it. I throw on a robe, open the bathroom door while toting my bag and call out to him, "The shower is all yours!" I place my bag on the bed and begin sifting through it. He walks through the bedroom to the bathroom, shirtless. *The sight of his magnificent physique never seems to get old.* I immediately lose focus on what I'm looking for within my bag. Everything feels like the first time with him, even his appearance. Each kiss has given me the same fluttering effect, but seeing him shirtless sends a different signal to my body. He shuts the door behind him, allowing me to regain my attention on what I'm looking for in my bag. I slip on the PJs that are packed and put the bag on the floor, holding onto my toothbrush and nightcap. I quickly brush my teeth and come back to shut the blinds and pull the coverings down the bed. I shut the room light off and climb under the blankets.

Eric shuts the water off and grabs his towel to dry off. Still troubled by Palidon's words, he rubs the moisture from the mirror and stares at himself. He shuts his eyes for a moment and takes a deep breath then mutters, "Don't get caught up." His eyes swiftly open as he presses his lips together and walks over to the bathroom door. Quietly, he opens the door and sees me lying down with all of the lights off. Very gently, he tip toes past the bed and into the living room where a small lamp is on to guide him. He quickly dresses in a pair of boxers and a shirt then pulls the blankets on the sofa bed down.

"Eric?" I call out to him from the comfort of the bed. I'm lying face up with my arms crossed over my stomach.

"Yes, Briellyn," he replies softly.

"Would you mind if I lay next to you?" I ask, remembering how great I'd slept with my head on his lap in the plane. He walks to the doorway of the bedroom and stands there.

"Why? What's the matter?" he asks, concern in his tone.

I lift up onto my elbow and gaze at him, "Nothing is wrong; it's just that I slept so well earlier knowing you were right there. After seeing Reilly like that today, I would just feel more comfortable if you were right beside me. But if that would make you uncomfortable…"

He flashes me a quick grin, "How about I come to you instead?" He strolls over and climbs into the bed as I scoot over to give him room. The king size bed is more than large enough for the both of us to remain on our respective sides without even having to touch each other. *If only it were smaller.*

I lay my head down while still lying on my side facing him, "Thank you."

He runs his hand on the side of my face, gently caressing my cheek. I close my eyes, embracing his touch.

He whispers, "It is I who should be thanking you."

Every part of me wants to pursue this moment further but my mind is telling me not to do it. I don't think I can take a rejection from him twice. My heart is beating faster with each longing touch to my face but I know this won't last. I grab his hand, kiss it, and whisper to him, "Goodnight," rolling over to face the other direction. He mutters it back to me and I can hear him get comfortable on his side. I stare at the wall for a little bit until my eyes grow heavy. Before I realize it, I've drifted off into a deep slumber once more.

* * * * * * *

Meanwhile in the room with Justin & Kalil…

Kalil

Justin has just showered, dressed, and continues to pace in the room. I glare at him while I sit at the table and go through the last bit of paperwork before going to bed. Justin stops and stares at me, "How long have you known?"

I put the last document down and look back at Justin, "Known what?"

"I know that you and Eric knew about my taps… question is, how long have you known?" He gestures angrily, his tone trickled with aggravation.

I underestimated him. I shake my head and chuckle, and then interlace my fingers. I look back up at him, "Does it matter?"

"I know somehow Eric used me to get Brielle to trust him that much more but I don't know why. All of the surveillance equipment came from guys whom I now realize work for Eric," he frowns. He shrugs his shoulders in disappointment. *"But why use me?* I thought Eric and I were friends. I mean I'm grateful that he helped saved my best friends life but this… I'm feeling slighted," he crosses his arms.

Hypocrite. I shake my head again, "Funny you mention thinking you were friends when you bugged Eric's phone. Either way, Eric had nothing to do with it." I can't help but laugh. He's barking up the wrong tree but I admire his spirit.

Justin exhales audibly, "Come on, give me a break, Kal. Stop trying to protect him for whatever reason. I thought you and I were friends too. And I didn't do it to betray his friendship, I did it to ensure Brie's security."

I raise my hand, motioning for him to stop, "I'm not sure how you realized we knew, but the men who gave you the surveillance equipment actually work for *me*. They know nothing of Eric aside from his name on their paychecks. If anyone set you up, it was me. But I didn't set you up technically."

Justin gives a unconvinced frown, "*Right…*"

"I didn't. When the men came to me telling me what you needed, I authorized it. I wanted to know what it was you were trying to do. And you did exactly what I thought you would with it. It allowed me to see if Brielle held loyalty to someone she's known her whole life or would trust a complete stranger over him. I was quite relieved she took your side."

Justin stares at him confused, "Wait, so you're trying to tell me that you *wanted* her to tap his phone based on what I told her?"

I nod, "Well someone who has no loyalty to someone they've known their whole life will certainly never have loyalty to a stranger. I was inadvertently protecting Eric, at first; just as you were protecting Brie."

"Protecting him from what? Brielle would never hurt anyone, not in a million years," Justin squints, frustration growing in his tone.

I laugh boldly, "I'm not afraid of her hurting him physically, Justin. Come on, you know as well as I do those two have an inexplicable chemistry. You had your chance with her and you blew it. *Get over it.*" I watch him carefully.

Justin gazes at the ground, remembering how Brielle's body language was when he first saw her interact with Eric. He smirks at the thought of how in denial she was. Deep down, he knew that Eric had a unique effect on her. He's never seen her act the way she does with Eric. He shakes off the bit of jealousy looming around him and stares back at me. "So you just used my own instincts against me... bravo," he sarcastically replies then claps his hands together. "Are you going to give me *all* the details yet? I think I've earned that right..."

"Sure, come sit down," I motion him over to have a seat with me at the table.

Briellyn

I begin moving around in my sleep; shivering, mumbling, and breathing heavily. Eric wakes up to my restlessness and looks over at me. I'm frowning with my eyes closed. Without hesitation, he slides close to me, pressing his body against the back of mine and wraps his arm around my waist. He whispers into my ear, "I'm right here. I won't let anyone hurt you." My restless movements cease immediately and my breathing slows back to normal. He snuggles closer to me and nestles his head behind mine. He breathes me in, the sweet smell of vanilla, coconuts, and hibiscus; smiling at the thought of doing this every night for the rest of his time with me, then frowns knowing his grandfather would never allow it. Subconsciously I slide my hand over his, embracing him completely. He smiles once more and lays his head down to go back to sleep.

*   *   *   *   *   *   *

The sun is peaking through the very small opening in the curtains. My eyes open to a still very dim lit room and a clock that says 7:27. I can hear Eric breathing directly behind me and notice my hand over top of his. I can't help but grin. I remember having an altercation with my father in my sleep last night and oddly enough, Eric was there to comfort me. Here he is, cuddled up next to me when I wake up and it's the best thing that I've experienced in my life… *thus far.* There were times in college that Justin and I would sleep in the bed together, that friend zone type of cuddle when he was in between girlfriends. *But this.* This is different for me. *Something about it much more sentimental for me.*

Of course my whole life I endure crappy relationships to then fall for an angel. *Literally, a freaking angel!* Sounds like a sad love song. Maybe this is what Rhea meant by experiencing love. Love doesn't last forever for anyone, but this may not last very long at all.

'It is better to have loved and lost, than never to have loved at all' is something my dad used to always say about my mother. He never got remarried; he never even dated anyone after she died. He used to tell me that no one could ever make him feel the way that she did. Is that my fate too?

Enough of the pondering about the future, it's about time that I start living for the now. Who knows, I may not make it out of this mission. I roll over onto my back and turn my face towards Eric. He looks so peaceful lying here next to me. No worry or panic about today's issues with the base or training, just relaxed and stress-free. I don't want to wake him but given the time he would probably want to be woken up. I gently touch his nose with my finger, "Wake up handsome." He doesn't move, he continues to breathe easy and sleep soundly. I place my hand onto his face and kiss his forehead and say his name once again, "Eric, it's time to get up." He begins to move around and slowly open his eyes. The little bit of sunlight coming into the room catches his eyes just right as they carry a gorgeous light blue shimmer. I have never seen them so light before.

Once his eyes adjust a little bit he stares at me, smiling. I smile back at him as he buries his face into my shoulder and continues to hold me tight. Every part of me could lay like this forever, but we both know there's a lot to be done. "Good morning beautiful," he mumbles, "I can't believe how comfortable you are. The only time I sleep seems to be next to you." He rolls over and stretches as I slip out from under the covers. "Where are you going?" he inquires, rolling back over and placing his hand on my spot of the bed.

"It's time we get the day started, I'm sure you have loads to do. And so do I," I stroll into the bathroom and shyly shut the door.

He rolls over onto his back rubbing his face and stares at the ceiling. Then he sits up. He clambers out of bed and walks to the parlor bathroom. I come back out of the bathroom and grab my toothbrush. Walking back into the bathroom, I pull the night cap off of my head and begin to brush. I need to make sure I look okay by the time Eric comes waltzing back in here. As I'm brushing with my right hand, I'm fixing my hair with my left; fluffing it to make it look fuller after sleeping on it. After a couple minutes, I'm done brushing my teeth but my hair is unacceptable. I grab a hair band and put it into a high ponytail. I wander back into the bedroom once again as Eric is now brushing his teeth in the parlor bathroom. I grab my phone and look to see if I have any messages yet. *Still nothing from Eryn.* I can feel my heart begin to race, worried that something may have happened to her. Seeing as demons came after my sister, I'm worried something could have happened to Eryn. Although Justin and I are wary of Eryn and the possibility of her being more than what we originally thought, I still have love for her. I decide to just dial her number.

"Hello?" a spry and chipper man's voice answers the phone.

I glance down at the number to make sure I chose the right contact for speed dial. *Yup, it's the right one.* "Hi, um, who is this?" I inquire, wondering who Eryn is messing with now.

The voice on the other side pauses for a moment and then begins speaking again, "Brielle…"

"I'm sorry, have we met?" I ask. The sound of my name coming from this person is all too familiar.

"Yes, of course, sorry. It's Fiore."

She is sleeping with him. I clear my throat, "Oh, um, hi. I'm really caught off guard by this... um... because it's so early there. Are you um, with Eryn?"

"Yes, yes of course I am. I have answered her phone, no? We are at the office already."

"Oh, wow. It's a bit early isn't it?" *And here I thought I was a workaholic.*

"I like to get things started early in the morning, leads to a much more productive day. Besides, I have a very important deal to keep with a certain CEO. I promised her results while she was gone and I'm a man of my word."

I can't help but giggle. *I guess he's not so bad.* Maybe even kind of charming, "I guess you do." If I'm talking to him, I know Eryn is fine.

"Things are great here though. We expected to hear from you sooner but we just assumed you were busy. How are things going?"

"They are... well... *complicated.* But good. I'm not sure how often I'll be able to call and keep in touch after this but, by all means, please email me," I remark as Eric comes back into the room. He gives me a strange look and quietly asks me who I'm speaking to. I put up my finger, asking him to wait a moment.

"We can certainly do that. I think you'll be happy to hear that I have your spring line being featured at Holiday Fashion Week in

Milan. It's sponsored by a certain favorite designer of yours with the initials C. L…"

"Oh my goodness, you didn't?!" my voice heightens and I begin excitedly running in place.

"Indeed I have my dear. He can't wait to meet you," Fiore chuckles.

"Well… I won't be able to physically be there but by all means please bring Julia. I'm sure between you and her, it'll be perfect. Has Stacy given you the last sketches that I was working on before I left?" *I hate that I can't be there for such a huge honor.*

"Why yes, of course. They are amazing by the way. I'm truly looking forward to working more *closely* with you when you return."

"*Ya know*… I have to say I was wrong about you Fiore. I'm glad that you have become part of our little family," I awkwardly smile, feeling bad that I misread him.

"Oh Ms. Donado, I certainly hope to become a more *permanent* member of it. Once I prove myself of course. I believe we can really get quite a few *other worldly* things accomplished. You know, really seal the deal."

"Oh yes, most definitely. But um, I have to go. Please give Eryn my love."

"I sure will. Don't forget to have fun. Chao," he replies smoothly.

"Chao," I chuckle as I finish the conversation and hang up the phone.

"You're in a great mood," Eric suggests as he walks closer and puts his toothbrush in his bag.

"That was Fiore," I smile and begin explaining why.

Eric rolls his eyes, "What'd he want?"

"I actually called him," I reply.

"*Why?*" he stops what's he's doing and looks at me. A hint of jealousy is present in his tone and body language. *It's kind of sexy coming from him.*

"I mean, I called Eryn and he answered," I correct myself.

"Are they…?" he suggests, looking upward.

"Oh no. I thought that too but no. Just getting an early start on work. Apparently my favorite shoe designer wants to feature some of my spring line at his Holiday Fashion Week though!" I begin smiling uncontrollably as I sift through my phone emails. Eric laughs at my childish grin.

"That's great Brie, I'm so happy for you," he continues filtering through his bag. He finds the shirt he's looking for and walks over to me. He presses his hand against my chin and looks at my jaw. The bruise is nice and dark now, incredibly easy to see now I've put my hair up.

I stop smiling and grow self-conscious. "Does it look bad?" I ask him, frowning while staring into his eyes.

He smiles, "Nothing on you could ever look bad, not even that." He walks into the bathroom and grabs a towel to wash his face. My heart rate surges from his compliment and my skin flushes with both anxiety and desire. Funny Fiore mentioned me having fun, *I was just thinking the same thing,* and Eric is allowing me to do just that. How is it that he always knows just the right thing to say at precisely the right moment? It's irritating and arousing at the same time. He finishes washing his face and walks back towards me, "Hungry?" He asks, smiling.

Not just for food. "Brie?" he asks again.

"Oh, um, I could eat. Sure," I smile and nod. "I'm just going to go ahead and shower once more. I'm feeling a little... *warm*," I unknowingly give my lip a gentle nibble.

He walks over to me and puts the back of his hand to my forehead, "You do feel a little warm. All that good news may have your energy levels out of whack. A shower should certainly help." Yes. *Something is sending my energy levels* through the roof but it's not the good news. I proceed to shower as he goes on to order room service, shutting the bedroom doors behind him.

Before Eric could call room service, he receives a call from Kalil on his cell phone.

"Hey there Kal, good morning," Eric greets him.

"Well good morning to you too. You sound... rested," Kalil replies, a smile heard in his voice.

"Indeed I am. I haven't gotten great sleep like this in ages," Eric smiles.

"I know. I'm so relieved to hear that."

"What's going on? I was just about to order Brielle and I some breakfast. Care to join us? As a matter of fact, round everyone up and we will all eat here in my suite. Go over today's schedule and what not. Is everything going as planned?"

"Yes. The remaining men and the cargo have all arrived. Everything has been unloaded, put together, and is clearing through customs now. They may be a little early actually."

"Fantastic! That sounds good, have everyone come by in about thirty minutes. I'll order pancakes, omelets, bacon, and what not."

"Ok then, see you in thirty boss," Kalil promptly hangs up. Eric places his cell phone on the end table then picks up the hotel phone to order enough food for everyone. He turns around to the sound of the bedroom doors opening. I'm standing there in a towel, peeking from behind one of the doors.

Eric strolls over, "Do you need something Brielle?"

I give a nervous chuckle, "Um. I don't have any clothes for the day. Would you happen to know where my combat attire is? All I have are undergarments and accessories in here."

"Oh," he walks over to a duffle bag near the door and zips it open. As he digs out my pants, a shirt, and my boots he teases, "Well, there's nothing sexier than a woman in lingerie with a gun holster and her weapon." He stands up and walks to me, handing me the items. I cross my arms and give him a seductive stare. He raises his eyebrows, "Here you are my love."

"Thanks," I nervously laugh as I creep from behind the door to grab the items. "I'll be out in just a moment," I grin at him and shut the door as he tries to steal a peek.

He walks away and grabs his laptop from the bag next to the duffle and sits down on the couch as he waits for me to finish getting dressed. "Don't get caught up," he mumbles to himself again. He checks his emails and any additional information regarding the status of the injured men from yesterday's attack.

I open the bedroom doors completely and stroll over to him. "Well, what do you think?" I ask him, posing very model-esque for the first time in the official mission attire. Black cargo straight leg pants; black boatneck, long sleeve dri-fit shirt; dark brown crisscrossed on the hip and leg gun holster; and mid-calf lace-up combat boots. I leave my hair up in a ponytail and used a little makeup to cover the bruises on my jaw and neck. Overall, I feel battle ready and prepared to kick some demonic mercenary asses. He raises his eyebrows and a grin creeps onto his face.

He puts his laptop down and stands up, looking at me from every angle. "You look amazing in a dress, but this is… this suits you. Hold on, one final touch," Eric gestures me to hold on and walks over to the duffle bag. He digs into the side pocket, pulling out a pair of gloves. He approaches me again and grabs my hand. He slips one of the gloves onto my right hand; they are fingerless and made from a material I've never seen or felt before.

"These are really nice," I grin at him and then look down as he continues to adjust the glove, "What are they made of?"

"It's a special man-made material that allows you to use your powers more freely through the fabric. It acts like a medium. I have a pair and when I found out that you could channel energy into an electric pulse, I had a pair made for you too."

I find his gift to be incredibly sweet. "You never mentioned being able to do more than see Empyrean symbols…?" I inquire. I know he's an Empyrean but he hasn't mentioned being able to do anything more than see Empyrean symbols.

"I know. It's not something I go around telling just anyone. I'm sure you'll see it… *soon*," he teases.

"You're seriously not going to tell me?" I ask, raising my eyebrow and crossing my arms, slightly aggravated that he won't come clean about his heritage.

"A man has to keep some kind of mystery about him, doesn't he? I can't have you losing interest just yet. I love keeping you on your toes. It's entertaining," he crosses his arms and grins, "You are so put together all the time and ahead of everyone else, I can tell it eats you alive when you're in the dark about things. It sounds bad, but you're cute when you're flustered. You twist your mouth and do this cute little thing with your nose…"

I blush while placing my hands on my hips, roll my eyes, and turn around to walk back to the bedroom to grab my phone. "Well, touché. Two can play that game, Mr. Windsor," I chuckle. I grab my phone from the desk in the bedroom and walk back out. *Knock, knock, knock.* I walk past the couch and head for the door, "Is that the food?" I ask, excited to eat something and enjoy our private time together for possibly the last time in a hotel. I swing open the door to be greeted by seven friendly faces. "Hey guys… *what are y'all doing here?*" I try to hide my disappointment of their presence.

Justin gives me a curious look and proceeds to enter the room first, as he's closest to the door. He immediately hugs me, kisses me on the cheek, then waves at Eric while Sheila and Joseph walk in behind him. I'm greeting everyone else as they enter the room and last to come through the door is Kalil. "Morning Uncle Kal," I say to him as he leans in to give me a hug.

Justin quickly turns around, "*Uncle?*"

I immediately frown, forgetting that not everyone knows this precious information. I shut the door, pat Kalil's arm, and walk to Justin. "We need to talk love," I mumble to him, grabbing his hand and bringing him into the bedroom. I shut the doors and ask him to sit down.

Eric clears his throat, loud enough for everyone in the parlor to hear. They all turn away from the bedroom doors and look at him, "Let's give them their privacy. I'm sure Justin has a lot of questions."

Danny flops down onto the chair and props his feet up, "Yeah, me too. Why did she call you Uncle, Kalil? I would say there is a detail or two that you have neglected to mention…"

Eric and Kalil exchange glances then Eric nods his head. "Brielle, as it turns out, is a great descendant of my sister," Kalil states, rubbing his hands together. "There's no denying it anymore that Eric and I are more… *seasoned* than any of you have come to believe," he puts his hands on his hips and looks down. Camille holds her breath and shuts her eyes, unwilling to see the expressions on Danny's, Dr. Strassmore's, Nick's, Layla's, or Jenna's faces.

"And this means what exactly?" Dr. Strassmore chimes in.

"Eric and I have been friends for well over two hundred years. We've been searching for the woman of the prophecy the entire time. Brielle happens to be a 10th generation descendant of my younger sister, whom was taken from my village and never seen again a very long time ago. We dug up the information when we traced back her lineage, as we have done with every prospect. Eric and I are immortals," Kalil presses his lips together in a hard line.

Dr. Strassmore squints at Kalil and then looks over at Eric. "And you expect us to believe this?"

Eric nods his head, "Of course, we have no reason to pull your leg. It doesn't change anything about us though. We are just older than any of you were expecting." He chuckles then leans forward, interlocking his fingers.

Jenna folds her arms and exhales rather loudly. "Wow," she mumbles and begins cynically laughing.

"What?" Kalil asks her.

* * * * * * *

Justin and I are sitting on the bed together and I grab both of his hands. "As you already know, I'm special. You've seen me and these wonderful things within me evolve into what they are today. I love you so much for accepting me for me. I'm sorry that you have been put through the ringer over the last couple of days. I don't know what all Eric has told you, or hasn't told you, but Kalil is indeed my blood relative. My great Uncle."

"How though? I know all of your family and I thought you, your sister, and the kids were the last of the Donado's?"

"Not exactly, um, Kalil is about two hundred and eighty years old. He's immortal," I stare into Justin's eyes awaiting his reaction. I know I had a hard time believing it, so I know Justin will too.

He looks back into my eyes, glancing from one eye to the other, searching for a trace of hilarity. He smirks, "You can't expect me to believe that..."

"I wouldn't expect you to believe in termagants, demons, and shape shifting sirens either but you've seen them all with your own two eyes," I try to remain as convincing as possible.

"Well, how long have you known this?"

"Since my fifth night of training…"

"Ah, of course. The day that you didn't use the pin in your hair," he rubs his knees and looks away for a moment, "Well did your precious Eric tell you that he knew you tapped his phone?" He shakes his head in frustration.

"No, he didn't… But I told him I did," I stare at him in confusion.

He looks at me aggravated, "Kalil told me last night that Eric knew. Kalil set it up… *to protect Eric.* Well, Kalil technically didn't set it up I guess, he just used my own insecurities against me." He sighs as he rubs his knees, "He then told me what the gems are really for and why it's so important for Eric to travel back in time."

"I was never told what the machine was. It's a time machine? When would he travel back to? Did he tell you?" my mind is now racing. Go figure. This entire mission is not only to help Eric to get home, but return him to a time where I will never see him again. *How bittersweet.*

"Eric has to travel back in time to make things right. He didn't kill Barbanon like he thought he did all of those years ago. As a result, the transport that allows him passage between his home planet and here was severed… trapping him here. Once he goes back in time, where does that leave the rest of us? We are putting our asses on the line, *especially* you, only for him to leave us; *to leave you.*" He stands up and begins pacing. I can tell he's very angry with the situation. It seems with everything new he learns, the more frustrated he becomes.

"Why are you so angry?" I stare, worried. I've never seen him so emotional.

"Because I…" he stops pacing and looks at me. He sits down next to me and grabs my hands, "I see the way you look at him, Brie. I see something in you that I've never seen before, when you're with him. He gives you a certain happiness that no one ever could, not even me. I don't want you to lose that." He glowers, genuine worry dripping from each word.

I twist my face slightly, "Are you sure that's why? This isn't about our conversation about being together is…"

"No," he interrupts, "I've only ever wanted to see you happy. I love you and will always love you, even if you're with someone else. You would think I'd be happy, him leaving and all. I know you would give my offer a genuine chance if he did. But it eats me alive knowing that he'll always be in the back of your mind, never to be seen again. You… always incomplete." He motions.

I gaze into Justin's eyes; I can tell this is hard for him to say. I'm speechless. I lift my hand up to hold his face, warmed by his words. "I can see now why God put you in my life. You've *always* been my guiding light, even when you don't ultimately benefit from the result," I give him an encouraging smile.

He grabs my hand, "I *would* benefit from it. Seeing you happy is one of the few things I've always cared about. You and Sky mean the world to me. And Marcus, he's a good kid." He gets a little teary-eyed, "Honestly, I'm just glad that Eric let me in on this mission. Now I can make sure you're good, without delay."

I wrap my arms around him, embracing him tight. "Thank you for your blessing," I whisper into his ear.

"Yeah, yeah, yeah," he jokes as he wipes his eye and hugs me back, "Enough with the sentimental shit. I hope you know that this means I don't give up my habits though."

I let him go and grin, rolling my eyes and shaking my head, "Of course." We smile at each other and get off the bed. "Let's go back and join in the festivities shall we. Oh, and I expect you to have my six at all times... *wingman*," I tease, bumping my elbow against his arm. I open the doors and see everyone pauses for a moment, then goes about their business. They are going over the problem points with the base and how the attack occurred.

Kalil walks up to us, "Do you feel better now pretty boy?" He grins at Justin.

Justin replies with a sarcastic chuckle, "Never better."

He flashes Kalil a fake grin and Kalil lifts up a brow in curiosity, "Come join us then." He motions for us to join the group. Eric waits for me to sit down next to him and then continues with his analysis.

"I believe that Barbanon may want part of this mission to succeed, for the sake that he wants the gems for himself. This leads Kalil and I to believe that he may try to come after us shortly after we've found all of the gems. Particularly after you, Brielle. Possibly even you Justin," Eric's eyes move Justin's direction.

Justin scrunches his brow, "*Why would they come after me?*" he queries, "I have nothing to offer them."

"Because of what you mean to Brielle. They may try to take you and hold you as a hostage to get Brielle to cooperate. Her sister's family was attacked. Now that they are unable to be found, he will most likely come after you. She is the only one who can find the gems, as determined by the prophecy. He will send different types of demons, possibly even possess animals or people to do his bidding. We must remain vigilant at all times. Brielle will be the *only* one who can physically retrieve the gems, as they will recognize her genetic thumbprint. Everyone else, prior to her moving them from their mounts, needn't touch them unless they want to crumble into ashes," Eric glances at me from the corner of his eye.

I swallow hard. At least I know that the first gem cooperated just fine so the others should follow suit.

"We will only be at the base long enough to assess the damage but we must keep moving. I doubt the next demonic mercenary party will be far behind. In all of my years of fighting off Barbanon's henchmen, I've never seen them display powers like this. It seems he's been very busy over the past two centuries. This entire time he's just been laying low, making Kalil and I believe we were successful in banishing his physical presence from this plane. Unfortunately, we see he's grown stronger than we've thought possible. Dark magic knows no boundaries, especially for an Ancient Empyrean. He must be destroyed completely. His body *and* his soul." Eric concludes.

* * * * * * *

Danny

There's a knock at the door. "Room Service!" a voice beyond our room yells out. Kalil quickly stands up, bumping my legs off of the chair in front of him.

"Hey!" I scold, then look blankly everyone.

Kalil opens the door and we hear a sharp whistling type noise. He groans and stumbles to the side, grasping his bleeding chest. A dark haired Latina dressed as the hotel help stands with a gun, muffled by a silencer. She rushes into the parlor. Jenna quickly gets up and runs towards her. "Don't leave her side!" Eric yells to Justin. Eric flips the coffee table as Justin attempts to cover

Brielle. Jenna and the assassin are fighting for only a few moments before she cuts Jenna in her side. Layla and Nick attempt to interfere and the assassin blows a dust from her palms that burns their bodies unrecognizably. She aims at Brielle with her gun but Justin pulls her behind him, taking the bullet.

"Justin!" she screams, trying to hold him and apply pressure to his wound. Everything is happening so fast. I do a running kick toward the assassin and begin hand to hand combat before Eric jumps in. She is fighting us both with no problem. Brielle stares at Justin as blood pours out from his shoulder. She holds him and continues to press her hands against his wound, attempting to stop the bleeding.

"Get out of here," he mumbles.

Briellyn

Danny looks at Kalil, who is about to open the door. "Wait," he quietly exclaims, jumping over the couch to walk to Kalil. Kalil stops in his tracks.

"What is it?" he squints at Danny. Danny pulls out his gun from his holster and looks through the peephole. It's the dark haired Latina. Danny, without hesitation, steps back and shoots through the door twice. Upon opening the door, the woman lies on the floor with a bullet in the head and another in her chest. Danny exhales loudly and looks up at Kalil and then Eric, "Those bullets work wonders Kal. She was here to kill us all," Eric rushes over. The woman's body shrivels up into a skeleton with leathered skin.

"Thank you Danny, your clairvoyance is quite useful right now it would seem," Eric states. "I think it'd be a great idea to remain at Brielle's side at all times."

Danny stares at Eric, he begins, "I can't."

Eric whips his head around and glares him, "And why is that?"

"I can't receive them when I'm around her or when it pertains directly to her," Danny grimaces, "I realized it in training. That night you came to the club. I didn't see it coming. *I should have.* I believe the only reason I was able to see this is because Kalil made direct physical contact with me in Brielle's presence. I may not have seen it otherwise," Danny raises his eyebrows and glances at Kalil.

"Either way, if he doesn't already know we are here, he will soon," Eric replies bluntly. He continues, "We must move. Kalil, find out where the transport is immediately and tell them we need them sooner than later. Everyone pack up. If an assassin has been sent, it means that we may have time to get out of here. Assassin's are sent alone when he's just speculating on location. I've seen this behavior before. Let's hope this one didn't send word back just yet. He'll know where we are soon enough." Eric tightens his jaw and walks back over to me. He looks at Justin, "You and I must remain more aware of her surroundings, now more than ever. I must request something of you that you may not like."

Justin comes to his feet and looks Eric sternly, "*If you ask me to leave...*"

Eric holds up his hands, "Not exactly. I remember you being quite the sniper. I've heard about your work with the Men of Echo. I could use those talents now." Justin shuts his eyes tightly.

"What?" I inquire, surprised by this new information. I stare at Justin.

Justin looks at me from the corner of his eyes, "Don't look at me like that."

He glances at Eric, Eric looks at me, genuinely surprised, "He never that's so thick, you could cut it with knife.

Justin turns his head to look at me, "I've wanted to tell you. It's the same people that gave me the taps so we could spy on *Prince Gallant* here. I was going to explain once all of this blew over. It was unnecessary information..." Justin's entire tone changes. I just stand there in disbelief. He turns back to look to Eric, aggravated that he would say that aloud.

Eric interrupts, "I would let you two hash this out but I'm not going to sugar coat it, we don't have time. Justin, if you don't give her the short version, I will. But I need to know if you're willing to do it. It may be easier for you to see things that we can't, from a distance. I'll give you some of my guys…"

Justin shakes his head yes and turns back to me, "I really was a sports therapist. But I did a few side gigs for about a year. Those times where you would call and I would tell you that I'm going out of town with a client for a week… those weren't therapy sessions."

I just nod my head in disbelief. "So are these people that you were hired to…" I'm having a hard time thinking of my best friend as someone who kills people. He was never the military type so this is hard for me to accept. The words feel like thorns prickling my tongue as they leave my lips, "were they at least bad people?"

"Of course," he tries to grab my hand but I gently pull it away. "I was protecting our country from terrorists," Justin pleads.

I force a fake smile, "Its fine. I'm sure you'll come in handy… *from a distance.*" I'm not even angry that he's been dealing expiration cards to terrorists or whomever; I'm hurt that he could hold on to such a large secret and not feel comfortable enough to tell me. *We've shared everything together.* I know every deep dark secret there is to know about Justin… or at least I thought I did. I was wary when he handed me the chip to tap Eric but I never thought it would be from this, I wasn't ready for that. I begin to walk away and turn around. "I don't know why you let me hear something like that at a time like this but uh, I hope you're as good as Eric thinks you are. Cause if you miss, I'll haunt your ass forever," I joke with a lenient smile, walking away trying not to show him how hurt I genuinely am. There are more pressing issues and I don't want to linger over it.

Kalil gets off of the phone and relays the information to Eric, "The transport is an hour out. I was able to call in a favor to get the customs check done a little faster."

Eric nods his head as he loads the few weapons he has on him. He grabs a vial from the duffle and walks over to the shriveled up demon, pouring the contents over the remains. I watch from a distance. The body begins evaporating, leaving nothing behind. No blood, no body, no clothes. "What the hell is that stuff?" I approach Eric.

He smiles at me, "Its equivalent to holy water, but it's blessed by Dionne. She is one of three oracles. I'll explain that to you later…"

"The one of Senon, right?"

"I never explained that to you, how do you know that?" Eric scrunches his brow.

"Rhea, she came to me during my unintentional meditation… or relaxation… *whatever you want to call it*. The night I began transmitting energy. I never had time to explain it to you because you weren't around," I sigh.

He holds my hands, beaming, "You've spoken to Rhea? So she *is* watching. That's wonderful news."

Eric's expression is different than any previous expression I've seen of him. Rhea means something special to him, but I'm not sure what just yet. I'm sure it has something to do with Empyria though. We finish gathering our things and make our way downstairs. Eric believes that another attack won't happen in public while we await our transport, so we are safest there.

* * * * * * *

Three hours later...

We have been traveling on the road for about two hours and finally we are only minutes from arriving at the base. Each of the range rovers has been specially equipped with bullet proof armor, advanced roll bars, and engineered for off road driving. Three of them have open trunks that hold additional seating for two more armed men. The base is tucked away in the middle of nowhere, so I see why the off road equipment is necessary but this kind of artillery makes me feel like we're crossing Afghanistan. I'm in the second car of the seven vehicle convoy, with Eric by my side and Kalil in the front seat. Justin and Nick are posted in the last vehicle and Danny is posted in the first, with everyone else scattered between the remaining vehicles.

We pull up to the base; taking notice the wall on one side is completely destroyed. There must be ten armed men guarding the same area. Security at the entry gate verifies the credentials from the first vehicle and guide us all in. The base is busy like a military base, every man and woman wearing their black long sleeve thermal shirts, dark digital camouflage pants, and headsets. This place has more guards than the White House. We step out of the vehicle and the moment my feet touch the ground, my energy level surges. I feel sick to my stomach and my head begins spinning.

Eric is walking around to the other side of the vehicle. Everything continues to spin and I find it difficult to keep my balance. Dr. Strassmore, who was in the car behind ours and on the same side as me, rushes over and lifts me from the ground. Once Eric sees Dr. Strassmore run by, he picks up his pace. "What happened?" Eric asks as he rubs my forehead. My eyes roll, making only the whites of my eyes visible to them. "Take her to my room here and treat her in there. I'll be along shortly," he commands Dr. Strassmore. A couple of men rush to Eric, wiring him up to be able to speak to every person on the base. Each of the remaining team members that just arrived is given their coms devices as they wait to hear from Eric.

"Com check Alpha, can everyone hear me?" Eric asks, adjusting the volume on his ear piece.

"Yes, Alpha leader, go ahead," the base commander replies.

"Everyone listen up. It's not by chance that this base was attacked yesterday. For those of you who are unaware, an assassin found us back in Quebec City. We were unable to get any intel from the demon but it's only a matter of time that this base is attacked once more, full throttle. I absolutely can not risk anymore of your lives. We depart at the first break of dawn tomorrow morning, at approximately 5:45am. We estimate this journey to take fourteen days to arrive at the closest, most outer radius of the first gems energy field. There we will set up base camp and begin our findings. Those of you who wish to go home to your families, I understand. I need only ten volunteers to join our crew. Everyone else may depart right away. I greatly appreciate the sacrifices that you all have made and continue to make. May those of you who depart, carry faith in your heart and send positive energy our way. For those of you who wish to volunteer, please come to the front of the main building where Kalil will be waiting for you. The rest of you, pack up. Your transport leaves in an hour," Eric glances at Kalil. "Get everyone set up and let me know who the ten volunteers are. I'm going to go check on Brie."

* * * * * * *

Dr. Strassmore lays me on Eric's bed, a small ten by fourteen room with a queen size bed, small desk and deluxe shower stall.

Everything in the room is either steel or wood, aside from the mattress. *Simplicity at its finest.* "Why is everything spinning? Make it stop, *please*," I beg Dr. Strassmore, my body in distress. The more the room keep spinning, the more painful it becomes. I begin screaming and my nose is bleeding once again.

Dr. Strassmore grabs something from his pocket and dabs some of the contents on my forehead, both wrists, and each ankle. Lastly, he pulls up my shirt and dabs the last bit across my chest, right above my heart. The pain begins to subside as the room slowly stops spinning. He grabs a washcloth and cleans my nose. "We really must see what these nosebleeds are about…" he suggests as my eyes come forward to see him clearly.

"What just happened?" I mutter, holding my hand to my head as I continue to lie.

"There's something on the grounds that is making your energy levels spike and then plummet, causing you to feel disoriented," he replies, his tone is certain.

"I thought Camille was the energy expert doc. Is there anything you *don't* know?" I softly joke as I try to sit up.

"No, no. Lie still. It'll take a few minutes for your body to regain its full upward mobility," he directs while assisting me to lie flat once more. "And I like to fancy myself as quite the sponge, absorbing as much information as possible."

I nod my head, frustrated once more. Every time I feel strong enough to handle a situation, something seems to knock me down again. These powers are becoming a pain in the ass and I haven't even unlocked the remaining three genomes! Doctor Strassmore places a folded, damp washcloth on my head as Eric slowly opens the door to his room. "Well doc, what is it? Is she going to be alright?" He asks, quietly closing the door.

I glance at him and grin. "I'm fine," lying through my teeth.

The doc looks back at him and says, "She'll be fine ... for now. She had an energy surge when she stepped foot onto the ground. It would seem that the mercenaries who attacked last night left a little gift for her. I suggest you get Camille to look around for a type of... small statue or trinket of some sort. It'll have a carved out chest, missing feet, and part of its head gone. It won't be very big, maybe about seven inches or shorter, so you may have to have a few people looking for it," Dr. Strassmore warns. Eric gives a gentle nod and copies the information through his headset.

"Will she be ok by daybreak?" Eric asks, walking closer to the bedside and cups my hand in his, smiling down at me.

"Maybe a little weak but she'll be 100% in about twenty four hours. She was in a weakened state before her surge. Given her previous injuries, her recovery may be slightly longer," he concludes.

I roll my eyes, "Ok, I get it. I need to take it easy. But given everything that is going on, how can I? I really want to help. I'm so past ready for this."

Eric sits down on the bedside, "I'll take it from here Doc." Doctor Strassmore slightly bows and walks out of the room.

"You don't have to be such a hard gunner all of the time you know. Even the best of us get hurt or need rest," Eric says to me. I look away from him. *Right*. I'm sure *you* don't Mr. Windsor. *But then again, you don't really qualify as us, now do you*. I remove the towel from my forehead and sit up, staring at him.

He sits back and stares in return, "What?" He grins, wondering what I'm thinking. I just continue to stare. "Do you know how awkward it is to have you just staring at me blankly like…"

"I know what you are…" I interrupt him mid-sentence.

"Excuse me?" he glares curiously.

"I know that you are an Empyrean…" I finish.

He chuckles and places his head into his hands, gently shaking his head. He looks back at me, "Kal told you…"

"Of course he did. He thought it would be good for me to know… *and for you.*"

"*Good for me?*" he blushes. He tilts his head, staring deeper into my eyes, "Now you understand why we can't be together then." He stands up.

"Is there some unwritten rule that Empyreans and humans can't mingle?" My question sounds unintentionally more like a plea.

He begins to pace as he explains, "I mean, there can never be anything serious between us. What would be the point? I go back to Empyria, you stay here. We're not even sure if God will reinstate the ability to travel back and forth freely. I am what my grandfather would call '*a God amongst me.*' Even if I stayed I would have to watch you wither away."

"I'm still willing to give us a try," I assure him.

He stops pacing and gazes curiously at me, "*Why?*"

"Because I believe that God has always guided me in the right direction. He's given me signs, *some perhaps more obvious than others,* but there's one thing he's never given me that I can't ignore."

"What's that?"

"True love."

Eric's eyes leave mine to stare at the ground, "I don't think I'm the one that will give that to you."

"You might not be, but I owe it to myself to at least try. No one has ever made me feel the way you do. I feel like the universe is kicking me trying to get me to listen and I haven't wanted to. Until now," I shuffle briefly in the bed, "I'm not saying I love you or anything. I just think there's something between us that neither of us should ignore." *Come on Eric, level with me here.*

"So, my immortality doesn't bother you at all?" he questions, the look on his face saying it all. He clearly wants this as much as I do, both of us too afraid to want to pursue it. Both of us thinking too much about the future and not enough about the now and enjoying each other's company before it's too late.

"Do you really want to live the rest of your life wondering what *could* have happened? I mean, you're immortal... *that is a really long time to have regrets,*" I tease, letting out a giggle.

He chuckles and exhales deeply, shaking his head, "No. I don't." He comes to sit on the bed next to me, once again. He stares into my eyes, thinking about Palidon's words one more time, *'don't get caught up.'* With everything out in the open he feels more inclined to further pursue his feelings, regardless of his grandfather's expectations of him. Even though deep down, he knows it can only lead to one possible outcome.

We both inch closer to each other. He places his hand on my face, gently caressing my jaw and neck. He pulls me in closer to him as I push up further from the bed, allowing our lips to caress. This is how our first kiss *should* have been. Our feelings clear, both of us willing. My skin comes alive with the touch of his lips on mine. He begins to glow, just like I had seen when he was protecting my niece and nephew. I slightly pull away and stare into his eyes, smiling, "Are those what Angel wings really look like? I saw them, back at my sister's house." He leans his forehead against mine, keeping his hand on my neck.

He gives me a nervous laugh, "Yes. They are made of light and energy that is attached to a select few of us. My grandfather has them as do his two brothers and my father."

"Sounds fancy," I joke as we continue to lean on each other. I inch closer and kiss him again. He lifts his other hand, wrapping it around my waist and scooting closer to me. With our lips still locked, he lays me down, deepening his kiss. I wrap my arms around him, bringing him closer to me. I playfully bite his lip and he slowly pulls away. He twirls my hair with his fingers and stares down into my eyes. I worry that he's feeling guilty again, "What is it?"

He smiles at me, "I want to know everything there is to know about you. What makes you laugh, what makes you cry, you're most cherished memories… how do we find time to do such things with all that's going on? I want to relish in every moment that I get to spend with you, every moment that *is* you." His eyes begin to twinkle.

"We will find time. Make it part of this quest. Between the hiking, the car, the plane, we have to figure out some way to pass the time don't we?" I blush.

"I want to show you something," he says, crawling over me to the other side of the bed. "Come close," he commands as he holds his arms open for me to lie on his chest. "I've never done this with anyone, but something about you tells me it'll work," his tone filled with excitement.

"Do what?" I ask curiously, reveling in seeing him come more and more to life with each second.

"Lay your head down, I'll show you," he replies, using the arm that I'm lying on to cover my ear with his hand. He begins taking deep breaths. His heart beat is strong, solid, slow and steady. "Close your eyes," he instructs as he guides my breathing through his own. His heart beat begins to further slow, until it beats only once every few seconds. Before I know it, it's silent.

XXI

The Stars

Palidon and Senon stand in a great room made of pure gold and black sparkling marble. At first sight, the room looks like it's suspended in a starry sky on a clear night. Pure gold pillars standing twenty feet tall holding up the sky to prevent it from falling to their feet. As they walk closer to the center of the room, the bottoms of their feet become submerged in water, a liquid version of the surrounding black sparkling marble, reflecting everything around it. Senon taps his gold and marble walking staff into the water three times, then twice. The water immediately fills the room, fully submersing the two Ancients in dark waters.

A beautiful woman approaches them, bringing the light with her. "Why hello there father… Uncle… what brings you two to the median?" Senon smiles but Palidon glares at her.

"Why Rhea, my darling daughter, my only child? Why must you play these games? You did not tell me the whole truth about the prophecy…"

"There are things that even I can not foresee, you're as shocked as I was," she replies, aggravated by his words. She continues, "I didn't realize certain details myself, father, until I saw her face to face a few nights ago."

"Indeed. I saw her last night when I visited Royce."

"Oh?! You visited him? How is he?" she inquires, trying to sound as reserved as possible.

"Fooled. The girls genomes are clouding his judgment. He needs to remain focused," Palidon replies, irritated.

"I assure you father, my son is never fooled by anything. He knows what he's doing. And he will help her fulfill the prophecy, exactly as it is told."

"He had better. Barbanon is gaining serious headway and has been sending his best to do his bidding. Is there anything else that I should know?"

Rhea sneers at her father, "*No.*"

"How could He grant me such a spiteful daughter?" Palidon rhetorically asks, turning his back to her.

"You know why Father… unfortunately, thanks to you. There are only four of us who know why. My dear sister, Dionne, weeps at what you've allowed to happen," Rhea's eyes narrow at her father.

Senon steps forward, lightly pressing his hand over Rhea's arms, "I, *more than anyone*, know of my daughters sorrows Rhea."

"I'm sorry Uncle; its just my father can be so stubborn. He needs to be reminded that he may have irrevocably caused more damage than good. Preventing any of us from ever being able to speak it besides himself… *and you.* You could do something about all this…" her eyes stare at Senon, filled with hope.

"My dear sweet Rhea, you know that I can't. We each have our own visions and I must trust in his reasons. More than anyone I want Dionne to feel comforted. Is she even aware of what's going on? Have you seen her? She hasn't come to the median since everything happened," Senon frowns, worrying about his only child.

"No, she has been unreachable for about as long as my son has been trapped on Earth. I've tried to reach her with no success. It doesn't help that my dear father restricts my ability to speak to Eric!" she raises her voice intentionally for Palidon to hear. Palidon turns his head just barely to acknowledge that he heard his daughter's plea.

"And this woman… Briellyn. Can it truly be?" Senon inquires.

"It is Uncle. She is exactly. I myself can't explain it. *She's remarkable.* You should go visit on the next full moon. I'm sure my son will be very happy to see you. Please tell him I'm thinking of him often," Rhea asks kindly.

"I think I shall, my dear. Please visit Briellyn soon and give her this," Senon hands Rhea a ring, "It's an ancient, very rare, black gold. It should help her with her developing powers."

"Of course, Uncle, *anything for you,*" she replies, giving her father one last look. She begins to swim away.

"Until next time my dear," he softly says to her as he taps his staff one last time, draining the water from the room and returning it to its original state.

"Brother. What has gotten into you lately? These last two centuries you have been, irritatingly different. More aggravated and terrible to Rhea… it's not like *you* lost…" Senon turns his body towards his brother and is interrupted by Palidon's words.

"I understand brother! It doesn't change the fact that our world is in grave danger. The fall of Empyria would mean the fall of mankind. The heir of our world stuck on Earth. It's the only place any of us are vulnerable!" Palidon scolds.

"I, more than anyone, know this," Senon sourly replies.

Palidon turns to look at his brother, holding his head down. "I'm sorry brother. You have remained remarkably judicious all of this time. You remain the crown and as long as you are well, I know Empyria has nothing to worry about."

Senon walks up to his brother and pats him on the back, "Indeed. I am the crown. I am the moon and the sun, the contributor of day and the purveyor of night. My memories represent the stars in the skies. The ultimate protector of mankind and yet, I still must have faith in Him. We are Gods amongst mortals but here... we are merely humbled servants. *We are not perfect.* We must continue to believe and grant our worries unto Him. We are all separated for a reason. I know your grandson will bring us honor. He will come back and take his rightful place as High Lord."

XXII

Briellyn

I can hear Eric's voice but I can't see him. I'm surrounded by a gray cloud and can't see anything. Suddenly, I see Eric's hand. I reach for it and he pulls me up. "Wow," I exclaim as I look around. We *are* on a gray cloud in a clear starry night sky. The vast universe and its stars shining bright, more beautiful than anything I could ever imagine. Ten silver pillars line the sides of this cloud, forming a giant circle. Smaller, fluffier clouds, about the size of silver dollars circle among the tops of the pillars with a large void in the middle. Past the pillars I can see the earth, darkened by the night sky and lights in all of the big cities, "Are we?"

"Heavens no," Eric laughs, "Pardon the pun. We are in my mind's oasis. I can't go home remember? It's why we are searching for the gems."

"So the gems are going to get you home?"

"Not exactly," he begins to explain as he walks around, "They are all of creation formed into jewels. They hold great power but transportation to another plane isn't exactly what they do. But in the right time in history, they will. The gems open a wormhole that goes as far back as the beginning of time. I need them to travel back to when I came to Earth to search for Barbanon in the year 1776. Apparently, my attempt to kill him was unsuccessful. But he's done an intricate job of making me believe I was victorious. Barbanon had done something so outrageous, He intervened. He didn't want Barbanon to be able to do it again so He closed all travel back and forth, leaving me stranded, unfortunately. So I need to go back and do what I was sent originally to do. Kill him, both physically and rid the world of his spirit as well."

"Well doesn't that interfere with the whole great balance of nature? Without good, there can be no evil; without evil, there can be no good." I'm genuinely curious as to how ridding the world of Barbanon won't somehow put the world in chaos.

"Interesting observation, Brie. The world is guided by rules of survival. But through advancements in technology and man's continued ability to make living longer more possible, I would dare say that something has been tipped on the scale. You're right, without one, the other cannot exist. But is it merely for the inescapable fact that you can only come to that conclusion by comparing it to the other? The great balance won't be interrupted by ridding the world's evil of its ruler. I'm sure a new one will rise, hopefully with a different agenda. And then we start this chess match over once again."

"Chess match," I snicker. It almost scares me that the world is like one big game. But it makes sense that with the wave of someone's hand, that the world could not be perfect. Being able to rid the world of all evil would be too simple. And if it were that simple, what's the say that someone equally as powerful couldn't rid the world of all good? I digress, "So once the gems are found, I say goodbye to you… *forever.*" The thought saddens me.

"Uh, not exactly," Eric replies, making his way towards me. "It is to my understanding that you must travel back in time with me, something about maintaining this very balance we speak of, the great order of things."

"What?" I laugh, "I can't go back in time with you. What about my sister? How would I get back to her?"

"The machine works both ways Briellyn, they won't even know we've gone," he smiles. I roll my eyes and sneer back, catching sight of one of the small clouds hovering above the nearest pillar. I can see a face in it.

I stare at it as I approach it, trying to encase it in between my hands, "Are these your... *memories?*" I think of my own oasis and remember the bustling river, carrying all of my recollections.

"Yes actually. Want to meet my family?" he asks, excitement in his tone. I nod my head and raise my eyebrows. When Kalil told me he didn't have any family, *he meant on Earth*. Poor Eric has been stranded without anyway to contact his family. I couldn't imagine the wreck I would be if I couldn't see or talk to my sister within a thirty day period, let along two hundred years. He whistles, calling all of the clouds down to a lower orbit. The baby clouds begin circling around us. I can see the faces of everyone that Eric has ever seen drifting within them. In amazement, I cup my hands around the little gray fluff and hold it closer to my face. I can see Rhea. "This is her, the one who visited me on my first night! *Rhea.* She's so beautiful and very sweet. Is she one of your peers?" I look at him and hope it's not an ex-girlfriend.

Eric replies with a robust chuckle, "Ha. Peers would be a matter of perspective I guess. She is my mother."

The smile disappears from my face immediately, "But she looks the same age as you do. I mean, aside from the white hair."

"Well, we *are* immortal," he replies sarcastically. My mouth drops and I turn to him, my expression still in awe. He nervously smiles, "What is it?"

"But that means... Palidon is your grandfather! *You're like Empyrean royalty.* That's why you have the wings," I can feel my heart beginning to beat faster. I inhale deeply and then exhale. I want to vomit all over again.

"Is that a problem?" he asks, noticing the change in my mood. His grandfather's words echoing through his mind once more.

"Well, yes and no... I mean. *I guess not*. It's just of all the people, in a matter of speaking, for me to be interested in... I mean. I could see your grandfather thinking of me as repugnant. I can look past your riches, even your Empyrean heritage. But your royal bloodline? That's a lot to take in," I feel my knees growing weak.

"I know, tell me about it. I live two hundred and forty years on Earth, never remotely interested in true companionship with any human and *boom*, here you are. I wonder myself what's so different about you. I'll admit, I'm dying to find out," he wraps his hands around my face and gazes into my eyes. His touch soothes my worries. None of the issues that we will face matter to me at this very moment. He leans in and kisses me once more, sending warmth throughout my body. I begin to glow, like one of the stars in the sky. He slowly pulls away and chuckles, "Even here you glow on your own."

I look down at myself. The glow appears different. It's more white than gold here. As I'm looking at my fingertips, I look past them to notice the same dark void among the rest of his memory clouds. I squint, lowering my brow to look closer, "What is that? It's surrounded by your other memories but there aren't any memories within it..."

"I don't know. I believe it to be part of my imagination or something; it looks quite similar to a black hole. It's been there though... *as long as I can remember*," he shrugs. He craddles the side of my face, turning it towards him and looks me in the eyes once more, "You know for every minute we spend here, it's equal to only one second in reality?"

I beam at him playfully, "No, I didn't know that." My voice softens as I wrap my arms around him, holding him close.

"Tomorrow night, I want to go into *your* mind. Get to know what makes you tick, what makes you so passionate, loving, and determined," he runs his fingers through my hair. Gently gripping it, he tilts my head back and kisses me again. "Kissing you is by far the most addicting thing that I have ever done. Every time I do, it's like the first time all over again. I have experienced many pleasures in my time, no one quite like you though."

I blush, "Hmmm, I would say I'm as dependent as you are. Maybe you can teach me a thing or two."

"I will my love, in due time. If kissing you feels like this, I can't imagine what…" he inhales deep and holds his breath for a moment then exhales, biting his lip. I close my eyes as my heart begins beating rapidly and my body begins to warm at the thought. I slowly open my eyes to look at him. He raises his eyebrows and looks down towards me, "Mmm, you have been, and are, well worth the wait. I want to serenade your curves, stimulate your intellect, wine and dine you. When I've conquered your mind, only then, will I conquer your body." He kisses me again, deeper and more passionately. His words are ecstasy and his kiss is my kryptonite. Every touch is intoxicating but his lips against mine are poetically perfect. My breath shortens and my knees grow incredibly weak. My heart beats slowly, with every third beat deeper and louder than the previous two. Our mouths are the mediators between my body and his, telling each other how deeply the other longs for them. They flourish when they are together, yet remain energetic when they are apart; two halves made entirely whole when they are together as one. I never want to leave his side and it's now that I know he may never want to leave mine.

We awake from our meditation, my head still cradled on his chest. I look around the room as my eyes adjust to the lighting. I lean forward, stretching my arms out. He rubs his hand on my back then comes to a sit up next to me. "Let's go grab something to eat. Meditation always makes me hungry," Eric says, looking at me with sexy, sleepy eyes. "This will be the last time you'll be able to eat quality food. Besides, I want you to come meet the other doctors. I'm sure they are waiting for us. How are you feeling by the way? Rested?" his eyes light up and his voice heightens as he crawls around me from behind and stands.

"Rested indeed, better than ever… Let's go," I eagerly answer, standing next to him. I still feel a slight dizziness but I don't let him see it. I'm high on everything that is Eric right now, my mind rambling through eager thoughts. He guides me out the room to the cafeteria. I get more lost in my thoughts while he talks about something, I'm not even sure because I can't hear him. If only he knew what he was doing to me, inside I think I already love him, but I know that's impossible. Love doesn't happen overnight or over the course of a few days. Maybe I lust for him and I'm confusing the two. I definitely know I *want* him. Either way, I love every moment I have with him. He's exciting, respectful, educated, funny, and the sexiest man I have ever had the pleasure to lay eyes on. Sure, he may be multiple centuries older than me but something about us just clicks. Besides, I'm sure I could think of a few ways he can put that historical knowledge to use.

He brings me to the study area, which is a decent sized room. There are four desks with comfortable looking chairs, charts on the walls with varying wave lengths, pictures of ancient dig sites and an odd looking picture of a metal alter on a dry erase board, scribbled Empyrean symbols all over the same board, and encased in a square glass holding container, floating, is the Aquari seraphic gem that I found back home. Four friendly faces stare back at me, one which I have come to know very well over the past week.

"Welcome to the lab," Eric lovingly expresses, pulling me further into the room. "Of course, you already know Doctor Richard Strassmore," Eric begins, Doctor Strassmore gives me a nod. Eric continues as he points at each person, "That is Dr. Jonathan Lannister there. He is our resident chemical engineer. And Dr. Marianne Reese is there. She is the Master historian. And lastly, Dr. Evelyn Teegrit, she is our Master of Mechanics." My eyebrows immediately go up the moment I realize the master of mechanics is a woman. Each doctor had a wildly different appearance. In comparison to Doctor Strassmore, Doctor Lannister is a little under six foot tall, short black hair, rich dark cocoa skin, wears glasses, and sounds like your typical scientist. I guess it makes sense for a chemical engineer to be the epitome of a nerd. He seems very sweet and quite handsome though.

Doctor Reese fits the perfect profile of a historian with her short whitish gray hair, pale skin, about my height, maybe around fifty years old, strong cheekbones and has a very sweet tone to her voice.

Doctor Teegrit, however, is the exact opposite of how one would imagine a mechanic. She has very full, curly hair with light bronze skin and a killer smile. She is soft and feminine where it counts, but still has a slight ruggedness about her. Her tone is commanding, even when she is simply introducing herself.

While introducing myself with each of the doctors, they ask me to call them by their nicknames. Doctor Lannister prefers to just be Jon, Doctor Reese prefers Mary, Doctor Teegrit prefers Eve, and then of course there's Rick.

"Well doctors, as you may have heard we depart at the first sign of daybreak in the morning. Are we ready to take this show on the road?" Eric asks, looking at all the papers everywhere.

"But of course, we've only been preparing for the past year... I can't believe she's finally here!" Doctor Reese gushes over me. "If only you knew how long I've waited for something as miraculous as this! I've studied the Empyrean word and matched it to so many languages. Translated ancient scripts. Different instances throughout history all pointing to one thing! Seeing that Aquari gem only brings to fruition everything I have ever dreamed, and that's not even the half of it," she explains. There is so much passion in her eyes and through her words; the way she stares at me makes me feel like a superhero. It gives me such confidence.

I'm startled by the opening of the door behind us. I turn around to see who. "Every great historian needs their sidekick," Mary adds, bringing her assistant close.

From the hallway enters three people; two men and a woman. The young woman stands next to Mary, "Haley meet Briellyn." I hold my hand to shake the young woman's hand. She looks to be a little younger than me, probably not by much. She has fair olive skin, freckles, curly hair, and brown eyes; of mixed race perhaps, she is very exotic looking. The two men who walked in with her stand behind her as if to wait their turn.

Eve walks to the man standing closest to Haley and pats him on the back rather loudly. "Well don't just stand there, Van. Say hello," she smiles at him and then over to me, encouraging him to speak up. He looks at her and gives a sarcastic look then holds out his hand for me to shake. Then in a strong southern accent utters, "I'm Eve's assistant, Van. How do you do ma'am?" He's about six foot tall, hazel looking eyes, strong chin, and muscular. It makes sense that Eve's assistant would be the muscle because she doesn't look intimidating whatsoever.

The final assistant comes forth, holding out his hand and in a shockingly deep voice articulates, "I'm Walker, Dr. Lannister's assistant. Nice to finally meet you." He stands at a little over six foot, light eyes, with boyish looks, but his voice says he's anything but young. I look behind me at the door once more, searching for another person to enter.

"If you're searching for my assistant, my dear, you'll be looking forever. I work alone, generally," Doctor Strassmore modestly states with a short lived smile.

This group of people has been behind the scenes piecing this mission together for the past year or two; along with Danny, Jenna, Camille, and Nick all contributing precious man hours for training others to protect these doctors on this mission. Not to mention, Eric and Kalil's time spent here looking for the one person, *the only person*, who can locate these gems accurately. I'm praying that I can get the job done and meet the deadline, for everyone's sake. It's amazing to think that they all know what the gems are for yet none of them seem confused or turned off by everything. They are 100% behind the idea. Being born different is one thing, but seeing these people come together for something they all believe in and haven't personally seen, is absolutely priceless. It gives me a big warm and fuzzy.

After we all chat a little bit, discussing all of the doctors hopes for the end result of the mission, we make our way to the cafeteria to finally eat something. Upon entering, Kalil is waiting for us along with ten personnel. "Here are our ten volunteers Eric, everyone else is packing and will be departing within the hour," Kalil speaks up as we move closer to him. The cafeteria is a very large room filled with plenty of steel seating.

On one end, the serving area is designed similar to a buffet with glass covering most of the top area of the food and warmers underneath. It smells of lemon fresh cleaning solution and garlic bread, hardly appetizing at first. But the closer we got to the buffet, the more it only smelled of garlic bread. My mouth begins watering.

Eric sizes up the ten strapping individuals; eight males and two females. "Thank you all for volunteering for the most crucial part of this entire mission. You have seen things, over the last couple of days, that hadn't been seen prior to this. You were made aware of the situation, *but seeing is believing*. I won't lie to you; during this journey you may see things much, much worse. I can't even promise that you will all come back, as I'm sure Kalil has already mentioned. You're bravery will be rewarded regardless and your families will be taken care of in your absences. The fate of mankind rests with the success of this mission. I appreciate you impartiality about our end result and your ability to remain silent on everything that goes on here, as crazy as this has all been," Eric trudges back and forth in front of them, looking them up and down.

"With all respect sir, it's easy to be open minded with the money you're paying us. I'd believe in the tooth fairy if you asked me to," one of the men jokes. Everyone in the room lightly quietly laughs.

Eric walks up to the man who made the joke. "And what's your name good sir?" Eric grins. The setting is pretty informal even though they are all standing next to each other in a line formation and their hands behind their backs.

"Matthew, sir," he replies, smiling proud after his comment.

"Matthew, I pray that you are able to maintain that amazing sense of humor when you are staring a demon in the face and it's about to eat you alive…" the edges of his lips curl ever so slightly. I look away to hide the smirk on my face. Matthew's smile is replaced with a straight face as he clears his throat.

"I'm just kidding," Eric comments, placing one of his hands on Matthews shoulder. Everyone giggles. "Each demon kills differently. But thankfully, none of them eat you alive," Eric yields a reluctant grin, "But I will admit that the things I'm seeing are new from Barbanon. Same technique mostly but different, more creative foes. We must be very careful, but not too careful; the job still needs to be done. I want you all to make this fun but remember this isn't a joke. Right Matthew?"

"Sir, yes sir!" he yells aloud.

"Former military?" Eric asks.

"Marine Corps sir," he replies.

"Oorah. You devil dogs know what I'm talking about," Eric nods. "Now let's eat!" he yells.

They leave their formation, motivated and enthusiastic. Watching Eric as the commander instead of the businessman that I've come to know entices me. *I'd let him tell me what to do.* I chuckle. I glance over at the volunteers and the thought that some of them won't make it through the possible debacle we will encounter saddens me. The cafeteria staff uncovers all of the food, allowing all of us to go ahead and dig in. Its chicken parmigiana with spaghetti, broccoli, garlic bread, and the desert is apple pie. The staff would be departing with the remaining guards that are being sent home. We have two cooks to travel with us but we won't have anything this tasty for the next month, give or take. It's only around 2pm so I decide to take an extra portion for Eric and I to eat later.

As we finish up, Justin, Danny, Layla, Jenna, Camille, Brendan, and Nick make their way into the cafeteria to eat. Justin looks over to me, but his expression remains serious. I wonder what's on his mind but he doesn't appear to be in a talkative mood. The doctors have all finished and returned to pack up their lab to take what's absolutely necessary. I indulge in the last bite on my plate before returning to Eric's room to sort out my thoughts.

Briellyn

In the comfort and silence of his room, I decide that I'm going to do some meditation. My sight and energy must be pristine prior to departure tomorrow morning. Besides, I've grown quite fond of utilizing it as a means of relaxation. I am already worn out from the day's events and this will be the perfect pick me up. My body has shown no signs of being able to open any more of my precious little treasure genomes, so I've decided that I won't concern myself with them. Instead, I just want to put my body in the most positive state possible, even if that means thinking of nothing at all.

I set a pillow on the floor and sit on it, leaving my legs over the edge. The lights are all off and I've rubbed one of the oils onto my collar bone to allow me to benefit from the smell and energy boost. Deep breath in through my nose and then an audible exhale through my mouth follows. The steady sound sends me off into a deep, relaxed state. My mind is completely blank and it's the most peaceful meditation I've had since my sessions began.

I'm lying down staring up at a clear blue sky, not one cloud in sight. I sit up to observe my surroundings. I'm back in my oasis but a little further from the river. The birds are singing and chasing each other through the sky. There are long stem ivory tulips surrounding me, coming up to the middle of my thigh. I take a moment to smell them before standing up, my own imagination forming the exact sweet smell of the flower. I know it isn't real but I indulge myself anyway.

"Do they smell as sweet as you remember??" a delightful voice asks from a distance.

I quickly lift my head up and look around frantically. Maybe it's the mother in my mind. I notice a woman sitting by the river, feet dipped into the bustling water. The white hair tells me exactly who it is.

"Well hello again, Rhea," I reply, walking to her.

She turns around and looks at me, smiling, "Hello sweet child."

Again with calling me child. I guess it makes sense. Compared to her, I'm just a baby. Still irks me a bit. *Just a tiny bit.* I squat down and sit next to her. "What brings you back to me?" I ask, staring at her glistening white hair as it reflects the sun.

"I wanted to give you something… and of course see how things are going," she answers softly.

I twist my mouth and look off into the distance. In a forgiving tone I ask, "Were you going to tell me that you're Eric's mother?" I turn back to look at her face.

Her eyes light up with joy, *"He told you about me?"*

"Well of course, you're his mother. Why wouldn't he?" I chuckle, curious about her answer.

"I haven't spoken to him in so long, I thought maybe…"

"He misses you a lot. Why don't you visit *him* when he's meditating?" I ponder aloud.

"It's complicated dear," she frowns as she looks away from me. *Now I feel like a jerk.* She reaches over to a rather large oyster and places it in front of me, "This is for you."

I look down at the oyster and think, what am I supposed to do with this? "Thanks," I mutter, holding the oyster up and faking a grin. I'm not sure what she wants me to do with it.

"No, silly. Open it," she laughs. I feel unusual opening this oyster, but I remember none of this is real. I pry the little shellfish open to reveal a ring. It's almost completely black in color but has a slight golden shimmer to it. The band is about a half of an inch thick and is formed to a sandy finish on the top side. It looks like a swirl of angel wings, pointed on both the top and bottom of the ring and the wings are studded with what appear to be tiny emeralds.

"It's beautiful but…" I begin.

Rhea gazes at me concerned, "What is it?"

"I can see that it's a ring. But why give it to me? It's not like I will have this once I leave my meditation…" I grin, trying not to sound like a smartass to her.

She begins laughing and shaking her head, "You have so much to learn still child. Please… put the ring on."

The moment I pluck the ring from the oyster, I feel my energy gush, circulating an electric field around me. My hair is flying upwards by the wind, coming from the ring as if it is it's the point of origin. Rhea's hair and clothing is blown in the opposite direction, she shields her eyes from the piercing light circling my body. As the burst closes in closer to me, it absorbs itself into the ring as I place it onto my finger, sealing it within me.

I sit in awe.

"It should help you hone in on your unique genomes, being able to utilize them in ways you haven't been able to yet. Maybe you should give it a try in the morning," she suggests, coming to her feet. She holds her hands out for me to assist me in standing up.

"I will," I manage to answer. She begins stepping into the river. I ask, "Where are you going?"

"I have other matters to attend to but don't worry, I'm only a thought away for you Briellyn," she says before her head disappears under the water.

Sad to see her go, I stare at the ring. This is exactly what I needed and I hadn't really thought about it. But how do I get it to come to realization once I leave my oasis? Maybe it's just a symbol in my mind that I use to focus my energy. I walk back over to the tulips and lay down. Staring at the sky once more, I admire the ring on my right hand and play with the amulet with my left. The sky grows dark and the field begins to fade as I slowly leave my oasis to return back to reality.

When I wake in Eric's room, I feel even more refreshed. I glance down at my right hand and the ring isn't there. *I didn't really expect it to be but I had hoped.* The overhead light begins to flicker and a gust picks up in the room. It begins very slow at first and then starts violently spiraling around me. My hair is flowing upwards as the winds origin appears to be me. When it's full force, my body is lifted from the ground and I begin to shine bright, killing all of the power to the building.

Still in the cafeteria with Danny, Kalil, Nick and Brendan, Eric notices the lights flickering. They stop chatting and look around briefly, and then the power shuts down completely. "Brielle!" Eric mutters, panicked as he frantically leaps to his feet from the cafeteria bench to get to his room, the crew following close behind.

With the energy pouring through me, a ring begins to appear on my right finger. Glitters of light piecing it together like a puzzle, it takes a few moments for it to be completed. Once the ring has solidified, it's sealed with an intense light.

Eric and the rest of our crew are at the door, now including Justin who rushed right over; weapons drawn and ready to kick open the door. On the count of three, Eric turns the handle pushing through the door. He stops in wonderment as the wind in the room begins to slow. I'm slowly lowered back to the ground, still beaming golden light. He holds out his arms to catch me, knowing that the surge would leave me temporarily weakened. The wind completely ceases and I fall into his arms.

"You're always there when I fall," I tease, flashing him a frail grin as he lowers me to the ground. The backup generators kick in and the lights turn back on. I grab onto his arm with my right hand, the ring practically in his face.

Shocked, he stares at the ring. He knows exactly what it is, "Where did the ring come from Brie?"

I try to catch my breath because I still feel winded. He sits me upright, everyone staring at me to see if I'm okay. "I'm okay guys, I promise. Just trying to get a handle on my powers is all. Nothing remarkable here," I drunkenly say. Kalil has the guys leave to give me and Eric a moment alone.

"Brie… the ring?" Eric sternly asks again.

I turn my face towards him and smile, "*Your mother.* Help me up would you." I reach my hand towards him while I try to stand. He comes to his feet and helps me along.

"When? *How?* Did she tell you what that is?" he sounds flustered.

"It's a ring to help better control my budding anomalies. And she just gave it to me, while I was meditating."

"Wait… so she came to see you once more while you were in meditation?"

"Yes."

Eric steps back from me for a moment, deep in thought.

I continue while I find my to the edge of the bed, holding my hand to my head, "I didn't think the ring would show up here. I mean, it was all in my head. And when I awoke from meditation, it was like my powers created it or something."

"That ring," Eric stutters, staring at me. "*That ring*, it belongs to Senon. Your electric power must be a direct genome from him. I know Camille explained that to you but its significance tells me that the same genetic anomaly that allows you transfer energy, is the *exact* one that Senon possess. Not some evolution of it that was passed down through thousands of generations. That would explain why you were able to manifest it to reality. But he had to have given it to her, to give to you." He frowns.

"That's a good thing right?" I inquire, grabbing the water bottle that was only a couple feet from me and sipping from it.

"Well yes of course," he adds, "but if my mother is able to make that kind of direct contact with you… I wonder why she hasn't contacted me the entire time I've been stranded here. *And* she must have had a way to see my grandfather without the help of the void. One that she's never explained to me."

"Void?" I look at him confused.

"It's the portal that allowed us to come and go from earth as we pleased," Eric says matter-of-fact, still deep in thought.

I gulp another bit of water, "Well I asked her why she wouldn't visit you during your meditation and she told me that it was complicated. I'd been down *that* road once with you already. I've had enough of your family secrets and folklore to last me a century," I chuckle, drinking some more water. His smile uneasy, he strolls over to sit next to me. His hands are cupped together and his head is down. I scoot next to him and then lean back to sit directly behind him, straddling him with my legs. I wrap my arms around him, under his arms and lay my head onto the center of his back. I just listen to his heart as I console him. It's obvious that he's hurt that I have encountered Rhea twice in the past week and he hasn't seen her once in over two centuries. I don't know how else to comfort him.

Eric lightly chuckles, "How are you doing that?"

I lift my head up, "Doing what?"

"You're..." he's trying to find the words to say, "It feels like you're draining my negative thoughts from me. You're making me feel better with just your touch."

I lay my head back down and squeeze him just a little tighter, "I don't want you to hurt or feel sad. I will help you get back to your family, Eric. I'm sure there's a good reason... *for all of this madness.* Mothers always have a great reason for everything, even if we children don't know what it is right away."

He lifts his hands to hold mine, closing his eyes for a moment and taking my affections in. My words seem to soothe his worries completely. It's the first time that I'm finally able to return the favor, for all of the kindness and comforts he's shown me.

Briellyn

Beep. Beep. Beep. Beep. Beep. Eric throws his hand over to his phone to shut off the alarm. I open my eyes and stare at the ceiling. *It's the first official day of the mission.* I'm actually really excited for this… yet nervous at the same time. I immediately sit up and stretch my arms over my head as Eric waddles out from the bed. I glance over at him, staring at his butt as he walks away. Smiling to myself, I yawn while I climb out of the bed behind him. "I hope you're ready," he mumbles to me, "It's going to be a really long day."

* * * * * * *

We are all packed up and ready to go. There are thirty-four of us and seven vehicles. Six passengers can fit into four of the vehicles while only four people can fit into the final three. We each have our own backpacks, which occupy the trunks of two of the vehicles. The third four passenger vehicle is carrying a deflated large occupancy raft in its trunk and hauling three snowmobiles. After a certain point, we must go by foot because it's unsure whether the terrain can handle the weight of the trucks. I clamber into the third vehicle with Eric and two security personnel while everyone else boarded their respective vehicles. By 5:50AM, we were leaving the now desolate base.

Apparently, the reason the driving portion would take so long is because the road to our location is mostly uncharted. We aren't able to drive over 30mph because of the rough terrain and could only drive during the day when there was more than enough light to the path in front of us with no issue. By 5:30PM, we make it to the first checkpoint. Everyone grabs their packs and we set up camp. It's a very chilling three degrees out here in the middle of an incredibly thick, snowy forest. Gray wolves can be heard howling in the distance. Brendan made it a point to assure me how fortunate we are that it's not colder. *Fortunate for who exactly?*

Kalil and Danny begin commanding their teams to set up a small perimeter and Justin is off with two other skilled snipers to keep an eye out on the camp from a distance through the night. The rest of us set up our tents as the two cooks prepare this evening's meal. Eric is off discussing things with Mary after the tent has been set up, so I decide to join the rest of the crew around the fire place.

"Is it cold enough for ya here Brie," Doctor Strassmore says smiling as he hands me a cup of hot chocolate.

My eyes light up, grateful for the hot beverage, "I thought with me being from the northeast, this would be a breeze. This is a whole other level of cold!"

He chuckles, "You know, I'm just guessing here but, I think you may be able to have a strategic advantage over the rest of us here." He sits down right next to me.

Shivering profusely and my teeth chattering, I glare at him in confusion, "Oh yeah? Enlighten me…"

"That's it almost exactly. I would think you'd be able to channel your electrical genomes to warm yourself up. It doesn't have to be extravagant or anything, so as not to tire yourself. But it would make sense. I believe that it's more of a lightning type charge that you give off as opposed to electric anyway, but I guess they can be one in the same. But lightning is hotter than the sun," he shrugs and raises his eyebrows at me, "Just a thought." He sips his cocoa. I look down and think about it. Maybe now that I have the ring at my disposal, it can help me channel something like that.

"Thanks Doc, I'll give that a try tonight," I reply happily, teeth still chattering.

"For now I guess, we can all just try to keep each other warm," he joyfully says wrapping his arm around me. It catches me by surprise.

He proceeds to whisper to me so that no one else can hear, "So, how are things between you and Eric?" I can hear the fire cackle when I turn my face to stare into his eyes.

I shrug my shoulders and reply, "I mean, we're fine. It's been an informative journey; finding out all of this information about him, this mission, and what really goes on beyond humanities giant walls. Why do you ask?" I try not to lead on the additional information that Eric has yet to share with the rest of the group.

"Oh, not to sound too personal but I just worry about you possibly getting pregnant is all," he begins. *If the rest of me is freezing, my cheeks are now the warmest part of my body.* He continues, "During your medical evaluation it didn't state that you were on any type of birth control. The hormones from pregnancy can potentially throw off your powers to find the gems."

My eyebrows raise and I look at him in astonishment. *Wow.* I begin shaking my head, realizing that he means it in the most professional and respectful way possible. I blush and whisper back, "We're not sleeping together… *yet.*" Yet? That came out wrong.

"Oh?" he looks surprised, "I just thought maybe… *oh dear.* I'm sorry. I must sound like such an ass."

I chuckle, "It's okay. If the roles were switched, I can certainly appreciate the concern and your position on the matter."

Eric glances over at us laughing about his comment. His arm is wrapped around me and he's extremely close. Everyone is having a good time. Eric finishes what he needs to do so that he can come join the festivities.

Ten minutes later, the food is done and we are each given a plate while Doctor Strassmore tells us all a joke. "So I ask the nurse how the little boy is doing, he'd swallowed ten quarters. And she simply says to me, 'No change yet'." Everyone laughs while Eric, Danny, and Kalil grab their plates to come sit with us. Eric asks Doctor Strassmore to move over so that he can squeeze in between. Doctor Strassmore graciously moves over as Eric wraps his arms around me, smiling, "Enjoying yourself?" *His subtle possessive ways are so sexy.*

"Oh yes, everyone is so funny… *and quite the lively bunch.* I never thought I would enjoy something like this but, here I am," I beam at him.

The next two hours went by fairly quick, hearing story after story of everyone's previous adventures and interesting things they'd seen. At about 8pm everyone began wondering off to their tents to get some rest for the journey tomorrow.

I scramble into my tent and lay facing the top of it. I glance at the ring and begin to focus on the thought of warming up without burning my tent to the ground. I immediately feel nice and warm and drift off into a peaceful slumber.

* * * * * * *

Ongoing flashes run through my mind. A chiseled physique lies beneath me as I straddle him with my naked body, his hands cupping my breasts. Our bodies glisten in tiny droplets of sweat as we enjoy each other vigorously. Upon climax, I roll over next to him, still breathing heavily. He sits up and rolls on top of me, passionately kissing me. While closing my eyes, I kiss him back. He enters me once more as he pulls his face away from the kiss. I open my eyes to stare back at his, but it's no longer Eric. The naked man on top of me is Barbanon but with a rich tan complexion and his physique looks like Eric's, even the same dark hair. "I'm coming for you," he whispers.

Breathing heavily, I sit up in my tent. Twisting the amulet in between my fingertips, I try to get Barbanon's face and words out of my head. I rub at my eyes as I attempt to catch my breath. The thought of intimacy with Eric right now is obviously on my mind. *But why does Barbanon keep showing up in my most private thoughts?* I roll my eyes thinking about how much I was actually enjoying the dream at first. I poke my head out of my tent to catch some fresh air. Everyone is sleeping soundly still. I lie back down and try to rid my mind of the lust-filled thoughts and focus on tomorrow's journey.

* * * * * *

Meanwhile, only three hundred miles away...

A whitish gray, nine inch wide paw stomps into the light snow; its huge snout sniffing close to the ground, its hot breath melting the surrounding flakes. It stands in front of the base, wide as a bull and seven feet tall. It's let's out a loud howl once it has picked up the scent of its prey. Two howls follow its lead. Their front paws return to the ground, running into the direction of the tire tracks we left this morning.

Briellyn

I awake to the hustle and bustle of the whole crew outside of my tent. Breakfast is being prepared and everyone is breaking down their tents and packing up the vehicles. I gather myself and step outside, zipping up my jacket. It's so early that no one is in the mood for exchanging words. Justin and his sniper crew have already returned and placed the snowmobiles up on their pallets for transport. I coyly wave at him; he acknowledges me with a halfhearted grin as he returns his focus to his task.

"Morning beautiful," Eric walks up from the side to begin breaking down my tent.

"Morning Eric," I blush as I momentarily remember the first part of that fantastic dream last night. I try not to lock eyes with his, afraid he might be able to read my fleeting, sexual thoughts. I quickly begin helping him break down my tent and gather my few belongings to steer my mind elsewhere.

"Are you okay?" he asks, staring at me strangely, "You seem a little… *tense.*"

"I'm great," I respond quickly, my voice almost cracking. I clear my throat then snicker, "Never better." It may not have been real, but it was certainly satisfying to an extent.

Once the tent is bagged and packed, I take all of my gear and load it into the vehicle. Eric wanted to do it for me but I insisted.

We have about a two hundred and fifty mile trek today and then we will make camp once more with the vehicles. Tomorrow morning, the remainder of the journey is on foot; approximately another eighty miles. They estimate that it will take us another five days or so to reach the most outer point of the gems projection field. From there, it could potentially take two to five days to uncover it and then our journey back.

Although I have mastered the warmth trick with the ring, I'm dreading being out in the cold for the walking portion of this undertaking. I'm praying the weather is on our side with how deep in the wilderness we have to go. We eat, get in the vehicles, and we are off once more.

* * * * * *

About twelve hours later, we make camp and reiterate the pace for tomorrow's walk to everyone. Two men will be left behind to care for the vehicles and wait for our return. The night went similar to the previous night and lights were out around 8pm.

The entire camp sleeps until about seven in the morning, attempting to be as rested as possible for the long walk. Each day we will go sixteen miles, stopping every three miles for rest. The sky is clear, *thank goodness*, and we are packed and ready to go. The three snowmobiles are loaded down with any extras and we each will take turns resting our feet by riding one as we go. We cross some narrow cliffs the first day, with thick trees and brush on the second and third day (including a light snow storm on the third day), and a small river on the fourth day. We have caught some fish and the chefs are cooking it up for dinner.

"Only sixteen more miles and we will reach the barrier. Thank you everyone for your contributions. This went much smoother than even I expected. Cheers to you all," Eric lifts his little tin cup in honor of us all. We each raise our cups in return, "Here, here!"

Kalil then grabs his ukulele and plays us a couple songs, like he has every night since we began the walking portion of the excursion. His chipper melodies seemed to lighten the mood and put everyone in good spirits before laying our heads down. Justin and the two snipers took two of the snowmobiles to scope out their perch and the rest of us gathered around the fire to listen to the music.

I catch a glimpse of Kalil and Camille laughing together. They are sitting close to each other, having a conversation, his arm wrapped around her and holding her close to keep her warm. Her eyes brighten every time she stares at him, and he's relaxed and confident staring back down at her. The connection between them is powerful on so many levels without one overwhelming the other.

I've grown very fond of sweet Camille. In fact, over the last few days she's been extremely helpful with helping me focus. The girl-talk about Eric certainly helps, but she has been more than that to me. Both a mentor and a friend, I imagine my mother would've been wise like her had she lived. She even lets me call her Aunt Mille sometimes. I hope that Eric and I could have that same connection as her and Uncle Kal one day, but I know deep down that can never happen. *Ironically enough, we won't have the time.* It's a lovely thought though.

Everyone in the camp is asleep. Justin, Wes, and one of the other snipers, are up watching either end of the camp while the third sniper sleeps. Justin radios Wes, "Hey I've got movement over here, Wes. Verify." Wes grabs his night vision binoculars. Justin gives him the location, "Trees, approximately one mile west of the camp site."

Wes adjusts his binoculars to see the area. The trees are moving. "I see movement but unable to confirm a target, J. Call it in," he softly speaks through his headset.

"This is Sniper J. Come in west base," Justin calls out over his walkie.

"This is west base, go ahead Sniper J," the guard responds.

"We have movement coming your direction about one mile out, can't make out what it is. Be on alert, over," Justin comments.

"Roger that Sniper J, over and out," the guard rounds up two other men and ready their weapons. Justin and Wes continue looking towards the area, trying to get a glimpse at what could possibly be causing that much movement amongst the trees. Justin sees the foot of what looks like a white bear while Wes sees the front claw of what looks like a large wolf.

"West base, be aware. Approaching target may be some type of large animal, now less than a half mile out," Justin states over the comms. He begins to worry. He is unable to get a clear enough visual to take a shot.

"Roger that Sniper J, stand by," the guard responds. As the *animal* gets closer, the sound of trees and sticks breaking in the distance become louder. The footsteps are loud, like colossal creatures from a dinosaur movie. The three men very slowly walk towards the noise to try and get a better look. They have red flashlights to try and see if they can spot anything. The noise of the forest stops completely. No footsteps, no branches breaking. The eerie silence causes the guards to carefully retreat as they continue visually combing the trees with their lights.

The middle guard believes he sees something, like heavy breathing. He carefully lowers his light inch by inch to reveal an eye. The eye is huge. The figure stands up on its hind legs, breathing deeply. It's breath being the only thing that the men can see. Terrified they continue to back up, attempting not to alarm the shadowed wild life. He can hear the animal sniffing.

"We've finally made it. Time for dinner," a deep, angry accent comes booming through the darkness. Three large, open mouths roar at the three guards and lunge at them. Four inch long claws on their front paws, shaped more like human hands with wolf-like characteristics; hind legs designed especially for standing upright and powerful jumping; long furry tails that can be used like a third hand; enormous elongated mouths and jaws with razor sharp teeth that are big enough to fit a grown man's head when opened wide; reptilian-like eyes that are black with green, reds, and yellows around the iris; their chests covered in metallic red armor; red Empyrean symbols tattooed all over their bodies; and white fur sprinkled with blood. It looks like a giant wolf-bear-human. The middle beast, which appears to be the leader, has a very definitive scar across both of its eyes.

The guards scream in horror as they begin shooting at the beasts while attempting to run backwards from them. The whole camp wakes up from the screams. The lead monster swipes at the guard standing closest to him, ripping his flesh from his bones. The other beast jumps at the second guard, encasing the man's head in its jaws and tearing it from his body; swallowing it whole. Blood squirts everywhere as his body convulses, eventually falling to the ground. The last beast uses his hind leg to push the last guard to the ground and digs his right paw into his torso, crushing his rib cage and ripping out his intestines to stuff into its mouth. Justin and Wes see the whole attack from the distance and try to find a good angle to take a shot.

Everyone rushes out of their tents, startled by the screams. The camps fire still burning in front of me, I crawl out of my tent and attempt to look past the flames. There is blood surrounding the beasts everywhere as they continue to eat the three men, tossing body parts to each other and laughing. *I've never seen so much blood before.* Traumatized, I stand there in shock. *No amount of training could have prepared me for this.*

I can hear a woman screaming and then a shot fired. The beast furthest to the left falls to the ground whimpering, black blood spewed everywhere from his wound. Justin very accurately shot the creature in the back of its neck. The lead beast roars at us and rushes over to his fallen brother. He looks up directly at Justin, as if he can see him, still perched in his sniper spot. "I'm coming for you," the beast mumbles angrily. His hand swipes over his brother, making him disappear within a red fog. He then turns to his other brother, "Finish the job here, Rwo. I have a bone to pick my teeth with from our sniper friend on the mountain."

Eric, Danny, Kalil, Nick, Brendan, Jenna, and five of the guards have armed themselves and are attempting to formulate an attack. The doctors, their assistants, and the remaining security have all retreated into the woods, awaiting further instruction. Before the lead beast departs, he proudly stands up and howls into the sky; the tone of it sounding increasingly angry and gut wrenching. The armor covering his chest begins to illuminate, like a fire within a sheer fur casing. His piercing shriek began to spew flames, encasing him and his brother in a fiery circle. Once he's done, he momentarily stares down at the campsite, breathing heavily, smoke simmering from his nostrils. He drops down to all fours and darts off into the forest, heading Justin's direction.

* * * * * *

Eric

"Change of plans," I tuck my gun into my holster and glance at Kalil, "I have to go after him. Can you handle this one?"

"No, I'll go. You're the only one capable of protecting Brie from this... *chimera*?!"

I continue to ready myself to leave, "It's not a Chimera, Kal. Its Barbanon's loyal pet; Ishtar. You might know him as Cerberus, the three headed dog from Greek mythology. I know I've never mentioned him to you, but I will explain to you later..."

"Do I even want to know?" Kalil loads his other weapon, gun in each hand.

"*Probably not.* But the one that is after Justin is the one that needs to be caught. If he's hurt, he'll call this one off. Keep him busy as long as you can!" I gaze at the ground for moment. My eyes become pearlescent white and a constant moving gold energy field surrounds each part of my body. I speed off quickly before anyone sees me leave.

Danny stands next to Kalil, ready to attack. Kalil asks, "Is this one in our favor? Can you see us winning this?"

"Visions are still pretty clouded. I can't see shit into the future when Brie is around. Looks like we are winging this one boss," Danny inserts a clip into his Beretta.

Kalil looks at the rest of the crew awaiting orders, "I'll attack first. Avoid the claws and teeth as much as you can."

"That's a given," Nick chuckles.

"We're just keeping it busy for now," Kalil continues.

"Ok," Jenna hesitates, "Keep it entertained and try not to die. Check."

Kalil tilts his head to the side and frowns. He runs out firing four shots, two from each gun. He manages to hit Rwo in the middle of his armor, collar, and his left arm. It distracts the beast long enough for Kalil to run and leap into a flying kick, knocking Rwo onto his back. The creature quickly recovers his footing, only to be met with Danny's foot to the side of his jaw. Rwo stumbles, shakes it off and notices that Kalil is charging at him. He drops to all fours, bracing for impact, tossing Kalil to the right using his own momentum. Kalil smashes against a nearby tree.

Nick approaches, shooting at Rwo's kneecaps. The bullets barely pierce the skin, mostly just crumbling and falling off, surprising Nick and stopping him in his tracks. Rwo backhands Nick, knocking him out cold. Jenna, who is now furious, charges at Rwo with Danny. Rwo slides down low at Danny forcing him to jump to avoid collision. As he makes his leap, Rwo lifts his whole body up, throwing Danny uncontrollably further into the air. The added height causing him more pain upon ground impact.

Jenna kicks at Rwo's gut, which forces him to hunch over. She then kicks his jaw, further pissing him off. She kicks again and Rwo grabs her leg, spins her around and tosses her into three guards who are rapidly approaching.

Camille and Layla run up to Briellyn. "Come on Brie, we have to get you some place safe!" Camille yells aloud as continuous shots are being fired towards the monster. Brielle continues to stand there in a daze, unmoved.

Rwo is growing angry from the constant fire, but nothing seems to be affecting him the way it did his brother. He drops onto all fours and viciously roars at the lot of men, slober and human blood being blown in the soundwaves.

"But what about the others?" Briellyn yells back to Camille when she finally regains focus. Camille and Layla attempt to drag her into the brush. She stares over at the men fighting; Kalil trying to get up, Nick still knocked out, Danny holding his ribs but coming to his feet, Jenna limping. The few men still standing, merely trying to keep the monster distracted with their firearms. Rwo happens to look over, *directly at Briellyn*. He sees the three ladies and leaps thirty feet into the air, landing just on the other side of the fire... *In front of Briellyn, Camille, and Layla*.

"Oh... shit," Layla utters as she stares up into the eyes of the monster while slowly backing up.

"Now would be a great time to run ladies!" Camille shouts pushing them the other direction. They all turn around and begin to run into the thicket. Rwo violently swipes his paw and grazes Camille's back just enough to tear into her skin and force her to fall forward behind Briellyn and Layla. She falls to the ground screaming. Briellyn can see Kalil in the distance shouting for everyone to get to them when he finally comes to his feet. Barely realizing how far ahead of Camille they'd gotten, Briellyn turns around to see Camille lying on the ground, unable to get up.

"Get outta here, Brie. GO!" Camille yells, swinging her arm around; fear and courage instilled in her eyes. It's the same look Briellyn's mother had the night she died when she told her to go.

* * * * * *

Briellyn

The creature slowly trots over to Camille to claim its second meal. I wasn't going to allow history to repeat itself. I could feel my body growing warmer with each leaping step I took towards her. Rwo stares carefully, with his snake like gaze, and mutters

smugly, "You're making this easy. Two, for the price of one."
He snorts, blood still dripping from his jaw.

I bring my left hand together with my right, using my index
finger and thumb to grip Senon's ring and twist it around my
finger, back and forth. I stand next to Camille, between her and
Rwo. "Brie what are you doing? He'll kill us both! Get out of
here!"

"I'm not leaving you," I declare, fear trembling down into my
bones. *I can't leave her like this.* A lightning storm quickly rolls in.
The wind is picking up and the smell of rain fills the air. The
beast squints at me, cocking his head to the right. He cracks his
knuckles as I raise my right hand into the air and close my eyes.
"Heaven don't fail me now," I whisper, allowing my body to
take control of the situation.

"I like my women well done," the creature grumbles as his chest
begins to glow and swell with fire. Kalil and Danny continue
running towards us, shooting the beast carefully from behind so
as not to hit myself or Camille. None of their efforts faze the
beast away from us. As he bends his head down to spew his fiery
breath, I crouch down over Camille to protect her. The fire
surrounds us, like a giant fire ball.

"NOOO!" Kalil screams, running towards the creature firing
every round he has. Danny and the others follow suit.

The creature finishes his scorching torment, leaving a raging fire
pit where Camille and I once were. He then turns around to deal
with the menacing bullets.

"Why aren't these rounds working?" Danny yells out to Kalil,
wondering why they are wasting their ammunition. Jenna
maneuvers around to the other side of Rwo to see if Camille and
I made it. There is nothing of us left, just a scorched area still

smoldering. She looks up and over at Danny and shakes her head. They are all in disbelief as they continue distracting the monster. The clouds overhead continue to grow dark, but the thunder has silenced.

Eric

Ishtar races up the side of the mountain to get to Justin and Wes. The third sniper, Chris, has joined in the shooting as the three are now together trying to decide if they should get back down to the camp. The three are unaware of the approaching creature but I'm not far behind, running tirelessly through the trees to catch up. *I look like a ray of light traveling through the dark, thick brush.*

The beast is quick, placing one foot in front of the other, snarling with each swift step. He approaches only but a few yards from the men, startling them with his presence. They turn to face the hideous monster, who creeps very slowly towards them. The creature anxiously gazes upon his prey, particularly Justin. "Yeah. You know who the badass is that shot your pathetic cub. You can get it too," Justin points his weapon at the animal's face ready to fire.

"Why you cocky little…" Ishtar snarls then lunges, claws out ready to tear him apart. *Not on my watch.* I rush in, colliding into the beast with my entire body, throwing him off to the side and through a couple of trees. I stand, where the beast once stood, looking over at Justin. My body is covered in glowing transparent golden armor around my torso, arms, and legs and my wings are easily visible to the human eye. Stunned and relieved, Justin lowers his weapon as he gives me a grateful nod.

"They could use the three of you back down at the camp, *go now*!" I command as the three men hop onto the snowmobiles and make their way back down. I turn towards the direction I threw the beast in.

"Ishtar, you know this is a fight you can not win," I call into the woods. I can see the beast slowly stalking towards me from the dark.

"If it isn't Royce Eryx. Fancy seeing you here. I was told you might give me some trouble. But I have just the thing to handle you," Ishtar loudly retorts, pulling something from the wrap around his right calf. It's a small vial that Ishtar opens and pours over his claws, "Now I can kill you."

I stare at him in confusion because I've always known that Empyreans can't be killed like humans. And since Ishtar is a product of Barbanon, he is unable to kill a direct descendant of any of Barbanon's brothers. *I'm not taking any chances.*

Ishtar lunges at me, claws elongated, teeth exposed. I hastily jump out of the way, pushing Ishtar further forward. I draw my baston from behind me and glare at the beast, ready to battle. The baston is a rich, blue, glass-like, five foot long, two and a half inch thick wood with golden pieces on both ends. With a twist, both ends transform into lethal blades. We slowly begin circling each other before I move forward to strike Ishtar over the head. Ishtar quickly steps to the side and kicks me in the ribs, sending me flying a few feet in the other direction. Ishtar then leaps into the air, coming at me from above. He lands on top of me as I hold the baston across my body, my arms extended upwards, preventing Ishtar from being able to bite my face. Ishtar continues to snap at my face and claw at my arm, scratching me just under my armor.

"Ahhh," I scream but manage to throw Ishtar off and smack him hard in the face with the end of my baston. Ishtar yelps like a dog and briefly retreats. I hold the baston behind me, ready to strike again.

Clouds are beginning to roll in, the wind is picking up, and lightning is striking every few seconds. I hear a man that sounds like Kalil yell loudly back from the camp. Distracted I turn away from Ishtar, fearing the worst. He takes the opportunity to attack me, low near my knees. He charges at me, picking me up and hurling me against a boulder. I quickly turn around as he tries to claw me once more but I bat away his right paw, then his left. Ishtar wraps his hands around the baston pushing it towards my neck while I struggle to push it back. I'm distracted still, worried about what happened down at the camp. It suddenly infuriates me.

The clouds grow dark but thunder silences as I stare into Ishtar's enraged, scarred eyes. The golden armor shines brighter, strengthening me enough to push Ishtar far enough away to then kick him twenty feet away. I then jump into the air, twist the baston to expose the blades and descend onto him to stab him in the stomach. Ishtar's roar is gut wrenching as I twist the rod further into his stomach. Ishtar reaches for the staff, trying to hold is as much as he can to prevent me from forcing it in further, "This isn't over…" He snarls before he swirls himself into a red fog to disappear, bringing Rwo with him. I drop to my knees, breathing heavily, and check my wound. *I'll live.* I need to get back down to the base to find out what happened. I race back down the mountain, slowed by my injury.

* * * * * * *

Briellyn

After Rwo disappears, the camp is quiet and distraught. Kalil drops to his knees, sobbing. "Is he gone?" I ask, my voice drawing everyone's attention toward the north side of the campsite. I'm limping into the camp, Camille in tow. A smile finds its way onto Kalil's face as he comes to his feet and runs over to us. "Oh thank God! How did you get over here?" Kalil asks as he grabs Camille from me to lay her on the ground near our tents.

Danny places a blanket on the ground for Kalil to lay her, he's obviously relieved too. "I'm not sure exactly. One second we we're standing there, and then next thing I know, we were almost fifty feet away." I'm still dazed and confused by it while I wipe my face clean. *More blood from my nose.*

Jenna hands me a handkerchief and gives me a friendly smile, "I'm glad you're not dead."

I sniffle, "Yeah, me too." I scan the camp and worry about all the damage those animals caused. Justin, Wes, and Chris pull up on their snowmobiles. And the doctors and their assistants make their way back to our ruined base camp.

"Doc, get over here!" Kalil hollers out to Doctor Strassmore, as he is the first to step into view. The doctor, Justin, Wes, and Chris run up to Kalil. Adjusting his back, Kalil groans to Doctor Strassmore, "Camille needs you, she's hurt." He then turns to his team of snipers, "Gather the available personnel and salvage whatever you can."

Danny helps me to sit down. I grit my teeth and squint. My head aches really bad.

"Just take a deep breath Brie," Danny coaches as he holds out my wrist to take my pulse. My heart is racing so my vitals are through the roof. "Slow deep breaths. Get back in control."

I feel drunk from all that power. *Maybe the correct term is hungover from it.* I'm not even sure what happened during those few moments between the creatures fiery breath and when we appeared in the woods.

Chaos ensues as people are trying to put out the fires and salvage any supplies that they can. Justin instructs a few of the men to lay blankets over the deceased, the sight of carnage too much to witness.

Doctor Strassmore examines Camille's back and determines that the beasts' claws were poisonous. Even though they weren't too deep, the poison is already wreaking havoc within her. "I will try my best to save her," he assures Kalil. Kalil kneels down next to her and holds her hand for comfort.

Eric arrives at the camp still holding his arm and breathing heavily. He walks towards me, relieved to see my face. He glances around the camp, then over at Camille. He kneels down next to me and looks at Danny, "What happened?"

"Camille was injured during the attack. The beast managed to get her. And Brie…" Danny smirks, "She saved her."

"Why am I not surprised…?" Eric smiles, sitting down next to me. I'm still unable to get my breathing under control. Eric holds my hand and gently squeezes it. Danny wanders next to Eric and glances at his arm. *"Ahh, it's nothing.* I'm alright," he mutters to Danny while never breaking his gaze from me.

"I'll get one of the corpsman to stitch you up," Danny insists as he comes to his feet and grabs one of the corpsman.

"Brie?" Eric whispers softly to me. His touch helps me to regain my focus. My energy is low but at least things appear normal once again. I turn my head to see Eric's face, blinking my eyes repeatedly.

"Are you alright?" I ask, my voice weak.

Eric raises his hand to my cheek and chuckles, "I'm fine. I'm more concerned with you. Are you going to be alright? Can you recall what happened? You're much more courageous than I originally thought. Think it's time you let me in there," he points to the side of my head, "And see what other surprises you might have."

I raise my eyebrow, "I'm not even sure how I did it." I stare at him confused.

He tilts his head back, squinting at me, "What are you talking about? That was all you, my love."

I close my eyes for a moment, trying to remember exactly what happened. It's all just one big blur. As if during the situation, my consciousness shut down.

I retort with a halfhearted smile. I can hear Camille coughing, causing me to glance over at her. I look back at Eric, "Help me up." He grabs my hand and helps me to my feet, walking me over to Camille. *Maybe she can give me some clarity, and hopefully I can comfort her.* Eric helps me sit down on the other side of Kalil, who flashes me a forced grin, trying to remain optimistic.

"Hey lady," Camille softly smiles as she glances up at me. She reaches for my hand so I grab hers, "Thank you for saving my life." She coughs, leaving a little bit of blood in the snow. "I would say you've mastered your genome now... or rather your genome has mastered you," she continues, sounding weaker with each word.

"Shh, you just relax. I don't need a lesson right now, I need to know that you're going to be alright," I stare into her eyes. Little by little her body is shutting down. I can see it. Like tiny particles of light leaving her forever. I look up at Doctor

Strassmore who comes rushing back over. "You're going to fix this right? Heal her like you did me?" I ask, worried yet hopeful.

"I'll certainly do my best," he forces a smile at me then focuses on Camille's back. Using some type of medical instrument, he attempts to scoop the visible traces of infection from the wound. There are four claw marks in her back, two of which are about a half inch deep and five inches long. The other two are shallower and maybe only three and half inches long. Camille uncomfortably fidgets as Doctor Strassmore attempts to remedy her wound. I hold her hand harder, hoping and wishing her pain would subside.

She looks up at me, stares into my eyes and grasps my hand gratefully, "Thank you." The expression on her face tells me that she is now pain free. I'm not quite sure yet, but it seems that the same genome that makes me glow and creates lightning, can enhance the moods of others too. I don't even know how I do it, but it certainly seems to be working in my favor.

Eric asks Kalil to stand up as the corpsman walks up to bandage his arm. Kalil is clearly worried but trying to maintain his focus on the goal of the mission.

"I need you tell me exactly what happened down here. Brie doesn't remember disappearing with Camille…" Eric conveys his concern to Kalil. The corpsman begins cleaning Eric's wound, which is already trying to heal.

"Our bullets didn't work on the creature. We tried our best to keep it distracted but it seemed to have its mind set on getting to Brie, Camille, and Layla. Not a tough guess as to who they were after here," Kalil explains, trying not to look over at Camille. "I mean, we got a little roughed up. After that… *thing* got wind of Brie trying to leave the camp, it went after her. He tried to roast her and Camille but Brie managed to escape it somehow. I'm not even sure because we didn't even see anything. Next thing we know, she's standing off on the north side of camp holding Camille. Luckily the beast disappeared. I'm assuming, thanks to you." He motions toward Eric.

"Hmm," Eric thinks for a moment as the corpsman finishes up his bandage. "Did Brie exhibit any of my characteristics, like when I morph? Wings, armor, or the white eyes?"

Kalil shakes his head no. Eric glances over at me as I continue to soothe Camille while Doctor Strassmore begins injecting the wound with some type of remedy. Danny and Justin run up to the two men.

Danny sums up the assessment of the campsite, "Just wanted to let you know, we have three dead and besides Camille, no one is really injured too bad. Nick is a little hazy, but his vitals are mostly normal. We lost six care packs in the fire, which means three of us have no other camp essentials. With this being said and if our remaining rations are divided evenly, we may fall short if the last part of this mission goes past the original timeline."

"Thanks for the update Danny. See to it that everyone is able to get some rest. I know Ishtar was extremely unexpected, but everyone including both of you, need to sleep. He won't be back tonight and we need this mission to move a little faster. Let us all pray that Brielle's new abilities lead us to a quick find," Eric presses his lips into a hard line. He gives Justin a quick nod.

Kalil places his hand on Justin's shoulder, "Can you hook up the mobile gurney to one of the snowmobiles? Camille won't be doing any walking tomorrow. And anyone else who may be hurt, make sure they won't have to haul anything either." Justin nods his head, catching a quick glimpse of Camille and I. "Don't worry, she's fine," Kalil finishes, referring to me.

The camp is finally calm after all of the chaos and most of the crew has finally fallen asleep. Camille is lying comfortably next to Kalil now, both cuddled up and warm. Four men are patrolling around us, sounding the alarm at even the slightest of movement.

I'm sitting on the edge of my ground mat just outside my tent. I can't get the blood and screams out of my mind; the scenario just keeps playing in my head over and over again. I couldn't sleep even if I wanted to. And the creatures voice, his distinctive accent, is oddly familiar.

"I'm coming for you," I mutter to myself, repeating the beasts' words from earlier. *Gasp.*

Eric sits down next to me, "What's the matter?"

"Do you remember the first morning after we'd met? I told you I'd received an odd phone call…" I begin. Eric nods yes. "The voice over the phone called me some weird name and mentioned it was coming for me. I ignored it because I assumed it was either a prank or a wrong number. But the accent from…" I try to think of what to call the monster.

"Ishtar?" Eric guesses.

"Yes, *Ishtar…* is very distinct. And it sounded the same just not as deep. I think it may be possible that had I met you or not, I had all this crazy shit coming," I frown, beginning to fiddle with my fingernails. After a moment or two, I throw my head back and squeeze my eyes closed really hard. I bring my head forward and stare at Eric, "What were those things?"

"Ishtar is known in Greek mythology as Cerebus, Hades three headed guard dog. He was never three headed but the bodies of the three beasts are all shared in a sense. The red symbols that

~ 419 ~

are tattooed all over them allow only one of them to feel any pain. Ishtar is the one you heard speaking, Rwo and Righ are the other two. Each of them can think on their own but all of them share the same heart, which is where the myth got the idea. Barbanon created that monster shortly after he was cast out. I've fought him before, a couple of times actually. Barbanon heals him and he always come back, a little stronger, a little faster. But he is unable to kill me. I think Barbanon may have figured out a way around that though. I don't think that Barbanon sent it to kill you though. I think he sent him to kill me," Eric frowns.

"I don't know about that. That thing seemed pretty determined to kill us all…" I state, recalling how Rwo made it point to try to set Camille and I ablaze.

Eric shakes his head no, "I keep forgetting, but you are covered by a protection spell that Barbanon himself has cast. He wants you *alive*. That beast must have known that he couldn't harm you which means it must have wanted to kill Camille. She can read the minds of both humans *and* animals so I'm assuming one of the three, probably Ishtar, knows something that she could relay to us. When he blew fire at you, he knew it wouldn't kill you. And Ishtar had some type of liquid that he applied to his claws before we fought; he said he can kill me with it."

I swallow hard; thinking what would have happened if I would have ran. I look over at Kalil and back to Eric, "Did you tell Kalil?"

He shakes his head again, looking in Kalil's direction, "No. I will tell him in the morning. He's got enough on his mind." He looks towards me again, "You really need to get some sleep though. Using that much power can't be a good thing for a beginner. I'll still be right here when you wake up." He grabs my hand and kisses the back of it. I slide into my tent, into my sleeping bag and attempt to get some sleep.

Three hours later, my eyes quickly open from a deep sleep, a flash of green within them. *Something is calling to me.* I must go… *right now.* The subtle whispers of high pitch voices come and go like the wind. It must be the gem; *I think it's summoning me.*

"Come to me. You must come alone. Only you can retrieve me." The words repeating, subtly, innocently, over and over again. Deep down I know the longer I stay the greater probability that someone else may get hurt or possibly die. My mother already sacrificed herself for me. I won't allow anyone else to follow suit, not when I know what I'm supposed to do. The sooner I get to that gem, the sooner we can find the others and get Eric back home and all this bad stuff goes away.

I pack my bag very quietly, leaving my tent up. One of the four guards patrolling happens to be near the snowmobiles. I hold my arms up over my head and pretend to yawn. Without saying anything, he sees the toilet paper in my right hand and my pack in the other. He doesn't think twice about it as he continues his patrol. I creep to the furthest snowmobile and hop on it. My eyes flash green once again, powering the machine without my having to turn it on, allowing me a quick and silent getaway.

Briellyn

Danny wakes up to do his round of patrol about two hours after I've left. Shortly after readying his weapon, he begins to step over to one of the men patrolling and has a premonition. At first, he doesn't realize it's a premonition because he hasn't had one since we'd began the journey and it is so subtle. The female guard he's relieving mentions to him that nothing out of the usual had happened over the past few hours and just a few people have woken up to use the *lavatory*.

"Alright, Nikki. Status report…" Danny asks the guard.

"Nothing out of the usual sir, just a few people have woken up to use the lavatory," her teeth chattering and her English accent have made Danny realize he'd just had this conversation… *in his head*.

"Oh shit," he rolls his eyes.

"Sir?" she inquires.

"Did you see Brielle get out of her tent?" he asks, worried.

"Um, I believe one of the other guards did…" she begins but Danny runs off as he tells her to remain on watch for a moment. He walks over to my tent and carefully opens the front. A note is lying on top of my sleeping bag. He shakes his head and clenches his jaw as he grabs it and looks at it.

'I had to. Don't follow.' Is all the note says.

Danny gets a little angry and quietly unzips Eric's tent. He taps him on the shoulder, waking him up. Eric squints with only one eye open as Danny hands him the note, "She's gone."

Eric frantically gets up and quickly reads the note. "When?"

"I'm not sure. Her sleeping bag is no longer warm and one of the guards thought they'd seen her get up and use the bathroom but never saw her come back. Couldn't have been more than a couple hours maybe. I realized it when I had a vision a moment ago."

"On foot?" Eric asks curiously.

"I would think so. The snowmobiles are loud enough where it wouldn't go unnoticed and no one reported anything out of the usual. I'll go check though," Danny leaves Eric and trots over to where the snowmobiles had been parked, a little past the camp. One is definitely missing.

"Damn it Brie," Danny mumbles to himself, turning around to run back. Eric is standing outside of his tent and packing his bag. He looks up at Danny coming from the other side and he shakes his head. Eric throws his pack over his shoulders.

"Well you can't possibly go after her right now…" Danny pleads.

"I have to," Eric replies flatly while walking to the remaining snowmobiles.

Danny continues, "But Eric, you know as well as I do how difficult it will be to follow her tracks right now…" Eric stops walking and gives Danny an irate stare. Danny holds his hands up and turns to walk away.

Eric grins, "Where do you think you're going? Those visions of yours are definitely going to come in handy right now."

Danny stops walking and turns around. He shakes his head, "Umm. What about…"

"Inform your guards to let the others know what's happening at first light. Kalil is an excellent tracker and will be able to find us. Camille needs her sleep if she is going to heal, as does Nick. Besides, we need to find Brie before she makes it to the gem." Eric situates his pack on the snowmobile as Danny runs off to inform the guard, Nikki, what the new plans are. He then grabs his pack and weapons, and heads back to Eric.

The two men push one of the snowmobiles far enough from the camp so to not disturb the others when starting the engine. Within minutes, they are on their way.

"Why do we need to find her before she finds the gem?" Danny yells into his headset to Eric, the wind whipping past their covered heads.

"The gems have a special protection function. They were never supposed to be wielded by a single person, unless of course it's God Himself. It prevents them from being taken by someone who wants the power for themselves. Even though it'll recognize her genetic thumbprint, she was never supposed to retrieve them alone. If she gets to the stone before we find her and she tries, the gem will see her as a threat and turn her into ashes too," Eric explains.

"Well isn't that just dandy. Why didn't you mention that precious little detail to her?"

"I never thought in a million years she'd venture off on her own. She's been a little reluctant this entire time. I didn't want to scare her off. She's becoming increasingly more powerful and finally embracing everything she is, which is great. But I fear she may not realize how vulnerable she still is. I'm sure I can guess her reasons for leaving…"

"Oh yeah, why?"

"She doesn't want anyone else getting hurt. She's carried such a heavy burden since all of this started. What happened to her family and Justin, she realizes those aren't just coincidences. If Barbanon chooses to retrieve her, she will be alone and she thinks no one can get hurt if there's no one else around. But I shouldn't have expected anything different from her; she is the same way with her business. Never take chances with those you care about. If she takes a risk, it'll be on her own. This way if she fails, she fails unaccompanied."

"Sounds lonesome."

"It is. I would know. But she needs to realize, she doesn't have to do that anymore. She has me. Deep down she doesn't *need* me, she's never *needed* anyone. Determined and stubborn as hell, she can't deny that she *wants* me around. Same as I do her."

"Can't say that I know what any of that mushy, love crap feels like," Danny asserts jokingly.

Eric chuckles, "Oh, that's because you haven't found the one that balances you out yet. She's out there. I'd pay to see her tame your crazy ass too." Eric laughs as he taps Danny's shoulders playfully, "I hope I'm around to see it!"

Danny simply shakes his head as they continue following the tracks. They are about to cross into the gems most outer projection.

* * * * * * *

The ride is steady and the moon is bright. The light of the stars allows me to see as best I can ahead for this time of night. The smell of the outdoors is almost overwhelming, pine trees and clean air. I can't go too fast, as some of the trees are packed tightly together. I have a map and a small compass to guide me. As I approach a very semi-transparent green wall, I stop the snowmobile and stare at it. I can clearly see through it. I assume that it's the outer projection of the gem. I glance at the snowmobiles gauge and see that it says 15.9 miles. I remove my right glove as I walk up to the wall. Very carefully, I try to touch it to see how tangible it is. When my hand crosses the field, the green wall bursts into millions of tiny particles and begins rapidly spinning around me. It looks like millions of tiny green lightning bugs slowly circling my body, reaching as high into the sky as far I can see.

After a transient moment, the particles disburse wildly into the air. Two of the pieces gently fall back down towards me, each one dropping into one of my eyes. I blink rapidly, trying to rid my eyes of the slight irritation that is caused by the flakes. The color of my eyes change from brown to green and I can see a clear path that leads me deeper into the midst of the gems projection, presumably to the gem itself. "This must be what Eric was referring to, the signs and projections may undoubtedly be unique only to me," I sneer, chuckling to myself as I board my snowmobile. I start the engine this time, following the lightened green path that the gem has so graciously bestowed upon me.

No longer does the gem speak to me, it now sings. The voice is heavenly, like the most beautiful opera serenade ever written. The words are in another language though, repeated over and over, slow, subtle, and beautiful.

Justin

Morning comes quickly for the rest of the camp, with me being the first to rise from my tent. I decide to breaks it down and do a quick scope around the perimeter of the base to make sure nothing is out of the ordinary. After last night, I didn't want to take any chances. I glance over to see one of the guards taking a seat but pay it no mind. The other guard, Nikki, the female who spoke with Danny and Eric when they left, approaches me. I raise one brow and stare at her.

"Morning Nikki, you take on a double shift last night?" I ask, breathing into his glove covered hands. I know I saw her take the first shift last night.

"Umm, no. Actually it would seem that Eric's little girlfriend ran off ahead of the group. Danny and Eric…"

I begin coughing and frown at her, "Excuse me what? You want to start over?"

"Ya know, the woman who is supposed to be leading us to the gem?" Nikki begins again, trying to sound more respectful. I nod my head and continue to stare. She continues, "She went off ahead of the group at some point last night. Took one of the snowmobiles. Eric and Danny went after her."

"How long ago?" I inquire, pulling the glove up from over my wrist to look at the time.

"Danny and Eric left maybe a little under two hours ago? *Maybe…*" she shrugs, "I was told to let Kalil know and he would know exactly what needs to be done."

"Indeed," I curl my lip, aggravated that she went off on her own. I won't panic though. Knowing that Danny and Eric are closing in on her brings me comfort. *You know, since Eric is apparently a certified badass.* But my anxiety rises while I wait for the rest of the camp to wake from their exhausting and frightening evening.

Kalil slowly opens his eyes and stares at the top of the tent. Camille is still tucked so neatly beside him and sleeping soundly. He doesn't want to wake her, so he tries to shift in an effort for her to remain comfortable. The moment he moves, she begins shuffling around and slowly opens her eyes.

"I tried not to wake you. How are you feeling?" Kalil looks at her lovingly, still concerned about her health.

"I feel a little better than last night. That remedy that Rick concocted must be working," she gives him a half-cocked smile but it's obvious she's still very weak.

"I'm going to go begin preparing the camp if Eric hasn't already started. The sooner we can get back to civilization the better. Ishtar can come back at any point," he says as he readies himself to walk out into the sunlight. She nods her head in reply and he leaves.

Kalil looks around the camp and sees me, waiting for him. I finish eating my apple and toss it into the snow. I trot over to Kalil.

"How's Camille doing?" I ask.

"She's much better," Kalil looks around, wondering, "Where is everyone? Where the hell is Danny?"

"*Well*," I begin. I explain everything that Nikki told me twenty minutes ago. Nikki then joins the conversation to cover any details that may have not been explained in her details to me. Once hearing everything, Kalil decides quickly to wake the rest of the camp and get everything prepared for them to move. In the event of bad weather, it'll be impossible to track anyone so getting started sooner than later is crucial. With us being down two snowmobiles, the camp will surely be slowed significantly. Kalil glances over at Camille, who is trying her best to get around stumbling about. He looks down at his boots and then back at me.

"Nick and Camille will be on the snowmobile. Everyone else will have to carry their packs and we will be walking double time. We have to try and catch up to them," Kalil commands to me before walking off to help Camille. I glare at him and briefly wonder what the rush is about. I go about my business, helping to prepare the camp to move and track Brielle and Eric's paths.

* * * * * *

Briellyn

Unknowingly, Justin and Eric are catching up to me as I come to my first stop. I can no longer go forward with the snowmobile, as the trees seem to be carefully grown out to cover up my path beyond them. I pull an MRE out of my pack and nibble on it while I look around. Beyond the trees lies a bridge that couldn't have been longer than twenty five feet but the cliff that it's connected to has a void so deep, that it's impossible to see what's at the bottom. With the sun rising, I thought I could see what exactly I'm crossing but no such luck. *It's not that important.*

I walk back to the snowmobile and pack the MRE tightly back into its packaging so it doesn't spoil. Placing it back into my pack, I put the pack onto my shoulders and secure it so that it doesn't cause my back any stress. I make my way back to the bridge, maneuvering through the over growth of trees. It seems like the trees have literally created a barricade, just barely big enough to fit a body through.

Once I reach the entrance to the bridge, I realize just how unique this connection really is. All of the trees that happen to be blocking the entrance to this *bridge* seem to have grown their roots out towards this cliff side. They have entangled each other to form the base of the bridge. One side has rope for a bannister and the other side is just open.

Reluctant, I stand there for a moment and catch my breath. I test the bannister rope for stability and take one step across the braided tree root bridge. My newly enhanced vision shows green footsteps across the bridge that appear in an odd sequence. Only three steps in and the footprints disappear, then reappear again... *at the end of the bridge.* There is about an eighteen foot difference between where the footprints end and begin again. However, the rope banister glows green the entire way.

I carefully hold onto the rope with my left hand, gripping it fiercely, as I take another step forward. I stop, look around for a moment, then take another step. I'm now at the point where the steps disappear. I look around, analyzing everything that I can see. I wave my right hand in front of me to see if anything happens. *Nothing.* As I turn my head to look back at the final footsteps, I realize that the last three steps curve. They appear to be coming from the left side of the bridge. It wasn't easy to notice because the bridge is pretty narrow, but I see it now. I grab a flare from the side of my pack and light it. Using the rope for support, I lean over to drop the flare over the left side of the bridge, still close to the edge. When I drop the flare, it doesn't fall to the bottom of the void. It disappears and falls on the underside of the bridge!

"*What the…?*" I'm amazed as I stare over the side once more and grab another flare. I light this flare and throw it directly in front of me. The flare falls… *up*. Up and over the right side of the bridge, I can see it falling deeper and deeper into the void.

My breathing quickens because I realize somehow I have to get to the underside of this bridge. My eyes see one thing but my brain is having a really hard time comprehending how this works. The general rules of gravity don't apply here. *And I prefer certain rules to remain unchanged.* I come down on to my knees and throw my legs over the left side of the bridge, still holding onto the rope. As I pull onto the rope to get down under the bridge, I can feel the ground shift beneath me. The bottom of the bridge tilts to the right. Moving with it to maneuver while it twists around, I realize I'm now under the bridge but *gravity* is keeping me upside down!

Clear as day, the remaining footprints reach the point of the bridge where the others had stopped. I stand up, grab the flare from my feet, and begin walking to the other side. Using the rope for support, *which is now to my right,* I reach the other side and use the same technique as before to make it to the end of the bridge. The bridge twists back, appearing as if I had never left the top part of it.

I inhale deep and swallow hard, taking my first step onto the land mass that is on the other side. The sun was shining bright on the other side, but here is dreary, drizzling, and foggy. From the other side it didn't appear like this. I assume it must be protected by other worldly forces, same as the bridge. The climate is also much warmer than the outside world; it must be at least 65 degrees compared to the 4 degree weather I've been subjected to for the past week.

I focus for a moment, ridding myself of the warm energy that has surrounded me for past few days. Then I shed my jacket and gloves, rolling it up and attaching it to my pack. I hastily follow the green path, sipping water every few minutes to remain hydrated. After walking around through the muddy grounds for a half an hour, I realize I'm back to the bridge.

"How in the hell am I back here?!" I ask aloud, as if the gem would somehow respond back to me. I look at the path and see that it's leading me in the same direction that I started off in when I first stepped foot off of the bridge. Tired and frustrated, I fall to my knees and put my hands over my face.

"Think Briellyn. *Think!*" I scream at myself as I poke my forehead with my right index finger. I hear something in the distance and lose focus. The sound ricochets through the void that separates this land from the mainland. After a moment or two, I realize that the noise is a snowmobile.

"No, no, no!" I gasp, realizing it must be the rest of the team, *"How did they catch up to me so quickly…"* I'm about to walk back across the bridge to ask the team to stay on the other side and realize the roped banister is on the left side. This *isn't* the bridge I crossed originally. If it were, the rope would be on the right side.

"Oh no," I mumble to myself, releasing my backpack to the ground and begin sprinting in the direction that I came from. If they try to cross that bridge, someone is going to fall into the void.

Why did you follow me guys?! I panic, mumbling to myself as I race back to the other bridge, praying I make it in time.

* * * * * * *

Eric and Danny pull up to my abandoned snowmobile. Eric practically leaps off of the back and takes his helmet off to look around. Slightly frantic, he begins looking around to see if there are any signs of a struggle. He finds himself relieved when he sees only one set of footprints; *mine*. Danny turns the engine off and joins him, leaving his helmet on the snowmobile. They can see that my footprints lead into the thick trees that are tightly grown together. They follow the very narrow path through the trees to find the entrance to the tree root bridge.

"Whoa," Danny mumbles as he takes a look at the land across the bridge and the giant void that separates them from it. He bends down to look at the base of the bridge, assessing the ground.

"I'm not having any visions here. I think we must be close. Judging by the disturbed ground, she was definitely here though," Danny looks up and over at Eric who is carefully analyzing the void. He walks over to Danny and looks down at the ground himself, nodding his head.

"Well that's good news Danny, but something doesn't sit well with me here," Eric mutters as he reaches down to the ground, swiping it with his hand and rubbing the dirt between his fingers.

"What do you mean?" Danny inquires.

"This bridge isn't man made... *well obviously*. I believe this may actually be spiritual grounds..." Eric continues, speaking very softly and continuing to analyze their surroundings carefully.

* * * * * * *

I'm breathing hard, running as fast I can. My chest tightens with each step, forcing me to stop for a moment. I focus my breathing and begin running again. "Eric! Please don't cross the bridge!" I yell as loud as I can, praying my voice would carry to them.

*   *   *   *   *   *   *

Danny stares at Eric curiously, "What are you looking fo…" Before he can finish, Eric turns around and tells him to be quiet. They both carefully listen as a voice in the distance yells out.

I yell out again as I continue running as fast as I can. My lungs and throat are on fire but I know I can't stop. "Don't cross the bridge!" I scream.

"What is that?" Danny asks, the voice still muffled and unclear.

Eric shakes his head, unsure.

"Danny, I'm across the bridge!"

Danny hears the words clear as day, "It's Brie!" He gets excited and attempts to cross the bridge. Eric places his hand on Danny's chest, preventing him from moving forward.

"Wait," Eric demands, still carefully listening to the words, "Listen!"

I'm almost to the bridge.

Danny looks across the bridge while Eric continues scanning the sky. Danny gets Eric's attention by tapping him on his chest and points, "Look…"

With a smile on my face, holding my waist, and the last possible breath escaping my lips, I'm finally through the thicket staring at the bridge. Across it, I see Danny and Eric standing there pointing at me. Relieved, I lean down onto my knees to catch my breath.

"Hold on guys… I'll come to you," I yell out in between breaths. Gesturing for them to wait.

"See… nothing to worry about," Danny states, beginning to walk across the bridge. I look back up to see him slowly step onto the bridge. My eyes grow wide as I sprint to the bridge entrance, throwing my legs over the side to get underneath.

Danny takes two steps and sees that I am no longer there. Eric is close behind, noticing that I jumped off the side of the bridge. As Danny takes another step, he floats up into the air. Eric tries to reach out for him but the gust is too quick and sends him under the bridge.

"*Gotcha!*" I say thankfully as I grab his hand before he continues to fall. I'm holding onto the rope with one hand as I hold onto him, my feet lifted up from the ground.

Eric looks over the roped edge to see the perplexing predicament we've found ourselves in. "Eric, come forward a little and carefully come to the side where the rope is to make your way to this side," I holler out to him, struggling to maintain my grip.

He quickly makes his way over and pulls me down, bringing Danny within the upside down gravity pull and he falls onto the bridge. Wiping himself off, he comes to his feet, "Thanks for that."

"No problem," I put my hand on my chest, "I just don't know why you didn't listen when I said I would come to you," I glare at him, happy yet aggravated about his impatience.

Eric and Danny exchange looks. Eric cocks his head to the side, "No, you said come over to you. So that's what we were doing…"

I place my hands onto my hips, "No I didn't. I said hold on guys, I'll come to you." I stare at him confused, thinking carefully about what I said. I continue, "Anyway, is the rest of the camp with you?"

"No, we came the moment we realized you were missing. Doubt they will be far behind though," Danny responds.

"Well I don't want the same thing that happened to you, to happen to any of them. You should both go back. I can handle this myself," I state angrily.

"No, you can't do this alone," Eric replies wearily.

"Of all people I would think *you* would believe in me on this. After all, *I'm doing this for you*," I scowl, irritated by his words.

"No, I mean *literally*. If you attempt to retrieve the stone alone, it will kill you. I will explain everything," Eric turns to look at Danny, "Danny, you go back to the snowmobiles and wait for Kalil and the rest of the camp to arrive. Let them know what's going on and not to follow. If it goes past forty-eight hours, come look for us. Use the flare gun if anything is wrong. I doubt the comms will work here," Eric points Danny back the other direction. Danny nods his head and grabs Eric's arm and my hand, "You two be careful. Come back to us in one piece." He carefully makes his way onto the right side up of the bridge as Eric and I find our way back to other side.

Angrily, I stare at Eric while he helps me to my feet. "Your eyes? *They are green…*" he begins.

I roll my eyes and step past him, "Look. I'm sorry I didn't mention this before, but the gems each have a protective function. If you find it, and you are alone, it will turn you into ashes regardless of your genetic thumbprint," Eric pleads as I begin to walk off. I stop and turn around, angrily staring at him.

"Damn," his grins.

"What?!" I ask, getting more irritated by the minute. My body begins to glow. Eric begins taking his jacket, gloves, and hat off; wrapping it all up and packing it. He looks at me carefully, still grinning.

"I hate it when you just leave, but love to watch you walk away. There's just something about you, ya know?" he tries to make light of the situation.

In the midst of everything, he has the nerve to be cracking jokes right now. *And to compliment me?* Ugh! I'm frustrated with him… *in so many ways.*

He holds his hands up and chuckles, "Look. I won't get in your way and I'm not here to tell you what to do. You coming alone was noble…" He brings his lips together, slightly curving them like he still wants to smile, *"And stupid."*

I glare at him and cross my arms, then look away.

He continues, "You know as well as I do that going at anything alone isn't the best option, unless it's you're only option. You need to get that chip off of your shoulder Brie. Regardless of everything that has happened, none of it is *your* fault. Your father, your mother, Reilly, and Justin; not once were any of those occurrences your fault. Barbanon has wreaked havoc on many men and women since the beginning. It just so happens that right now his sights are set on the people you care about. So stop blaming yourself. I have your back in this, whether you like it or not. I know you aren't some damsel in distress who needs rescuing. But I'm here, willing to help. We can reach this goal, *together*. After all, it *is* my fault you're out here."

My expression softens with every word he says. I exhale audibly, and uncross my arms, "Ok." It's all I can think to say. "Let's go, we don't want to waste any time," I turn around and begin leading the way. Eric follows close behind.

"How fast were you and Danny going to catch up to me so quick by the way? I had only been here about a half an hour when I heard your snowmobile arrive. Thought I would have at least a two hour start on you. You know, until the shift change." I quickly stomp through the muddy grass, pushing leaves out of the way.

Eric glances at his watch, "Well I'll be damned. We're in some sort of time lapse here. Time seems to actually be moving slower. Might explain why none of our electronics work here."

I peek over my shoulder, "We just have to retrieve my pack. I left it when I heard you pull up. Needed to lighten the load to back track faster."

"Ahh," he gasps while he tries to adjust his pack on his shoulders.

"Are you okay back there?" I chuckle.

"Yes, of course. It's nothing," he replies, grabbing at his bandaged arm.

"We're not far. Shouldn't be long," I assure him. Ten minutes later we reach the *other* bridge, where I left my backpack. I stop cold in my tracks and quickly look around. It would appear someone had been rummaging through my pack because the things that were tucked inside are now scattered about. I search the area for any animal large enough to cause such a disturbance. When I don't see anything, I then proceed to the backpack to put everything back in it. Eric cautiously looks around and then proceeds to helping me gather the things that were left about.

"We should definitely keep moving," he suggests after handing me the last item.

I realize, "*My MRE is missing*. I had eaten a little bit before I crossed the bridge, but it's not here."

He smiles at me, "You can share mine. Aren't you happy I came now?"

I roll my eyes then squint at him. "Mmhmm," I coyly reply under my breath. "Okay, this way," I begin in the continued direction of the green path. The plants are getting more and more dense; slowing our pace drastically. After dealing with pushing endless foliage out of my way, we finally come to a clearing.

The skies are still dim but the sun is trying to find its way through the thick gray clouds. In the distance where our path leads, there are some type of long stemmed ivory colored flowers bunched together. We make our way through the field.

"Aww, I love tulips. Especially ones this color," I coo over the flowers as we step through trying not to destroy them. After walking through them for a few minutes, soaking in the delightful smells, I look up. Eric and I gasp at the same time. "I know this place," we both say aloud, astonished at the sight.

Briellyn

We look at each other in confusion and ask at the same time, "How do you know this place?" I smile and tell Eric to go first because I'm extremely curious as to how he could possibly have seen this place before.

"My mother used to bring me here as a boy. She would tell me it was one of her favorite places as a little girl because her and my Aunt Dionne would play here for hours. I feel like I have other memories here, but it's a little fuzzy right now. How on earth do *you* know this place?" Genuine interest is written all over his face, anxious for my response.

"This happens to be my oasis when I meditate… *Rhea never mentioned it being a real place though,*" I step forward and avoid making eye contact with him, "Strange that I imagine something that I've never seen before that happens to be a real place. The more I feel like my life is beginning to make sense, the more is doesn't." I glance toward the ground and think hard. Eric walks up and places his hand on my back.

"My mother told me that Senon created this place for Dionne. A place for her to come and play freely with no distractions, interruptions, or danger. For the longest time, if you couldn't find her anywhere, you knew to find her here. I never knew how to get here without the help of the portal though. I guess I always kind of thought it was never really on Earth," he reluctantly grins and I give him a skeptical stare.

I place my hand on his chest and tease, "I would still like to think of Earth as the only place that has life on it and Heaven as a place in the clouds. The thought of life on other planets is still very… *bizarre.* So uh, *let's keep those comments to yourself for a little longer shall we?*" I press my lips together in a hard line trying not to laugh.

He raises one eyebrow and cracks a smile, then just begins laughing, "Sure."

I turn around and begin walking again, slowly. I want to hang around in this place for longer but I know we need to find this gem. The green path leads into the middle of the running water. The bustling brook is crystal clear and then gets really deep in the middle. Across the brook is that same tree, the one my mother was standing under, the one where my locked genomes are… *the one where that fawn died.* I gasp in horror and begin shaking my head.

"What is it?" Eric asks concerned as I begin stepping away from the water. I continue shaking my head and begin slightly trembling. "Brie? Talk to me…" he insists, walking towards me as I continue taking small steps back.

"It was a sign. It had to be," I reply horrified as I stare at the water as it changes from clear to stained with red.

"What was a sign?" he asks, reaching for my hand.

"The night I met you, I had a dream. I was here, standing right here. And everything was beautiful and perfect and then it grew dark, like it is now. There was a fawn across the way, there by that tree," I point, "It fell over and was bleeding out. I tried to get across the water to get to it and help but something pulled me under. And there was definitely a termagant standing above the water watching me drown. I'm not going in there, I'm sure there's something that will kill us," I chuckle to lighten the mood, trying to hide my fear and reluctance. I can feel my heart pounding, my breaths shortening, and the dizziness from heightened blood pressure.

Eric grabs my hand and surrounds it with both of his. "Well what if I see your... *dream*, from a different perspective?" he asks, drawing my attention to him. I squint, confused as to how it could possibly be different. "What if the *thing* that pulled you under, was actually trying to protect you?"

"How do you figure that?" My tone sarcastic and unconvinced.

"Termagants are subject to earthly restrictions. I'm sure Barbanon never intended for it, but it's present within them none the less. They can't fully submerse into water. They can possess someone and then go into water but can't do it alone. I believe that there's a strong possibility that whatever pulled you under was actually trying to save you from the termagant's wrath by drawing you under," he raises his eyebrows, "*Just my thoughts.*"

I curl the edge of my lip up and glare at him. *Who asked you anyway Eric?* I know he's only trying to help. Could he be right though? He would certainly be the expert in this other worldly stuff though. I exhale loudly and begin to take off my backpack.

"Now what are you doing?" he asks as I take my long sleeve shirt off.

Nervously I reply, "I guess there's only one way to test that theory right?" *I'm terrified.* Everything within me screams this is a bad idea. I'm not a strong swimmer and the water has too many unknowns. I don't like taking big risks and this place has been eerie since the moment we stepped foot off of the bridge.

"I can think of a million reasons why I should turn back and say 'screw this,' but I only need two reasons to go through with it... drop your pants," I say while unbuckling mine.

He quickly shakes his head, his eyebrows raise, and he can't help but awkwardly smile. He begins unbuckling his pants and says, "You don't think this is a little... *sudden*? I mean I..."

"No, I didn't mean like that," I laugh. *He knows what I meant. I think he's trying to make me laugh. It's working.* He shakes his head and mumbles he knows while chuckling to himself. We strip down to the undershirts and long compression shorts that were underneath our clothing. Our backpacks have a pair of aqua shoes tucked at the very bottom. They were meant for the next mission but they are coming in handy right now. Eric steals a glimpse or two of my extremely tight shorts just before I step into the warm water. It gets deep really quick so I take a deep breath and submerse myself, Eric following close behind.

The water is crystal clear as the green line guides us down about thirty feet. It leads us to a cave dimly lit in amber colors. As I attempt to swim into it, I fall flat onto the brown stone surface of the floor of it. Coughing and hacking, I try to catch my breath as Eric steps in next to me. He helps me to my feet, my face flush with embarrassment. The area is completely dry. Looking back at the entrance, the water is held by some kind of barrier. I turn around to see the cave is lit by a very old looking wooden torch. I dust myself off and give Eric a reassuring grin. The green path leads further into the dimly lit cave, I hope the gem is at the end of this so we can begin making our way back already.

I glance over at Eric, *who now appears to have a slight greenish glow himself,* and admire his damp face and soaking wet hair. His drenched shirt shows just the right amount of his muscular physique underneath. He runs his hand through his hair to get the top off of his face. His physique makes sense now; warrior, God, angel... *need I continue?*

Focus Brie. I try to adjust my ponytail to make it more comfortable. Eric glances over at me and takes notice of my shirt. Even with a sports bra, the slight chill in the air is quite noticeable. I bend over to adjust my shoes as he enjoys the view that has now been bestowed upon him. I stand upright and adjust my shoulders, "Ready?"

He looks into my eyes and nods his head, "After you, my lady."

We follow the cave down as far as it can go to a vast room that is filled with gold and jewels as far as our eyes can see. I shake my head in confusion, "What *is* this?"

Eric shrugs his shoulders, "Sacrifices? Gifts to the Gods, maybe?"

"There is only one God," I mutter, correcting him.

"Well, yes that's true. But you know as well as I do many cultures have believed in many supreme beings."

"I wonder who gave them *that* idea..." I tease, "Angels among us, which I'm sure other people interpreted you 'Empyreans' as gods. Parading around here like you own the place. Let's find this gem and get out of here *Ares.*"

"Hey now, I prefer Mars to Ares. Either way, I think my story is seriously confused. Everyone always getting me mixed up with my father," he defends himself. "Finding the gem would be like a needle in a haystack in here. Where is the path pointing us now?"

"I have no idea..." I answer, looking around the entire room, "Everything is glowing the same now."

Eric grabs one of the torches and begins walking into the room. It's so large that the few torches present don't light the room enough for us to see everything very well. As we make our way to the apparent center, there are continued piles of gold and jewels everywhere.

"If you're right and these are *gifts* to the so called gods, aren't you wondering how they all got here?" I inquire, dreading his reply.

"The thought crossed my mind, yes," he retorts. We continue wandering, both looking in opposite directions. Upon reaching the center, the floor changes to a stained glass about ten feet in diameter. In every direction, there is just more jewelry, art, and statues.

I crouch down to sit, both mentally and physically exhausted. I huff noticeably, feeling defeated, "This could take *weeks* to go through. We just don't have that kind of time." *I feel pretty silly now, doing this alone would have been no good.*

Eric looks down at me and squints. He lifts his head and pretends to glance around, "Um, Brie?"

"Yes?" I respond, still looking off in the distance.

"I need you to stand up… *very carefully.* Whatever you do, don't look down and no sudden movements," he says to me softly, still looking in the distance.

My body stiffens while my mind panics, somewhat curious to look down and horrified to think what I might see. As I find my way to my feet, it would appear that the floor is moving. But it isn't the floor itself. A large dark figure is underneath the glass, moving every direction I attempt to step in.

I whisper to Eric, "What is that thing?"

"I believe it's a baugoreast. I haven't seen one in a very, very long time though. So this is a bit of a shock. However, it explains all of the gold," he replies calmly, trying to find a good place for us to run to.

"Do I even want to know what a baugoreast is?!" I quietly respond, trying my best not to look down to see just how large this thing is.

"You won't like it, but I'm going to tell you anyway. It's an ancient animal created to protect Empyrean artifacts but because it had very violent tendencies, it was decided to force them into extinction. Apparently this one got away," he spots the best pathway for us to run to.

"*Oh great*," I mumble sarcastically.

"That's not the worse part. Civilizations did more than just offer gold to the gods… they offered women, *virgins*. I will not go into the vulgar details of what it does to women but I will say that it thinks of you as somewhat of a toy," Eric slowly takes off his shirt. I can hear the beast sniffing the glass where I'm standing.

"Now when I tell you to go, you're going to run down the pathway that's at my nine o'clock. Take your shirt off and put mine on," he hands me his shirt, "The beast has locked onto your scent so toss your shirt some random place as soon as possible. Run as fast as you can and don't look back. Find some place to hide. There is clearly a lower lair, possibly a catacomb beneath this floor that I can bet you is where the gem is. The baugoreast will try to find you, *hopefully*. He knows that there are two of us, so with any luck you can draw him out for me," Eric's eyes turn white.

"*Hopefully?!* You're seriously going to use me as bait?!" I ask, hating the idea. I can feel my adrenaline kicking in.

"It should bring you great comfort that he won't try to eat you."

And that's supposed to make me feel better!? "Oh right, I'm just a giant moving toy for him. Like a cat and a mouse."

"Ok, maybe *toy* wasn't the right word. If he catches you, he will bring you back to his bed and try to mate with you."

I gasp, "*Are ya fuckin' kiddin' me*!? Why would it do that?!"

"Well, a baugoreast is… well, a mutated man. Hopefully he's more horny than hungry; being down here all this time, there's no telling when the last time he…"

"And yet you're hopeful once again," my words dripping with sarcasm. "It is so very important that you not finish that sentence."

"*Right*. Are you ready?" Eric's armor is now circling his body. He hands me the torch.

I cringe at the thought that this creature may catch me. "You're not going to let it catch me right?" I ask as my heart begins beating out of my chest, the adrenaline kicking in to suppress the fear. I glance at Eric to see his golden armor and the wings spread behind him. I can barely see his face through his helmet, the armor visible yet pulsating to a transparency.

"Go!" he yells as I sprint as fast as I can down the pathway he indicated. With a sudden burst, Eric is gone and the creature is making his way under the catacombs to find me. I can hear its claws crushing into the stone and its wings flapping, like a giant bat of some sort. I remove my shirt and toss it away, slipping on Eric's shirt right after.

I find a small room and squeeze into it, taking a moment to try and catch my breath. When I look behind me, a skeleton is lying

~ 447 ~

there. It took everything in me not scream, including dropping the torch and covering my own mouth. The rib cage is crushed in and it's wearing some sort of headdress. I'm unsure if it's a man or a woman's skeleton. The flame from the torch fizzles out and I press my back against the wall. Trying not to panic or make any noise, I remain quiet hoping my hiding place will keep him busy for a bit, while Eric finds the gem.

A Spirit Near Camp

"How long has it been since they've gone in there?" Kalil asks Danny, growing impatient with each waiting minute.

"It's been almost nine hours. I know you want to go in there, but Eric specifically asked us to stay out of this one," Danny replies, "It would be impossible to track them in there anyway. There's a lot of things that you nor I can see."

"Yeah," Kalil retorts. The rest of the team has settled in and set up their tents. It's not quite dark yet but it will be soon.

Camille has been trying to get some more sleep but she has been in and out of fever dreams. She manages to get comfortable enough in the medical tent to fall asleep once more.

Ishtar kneels in front of a dark cloaked figure. "Do you understand your orders? I'm counting on you to get this right..." the dark cloaked figure says to the beast. Ishtar nods his head and looks up into the figures eyes. The figure removes the hood that is covering his face to reveal his true form. Barbanon. He pats Ishtar on the head as he completely disrobes, morphing into a completely other person, someone Camille knows quite well...

She wakes up in a fright. A man's figure is standing above her bed.

"Sorry for this love," the figure says before proceeding to place his hand over her mouth. With a wave of his hand, he temporarily paralyzes her with his mind and grabs her wrist. Pricks it with his thumb nail, he begins to drink her. Slowly, her energy is absorbed completely within him, taking her life force with it. He can see every thought she's had, every intimate moment, everyone she's ever loved; getting all of the information he needs. Her skin turns an odd shade of gray and the veins become more noticeable. "Pity, I was actually quite fond of you too," the man mutters. With another wave of his hand, her skin restores to a more vibrant state. Her eyes open wide, the color of them a rich shade of red then fading to brown. He rids her of any markings on her wrist and heals her back wounds. "Now you can parade around freely, you know what I need you to do. Don't disappoint me," the man says before he disappears in a red mist.

Doctor Strassmore walks into the medical tent to check on Camille. He's stunned to see her sitting up. "*Well,*" he stops for a moment and then proceeds over to her, "How are you feeling?" He places his hands on her neck to take her pulse and then looks at the scratches on her back. "*Amazing*... my serum worked much better than I thought it would," he mentions.

"Well, what can I say. You're a miracle worker Doc," she replies in a soft tone. Kalil walks in just as Rick finishes up.

"You're awake," he slightly grins, "I just wanted to check on you." Kalil walks over and caresses her head and then kisses her cheek.

"She's healed very well. I don't think we have anything to worry about," Doctor Strassmore adds. He places his stethoscope down and removes his rubber gloves.

"I've been looking forward to seeing you, my love," she smirks at Kalil as Doctor Strassmore leaves the tent.

Briellyn

I peek into the main room through a small crack in the wall. I don't hear or see anything. As I gather my courage to step out and possibly seek out the beast, I can feel heavy breathing on the back of neck. I swallow hard and look far to my left, attempting to turn around. Very slowly, I turn around to see its big light brown eyes staring into mine.

The baugoreast is a little over six feet tall but quite wide looking. His face and body were similar to that of a gorilla but not quite as large. His bottom incisors elongated, poking over his top lip. His arms long and muscular but connected to his torso by a thin skin to form wings like a bat. A golden cloth is covering his nether region and he has a collar around his neck. He had thick dark fur covering most of him, with the exception of his chest and stomach that was thin enough to see the brute powerful frame underneath. The creature is clearly created for one thing.

It takes everything within me not to scream as he comes closer and continues to sniff me. With his long tongue, he licks my chest to my neck and presses his body against mine. He then grabs my wrist, turns around, and begins to walk away. Reluctant, I attempt to pull away only to be met with a growl and be thrown over his shoulder.

I can't believe Eric has not only used me for bait, but has allowed me to be captured by this… *animal*. I try to focus my attention, and energy, into sending a painful shock to the beast to force him to let me go. Every effort proves useless, as I can see the electrical pulses that leave my body are absorbed into the collar he's wearing.

After walking with me for a few minutes, we reach a well-lit room that has a rather large pile of fine linens on what appears to be a very ancient looking bed. I look to my left to see the rotting corpse of a woman, mostly still intact. No I start panicking, "*No, no, no no*," and begin desperately struggling to free myself from his iron grip. The baugoreast throws me from his shoulder, slamming me down onto the bed.

My heart is going a million miles a second as I begin praying for Eric to rescue me. I kick the beast a few times only for him to settle himself between my legs to prevent further assault. Just as the baugoreast tries to fully restrain me, Eric shows up in the doorway holding some sort of golden scepter. The same inscription on the beast's collar appears on the staff as Eric walks in holding it out in front of him. His eyes are still white and his armor present.

"Release her and back away," he warns as the baugoreast lets go of my wrists and proceeds to walk towards the wall away from me with his head down. I get up and run over to hide behind Eric.

"Nacletus, reveal yourself," Eric mutters.

The baugoreast begins shedding his fur and animal physique to reveal a tanned skin man with dark hair, blue eyes and athletic frame. He drops to his knees and then to his hands.

"My lord I didn't know that she was yours. Please forgive me," he begs. His voice is monstrously deep, unlike anything I've ever heard.

Eric retracts his armor and his eyes return to their natural state. His expression softens as if he's in shock.

"Aldric?" he asks as the cowering man looks up in reaction to the name. Eric clenches his jaw and walks over to him. He uses the end of the scepter to hold the man's chin up

"My Lord Royce, I swear I didn't know it was you. Nor did I know that this was your mudra..."

Eric frowns angrily, pushing the edge of the scepter into his throat, "You will hold your tongue when speaking of a chosen one. She is no mudra, she is my equal. Show her some respect."

Aldric scowls at Eric then slightly whimpers.

"I'm sorry, my lordess," Aldric looks at me, "It's been very long. I didn't think anyone would ever come. I didn't know that it would be *you* My lord."

"*You knew we would come?*" I ask, curious.

"Why yes lordess, it's been prophesized and written on the wall that someone would come to retrieve the stone. Many have tried..."

"What wall?" Eric interrupts.

Aldric points his finger to the right, "Through that barrier my lord."

I look over at the stone wall he pointed to and begin touching it. My hand would go straight through, making the wall liquefy. I walk through it without a second thought, hoping for answers. The room is completely encased in polished lava stone from the floor to the ceiling. It's graciously lit green by something floating in the middle of the room a few feet above eye level. It looks like a sequined disco ball. On the far wall, there is Empyrean scripture.

"Eric, come look at this," I yell out for him to join me.

He walks in with Aldric and reads the scripture aloud, "Only two may come for the gem. It's really for her but she thinks it's for him. All will show itself in time. For now with hopes he will decline."

"What does it mean?" I ask as I touch the wall. The green sequined ball immediately dissipates, leaving glowing green bits scattered around the room.

"*The Emaldi gem*," Eric whispers. The gem lowers itself to me, beckoning me to take it. I look to Eric for approval and he nods his head. I take it as it glows brighter for a moment and then dies down. My body feels more energized, more in sync. Aldric begins snickering aloud, his laugh disturbing and vile. The collar from his neck disappears.

"Thank you, I'm no longer under the control of that stupid scepter," he comes to his feet and knocks the scepter from Eric's hand and pushes him back through the barrier. He turns to look at me.

"Lordess, your scent is so intoxicating. I'd never forget it. Might I have a bite?" he morphs back into his hideous form and charges at me. My first instinct is to electrocute him. *And it works*. The collar shielded him from my gifts but now that he's free from it my powers work. He collapses to the ground; the pulses making him twitch momentarily. I run out to the other side of the barrier as Eric comes to his feet.

"Let's get out of here," he says to me relieved. I nod in agreement. Eric grabs the scepter from the ground and we run out of the room. He has me stop just outside of the room as he waves the scepter over the doorway, creating a metal door that is latched shut. He throws the scepter and we continue running out of the catacombs, back to the main floor.

I can hear Aldric banging hard against the door, eventually bursting it open while we make our way back to the entrance of the great room. The water barrier is now directly at its entrance.

"We'll never make it. I can't hold my breath that long. I was struggling as it was," I begin to panic, terrified by the thoughts of what will happen if Aldric catches up to us.

"You trust me right?" Eric says. The determined look on his face tells me that I should shake my head no because he's going to force me to do something I won't like. I can hear Aldric making his way through the catacombs below.

"He can't follow us in the water Brie, please trust in me," he reaches out for my hand. Feeling reluctant yet willing, I grab his hand just as Aldric finds his way into the great room and is quickly flying towards us. Eric pulls me through the water barrier, submersing us entirely. The pathway through the cave is at least two hundred feet long. I swim with vigor as the gem lights our way through the cave. Eric is clearly a much stronger swimmer than I, he glides through the water the way an eagle does the air.

We are only half way through the cave before I come close to losing my breath. Eric looks back at me as I slow my strokes. He swims over to me and pulls me close to him. His lips press hard against mine, breathing fresh air into my lungs. My eyes spring open, surprised in his ability to give me oxygen and still have air of his own. We continue swimming, approaching the opening of the cave. He brings me close once more, breathing the goodness of his air into my lungs. I know I can make it from here. I am close to the surface, ready to breathe in the fresh air.

When I break the surface, I close my eyes and inhale deeply. Before I can adjust myself, I am pulled back underwater. Staring up, a large dark figure is hovering at the surface. Eric pulls me close to him to guide me in a different direction. We swim further down the river and find our way out of the water. It's Aldric who is hovering above the water where I surfaced the first time. *Eric was right.*

He helps me to my feet when the winged beast realizes where we are. Eric focuses his energy and surrounds himself with his armor once more, his eyes glowing white, his wings made of energy spread wide. Aldric flies to us and lands in front of Eric, commencing in hand to hand combat. As they fight, I run over to our bags and slip the gem into the front pocket.

"Feeling a little weakened my Lord? After I kill you, I will ravage the Lordess in your honor. I will cause her as much pain as you have caused me," Aldrich threatens in his deep beastly voice, aggravating Eric that much more. The fight is brutal, Eric beating, kicking, and punching Aldric, and in return receiving several hard blows himself.

I stand off to the side, unsure of how I can help. Eric takes notice of me waiting for him and calls out, "Go Brie, get the gem to Kalil. He will know what to do from there."

Although I nod acknowledging his words, I disregard his request, "Forgive me Eric, I'm only following your advice." I run over to them and ready myself to project a deathly charge toward the beast. Aldric currently has the upper hand, pushing Eric's face into the ground while they both stare up at me. My heart hurts at the thought of potentially losing Eric.

"Oh look, she'll get to watch you die," Aldric comments smugly as Eric attempts to free himself, "It would seem the odds are not in your favor my Lord Eryx. Ishtar has made this that much easier for me. *Maybe I won't kill you.* Maybe I'll just permanently disable you and make you watch me with her."

Eric yells out angrily and manages to free himself. *"You will never have the chance!"* he screams at him. He maneuvers around and kicks him off, "Now Brie!" I gather all of my energy and project a vast, powerful bolt at Aldric. His fur catches fire as he falls into the water. I fall over from the exhausting ordeal as Eric makes his way over to me, dropping to the ground opposite of me. He reaches his hand out to me and I reach mine to him, as we both lose consciousness. Like yin and yang we lie there, connected by only our hands; opposites that are incapable of letting go. Man and woman, black and white, mortal and immortal yet so perfectly in sync with one another; tucked under the same tree where my visions all began.

Briellyn

It didn't feel like much time had passed before I woke up in the field of ivory tulips once more. The sky's crystal clear and the sun's warmth on my skin. "You sleep like the dead. You must have really needed it," Eric teases as he walks over to help me to my feet.

Holding my head as he helps me up, I mutter, "How long was I out for?"

"Almost nine hours," he replies simply.

"What?! We have to go. The others will be worried…" I begin but he shakes his head. "What?" I ask.

"We are both in a comatose state," he grabs my hand, "This is your oasis, not the actual field. It happens sometimes when too much power is used at once. While your mind's been mostly at rest, I've had the opportunity to observe your many memories and explore your past."

Nervously, I pull my hands away, "Will we ever wake up?"

"Of course. Your body is merely trying to recuperate, shouldn't be much longer now that you are actively awake here. But while we wait, I thought I might take the opportunity to get to know you better," he guides me over to the water and we have a seat.

We begin talking about my childhood and the few happy times that I had when my mother was still alive. I tell him about the good, the bad, and the ugly that has been my life for 28 years.

There were moments of laughing so hard that we would cry, moments so sorrowful that I couldn't bare to look at him, and moments of pure bliss where staring at each other was the most welcome feeling in the world.

"I knew that's why I couldn't leave you. If I never saw you again, *ever*, and I knew that I could have done something to have prevented it... I think I would just lose my sanity completely. But you know that's why I left. I want to help you get back home but I thought I could do it alone. Not risk anymore lives," I wrap my arms around my knees and stare at him. I can't get the thought of all the blood during Ishtar's encounter out of my mind.

"Everyone, *and I do mean everyone*, who is on this mission knew of what the dangers were. No one is here because they are being forced to be. After seeing and hearing your past..." he sighs, "I can see why you are so guarded. You still manage to forgive those who have wronged you, give to those who you know are undeserving, and yet still find it in your heart to love and still hope for love even though you've never received it. You just distract yourself with countless hours of designs, ideas, and deadlines. *Honestly*... I was quite shocked that you were unwed when I found you. Any man would be quite lucky to have you."

I blush and look away. Compliments have always been so difficult for me to accept. I find a way to change the subject, "And what of you? Do you not have someone waiting for you in Empyria? Surely the God of War has his Aphrodite?"

"*Ha!*" he scoffs, "First off, I prefer the stories of the Angel Gabriel than the God of War. My father was the one in charge of overseeing the affairs of men. When you have lived as long as I have, you see the countless lives taken over stupidity and realize that even as supreme beings, we are powerless to stop it.

Only intervene where we see most just. But even then choosing a side has always been difficult. And no…" he turns his head to look at me as he lies there, upper body held upright by his right arm picking at the grass, "*There is no one else.*"

"Well do Empyreans feel emotions like humans do?"

"That and more, much more. We have desires, emotions, and feelings just like you do but they are so much deeper. When we love, it's forever. When we make love, it's transcendent."

I swallow hard and begin slightly fidgeting. Clearing my throat I reply, "I see."

"None of us are perfect Brie. *I am most certainly not perfect.* I've had my so called 'fun' over the centuries, merely to fill some kind of hole within me and my longing for home. But I've been mostly reserved and deep in thought," he throws another blade of grass.

I chuckle, "We all have our flaws I guess. To err is human, after all. You are merely *super* humans, but the word human is still there."

"Indeed," he beams, "You have a beautiful mind Briellyn. And one of the most loving hearts I've ever had the pleasure of feeling. I'm not only honored to call you my friend and have you as a part of my life, but everything you are makes me want to change where I see myself in the near future." He sits up and scoots closer to me. He places his hand on my cheek and stares into my eyes. He makes me feel so alive yet leaves me breathless with his words and his touch.

"My dear Brie, Empyreans can only love one person in their lifetime… *just one,*" he breaths in while I hold my breath, "Supposedly Empyreans can only have that connection with another Empyrean. Like you, I've never known that kind of love. But with you, everything is just so easy."

I close my eyes and focus on his touch, losing myself in his words.

He sighs, "With everything that you have already done, I need to ask you another favor."

I open my eyes and take his hand into mine, "Anything."

"I will not wake when you do," his eyes fall to the ground.

"*Why?*" I ask nervously.

"I've been poisoned by Ishtar," he says regrettably.

"*But I thought...*" I begin.

He stops me, "I know. Apparently Barbanon has figured out how to supersede the laws of nature. But I believe there may be a solution."

"What do I need to do?" I can feel my throat begin to swell.

"Use the gem. The Emaldi, also known as the earth stone, was wielded by none other than Senon. It connects everything that's living together. Supposedly it carries with it a natural healing ability. I'm hoping that it will allow you to wield it as well, seeing as you must be Senon's descendant somewhere down the line. I believe the blessings that come with that ring will help. I can't recover from my coma without an antidote. That's why I've remained busy, keeping my mind from slipping away."

Saddened by this news, I stare at him, "How do I use it?"

"Let your heart guide you... anything done out of pureness... or love, will be allowed to use the power the gem possesses. Which may explain why you are the one the prophecy chose to find them. They are drawn to you as you are to them," his voice begins to sound weak.

"What if it doesn't work?" I further inquire, worried as hell now.

"I believe in you. *Always have.* If it doesn't work, reach out to my mother. But I know you will figure it out. I have a good feeling about it," he grins at me, trying to seem lighthearted about it. I'm genuinely worried that it may not work. Is this it? Will I ever get to enjoy his contagious laugh once more or feel the warmth of his touch on my skin? I try to rid myself of such selfish thoughts. I inhale deeply and close my eyes, forcing myself to wake up.

My eyes open wide as I stare at Eric who is still curled up and holding onto my hand. I look up at the sky which is already dark but growing more cloudy by the minute. I run over to the bag and grab it, rushing back to Eric's side. I rustle through the bag to grab the gem from it.

"God please allow this to work," I whisper to myself as I unwrap his bandaged arm. The poison is very apparent and similar to the way my injury looked when Doctor Strassmore determined I was poisoned. I place my hands together, palm to palm, encasing the gem between them. I lightly rock back and forth, my eyes closed, muttering a prayer.

"If anyone should lose their life, please Lord, let it be me. I would give it a thousand times if I knew it would protect those that I love and care about. I would give it a thousand times to protect this man. I know him and though we may not belong together God, as you have created us differently, I feel something remarkable for him and I can't deny it. Don't let me believe that this is what love is only to take it away before I am even able to truly *feel* it. Please..." I pray, whispering the words and trying to find the power to wield the gem. *Nothing.*

I begin to lose faith in my ability to use the stones power to heal him. A tear escapes my eye, falling down my cheek and into my palm. The Emaldi begins to glow, ever so gently. I sniffle and stare at the gem. Hypnotized by it, I bring it to my lips, kissing it softly. I then place the tip of it to Eric's poisoned arm, holding it carefully with my other hand. The glow absorbs into his skin and the gem fades once more. I wait, watching his face carefully, waiting for him to open his eyes. *Still nothing.* I lay my head down onto his chest as tears begin to steadily stream down my face, "No, I can't lose you." It begins to drizzle as I cover him with my body. I kiss his lips and press my ear to his chest. His heart rate is extremely slow. Each beat taking longer than the last until it stops. *He's gone.* I begin crying profusely as I attempt to cover him up with his jacket from my pack. The rain is growing progressively heavier and thunder sounds within the clouds. My tears get lost between the drops of rain trickling from my face. A large lightning bolt hits the ground where we are, carrying us back into the clouds from which it came.

Briellyn

"What's the matter?" a voice breaks my thoughts. Nothing but a gray foggy cloud surrounds me.

I sniffle. "Whose there?" I ask cautiously, as I look around trying to see through the denseness of the cloud.

A familiar laugh intrudes and then a hand to help me up. I leap to my feet as the hand brings me above the cloud. My arms spread wide, "How are you here?!" I rejoice as I embrace Eric.

"You remember when I brought you into my meditation the first time?" he asks.

I smile and recall his heart stopped beating during the transition, "I had forgotten actually. But I'm relieved now. I thought I had failed you." I look up at him.

"I heard your prayer," he begins. I release the hug and look at him shyly.

"You what?" I ask.

"I heard your prayer and what you said, did you mean it?" his expression tells me he's curious about how I'll answer.

"Of course I did," I reply looking away from him. Sentiments aren't my strong point and I get very nervous when discussing my feelings. I turn away from him, "There isn't anyone that I have had the pleasure of meeting and getting to know that makes me feel the way you do, not even Justin. I think I…" I rub my hands together out of uneasiness. Eric walks up behind me and wraps his arms around my waist.

He leans in close to my ear and whispers, "You don't need to say it until you know it to be 100% in here," he presses his right hand on my chest over my heart. "Trust me, you'll know."

I turn my face towards his and lean closer . Our embrace feels so perfect, like I belong there. No man has ever given me such a heartening and confident feeling, when he holds me there is never any doubt within my mind. I get butterflies deep within me, my mind goes blank, and all I can hear is my heart beating and my shortened breaths. Deep down I believe he's the one. My perfect match yet my complete opposite, star-crossed lovers destined to love from a distance like some sad Shakespeare story.

He turns me around so that I can see into his eyes. He presses his hand under my chin so that I don't look away. "Thank you for saving my life. Had you not believed, I may have been in a coma forever. But I must let you know that I won't wake right away. I can feel my body flushing the rest of the poisons out," he says to me softly.

I swallow hard, "So how long until you wake?"

"Who knows, maybe a week, maybe longer… you can visit me here though, whenever you like. And I can hear everything that's going on outside so if you can deliver messages from me to the others, I'd be grateful," he assures me.

"I'll visit every day," I promise, trying to hold back the tears knowing that I won't feel the warm comfort of his skin outside of this dream world.

"I hope you will," he looks deep into my eyes. He brings his hand from under my chin to the back of my neck and his other hand slides over my behind as he leans in swiftly to kiss me. Deeply and passionately he massages my tongue with his while he caresses my ass. I wrap my arms around him to embrace his touch that much more. I can't even feel my own heart beating anymore as its dominated by the strong thumping of his, like our hearts are in sync with one another.

He stops kissing me and just stares into my eyes for a moment. I feel like something is pulling me away from him. Before I realize it, he's out of my reach and I fall beneath the cloud. I try to scream his name but no sound leaves my lips. Everything grows dark just before I open my eyes to see the sky once more. I'm shivering, freezing from the cold and the snow, as a man picks me up and throws a jacket over me. Once my eyes adjust, I realize its Justin.

He brings me into the medical tent where it's nice and warm. Right behind us are Kalil and Brendan carrying Eric in. Justin lays me down on the bed and quickly covers me with several blankets.

As my teeth chatter, I manage to ask, "How did we get here?"

Justin smiles at me as he rubs the blankets trying to warm me up faster, "You and Eric arrived just after a bolt of lightning struck the ground. New powers you care to tell us about? Always have to come in with a bang… or in this case a crash and crackle." He chuckles as a single tear falls down his cheek.

I try to focus so that I can warm myself up but I feel a little off. Doctor Strassmore comes in and first takes assess Eric's condition, opening each eye and flashing a light in them. "Is there anything that I should know Brielle? What happened?"

"We are both fine... *well mostly*. Eric is in a coma thanks to the scratch he received from Ishtar. He will wake soon though," I mumble as I reach into my bra to recover the gem.

"How do you know he will wake soon?" Doctor Strassmore asks curiously while listening to Eric's chest.

I pull out the gem and show it to the men, "Because I was able to heal him with this. Now the remaining poison is just being circulated out of his system. He can hear everything that's going on and I can talk to him through meditation." Justin grabs my hand between his and kisses it as Kalil walks over and takes the gem from me.

Kalil rubs my forehead, "I'm glad you both are ok. Did he mention to you what we should do next? Go on without him?"

"He said you would know what to do with the gem and for us to keep going for now. At least to make it back to Quebec City," I tell him. Kalil takes Brendan and immediately leaves the tent to begin packing up the camp for our departure. I look at Justin's expression, "What's the matter Justin?"

He doesn't turn to look at me, as he continues to hold my hand in-between his like he's praying. He swallows hard and attempts to speak but his words are difficult to pass his lips, "I'd thought... *I'd lost you*. You looked so... *lifeless* lying there... in the snow." He sniffles. "I'm sorry I didn't tell you everything. Please don't be upset with me anymore. I just didn't want you worried. I hate seeing you worry," he places his forehead against our hands.

I softly smile at him, "Oh Justin, I was never angry. A little hurt maybe, but you know I could never be truly upset with you." He finally turns to look at me, with a saddened smile, relieved. I glance around the tent and notice that it's only Eric and I as patients in it. "Where's Camille? Is she...?"

"I'm here, I'm fine," her voice interrupts from the entrance of the tent. I lean up to see her, relieved that she is walking and getting around just fine. She quickly walks to the foot of my bed and softly mentions, "We'll talk once you've warmed up and we are back to civilization." I nod my head in and stare back to Justin.

"I'm fine, I promise," I begin, then explaining what happened and why I left initially. Once I warmed up, I helped break down the rest of the camp. Before long, we were on our way back to civilization.

*   *   *   *   *   *

It took us another five days to reach the vehicles and then another three days in the vehicles to get back to Quebec City. I never leave Eric's side, hoping I will be the first person he sees when he finally wakes up.

When we arrive in the city, Justin's brother, Marcus, is waiting for us. "Is that...?" I ask Justin as I lean forward trying to make out the man's face.

"Yup, it's my baby brother," Justin happily says. We had to stop to make a pickup prior to seeing my sister. I'd managed to convince both Eric and Kalil to allow Justin and I to spend a week with my sister and her family for the Thanksgiving holiday. *Apparently, Marcus is joining us.*

Marcus is a little shorter than Justin but they look like twins, both resembling their father. "He'll be joining us to find the last two gems," Justin adds. I give him an awkward look and then remember Marcus' military background as a diver. I hop out of our vehicle to give him a big hug after Justin greets him.

"I'm excited you'll be joining us, both for the holidays and for the rest of our journey. This is certainly turning into quite the family affair," I joke as Marcus hands Justin his bags. Kalil leaves his vehicle to formally introduce himself.

"Hi Marcus, I'm Kalil. We spoke over the phone. I'm glad you made it," Kalil is cordial as he shakes hands with him.

"How could I turn down something so exciting? I'm honored to be here," Marcus replies.

"You'll be riding with Camille and I in this vehicle. Justin and Brie are carrying precious cargo and have no additional seating," Kalil mentions. Marcus nods, fine with the driving arrangements. We load up and continue on to my sister's safe house.

* * * * * * *.

We arrive at the safe house, which is guarded by twenty of the best trained security guards at all times. Two of the guards help us to unload our precious cargo and set him up in one of the vacant rooms. Thankfully, Reilly is getting around a little bit better now that he's had two weeks to heal. He's having a great time chatting it up with Justin and Marcus.

I kiss Eric on the forehead and whisper to him that I won't be far and will check on him every hour, hoping he'll wake up. "Love is a strange thing, isn't it?" Skyla mentions as she catches me in the act of showing Eric affection.

I look over to her and stand, "I'm not sure what you mean." I try to play dumb as I walk out of the room and close the door behind me. A guard is posted just outside of the room.

"So what happened in the last two weeks that gives you this glow? Are you and Eric…" she playfully bites her lip and motions a hump. I laugh but elbow her to stop, even though I find it funny.

"If you must know Sky, we haven't had time to do *anything* like that."

"I'm *just* kidding Brie. I know how you are. But there is something different about you in the short time since I saw you last. I know it was kind of a crazy escape but I know a difference in my sister when I see one," she continues lovingly.

"Well," I roll my eyes, insanely anxious to tell her my feelings about Eric, "I'm definitely in love with him." I close my eyes and shake my head as if I'm still in denial. "I've never felt anything like this before. I mean, I love you and the kids… and that goofy husband of yours but to be *in* love with someone is quite different. We haven't had sex or anything but when we kiss it's like, the most intense interaction I've ever had with anyone *ever*. Certainly more intense than any sexual encounter I've ever had."

Skyla's eyebrows raise and she appears taken back by my comment, "I don't think that to be possible Brie, unless every guy you've ever been with… grand total of three, has severely sucked. And even with that, how do you even compare the two?"

"Easy for you to say Sky, being with someone for a while has its advantages. Your husband knows exactly what makes you tick, what turns you on, your weak points… ya know what I mean. Anyway, I've never been *that* close with anyone. The closest was probably Justin but you know what happened there."

"Mmm," she mumbles, crossing her arms, "Well I would say that Eric is one lucky, *and apparently very talented*, guy. You might as well be a virgin," she jokes, smiling at me innocently as she intertwines her arm with mine.

I giggle at her response, roll my eyes and reply sarcastically, "Whatever you say oh wise one." I proceed to tell her all of the wonderful things that Eric has said to me and how we communicate on a different level. I even told her about half of the sex dream I had about him. Overall, her and I had a great time catching up and I am so glad that Eric and Kalil agreed to allow us all to be together once more for the holidays. I even told her Kalil's relationship to us through genealogy and she welcomed him with open arms.

* * * * * * *

It's the last evening we are to spend the night with the family and I indulge myself in all of the delicious food. Skyla and I whipped up an amazing feast for everyone for the Thanksgiving holiday. We had chicken and turkey, roast beef, stuffing, collard greens, sweet potatoes, and macaroni and cheese, just to name a few. After we eat, Skyla and Reilly go off to put the kids to bed. I kiss them all good night just in case they happen to fall asleep.

In the meantime, I make my way to my room to check on Eric, growing worried about him waking up soon. I'd really hoped he would wake up before we left Sky's house but it seems that may not happen. I stare at his still body lying on the bed and stroll over to him. The moon is shining through the window, its milky white color giving the room a subtle hazy hue. Eric's face looked perfect, so peaceful and rested. It reminds me of the first night we met on the drive home.

I sit down next to him and place my hand on his face, cupping his jawline with my right hand. For a man who is well over a few centuries old, he barely has a wrinkle to show for it. "I know you've told me you'll wake up when your body is ready, but I need you to sooner than later. Even though we can still speak, you're physical presence is something that we all could use right now. We don't want to get on that boat without you…" I softly whisper to him.

"Have you had fun this week?" Camille mentions, startling me half to the death. I jump up off the side of the bed before turning around to look at her, hand over my chest.

"Oh geeze woman, you've been so quiet since you've gotten better. You scared me half to death there," I smile at her, trying to laugh it off.

"Can't have that, now can we?," she replies softly as she makes her way over to me, "Still no signs of him waking up, huh?" She grabs his hand and frowns. She clearly senses my longing for him.

"No, but I'm sure it won't be much longer," I assure her, "I have a good feeling it'll be soon." I don't know if I'm trying to convince her or trying to convince myself.

"You should really try to get some sleep. We have a long drive tomorrow," she suggests to me while rubbing my shoulders.

"I'm really not quite tired just…" I begin before she embraces me suddenly.

Holding me close she whispers, "I wasn't asking…" I feel a subtle pinch on the back of my left shoulder then grow incredibly tired, practically fainting. She holds me up and pulls me onto the bed next to Eric. "What…" I begin softly whispering a few additional inaudible words before drifting fast asleep.

Camille then opens my mouth and places a small pill under my tongue and proceeds to do the same thing to Eric. She then pulls his sock off and pricks his big toe with a small needle. She grabs me, lays my head onto Eric's chest and wraps his arm around me, the same position we do when we meditate. "You two need to start seeing each other a little differently so my master can get what he needs from you," she whispers into my ear so that only I can hear, "You want him and he's wanted to take you the moment he laid eyes on you. Don't let him fool you. Think of the sexiest lingerie you've ever seen and dress in that to meet him in your dreams tonight. You'll find he's much more willing now."

She snickers and raises her eyebrow at the two of us. Crossing her arms she mumbles to herself, "Almost too easy. Never send a man to do a woman's job." She proceeds to walk out of the room, shutting the door behind her. She glances at the guard, "No matter what, you open this door for no one. The love birds need their sleep." She smiles at the guard innocently and walks off to meet Kalil in the den by the fireplace where he, Justin, and Marcus are all still chatting.

"Where's Brie?" Kalil asks.

Camille grabs her wine glass, "Oh the poor thing was so tired she practically fell asleep talking to me." The evil smirk she gives Justin makes him feel incredibly uneasy. But Justin knows that if he questioned Camille in any way, he would have to deal with Kalil and that's not something he wishes to do again. Justin stares at her as she begins distracting Kalil by nibbling on his ear. He scrunches his brow and his brother takes notice. Kalil picks her up, "We shall see you boys in the morning. I think we are going to take advantage of our last night in a real bed above water." Kalil smiles as he hauls her off in his arms as Justin and Marcus raise their glasses to him. Justin can't help but think something more is going on but he just sips the rest of his wine before he and Marcus decide to retire for the evening as well.

* * * * * * *

The twinkle of the stars is the first thing I see. The sky is a rich midnight black and the stars seem brighter than I have ever seen them. I take a deep breath and sit up, immediately taking notice of the low cut, short, satin slip-on that I'm wearing. It happens to be red. Not just any red though, it's a deep passionate seductive red. It's the color of blood, with a beaded neckline and beaded waist. It drapes down just past the bottom of my derriere and makes my breasts look amazing. My hair is straight and down with beautiful wisps in the front and layered curls in the back.

I look over to my left to see that I'm slightly propped up from the base of the cloud. I carefully turn my body and place my feet to the floor. As I stand up and take one last look at myself, my thoughts are derailed by Eric's voice. "And here I thought I couldn't get any more attracted to you," he says as he leans against a nearby pillar. Nervously I wrap my arms around my bust to attempt to cover myself up.

* * * * * * *

Eric

"I, uh, don't know how this happened. Wardrobe malfunction I guess," Briellyn tries to make light of the situation. She glances at me as I creep closer to her. I can see her holding her breath as she stares at me in my rich ocean blue satin pants and completely unbuttoned matching shirt. I tuck my hands in the pockets as I creep closer towards her.

She is breathtaking in her satin red night gown and her hair down. But what makes her that much more attractive is her shy body language. Here is a woman who has shown tremendous confidence and courage but immediately becomes timid when I'm around.

I stand directly in front of her and carefully place my hands over her shoulders, rubbing them up onto her neck and then back down around her arms. Her skin is soft and smooth. I marvel at its beauty. I stare at her face as her eyes close while I continue to touch her. Her glow appearing whiter than it had before. She's still nervous, trying to cover herself from me. "Relax," I whisper to her, taking her hands within mine and pulling them to her sides. I hear her breathing quicken as she refuses to open her eyes, still nervous.

I cradle her face, gently guiding it to the side, exposing her neck. *That beautiful neck that beckons for the touch of my lips.* I kiss it carefully and place my hand on the middle of her back, pulling her closer to me. Her scent is intoxicating, that hint of coconut and vanilla that I can't seem to get enough of. With each tender nibble, her body reacts with a slight shudder and approving groan. I can feel her nervousness begin to subside as I make my way back to her mouth. *Those luscious, soft lips.* And begin to kiss her, using my tongue to guide her mouth open to let me in. *Her walls are down now.* While I continue to kiss her, I lift her off her feet and carry her to the bed, cradling her within my powerful arms. Her body is soft nestled next to mine, relinquishing all of her worry to allow me to be her defining strength.

I place her back onto the bed cloud. I stand in awe of her splendor, taking in every inch of her delectable bronze skin, from each hair on her perfect head to her perfectly manicured toes. She's staring at me; those brown eyes that make me weak. She bats them at me; those long curly lashes that could cause the most anchored man to blow over and bow to her every whim. Her cheeks rise up like perfect ovals to display delight in our shared moment. She's smiling, parting those lips just enough to show her beautiful, white teeth. Born to perfection, the contrast of those pearly whites to the golden hue of brown that is her has my eyes drunk with enchantment. And those perfectly shaped, full lips, that are smooth as silk and softer than the finest cashmere.

She reaches, pulling me closer to her. My eyes can't help but take the rest of her in. My gaze falls to her breasts. *Oh they are magnificent.* I lay myself on top of her, pulling the straps down the side to expose them. Supple and round like caramel mountains topped with Hershey kisses. I want to bury myself in them, hold her close and listen to her heart beat hasten with each stimulating touch.

My eyes come back to meet hers as I slip my hand between her long legs, gently prying them apart so that I may feel her anticipation. She allows me to do so willingly, her expression filled with desire. *She wants me.* I remove my shirt allowing her eyes to take in my physique, the way I have indulged in hers. She bites her lip in approval as I slip my pants down and lie next to her. I continue to run my fingers up and down her body, which is now overflowing with zeal. I turn her onto her side, facing away from me, so that I may continue to kiss her neck and nibble at her shoulders.

I lift her satin gown, placing my hand over her stomach and pulling her closer to me so that we are spooned next to one another. I clear my throat.

"Can I have you?" I whisper into her ear as she reaches over her head to pull my head in closer to her neck.

"Yes," she mutters as my hands continue to explore her body. I find my way back to her panties. My desire for her is unsettling. I want to know how she feels. I want to know she is mine before I move forward. I need her to be mine forever and *only mine*. I tug her panties upward, sending her body into ecstasy. Her eyes fly open as I say to her, "I want you to belong to me. *Forever.* Marry me." I continue to kiss and nibble at her, waiting for her answer. She seems lost in the moment so I tug her panties once more, "Say you'll be mine. I won't have you now if I can't have you for eternity."

She bites her lip and places her hand over mine, as it's still wrapped around her panties. Her lips part to finally give me an answer, "I've always been yours, I was made for you." I pause for a moment and take in her words. They made me feel strong and desired.

"So you'll be my wife," I ask once again, to ensure I have her definitive answer.

"Yes," she whispers. My hands journey from her hips to her beautiful face; pulling her toward me so that I may kiss her vigorously. *Something about her being made for me is too much to resist.* She slips off her underwear and presses her ass against me.

I start slow, careful not to hurt her as she slowly opens up a little more for me to bury myself deep within her. I've experienced her beauty and her intellect. *And now her body is more than I ever could have imagined.* Hearing her moan is better than the finest symphony. Her body delighted with me so alive within her, her neck cradled back and her eyes screaming with pleasure whenever they open to greet mine. I'm lost in her expression, her shy demeanor has been replaced with desire. *The desire that she will only allow me to give.*

As we both climax, we are jolted out of meditation and wake up suddenly. We both sit up, breathing heavily, bodies still hot from our heated session. I stare at her, still lost in thoughts *of her*. Between breaths, she softly says, "You're awake."

I sweetly reply, "Yes. And you're going to be my wife…"

Enjoyed the read?

Please Write a Review!

Thank you for reading the first book in the *Beyond the Balance* series! If you are hankering for more background information, deleted chapters, and more indulgent details, please check out **www.pasclo.com**. It has more juicy details, hidden chapters, and character background stories!

Balance Interrupted, book two in this series is now available for preorder, be the first to receive it the day of its debut, September 7th on Amazon.

Join us for a book release celebration for the third edition in the series, *Restoration of the Balance*. Check out the website!

There's nothing more encouraging and supportive to me as an author than hearing the thoughts of my readers. Please take a moment to write a review on Amazon and Goodreads. I love getting to know my readers and respond to all inquiries, messages, and comments whenever I can. Spread the word about the book if you love it!

Find Her on Social Media

Like her page on Facebook:
www.facebook.com/pasclo.tadavenport

Follow her on Twitter: @TADavenport

Cosplay & story pictures on Instagram:
www.instagram.com/t.a.davenport

Visit the website to read behind the scenes notes about the book and sign up for the newsletter to find out the release dates of the next book or special extras or visit us at: www.pasclo.com

Character References

*This list was created for visual reference only. The author had specific people in mind when describing certain characters. Feel free to use this list to engage in a more enhanced reading experience.

Royce Eryx (Eric) Windsor	(Henry Cavill)
Brielle (Briellyn) Rene Donado	(Terrene Davenport)
Kalil Roketi	(Dwayne Johnson)
Justin Vandegrift	(Chris Pratt)
Marcus Vandegrift	(Sam Worthington)
Father Donado	(Morgan Freeman)
Skyla Donado – Matthews	(Meagan Good)
Reilly Matthews	(Charles Michael Davis)
Eryn	(Rooney Mara)
Barbanon	(William Levy)
Fiorello	(Tom Hiddleston)
Senon	(Dennis Haysbert)
Palidon	(Mark Harmon)
Dr. Richard (Rick) Strassmore	(Lee Pace)
Daniel Rodgers	(Chris Evans)
Jenna Fauxx	(Rhonda Rousey)
Camille LeVonn	(Deepika Padukone)

Dominic Lopez	(Benjamin Bratt)
Tanith	(Rita Ora)
Rhea	(Evangeline Lily)
Dionne	(Paula Patton)
Dr. Jonathan Lannister	(Lance Gross)
Dr. Evelyn Teegrit	(Denny Méndez)
Dr. Marianne Reese	(Melissa McBride)
Van	(Michael Levy)
Walker	(Jensen Ackles)

About T. A. Davenport

As a New Jersey native, Terrene has had her fair share of city life. She's lived in New York, Miami, and San Diego. She's even had the luxury of seeing South America, the Caribbean islands, Japan, and the tiny island of Guam.

She is a proud mother of a little boy and happily married to a sailor. As a veteran herself, she took her creative mind, her adventures, and her dreams, and turned them into something that all may experience through this magical tale.

She possesses a Bachelor's and Master's in business fields. With no formal experience with writing, she is hoping to take her love of telling stories and creativity to another level. One must have passion and endless pursuit to achieve success! She loves to give back and never forgets those who have believed in her. Her faith and beliefs have always guided her in the right direction.

Proceeds from the book sales go to allowing Terrene to help inspire the lives of youths and help enrich their young minds to strive for their dreams and have an additional positive role model in their lives.

Made in the USA
Columbia, SC
14 December 2018